After taking a Moder
Elizabeth James taught
and also worked with m
a bookshop with her hu
been writing full-time.

By the same author

Life Class
Life Lines

ELIZABETH JAMES

Lovers and Friends

GRAFTON BOOKS

A Division of the Collins Publishing Group

LONDON GLASGOW
TORONTO SYDNEY AUCKLAND

Grafton Books
A Division of the Collins Publishing Group
8 Grafton Street, London W1X 3LA

A Grafton Paperback Original 1989

Copyright © Elizabeth James 1989

ISBN 0-586-20435-0

Printed and bound in Great Britain by
Collins, Glasgow

Set in Times

To Judith Kendra
With thanks for her encouragement and support

1950

1

Paul Macdonald and Ruth Law stared at the camera, their eyes half-closed against the dazzle of the sun. Behind them the sky was a light and transparent blue, blending in the hazy distance with the line of the sea. Far off to their right the Arabian Nights shape of the pier shone enticingly.

Rebecca wasn't satisfied. 'Say cheese, for goodness' sake. You look so . . . po-faced!'

Obediently they donned broad smiles. Hand in hand they stood in the shallows, the glittering, to-and-fro rush of the waves skimming their ankles. Ruth's pale hair was whipped by the wind. Below the hitched-up skirt her legs were long, slim and white. Paul was bare-chested, his trousers rolled to the knee. He'd knotted a handkerchief at all four corners and wore it as a makeshift sun-hat in parody of the traditional British holidaymaker. Even smiling he managed to look somehow sceptical.

'That's more like it.' Rebecca clicked the shutter. 'When you're both famous I'll sell this picture to the papers and make lots of money.'

'Or blackmail us with it,' Ruth laughed. Tiny golden hairs gleamed on her slender arms as she held the bunched skirt negligently against her thighs. She turned her face up to the sun with a dazed, dreamy air. Among the buckets and spades, the sandcastles, the families from Macclesfield and Chorley, she seemed out of place, Rebecca thought, sort of . . . ethereal, somehow aristocratic.

'No, the photo'll come in handy when I peddle my story to the highest bidder.' Paul printed imaginary tabloid headlines in the air. 'Youthful indiscretion of Britain's best-loved actress.' He looked at Ruth sideways, good-natured but perverse.

'Cad!' She kicked water at him, spattering his rolled trousers. He made a lazy grab for her, but missed.

In Rebecca's company they made no bones about the fact that they were lovers. She was a little shocked, but pleased and flattered by their openness. She wasn't used to such candour. It made her feel older and more worldly. Ruth and Paul included her in their irreverent joking too, usually at the expense of the holidaymakers they entertained down at the theatre, taking for granted that she'd share their own flippant attitude.

The three of them dawdled along the beach, chatting idly, carrying their shoes, laughing companionably at whatever struck them as funny. Rebecca had her father's camera slung from one shoulder. She kept a sharp eye on the time. She was wanted back at her mother's guesthouse at midday to help with the lunch.

Lying in bed that morning she'd been thinking about Ruth and Paul, her new summer friends, and in a flash of realization it came to her that any sparkle, any excitement she anticipated from the day ahead sprang directly from the prospect of seeing them. In some way they personified her future, a freer, sharper way of living. But they'd be gone in a month or so, leaving her world as it had been before – not unhappy, but stale with routine and familiarity. It was then she decided on the photograph. It would be a souvenir, an inspiration, a reminder through the coming year that she, too, was heading towards a more spacious life.

And now, on the beach, without warning, her thoughts spilled over into words. 'I hate you two. You'll be going soon and leaving me to moulder.' The accusation sounded petulant and jarred on the careless tone of their conversation.

10

Smoothly Paul side-stepped. She'd noticed before that he steered clear of any serious dialogue with her. 'We're rolling stones, Becky. Even the charms of Llandudno can't hold us for long.' He gave her one of his odd, twisted smiles. She used to think him ugly but had progressed to finding his looks interesting.

Ruth smiled sympathetically. 'It's only a year. That's not so long.' She'd once told Rebecca that she reminded her of herself at seventeen. 'You've got brains. You'll get to university and then the world'll be your oyster.'

'But a whole year. It'll be like doing hard labour.' In her mind's eye an image rose up, a contrast to the sand and sun, their barefoot sauntering. She pictured a winter-white sky viewed through a rectangle of classroom window, and inside the stuffy, chalk-smelling tedium of a late-afternoon maths lesson.

'You're not the only one. We've all done our porridge.' Paul remained callous towards her gloom. 'Thank your stars you're a girl. At least you won't have National Service to do.'

Rebecca shrugged, reluctantly recognizing the truth of his words. Paul knew what he was talking about. As well as his eighteen months in the army he'd completed three years as an apprentice plumber. And all the time the siren rhythms of his jazz piano had played inside his head. He'd always known what he wanted to do. She, on the other hand, had no clear ambition. Just vague, urgent, contradictory longings.

They reached a likely spot towards the end of the beach. Ruth and Paul settled in the sun. They weren't wanted at the theatre till early afternoon. Ruth began to unfold a newspaper. It flapped in the summer breeze. Ignoring the Korean war on the front page, she searched for the horoscopes.

Rebecca wished she could stay, but time pressed. Already she was cutting it perilously fine and it wasn't worth risking her mother's ill humour. She sat down to brush the sand from her feet and put her shoes on. 'I'd better be getting back to the rissoles and custard.'

'Tell your ma I won't be home for supper.' Casually Ruth looked up from her reading.

'Okay.' Rebecca began to walk towards the steps that flanked the beach.

'And come down to the theatre tonight if you like.'

Rebecca was pleased. 'I might.' Crossing the road, she began to make her way back to her parents' guesthouse. As she walked through the familiar streets her thoughts were still full of the couple she'd left behind on the beach.

She pictured Paul as she remembered him at a party her parents had given three weeks earlier for their twenty-first wedding anniversary. There had been a slightly uncomfortable mix of neighbours, relatives and guest-house residents. The gathering was politely conventional. Paul had been invited as a friend of Ruth's, though he lodged elsewhere. Towards the end of the evening he was prevailed on to give them a tune on the neglected upright piano that stood in one corner of the lounge – Rebecca's own lessons had come to a halt at least five years earlier. He ran his fingers experimentally across the keys and pronounced the tone rotten, but placed his tankard of beer on top of it in the approved bar-room style and began to play.

She could see him now, with a cigarette drooping from his lips and his muscular hands spread across the keys, pounding out a driving boogie. It was irresistible. Unusually, her mum and dad, as well as the assembled guests, had had a bit to drink. People began to dance, self-consciously at first, but gradually letting their hair down. She and Ruth had performed a smooth and seam-less jitterbug. Her mother had looked young and happy, kicking up her legs in a sort of old-fashioned Charleston, losing the harassed air she wore most of the time in summer. The tinny sound of the instrument made the music better in a way, like something out of a speakeasy in a gangster film. The impersonal guesthouse lounge had never been so animated.

Paul played for three-quarters of an hour or more, a lock of curly brown hair bouncing on his forehead. His face was expressionless as he concentrated on the music. It wasn't his style to grin as he played, like some musicians did, but she could tell he was pleased with the atmosphere he'd coaxed out of the politeness and caution.

'Funny-looking chap, isn't he?' her cousin, Dot, had remarked. She claimed he had bedroom eyes. Rebecca detested the expression and disagreed forcibly. Still, she had thought of him somehow differently since then. His eyes *were* his most compelling feature. Baggy rather, although he was only twenty-three. They were brown, the colour of the dark sherry their next-door neighbour kept in a small decanter to offer to visitors in thimblefuls. Rebecca supposed he was funny-looking, but she could see why Ruth might find him more interesting than Teddy, the handsome juvenile lead from the theatre with his blazer and his blond quiff.

'Off in your own little world, then?' The face of one of her classmates loomed in front of her. It was Vicky Williams, grinning, made up like Ava Gardner now she was out of school. Rebecca remembered that in the holidays she helped out down at the whelk stall on the front. Vicky looked blooming, as though she were off on a date rather than to an afternoon spent handling smelly shellfish.

'All right, are you?' Rebecca was in too much of a hurry to stop and talk. And besides she hadn't the inclination. She was happy with her thoughts.

'Grand.' Vicky always had the irrepressible air of living in the best of all possible worlds.

'Must rush.'

'Guess what, Becky!' The appeal stopped Rebecca in her tracks. 'I was down at the theatre last night.'

'Oh yes?' Now she was interested.

'I saw that Ruth, the one who lives with you. Ruth Law. Good, isn't she? Quite a character.'

Rebecca was gratified. 'I'll tell her.' Vicky nodded benevolently and walked on.

Becky reached the steep road that led to the Crow's Nest Guesthouse. Ruth had complained that the walk had added a good inch to her calf muscles. It was funny, Rebecca thought, that Vicky should have called Ruth a character, since she'd been taken on originally to provide the glamour ingredient in this summer's concert party. She was slim, blonde and decorative, and she'd been engaged to play the pretty *ingénue* in sketches opposite her male counterpart, Teddy; to sing sweetly and dance with a well-bred competence.

However, Ruth lacked the necessary docility, and constantly found ways of modifying her role until it became something quite different. She had a spot in which she was required to sing a medley of mellifluous love-songs – 'Blue Moon', 'He's Just My Bill', 'This Is My Lovely Day' – while Paul tinkled out a silvery accompaniment. One night she appeared dressed as a charlady in wrinkled stockings and slippers, her hair tied up in a check duster, and sang the songs like that. Mr Murphy, the boss-manager, was aghast as he glimpsed her, too late, from the wings. But her turn brought the house down and rather huffily he ordered her to carry on doing it that way.

She'd also introduced a spoof on Marlene Dietrich in *The Blue Angel*. In a top hat, with her stocking suspenders showing, and leaning in a sultry fashion on Paul's piano, Ruth sang 'I Can't Help It' in a throaty, aggressive parody that stopped just short of caricature. Mr Murphy appreciated this particular notion somewhat better. The glamour element was still there for all to see. Rebecca thought

Ruth looked beautiful in her top hat, with her straight, shining blonde hair touching her shoulders, and a laughing, challenging look in her eyes.

To the tune of 'Let's Face The Music And Dance', played on a gramophone from behind the scenes, Ruth had worked out a Rogers-Astaire routine with Paul that was stylishly inept, a masterpiece of comic mistiming, without ever quite descending to farce. The audience lapped it up. Ruth's classic looks made the joke all the richer. It was as if some wayward princess had thrown aside her dignity and come down to their level to entertain them.

Ruth still had to take part in dated, hastily written sketches, bristling with words like 'ripping' and 'top-hole', but even these she invested with a vaguely fractured charm that transcended the material.

Rebecca had met Alice, a busty, brassy trouper with dyed jet-black curls and muscly dancer's legs, a veteran of more than twenty years of summer shows, who in the early days had condescended to Ruth with her inexperience and her RADA training.

'What you need is oomph, dear,' she used to tell her in a voice languid with experience. 'And you've got to love the punters. Believe me, they can always sense it.' She confided to Ruth all the little ploys she used to get the audience eating out of her hand, as she put it, though she found Ruth a mite unresponsive as a pupil.

'But nowadays she treats me like a mate,' Ruth had told Rebecca a few days ago, with a look of sly amusement in her eyes. 'She calls me a giggle and a caution. Actually I think she's a bit miffed because I go down well with the audiences too. But she's got no reason to worry. They still love her Tessie O'Shea impersonations. Always have, always will.'

Rebecca was enchanted with the crumbs of gossip she

gleaned about the company, repeating them to her mother who was almost as fascinated as she was.

She glanced at her watch as she neared the house. Five minutes to spare. She could afford to slow her pace and give the impression that the question of her arriving on time had never been in any doubt.

Although her mother, Marie, was intrigued by the theatre people and gratified when any of them chose to stay at the Crow's Nest, she was beginning to hint that Rebecca spent too much time with Ruth and Paul and had come too far under their spell. She was on the lookout for any small signs that confirmed her misgivings. Unpunctuality was a case in point. If Rebecca was late it proved that she was thinking too much about her friends and too little about her obligations to her family.

You had to go up a flight of five stone steps to reach the front garden of the Crow's Nest. All the houses in this steep part of town were built on terraced ground. Tucked under the Orme like Indian ruins, Ruth said. Now Becky strolled unhurriedly down the crazy-paving path, secure in the knowledge that she had seconds, if not minutes, to spare.

The front door was flanked by two wooden tubs of red geraniums. Marie hoped that their cheerful welcome would draw guests' attention away from the fact that the house could do with a lick of paint. Even now, five years after the war, so many things were hard to come by. Marie and Len, Rebecca's father, haunted the local auctions in winter, looking for cheap secondhand buys that might add a little lustre to the Crow's Nest's shop-worn fixtures and fittings. Marie slaved to make up for the dilapidated air of her guesthouse with a scrupulous cleanliness. Visitors noticed the smell of soap and polish the moment they entered the front hall, though just now it was overlaid with the homely aroma of vegetable soup and roasting potatoes. The hall floor was covered with a kind of large-scale patchwork of the good bits of generations of carpets. This theme was repeated in the dining room and in the bedrooms nearest the top of the house.

Double-checking, Rebecca glanced at the clock on the wall. This timepiece ruled the routine of the guesthouse, and it had hung there ever since she could remember. She'd never seen one like it. A bas-relief village landscape, painted in colours that verged on the garish, featured as its focal point a church tower with a clockface that actually worked.

'Will I have the hall clock when you and Mum die?' she'd asked her father wistfully at the age of four or five. The question had gone down in family history.

To her left was the lounge. She turned right into the dining room. Her first job was always to lay the tables, peering at the cloths to check which were unstained and could be used again.

'That you, Becky?' Marie put her head round the kitchen door. Fronds of her dark hair had curled round her face in the steam from the cooking. She wore her busy look. It wasn't that she was flustered – she was too well-organized for that – but she had a fixed, preoccupied air that blocked out all distraction. It was no good trying to tell her anything when she was like this. Nothing registered but the task in hand.

'Go upstairs, would you, Beck, and get the green gingham cloths. It's no good. I might as well change the lot. Oh, and put the old ones in the dirty-bag.'

'Okay.'

Deftly Rebecca began to collect up the used linen. It was time to change gear. Regretfully she abandoned her infinitely absorbing daydreams, re-entering the worn, familiar groove of her everyday life.

2

Paul smiled at her in the muted light that filtered through the thin, floral bedroom curtains. Ruth was endlessly fascinated by his smile. It had a quality she found hard to define. A bitterness? No, that was too harsh a word. A ruefulness maybe. At the same time she imagined she saw a flicker in his eyes, an almost imperceptible refocusing of his attention, as though his thoughts had been elsewhere.

'What are you thinking about, Marlene?' He called her that sometimes when they were alone. A private joke, a pet name, a reference to her *Blue Angel* role. He turned to lean on one elbow, lying alongside and half above her, looking affectionate now he'd remembered that she was there.

'Nothing. Just lying here and feeling satiated and wonderfully languorous.' Her reply had a teasing edge. That was their relationship. Always a tinge of defensiveness between them, as if by tacit agreement. In any case it was hard to feel languorous in this grim little bedroom.

In fact she'd been thinking about Paul himself. Wondering what he imagined when they made love. As they twined and caressed, his attention seemed inward, as though he wasn't seeing her, but some imagined parallel world. It didn't offend her. They weren't in love, they'd agreed on that too.

She was interested, though. Paul interested her. He seemed to live his life somehow in a fantasy of his own making, assimilating the commonplace into his own world, reinventing it. He read constantly when on his own: French existentialist novels, which he struggled through dedicatedly, with the aid of a battered dictionary;

James Joyce, Hemingway, Henry Miller. The aura of their writing enveloped him – it seemed to Ruth that he viewed his actual surroundings as if through a misted window-pane.

Once he lent her his treasured copy of *Tropic of Cancer*. It was a French edition – the book was still banned in England. She read it through the night. Miller's mythology seemed alien and brutal to her. But perhaps when Paul held her, looking fevered and distant, his eyes closed, he was imagining one of Miller's lewd and graceless whores. She smiled dubiously to herself at the thought.

His lips brushed against her neck and shoulders. He murmured, 'Yeah, but don't get too settled. We don't want Jim and Shirl walking in on us. They'd drop dead on the spot and how would we explain that to the ambulancemen?'

'God, what's the time then?' Awkwardly she lifted her head, trying to peer at her watch on the bedside table. On afternoons like this she lost track of the hours passing.

He laughed softly with playful malice. 'Keep your hair on. Nearly an hour before we need move.'

They could really only make love when Jim and Shirl Evans, Paul's elderly landlord and landlady were out. Ruth's room at the top of the Crow's Nest was out of the question. The house bustled with life until late at night when the front door was locked. Paul was the Evans's only lodger. They were a placid, home-loving couple who rarely went anywhere, but once a week or so they visited Shirl's sister in Bangor, returning on the early evening bus. Then Ruth and Paul could snatch a few hours together between the afternoon and the evening show.

Ruth suspected that Paul relished the nervous clockwatching atmosphere of these encounters, as well as the discomfort of his narrow bed and the disapproving presence of the framed, yellowing biblical texts on the walls.

His perversity puzzled her. She disliked his room with its blotchy brown lino, the flattened, brick-coloured rag-rug and slippery pink quilt, but its very ugliness seemed to heighten his desire.

'Becky was in an intense mood this morning,' he said suddenly, out of the blue. 'She's a funny kid.'

Ruth smiled as she thought of Rebecca. 'It's her eyes that get me. They're so direct. Uncomfortable sometimes. They show everything she's thinking.' Sometimes when Ruth got home at night she and Rebecca talked till the small hours about everything under the sun. Then the girl's face shone with eagerness and pleasure at the privilege of having Ruth to herself. It was flattering, she admitted, and touching too. 'She says you and me are the only people she can talk to here. She has to shut down her innermost self, because if she says what she's thinking half the time people look at her . . . as if she was a bit unhinged. But with us . . .'

'She's safe in the knowledge that we're unhinged too.'

Ruth's room was next door to Rebecca's at the top of the house. During the spring and winter the girl slept in one of the larger, lower rooms, but in summer she retreated to the attic to make room for the seasonal guests. They usually talked in Ruth's room. Often Rebecca would knock on some pretext or other and Ruth would ask her in. She always sat on the floor, propping a cushion on the square of wall under the dormer window. Ruth could picture her, with her skinny brown arms circling her knees, hair straggling over her shoulders. She always leaned forward a little as the confidences poured out in a pure stream of consciousness. Her parents were from Lancashire originally, and her soft northern vowels were overlaid quaintly with an acquired Welsh veneer. And all the time her steady, dark, slightly prominent eyes glowed in her small, smooth, suntanned face with a quiet animation.

Paul lay back with his hands behind his head. 'The other day she was talking to me about Klaus Fuchs and Russia and the atom bomb. Just a kid and she knew so much. A hell of a lot more than I did.' He grinned reminiscently. 'She was disgusted with me. "God, you're an ignoramus."' He imitated her quiet vehemence.

'She's been brought up to it. The political side. Her dad's always off at Labour Party meetings and things, and ever since she's been in her teens he's taken her canvassing and leafleting and such like. I think she takes it all for granted.' As she spoke Ruth traced the outline of Paul's lips delicately with one finger. They were full and warm with a downward curve that she liked. Teddy Horn at the theatre had such a ready, easy smile. A surface smile. Likeable, but available to all.

Her mind went back to Rebecca. 'It's odd, you know. Although she's such a seething mass of anger and adolescent yearning, there's something terribly practical about her. She makes me feel . . . Sometimes when I'm rabbiting on about Shakespeare or Ibsen I feel like some willowy aesthete with my head lost in the clouds.'

'No comment.' Paul gave her an amused, appraising look. It was clear that his attention had strayed from their conversation. With a sensual movement he pulled her towards him. She responded to the contact of their skin with a lazy blooming of excitement. His lips brushed her neck and began to travel down towards her breasts.

When Alice nobbled her, as she tried to do quite often, to talk about the warm and wonderful ways of Joe Public, about loving your audience and getting them to eat out of your hand, Ruth was inclined to back off, unwilling to associate herself with such thumping clichés. Privately, though, she admitted to herself that, more than most, the veteran trouper knew what she was talking about.

In some ways Alice herself was a walking cliché, with

21

her corseted hourglass figure, relentless matinees, dry, rich voice and the slow, cocky, plum-coloured smile that caught your attention even before she spoke, so that she was able to place her words with deliberate care like books on a shelf. But there was more to her than that, Ruth came to realize.

On stage the actress had a genuine originality, a daft and dizzy eccentricity that shone through the hackneyed material she performed. She could speak her lines in totally unexpected ways and make them irresistible. Alice had never lost a certain vulnerable air, and an open, almost girlish pleasure at the audience's reaction to her.

Ruth's other colleagues were different. She soon became all too familiar with the check suit and tough, glazed, professional smile of Mr Murphy, the Master of Ceremonies. Eric King, the company comedian, had pursed lips and stylized camp gestures. Teddy Horn sported a boyish grin and an air of bewildered mock-innocence. They saw themselves as types and lost their identity in the process. Their timing might be spot-on, but they never related to the public the way Alice did.

Sometimes Ruth thought she sensed a kinship between herself and Alice, a sort of unspoken recognition. At other moments she told herself she was imagining things. As she settled into the Illyria Theatre Company Ruth began to notice, as she'd noticed in other jobs ever since she started acting, that somehow the audience seemed to single her out, to show special pleasure when she came on stage, to clap her more wholeheartedly than they clapped the other entertainers – with the exception of Alice.

One night, about a month after she arrived in Llandudno, Ruth came off-stage in her charlady's outfit to find Alice standing in the wings. In her rosy theatrical make-up and striped Tessie O'Shea costume, she was poised to go on. 'They like you,' she commented to Ruth, nodding her head briefly in the general direction of the stalls. Ruth

22

was struck by the straightforward honesty in her voice, the absence of the heartiness which Alice usually injected into her smallest utterance.

'You too,' Ruth wanted to say, but it would have sounded lame and insincere. Instead she grinned sheepishly as she passed on her way back to the dressing room.

Rebecca stood leaning on the plush-covered rail at the back of the stalls. In the semi-dark in front of her, rows of heads focused silently on the amber-lit stage.

A few minutes back she'd been sitting in the women's dressing room chatting to Ruth and Sheila, one of the dancers. There'd been a loud knock on the door, and before anyone could answer, Mr Murphy had peered in, looking benevolent and slightly drunk.

'Come here, kid,' he said, and Rebecca realized with a start that he was addressing her. She stood up and crossed the room. Mr Murphy put a kindly, patronizing hand on her shoulder. 'Nip round the front, would you, Becky, and tell us what you think of the new routine.' Rebecca was acutely conscious that behind her Ruth would be watching with a shrewd, mocking eye. Red-faced, jowly Mr Murphy was a favourite target for her wit.

He called out to a passing stagehand, 'Derek! Let this kid in round the front, will you?' He winked at Rebecca like a kindly uncle. 'Don't forget, now, I really want to know what you think.'

Rebecca had followed Derek, feeling a touch bemused. Until this moment Mr Murphy had always seemed to regard her as a bit of a nuisance, hanging about the dressing room and laughing with the girls, though he'd never actually said as much, and now here he was, asking for her opinion.

On stage Ruth kicked up her legs with the five female dancers in the company. All were dressed identically in red shorts, tap shoes and white sweaters. Paul played

23

'Keep Your Sunny Side Up' on his piano in a sprightly fashion and the dancers performed a precision routine, making a chorus line, with their arms round each other's waists, high-kicking, wheeling in formation, goosestepping across the stage, each dancer with her hand on the shoulder of the girl in front, even executing the occasional synchronized cartwheel.

Throughout it all Ruth contrived to be a shade behind the rest, wheeling just too late, tottering hastily to catch up, becoming wrong-footed, sneaking quick, anxious glances at the other dancers in an attempt to imitate their blithe strutting and tapping.

Although seeming to ignore the audience, she had already got them on her side. They giggled and guffawed at each new blunder. Rebecca heard isolated cries of 'whoops' as they lived Ruth's predicament along with her, grinning delightedly at the expression of earnest effort on her face.

'She's a character, that one,' Rebecca heard a woman in front of her comment to her companion, unconsciously echoing the remark her classmate, Vicky, had made that very morning.

The chorus line had reformed along the front of the stage, a row of fixed smiles and clockwork legs. At one end, apparently oblivious, Ruth faced the opposite way and was directing her strenuous high kicks towards the back of the stage. The appreciative chuckles combined into a gale of laughter. It had always surprised Rebecca that Ruth, with her aspirations to a modern, experimental sort of acting, was capable of entering with such manic energy into this kind of foolishness. Rebecca envied this lack of inhibition, knowing that never could she be induced to make such an idiot of herself on stage.

She remembered now that Ruth had told her about this new act, rather scathingly – she had no great opinion of Mr Murphy's professional acumen.

24

'He's insufferably pleased with himself,' she told Rebecca one evening. 'Now the season's half over he's finally twigged that I'm good for a spot of comedy, but the best he can come up with is a blatant copy of my Rogers-Astaire idea. And he thinks it's a brainwave. He's like a dog with two tails.'

On stage, though, her reservations didn't show. Now she embarked on the final stage of the routine – a rapid, swooping tap dance – with a wild verve, before colliding ignominiously with the girl next to her. Finally the dancers strutted off, waving to the public as they disappeared into the wings. Ruth followed several paces behind, kicking her legs up behind her in a comic, music-hall fashion, and waving warmly as she was cheered from the stage.

A second or two later she reappeared, flushed and dishevelled from her exertions. Her eyes shone with pleasure and suppressed elation as she fanned herself with one hand, miming exhaustion. The ovation redoubled. Somehow Ruth looked smaller now, Rebecca thought, pretty, modest and unassuming. She blew kisses with the naturalness of a child. The audience was charmed. The woman in front of Rebecca aah'd as if at some small, cuddly animal. Finally, absurdly, in her shorts and tap-shoes, Ruth dropped a curtsey, smiled impudently, and quit the stage, leaving behind her an atmosphere of warmth and total affection. It was a *tour de force*.

Rebecca clapped with the rest, dazzled. When she wasn't on stage, Ruth was often dreamy and absent. In fact she made quite a fetish of her own lack of the practical, everyday virtues. But with the stimulus of the footlights she became vibrant, concentrated and effective. She was canny, with a kind of sixth sense, able to calculate to a nicety the effect she was having on her audience. In some ways the reassuring modesty and ordinariness of her final appearance was as much of a mask as that of the

25

earnest, slightly crazed chorus girl, or any of the other roles she played.

'Thank you, ladies and gentlemen, thank you . . .' Mr Murphy appeared from the wings, wearing his infamous check suit and holding up his hands to quieten the tail-end of the hubbub. He looked beery and ruddy and full of professional bonhomie. He proceeded to tell an improbable and mildly off-colour joke about Mr Attlee, the Prime Minister, and his secretary, then announced Eric King, the company's stand-up comedian.

King teetered on, the epitome of a theatrical pansy, though according to Ruth he was having an affair with one of the female dancers. He pouted coquettishly, wide-eyed with mock surprise at the applause that greeted him.

'Well, you're a rum lot,' he announced, bridling foxily. It was his catchphrase. Those in the know acknowledged it with a ripple of clapping. It was interesting, Rebecca thought, how the audience's reaction differed from performer to performer. Their laughter at King's petulant posturing had a mechanical quality. It was what was expected of them, a conditioned response, with none of the good humour and genuine delight she had seen in their appreciation of Ruth.

'I say, to look at me, to look at me, boys and girls, you wouldn't think I was a married man . . .' The comedian put his hands on his hips and ogled the front stalls provocatively. The spectators tittered obligingly.

Experimentally Rebecca put her fingers in her ears and watched King as he paraded back and forth, gesturing limply with his hands, grimacing towards the wings as though he had accomplices there, emphasizing the punch-lines of his jokes with a shift of the hips, turning away from his public, then looking at them over his shoulder, sly, conspiratorial, lecherous. He affected to be surprised at the meanings the audience found in his words, pulling faces that were shocked and suggestive at the same time.

The performance was a kind of flirtation. King was poetry in motion, the living embodiment of the music-hall tradition. Normally Rebecca was unimpressed with his jokes, but she enjoyed watching him like this, soundlessly, as if through the wrong end of a telescope, concentrating on the capering of his distant marionette figure.

Ruth was quite fond of Eric. In private life he was a quiet man with regular habits. He liked a pint at lunchtime and at seven o'clock, before the evening show. He bet on the horses most days. It was another custom of his, but he seemed unaware of the forbidden thrill of gambling. 'Over the season I reckon to break just about even,' he'd told Ruth one lunchtime with an air of flat indifference, as he calculated the previous day's profits and losses, columns of small, pencilled figures in the margin of his newspaper.

His supposed affair with the dancer, Mavis, was conducted in the same routine fashion. Two or three times a week they left the theatre together, arm in arm, quite openly, King looking as expressionless as a lizard. On other days he treated the dancer without special partiality. It seemed his professional verve was simply something he'd learned by rote – unless, as Ruth had suggested, he was acting out some deeply buried fantasy on stage.

Rebecca removed her fingers from her ears. Something in King's movements suggested to her that his act was drawing to its close.

'Do what you always do,' he was declaring aggressively. 'Tell 'im you've got a headache!' It seemed to be the climax of his final joke. There was a moderate crescendo of laughter and some clapping. The comedian gave one last glare of mock outrage. 'Well, you're a rum lot,' he repeated. The clapping was renewed, along with the odd whistle, as he minced from the stage. King wasn't inspired, but he was reassuring, Rebecca thought. He gave people what they expected and, unless the world changed drastically, he'd never be out of a job for long.

It was Paul's turn now. His solo spot ended the first half. Rebecca knew that these few minutes were the high spot of his day. Unlike Ruth, he resented a job that he'd taken out of financial necessity. Paul pictured himself in some Soho cellar, playing jazz with a group of like-minded companions, yet here he was, tinkling out bland accompaniments for the likes of Alice.

Ruth saw the work here as a light-hearted interlude. Even so, she'd learned lots, she assured Rebecca. And she had a definite post lined up come January with some arty, experimental theatre company. Till then she was contentedly marking time. Paul's future was far more uncertain, and he saw the cheerful mediocrity of the Illyria Company as vastly more of an affront to his vanity. For him, those moments when he was allowed to play what he liked how he liked were the one redeeming feature of his present job.

The stage was darkened dramatically. Then a single bleached spotlight picked out the dully gleaming grand piano. Under cover of the blackout Paul had already taken his place. He was sombrely dressed and in the white glare his face managed to look both youthful and ravaged. True to his own image of himself he neither smiled nor bothered with the usual ingratiating line of patter. Immediately he launched into a rocking version of 'Viper's Drag', and left his music to speak for itself.

The theatre's loudspeaker system was really quite effective, and the heavy, insistent rhythm began to reverberate round the darkened womb of the theatre. Rebecca started to move her feet to the beat. You couldn't do otherwise. In front of her she saw shoulders beginning to twitch. The music had an insinuating power. It made you smile. It unlocked a mood, careless, exhilarated.

'I play good-time music,' he'd told her and Ruth once,

during one of their many idle strolls along the beach. He said it gravely, almost as though he were talking about his life's mission. Then he smiled his odd smile as if to make fun of his own solemn statement. The phrase came back to her whenever she heard him play.

The effect of the rhythm was cumulative. It seemed to gain a momentum of its own, so that Rebecca had the queer, fleeting impression that the walls of the theatre were resonating with it. On stage Paul looked pale and somewhat innocent, as though divorced from the action of his hands, and it was hard to believe that he was the author of this potent sound.

He played four more numbers. Rebecca recognized 'Honeysuckle Rose' and 'Tiger Rag', but she didn't know the others. People moved their bodies – feet, fingers, shoulders – more and more freely, as if chafing against the restraint of their chairs. The air seemed thick with the music and a kind of tension, and an almost tangible feeling of happiness.

Paul's finale was a tune she knew but couldn't name. His hands moved with dizzying speed and nimbleness across the keys. The excitement rose. There were audible gasps at the sheer dexterity of his fingers as the music increased in pace. Paul was hunched over the keyboard now, his hair in his eyes. The detached air had vanished. He played a passage that had Rebecca transfixed – how could he control his thoughts, movements, reflexes at that speed? Then finally, abruptly, the music climaxed and stopped. There was a split second of incredulous silence, then the theatre erupted in cheers. It was the most dramatic ovation of the night.

A couple of minutes later she met him backstage. He was leaning impassively against a wall, smoking a cigarette, while Alice explained to him some change she wanted incorporated into her pearly queen act.

She was already in the costume, a black dress and a flat hat, stiffly studded with hundreds of pearl buttons, but on her feet she wore an incongruous pair of beige wool slippers with pompoms on the uppers.

'You'll have to take it slower, dear,' Rebecca heard her say as she approached. 'Old Murphy keeps falling behind. Can't remember the steps unless he has all the time in the world. We'll just have to slow the whole thing down, specially the bit with the little shuffle.'

'You've left it a bit bloody late to tell me,' Paul was protesting.

'Yeah, well, just do it, dear, all right?' With a bored steeliness Alice pulled rank. Already she was moving away. 'And don't worry about Murphy. I'll sort that out with him.'

Rebecca grinned conspiratorially as she joined Paul. He aimed an expression of mock venom at Alice's retreating back.

'Are you happy in your work?' she asked, amused.

She expected him to reply in kind, cheerful, inconsequential, but her question seemed to touch him on the raw. He grimaced despondently and took a long drag on his cigarette – Rebecca admired the gloomy panache with which he did it. Then he said flatly, 'I don't think I can take much more.'

'Alice got you down?'

He shook his head. 'No, it's not her. She's okay. It's everything. What we're peddling here is the uttermost corn. The dregs. I mean if I wasn't working here I wouldn't come within a million miles of the place.' She was taken aback and rather impressed by the savagery of his tone.

Behind him she glimpsed Teddy Horn's blond hair and heard him exclaim testily, 'My sodding cigarette holder's gone missing again!'

Paul grinned for the first time that evening. Rebecca

suppressed the urge to giggle stupidly. Both of them moved closer to the wall as Derek, the stagehand, walked by carrying a plywood tree.

Rebecca returned to the thread of their conversation. 'But you've always known this wasn't your cup of tea. You're only here for the cash.'

'You're right.' He turned his dark-brown eyes on her with a rueful look. 'But you get days when it all looks worse. Tonight, watching those damn dancers with their lipsticky smiles, and Murphy with that tired old Attlee joke, and Alice being all cosy and matey, I felt like murder.' He shrugged with a glint of frosty humour. 'I think I've seen it all just once too often.'

'But what about your bit? Your solo? I mean the rafters were positively ringing with cheers.'

'I know. I was showing off.' He smiled wryly. 'Man with the flying fingers. That's not what I want.'

Over Paul's shoulder Rebecca caught sight of Mr Murphy's brown and white dogtooth suit. 'Oh God!' She put her hands to her head. 'I bet he's looking for me. I've got a feeling he wants a long talk about the new chorus-girl sketch, and I don't have the time.' She stood poised to rush. 'I daren't be late home. Tell Ruth I've left, would you? Maybe I'll see her later.'

Paul turned his body as though to shield her from Mr Murphy's approaching bulk. 'Go on, then. Bugger off,' he said amicably.

3

It was a warm, muggy night. Rebecca said goodbye to her father, Len, on the corner of Chapel Street. 'I'll just pop in for a quick one,' he said. 'Tell your mother I'll not be long.' A good debate at the Labour Club always gave him a thirst.

Marie and Rebecca joked that he never mentioned beer or drinking. And he never went anywhere, always popped. Down the road. Round the corner. In for a quick one. 'Makes it sound nicer somehow,' Marie said.

'Bit of a departure from tradition,' Rebecca teased. She looked affectionately at his large, blunt features and wavy grey hair. They were always good friends after an evening of politics. It was what they had in common. A bond between them. Marie was too busy to bother with any of that, as she reminded them often.

He was sweating profusely, though he'd removed his jacket and was carrying it over his arm. His blue shirt, though, was buttoned up to the collar, down to the cuffs. And the navy tie was in place. He'd never dream of going anywhere open-necked.

'You'll be all right for the rest of the way?' he asked. It was a silly question, posed for form's sake. She was allowed to be out any time up till ten in the summer.

She couldn't resist saying waggishly, 'I don't suppose I'll be raped more than three times between here and the Crow's Nest. No cause for alarm.'

'Beck! There's no call for that.' He was easily shocked, but at the same time he smiled reluctantly.

'Bye then.'

'Bye, love.' He turned on his heel, then paused for a second. 'Oh, Beck.'

'What's that?'

'Good point you made. About Bevan.'

She grinned, pleased. 'I thought it was quite telling.'

It felt airless as Rebecca began the usual uphill haul. They could do with a good thunderstorm. Her mind was still full of the arguments she'd heard that evening. Len had got quite worked up. He was all in favour of the government's hefty defence spending and it made him mad to hear people say that everyone would be a lot better off if the country laid down a significant part of this particular burden.

He'd shouted at one such doubting Thomas, 'You're living in blooming cloud c-cuckoo land!' Len stammered when he was roused and his face flushed angrily. 'Blooming' was strong language coming from him. Watching, Rebecca felt, as she always did, a mixture of embarrassment and pride.

She was inclined to disagree with him though, and in fact she'd argued against him tonight. Some of their fellow members, especially the men, had found that funny.

'You tell him, Beck,' Harry Marwick had joked. He worked with Len down at the Post Office. The comment had annoyed her – he wasn't taking her reasoning seriously. He hadn't called out like that to any of the men. She was consoled a little when Len told her afterwards that he thought she'd made a good point. She knew she had.

Rebecca found herself wishing that she could talk to Ruth about this evening's debate. But it was no good. She could tell her anything personal and Ruth would listen with endless patience, never treating her as a child or belittling her problems. She would fix her grey eyes on Rebecca's face and work things out with her slowly and seriously. But she switched off when it came to anything political.

Once Rebecca had pointed this out. Ruth had shrugged as though the reproach was supremely unimportant. Then she smiled, languorous and irresponsible. 'Oh Becky, leave it to the experts.'

Rebecca paused for a moment at the corner of her street. You could look out from here and see all of Llandudno spread out in front of you, grey-blue in the dusk like a cubist painting, ending in the flat expanse of the sea. The lights down by the shore added a touch of glamour and drama. She felt friendly towards the town tonight. Perhaps it wouldn't be so bad, the one year that remained before she could strike out on her own.

Back at the Crow's Nest she helped Marie with the washing-up and laid the tables for breakfast. Then she went upstairs. Might as well go to bed early. There was nothing really she wanted to talk to Ruth about tonight.

She'd been asleep some time when she became aware of a knocking on her door. She had the drowsy impression that it had been going on for some while. She managed to rouse herself enough to frame the words, 'Who's there?'

'It's Ruth.'

'Oh.' Rebecca dragged herself into a sitting position. The room was dark, illuminated only by the diffused, filtered light of a street lamp a little way down the road.

'Can I come in?'

'Yes.' Her voice sounded oddly thick to her.

'Did you say yes?'

'Mmm.'

The door opened and a black figure appeared in the slit of light. 'You sound drunk.'

'I'm asleep.' She blinked at Ruth's silhouetted shape. The light disappeared as Ruth closed the door. 'Just a mo.' Rebecca couldn't face the glare of an electric light.

She fumbled and found matches and a stump of candle kept on the table by her bed.

She struck a match. With a hissing sound it flared into life and she held it to the wick of the candle. A pale, flickering flame revealed the sloping contours of her room, the solid outline of a chest of drawers, a wardrobe. At the same time she noticed rain driving against the window. Drowsily she saw that Ruth wore a dressing gown and had a towel wrapped round her head.

'Did you get drenched?'

Ruth nodded, seeming indifferent to the fact. 'Listen, Becky, are you properly awake? I've got to talk to you.' An unusual note of urgency in her voice roused Rebecca to a higher level of wakefulness.

'I'm listening.' She settled on one elbow as Ruth sat down on the end of her bed.

'It's about Paul.' Ruth lifted her legs on to the bed and wrapped her arms round her knees. 'He's gone! Just upped and left.' Her voice held a mixture of outrage and excitement.

'Why? When did he go?'

'This afternoon. And he didn't tell anyone at the theatre. It's been chaos down there.'

'How on earth did you manage?'

'Bronwen in the box office. Her next-door neighbour teaches piano. She ran home and fetched her. Took a bit of persuading, by all accounts.' Ruth's eyes shone in the candlelight with gleeful malice. 'A big, buxom woman – what you'd call ample – with a tweed skirt and a moustache and a pork-pie hat. She kept it on all through the performance. And she was bossy, too. Had us all running round in little circles . . .'

'And she saved the day?'

'Yes, in a plodding sort of a way. She's no virtuoso but she did her best. And she's agreed to fill in till we can get someone else.' Ruth removed the towel from her head

35

and placed it on the floor by the bed. She ruffled her hair. 'Except Tuesdays.' She smiled mischievously. 'That's her Workers' Educational night.' Her hair stuck out round her face, damp and still tousled.

'My God!' Rebecca was struck again by the enormity of Paul's defection. There was a moment's silence between them. Then she said, 'When I was down at the theatre the other night he seemed really browned off with it all . . . I mean more than usual. Quite savage he was.'

Ruth nodded. 'He's been grouchy for a few days. I've been rather pissed off with him. We had a tiff today. Over spam sandwiches in Haulfre Gardens.' Beadily she looked across at Rebecca. 'I didn't tell them *that* at the theatre, though. They might have thought his leaving was all my fault.'

'What did you quarrel about?'

Ruth shrugged. 'I can't remember how it started. Something silly, I expect.' Rebecca had the impression that her indifference was studied. It didn't ring quite true. 'At some point he said something rude about the show and I lost my temper. I told him he was negative and hypercritical . . .' She tucked the hem of her dressing gown round her bare feet. It was cold for a summer night. 'I probably sounded totally smug, lecturing him, trying to convince him that the job's what you make it, all experience is good experience, etcetera, etcetera . . .' She gave a terse little laugh and added drily, 'He didn't take it too well.'

'I think he'd have stuck it out if he was like you, with a job lined up. A job you really want.'

Absently Ruth ran her fingers through her hair again. It was beginning to dry. She looked young in the pale light with her spiky locks, and somehow hurt.

'Paul's trouble is that he lives in a world of his own,' she said pensively. 'He's an anti-hero, an existentialist, that's how he sees himself, and the Illyria Theatre's hardly the ideal setting . . .' She was quiet for a moment or two, then she said, 'I find that appealing in a way, and I understand it. It's like acting. He's impatient with reality. But it's maddening too.' She shrugged. 'I'm not surprised he's left. But he *has* let everyone down and that's bad of him. I told Murphy on the quiet that Paul's mum was poorly . . . Maybe he'll be back in a day or two and they'll make allowances . . . They're not going to find anyone as good . . .'

'What about you? How do you feel?' For the first time Rebecca sensed a fragility in Ruth. Normally she seemed protected by a carelessness, a lazy humour.

'Oh.' Ruth shook her head dismissively. 'Paul and I are free agents. We're not in love. I'm fine. I'll probably get some silly letter from him in a couple of days and he'll be in Paris or somewhere. He likes it there. The jazz clubs and all those intense people in black sweaters. It's a fantasy world just made for him.' Her voice tailed off. She stood up. 'I'd better let you get some sleep.'

'Sure you're okay?' Rebecca was hesitant about asking again. Ruth had always set limits on their intimacy.

But Ruth just smiled down at her, vaguely affectionate. 'I'm fine, Becky,' she repeated. She paused, then added awkwardly, 'I loved someone once. A boy in the war, when I was younger than you. And he died.' She shook her head. Her eyes were bright. 'I don't want to feel anything like that again.'

4

A few days later a letter with a French stamp lay on the breakfast table next to Ruth's plate. Her first amazed thought was that Paul had indeed written from Paris, but in almost the same instant she realized that the letter was from her mother, Sarah, who lived in southern France. She experienced a twinge of guilty disappointment.

'Porridge?' Rebecca was waiting at table. She was in black with a white apron. The outfit had come with a starched white cap, but she refused to wear that.

'Yes. Thanks.' There was a depressing cosiness about the dining room at breakfast time. People discussed the weather *ad nauseam*, and their plans for the day ahead. Everyone looked fresh, rested and well-groomed. Sometimes, with private amusement, Ruth imagined how it would be if the guests came downstairs as they probably did at home, yawning and unshaven, in down-at-heel slippers and creased pyjamas, or flannelette nightgowns and pin curls.

The breakfast hour was almost over. Ruth usually put in a late appearance. She preferred stewed tea to the bright, enforced conversation. Only one family remained at table. The father read his newspaper in majestic peace, while his wife, anxious and fussy in a plaid two-piece, struggled to control three young children brandishing jammy fingers of toast perilously close to the yellow seersucker cloth.

Rebecca brought porridge and tea. 'Look at that pig sitting there like the Great Panjandrum,' she whispered. Then she whisked off, deft and efficient, to clear some of the other tables.

38

Ruth slit open the letter. Sarah and her French husband, Guy, lived just outside a small, unspoiled, intensely photogenic village in the Lubéron Valley. Ruth had been there often for long stretches, so she was always fascinated to catch up with the latest gossip about the locals. To find out who had married, been born or died, who had quarrelled or fallen in love with whom.

Both Sarah and Guy were painters. They'd married only four or five years ago, soon after the war had ended. They relished passionately their new shared life, the companionship, the rustic house and garden, the constant exchange of ideas about their work. Her mother's letters radiated a contentment that often left Ruth wistful and mildly envious.

The remaining family finished breakfast and got down from the table. The children pushed and scuffled their way to the door, followed by the ineffectual reprimands of their mother and the lordly disapproval of their father. 'It's about time you took these kids in hand,' Ruth heard him say as they left the dining room.

Marie appeared from the kitchen, trim and fully made-up. Her dark hair, only lightly flecked with grey, was pulled back tightly into a stylish pleat. As usual she was preoccupied, focused on the day's duties, giving orders. 'Becky, don't forget you've got to sort out those ration books for me, then run and fetch the grocery order . . .'

With tart emphasis Rebecca held out a trayful of used crockery she'd collected. 'One thing at a time, Mother.'

'Just don't forget. We're down to half a packet of sugar . . .' Running a guesthouse under the stringent rationing that prevailed nationally took a great deal of ingenuity. Marie was resourceful, but constantly harassed. She noticed Ruth and greeted her vaguely, her mind elsewhere. 'Oh, a letter. Nice.'

'Mmm.' Momentarily Ruth lifted her eyes from the

paper to smile at Marie. Then she turned a page. Sarah wrote infrequently, but usually at length.

Her mother had been born and brought up in a small mining village in South Wales. She'd been married there briefly, but the relationship had failed and at the age of nineteen she'd left to study art in London, afterwards earning her living as a painter. In the late Twenties she'd been married again to a writer, Stephen Law. For two years they'd been close and happy. Ruth was born. Then Stephen became seriously ill and, rather than continue as an invalid, he'd killed himself. For years Sarah had existed with the pain of his death.

Now she lived surrounded by her new husband's French heritage, and in spite of her contentment Sarah had begun to hanker after her own roots. On a trip to Britain she revisited Carreg-Brân and what was left of the world of her childhood, resuming a tentative friendship with Holman, her first husband. They corresponded regularly, and by letter Holman fed her newly aroused curiosity about her own village. Occasionally she reported his gossip secondhand to Ruth.

Today, though, there were no anecdotes, just a casual postscript. 'I'm afraid I may have landed you in it, love. Rashly I mentioned to Holman that you were working in Llandudno. As it happens a young man from the village – a sort of protégé of his, I gather – is spending a climbing holiday nearby. Holman's encouraged him to look in on you. I hope for your sake that he's interesting, attractive and entertaining rather than the opposite. Sorry! Mum.'

Ruth folded the letter. She was sceptical about the prospect of this unknown young man actually appearing in the flesh. In her experience this kind of vague arrangement rarely materialized. Irrationally she had pictured him already, with distaste, as carrot-haired and moist-eyed like a boy from Swansea who'd been in her voice production class at RADA.

40

Rebecca appeared at once and began to clear the table. She was flushed with hurrying, and one lock of her dark hair, which she scraped back when she was waitressing, had come loose and hung wispily down one side of her face. In the severe black outfit and apron she reminded Ruth momentarily of some young Victorian parlour maid. 'Lucky devil,' the girl growled *sotto voce*, as she clattered cutlery and condiments on to a tray. 'Off out while I stay here and cut bits out of people's ration books while Mum hums and hahs about how to make them stretch to a week's worth of three-course meals.'

Guests surrendered their books to Marie on arrival and for the rest of the week checked, eagle-eyed, that they were getting their fair coupons' worth. On Monday mornings Marie drew up her menus. For Rebecca this was the worst time of the week. Her mother became indecisive and tetchy with the effort of trying to get a quart out of a pint pot, and the deliberation took forever.

Ruth patted her consolingly on the shoulder. 'You don't know when you're well off. Think of me being bossed all morning by a mediocre pianist with delusions of grandeur. *And* trying to get Teddy to act the fool for just one second . . .' Teddy was standing in for Paul as Fred Astaire. He was a poor substitute, stiff and on his dignity. 'Honestly, Becky, he's useless. Trying to be dead suave all the time.' She demonstrated Teddy's boyish, self-congratulatory smile and Rebecca snorted with laughter.

Ruth wouldn't admit to missing Paul in any personal way, but she was frank about the gap he'd left down at the theatre. Even Alice, who'd never had much time for him, confided to Ruth that she'd never realized how bloody good he was until it came to explaining what she wanted to Florence, his substitute. 'It's not just that she can't play very well. She just never understands what I'm

41

getting at. One word, that's all it took with Paul, and he knew exactly what I meant.'

Ruth had her own reasons for feeling bereft. Paul had been the only person at the Illyria who was on her wavelength. There was no one now to laugh with or pull faces at on the quiet when Alice or Mr Murphy became too preposterous. She and Paul used to sit together at lunchtime and share their sandwiches while they bounced ideas around for new sketches, often developing them into bizarre private jokes, but salvaging a constant stream of realistic, usable suggestions to brighten up Mr Murphy's timeworn theatrical precepts.

'I bet you miss your partner in crime, don't you?' Eric King had remarked, to her surprise, a couple of days ago. He invited her for a consoling pint and entertained her with a string of wry theatrical anecdotes. Ruth was touched by the gesture, but kept thinking how much Paul would have enjoyed the stories too.

'Someone's been asking for you. A man.' There was just a shade of displeasure in Teddy's voice, but nothing you could put your finger on.

'Oh?'

'He says he'll come back at midday. Name's Owen or something. Owen Roberts?' He looked at her with interest to see how she reacted.

Ruth shook her head. 'Never heard of him.' She was intrigued. 'Young or old?'

'Youngish.' Teddy wore his sulky look. Like that he reminded her irresistibly of the hero of *Maitland Makes Good*, a patriotic schoolboy story someone had given her as a child. In the line illustrations Maitland had been high-cheekboned and rosebud-lipped, with a sweeping crest of blond hair. Impossibly handsome, she'd thought at the time. Now, foolishly, the unwitting resemblance always made her want to grin.

She shrugged. 'Can't imagine.'

'What sort of a time d'you call this, my lady?' Alice hectored good-humouredly from the front row of the stalls where she was sitting with Eric King. Her short, muscular dancer's legs, trim in grey slacks and stack-heeled shoes, were crossed one over the other. Her arms were spread along the backs of two neighbouring seats. There was a commanding set to her body, Ruth thought. Her black hair gleamed in corrugated rows of curls. She'd already been to the hairdresser's for an early shampoo and set.

'I can explain.' Ruth threw up her hands as if at gunpoint and walked to the front of the stage. 'I called in at the antique shop about the rocking horse. They dithered for ages but in the end they surrendered to my charm and agreed to let us borrow it.'

Alice nodded approvingly. 'You're not as daft as you look.' She stood up. 'Ready everyone? We're doing the kiddie sketch this morning.'

Since the beginning of the season Ruth and Paul had watched, fascinated, the slow but inevitable transfer of power from Mr Murphy to Alice. Nowadays it was usually Alice who decreed what they'd rehearse. It seemed only natural. She was brisk and decisive, and Murphy seemed as content as anyone to follow her lead. Currently he lurked, in a yellow cable-stitch sweater, to one side of the stage, discussing lighting with Derek, the stagehand. He seemed happier when dealing with practical matters. Since the chorus-girl inspiration he'd not come up with any new ideas.

'All right, Florence.' Alice turned to the substitute pianist who sat silently thumbing through assorted sheets of music. 'Could you play the introduction, please?' After more flicking and riffling Florence found what she wanted and thumped out the opening bars of 'The Teddy Bears' Picnic'.

The kiddie sketch, for which the rocking horse had been reserved, was Alice's brainchild. She'd done something similar in Scarborough the year before last and it had gone down a bomb, according to her. All the members of the cast would be dressed as children. It was Ruth's least favourite role. When they got to the dress rehearsal she'd be required to wear white knee-socks and suck a lolly. One lunchtime, over a draught Bass, Mr Murphy had become embarrassingly enthusiastic at the thought.

The rehearsal of this scene took them up to lunchtime. Everyone made suggestions which were lengthily discussed, tried out, amended, and finally accepted or rejected. And there was a silly dance routine to be learned to the tune of 'Three Little Fishes'. It was a morning when Ruth could readily sympathize with Paul's abrupt departure. She kept picturing the ascetic-looking person who'd auditioned her for the Manchester Experimental Company, and wondering what he'd think if he could see her now.

Usually they took a break around midday, but today they overran. Alice and Mr Murphy became involved in an interminable impasse over his part in the dance. She kept demonstrating a complicated series of steps, which he imitated haphazardly but with great good will, like a docile dancing bear. Generally he coped with his routines in this fashion. But this morning Alice wasn't satisfied. She was determined that he should do the thing properly. As director of choreography she was within her rights to insist. The rest of them watched with increasing boredom.

'He's there or thereabouts, Alice,' Eric King remarked mildly. Ruth could see he was eager for his pint and his bet.

'There's a right way and a wrong way.' Alice was feeling bloodyminded. She kept on until Murphy got it right, then insisted on a complete run-through for everyone else. Towards the end of the dance, as she wobbled her hands in the direction of the auditorium, with sinuous, fishy movements, Ruth became aware of a stranger standing by the wall four or five rows back on the right. A silent figure, bearded, and wearing dark clothes.

Teddy nudged her as they approached the footlights for the finale. 'That's him. The bloke that was asking for you.'

The knowledge made Ruth a touch self-conscious as she and the other performers dropped to one knee, arms raised in a sort of triumphal salute, and smiled warmly towards the empty rows of seats. She wondered how long he'd been there watching them.

'He's a bit of all right,' Sheila, one of the dancers, murmured. Alice called for a break.

Ruth climbed down from the stage and walked towards the newcomer. She tried to look nonchalant, but she could picture all too clearly the glances of speculative interest that would be following her. The stranger watched her approach with a self-contained smile.

She stopped a couple of paces away from him. 'I'm Ruth Law. I was told you were asking for me.'

He stepped forward. 'I guessed you were.' He was tall, about six feet, and slim. 'My name's Owain Roberts.' He stuck out a hand as if to shake hers. She took it, belatedly. He went on, 'I apologize for arriving out of the blue like this, but I promised someone that I'd look you up . . . If you're too busy to see me I'll understand . . .' He seemed to step backwards a little as though to demonstrate his readiness to withdraw. His voice was pleasing, quiet but firm, with a distinct southern Welsh intonation.

'I'm afraid I don't . . .'

'I'm sorry. This'll take a deal of explaining. You see I'm a friend of your mother's first husband. From Carreg-Brân. When he knew I was holidaying here he seemed

45

really keen that I look you up . . .' He grinned, as though taking her into his confidence. 'Well, he's a nice old boy . . .'

'Of course!' Realization dawned. It was the young man threatened in Sarah's letter. She was amazed at the timeliness of his appearance. 'You're right on cue. I heard from my mother only this morning saying you might . . .' He was very different from the carroty-haired youth she'd pictured herself being obliged to humour.

He was visibly relieved, and fixed her with enquiring greenish-brown eyes. 'I was wondering, do you eat lunch? Are you allowed out?'

'Sandwiches.'

'Only that?'

She shrugged amicably. 'You can share them if you like. On the beach?'

He seemed amused. 'Fair enough. Perhaps I could buy us some dessert on the way.'

'I'll have to change.' She was wearing her practice shorts and plimsolls. 'I'll meet you outside. I can take an hour or so. We've got a show this afternoon.'

Sheila squeaked appreciatively when Ruth told her what they'd planned. 'Ruth, he's smashing. Who is he?'

Ruth buttoned a blue skirt over a white cotton sweater. 'Just a friend of a friend.' It would take too long to be specific. Sheila's enthusiasm had taken her by surprise. It hadn't occurred to Ruth yet to react one way or another. She leaned forward to brush her fair hair in the dressing-room mirror.

'Put some make-up on,' Sheila urged. 'He's worth it.'

'Can't be bothered.' Ruth smiled at her provocatively. The dancer was always reproaching her with not making the best of herself. Sheila toted a heavy, pale-blue plastic vanity case filled with cosmetics of every colour and description. She regarded her face as a virgin canvas to be embellished with stony-eyed concentration.

46

Owain Roberts was waiting outside, hands in pockets, his hair blowing in a slight breeze. Ruth looked at him afresh in the light of Sheila's frank admiration. With his clipped beard and black shirt he did cut an intriguing figure, making her think of some brooding nihilist in a Russian novel. His face was on the thin side, oval and regular, his skin pale but lightly tanned. In the daylight his eyes seemed lighter and luminous, green rather than brown. His dark hair was cut short and lay across his forehead like a Roman emperor's.

They began to walk along the front. He noticed a grocery a little way up a side street and went to buy some extras for their picnic. He emerged with a couple of cakes, some apples and a bottle of fizzy red Tizer. He held it up. 'I took a chance. Can you drink this stuff?'

She smiled delightedly. 'It's a passion of mine. A depraved one. I don't usually give in to it.' The drink looked incongruous in his hands. She liked him for buying it.

They strolled on. Ruth had become fond of the promenade, with its long crescent of tall hotels on one side and generous curved sweep of sand on the other, and beyond that the sea with all its varying moods. Today it looked blue and cheerful, its surface lively with the white crests of many small, scudding waves.

'How's about here?' They'd reached a spot where she used to eat sometimes with Paul. They went down a short flight of steps. The beach was beginning to fill up with picnicking families, but there was still plenty of space. They found a spot and settled themselves. Ruth opened her sandwiches and offered him one. 'Egg and cress. Lots of cress, not much egg.'

They began to eat. The air was bright and clear, and there was an off-shore breeze. Ruth watched a red kite dipping and rising against the tender blue of the sky. She grinned at Owain, her hair in her eyes. 'You never said. What did you think of the show?'

He turned to look at her with a sort of humorous reserve, as though he feared to hurt her feelings. Then, irrepressibly, his mouth and eyes formed into a smile. He hesitated. 'Interesting,' he commented. 'And lively.' She was charmed by the way he said it, a compromise between tact and honesty. Their eyes met and they laughed spontaneously. It was their first moment of real contact.

'You're good though,' he said quickly. Then, 'You really are. I'm not just saying that.'

'I can't see how you can tell. Not from what you've seen, I mean.'

He shrugged. 'You can always tell.' He didn't pursue the subject, but broke open the Tizer and courteously handed it to her first. 'You're at the Illyria because you need the work, I gather, but in an ideal world what would you be doing?'

'I'm joining a new company at the end of the year. In Manchester. It's going to be very avant-garde and experimental.' Rather against her will she felt the need to impress on him that the concert-party was far from being the height of her ambition. 'We've got Arts Council funding and we'll be doing Brecht and Pirandello . . . and lots of improvisation. It's the sort of thing I'm good at. There are some brilliant people in the company and I'm just so . . . honoured . . . that they've chosen me.' She noticed suddenly that his smile was amused and indulgent, almost as though he were listening to the outpourings of a child. It froze her. Soberly she upended the Tizer bottle and took a long swig of the nostalgic, fizzy sweetness, then wiped the neck of the bottle carefully on the hem of her skirt. She went on more slowly, and without her former rush of enthusiasm. 'In answer to your question, in an ideal world I'd settle for the same job.'

'So don't you feel very frustrated here?'

She shook her head. 'Not really. Most of the time it's fun. And I'm learning constantly. Things you don't pick up, say, in ordinary repertory. I don't think you should ever despise experience.' He raised the bottle to her with a grin, as though acknowledging this lesson in life.

Ruth leaned back on her elbows, turning her face to the sun. She experienced a sudden fierce sense of being enviable. It had come to her as she explained herself to Owain Roberts. Her future had sounded spacious to her, full of promise and purpose and pleasure. She enjoyed the privilege of doing what she wanted in life and she believed that she could do it well.

A few yards in front of them a fat toddler sat playing with the sand. Oblivious to everyone, he prodded and moulded its damp grittiness, patting it into a shallow plastic bowl and plopping it out again. Destroying his little castle with a vague swat of his hand. Gingerly tasting the grains stuck to his plump, pink fingers, then scooping up another handful and rubbing it into his bare legs. Chatting to himself continuously as he did so. As she watched him, Ruth suddenly identified vividly with his grave and simple pleasure.

Owain said, as if he read her thoughts, 'You seem happy.' It was a statement of fact without flattery or envy.

She was startled out of her absorption and smiled almost guiltily. 'Yes.'

5

As she changed into her costume for the first number of the show Ruth thought about Owain Roberts. She was rather taken aback by the interest he'd aroused in the rest of the cast. Some, like Sheila, asked questions eagerly, frankly. Others displayed a more discreet nosiness. The whole company seemed rather impressed with him. Ruth was a little irritated by their curiosity. It was as if they were taking the measure of some new boyfriend, but he was only someone who'd looked her up out of duty.

She found herself comparing their attitude towards Paul. The feelings he aroused had always been far more ambiguous. Frequently he rubbed people up the wrong way, herself included, and his looks were most definitely an acquired taste. Objectively speaking, his nose was too big, his eyes baggy. Sheila had always said he looked decadent, and there was no hint of sneaking admiration in the description. Yet Ruth thought his face interesting, watchable. His reactions were close to the surface. There was always an intensity about him. She couldn't imagine him, like Owain today, making contact with an unknown woman, encouraging her to talk about herself, and playing down his own thoughts and opinions. Paul would have thought it necessary to challenge and provoke her.

Of course, Owain was older – twenty-seven, she'd discovered, five years her senior. He was a journalist in the political field. The information had little meaning for her. She deliberately hadn't asked him much about his work. She'd never enjoyed faking an intelligent interest where none existed. But she made a mental note to mention his name to Rebecca and find out whether she'd heard of him.

He had asked, out of the blue, if he could wait and see her again, late, after the second show. She was surprised and quite flattered. She knew he was intending to go back to Capel Curig, where he was staying with friends, on the afternoon bus.

'It'll be late by then,' she'd warned. 'By the time the show's over. After ten, and things close down . . .'

He'd replied with a grin. 'I don't mind if you don't.'

Ruth was really quite excited about seeing him again. The striking looks that so appealed to everyone else weren't totally lost on her. She'd get him talking about the sort of things that interested her, like his childhood, his favourite films and music, maybe even his love affairs . . .

'Look.' Ruth peered in through the lighted hotel window, feeling vaguely like one of the Dickensian poor.

Owain joined her. 'Good God!'

Inside was a large ballroom with a polished floor, chandeliers, and couples dressed to the nines. The men sported dinner jackets, the women full-skirted net, chiffon and sequins, their faces powdered and rouged, their hair formally set and teased. All the couples were in their sixties at least and many appeared considerably older. They danced, with expertise and flair, in studied, correct formations, while a four-piece band played silvery strict-tempo dance music. Few talked or smiled as they glided across the parquet flooring. It was as if the dancing was an end in itself, a ritual rather than a social activity, though the couples sitting out in chairs round the perimeter of the room chattered animatedly enough.

'They dance here like this pretty well every night.' Ruth and Paul had come upon this singular spectacle walking home one evening after the theatre. After that they often passed by and stopped to stare companionably, hand in hand, outside the window. Now she offered the discovery to Owain.

'It's like a dance of death,' he said, awed.

Ruth looked at him in surprise. 'I've never seen it that way.' She and Paul had always viewed the elderly dancers with affection and pleasure. She was startled by Owain's morbid view of them.

'Come on.' He took her hand. 'Let's go.' They hadn't touched before. He pulled her with him. She didn't resist. He seemed genuinely eager to get away.

Most of the town's amenities were closing down for the night, but the air was still mild, the sky dark-blue and starry. Ruth felt very awake, and curious to see what turn the evening would take.

She probed gently. 'How are you going to get home?'

'First bus tomorrow.' He gave her a steady look as if to emphasize that he was levelling with her, but there was a hint of challenge in his eyes. 'Listen, Ruth, I'll take you home just as soon as you want to go. You're under no obligation. But I'd like to spend time with you, as much as you can spare . . . And don't worry about me,' he added. 'I've never kept regular hours.'

'That's fair.' She shrugged, as though joining him in disclaiming conventionality. 'We'll play it by ear.' She was intrigued by his offer, which made the night seem a potential adventure. They drifted across town towards the West Shore.

'If you're feeling energetic,' he suggested, 'we could walk round the Orme.'

'Why not? I've never done it, although I've been here for most of the summer.'

They began to ascend the narrow road. Apart from their two figures it was deserted. You could smell and hear the sea down on the left, and if you looked over the railings the bone-white rocks of the shore gleamed in the moonlight. Above them the dark shape of the Orme loomed and the etched black lines of branches cut across the sky. Ruth felt elated with the solitude and the vastness. She took in a deep breath of the fragrant air. 'I should have come up here before. Funny how you scuttle from place to place doing all the things you've got to do and never go out exploring for the simple pleasure of it.'

Across the black bay the lights of Penmaenmawr twinkled. Ruth stopped to gaze. 'It looks so enticing over there, sort of mythical, like a promised land.'

'Don't you believe it,' he replied with a damning certainty. 'Those are just the street lights. Everyone's been in bed since nine-thirty.' He added offhandedly, 'Like where I come from.'

She laughed. 'You don't sound very keen.'

He was dismissive. 'Doesn't matter now. I don't live there any more.' He turned and perched on the wall that bordered the road at that point. He was facing her, his face pale and indistinct in the dark. 'Your own village is a bit like your parents – it's easy to see the bad in them, and the good sometimes gets taken for granted.'

She nodded, interested. 'I think my mother found that. She never went there for years. Never wanted to. Remembering the bad things, you know. But now she's got the urge – very strongly – to get to know it again.'

'Your mother was a bit of a celebrity when I was growing up.' There was a new spontaneity in his voice, making the Welsh speech more pronounced. 'A bit scandalous – divorced, like. And a painter. Sometimes there'd be a piece about her in the papers and we'd all show each other.' He laughed briefly. 'You know, I always thought my dad had a bit of a soft spot for her. Very interested he always was in her doings.'

'He's a miner, is he?'

'Yes. And he's been active in the Union all his life. He

used to be quite well-known in his way. Ianto Roberts?' He made the name a question.

'Don't know him.' Ruth shook her head and smiled. She'd already made clear to him her lack of enthusiasm for the highways and byways of politics.

'No reason why you should.'

She hastened to ask another question, to keep alive the new current of communication between them. 'What's he like, Holman? My mother's first husband?'

'I'm fond of him.' Owain's voice softened. 'He can be a bit of a fussy old bugger, but he's been good to me. Good *for* me.'

'In what way?'

'Well, I went to the Grammar. And I got interested in books and music – nancy stuff, so my dad thought.' There was a note of satire in his voice, as though he considered his story almost too trite to be told. 'But Holman used to lend me books and records. Never pushed them on me. But they were there if I wanted. He and his missis never had any kids. He's a nice old boy . . .' Unconsciously he repeated the phrase he'd used to describe Holman earlier in the day, when he first introduced himself.

Sarah had talked to Ruth only once or twice about her first husband, but her account of him had been strikingly similar. Ruth could remember her mother saying, 'If it weren't for him I'd probably still be working in a grocer's shop, with four or five kids to my credit.' Sarah had been his wife, briefly, and Owain, it seemed, a surrogate son.

'So you don't hit it off with your dad?' Questions like this always fascinated Ruth. She wanted to know the truth about people, and was impatient with anything she considered abstract or theoretical.

'I play rugby still. He can relate to that.' She sensed a bitterness in his attitude. 'And we've always had politics in common. We get by. I respect him in certain ways. But there've been times when we detested each other.'

He reached out, circling her wrist with one hand. 'And what about you?' He sounded wryly accusing as if, by drawing him out, she'd caused him to be indiscreet.

A car approached, its headlamps flooding them with light, so that for an instant his thin, watchful face was revealed to her, and she realized in that moment, almost with surprise, how attractive she found him. She smiled. 'We talked about me this morning.' She had a sudden mental image – Owain bending towards her, kissing her on the lips. For a second she wanted it fiercely, but, tantalizingly, he made no move.

They had strayed from the road and now sat in a sheltered hollow on the soft, wiry grass, looking towards the sea, black, vast and rustling. Above it the moon hung, a white near-orb, enveloped in a silver-grey haze.

'Magic.' Ruth lay back on the grass. The two of them seemed hugely isolated from everyone and everything, close only to one another, their closeness seeming charmed and fragile because of its very unexpectedness. There was a certain tension in the air, as well as an electric awareness of erotic possibility. Ruth remembered, with a ripple of surprise, that it was only that morning she'd read about the vague possibility of Owain's arrival. She had the impression that he'd been a fact of her life for much longer.

Now he reached for her hands and scanned them in the moonlight. 'Married? Engaged? You never said.' The joking tone seemed alien to him, awkward, as if he'd told himself that he must raise the question but didn't quite know how.

'Not till I'm thirty at the very least,' she said, with certainty.

'You've got it all worked out then.'

She shrugged off the banality of the remark. 'I need to be free with my work. I go all over the place. I couldn't

55

give up acting and it wouldn't be fair to expect someone to wait . . .' Ruth left the sentence unfinished. 'What about you, anyway?' she asked.

He smiled with a kind of complicity. 'I'm in no hurry either.' The tone of his voice, somehow meaningful, excited her.

They lay side by side in a charged silence. Owain said, 'Ruth . . .' A questioning inflection. A vulnerability in his eyes that she found touching, alluring.

He laid a hand on her upper arm, then moved it upward to her shoulder, her neck. His lips came down on hers smoothly, bringing relief, an end to waiting. He caressed her slowly, offering her the possibility of turning away. But she began to respond, with cool, measured movements, enjoying his lips and the controlled urgency of his body. She held him, kissed him, while a part of her looked on, marvelling at the beauty of the whole tableau, the huge, black, starry sky, the sea, the dark hillside, the ritualized movements of their two bodies. At the same time she savoured the texture of the rough, slippery grass beneath her legs, the damp, earthy freshness of the air – a montage composed of separate, kaleidoscopic elements.

Now she felt Owain's hand on her thigh under her skirt, and on the edge of her consciousness, an alarm sounded. No words, just a sudden sharp remembrance of the future she wanted so badly, and how easily it could be destroyed. She'd never been preoccupied with pregnancy. In the past she'd been rash and lucky at times. But recently there was too much at stake. She could stop him now, still, in fact she must, though a passive, sensuous languuour sapped her will.

Nevertheless she pushed at his hand. 'No, it's not safe.'

A whisper came in the silence, practical, reassuring, at odds with his passion. 'It'll be safe. I promise you I'll make sure.'

She abandoned her resistance then, making her decision like a swimmer striking out from the shore into a turbulent sea. There was the darkness and the texture of his skin, his whispered urging, the cool grass and the heat of their flesh, then a gradual reckless excitement as Owain moved convulsively above and inside her. She arched to meet him, craving his violence. He came with a harsh, groaning spasm, then lay covering her body as if he owned it, pressing it down into the hollowed earth.

Afterwards he lay beside her and kissed her gently. 'I love you.' She lifted her hand to touch his cheek, his lips, but didn't reply in kind. To her the words were taboo, though she'd discovered that some people used them more lightly.

Gradually they began to talk again, softly and inconsequentially. He said, 'I managed to get a ticket for the evening show, you know . . .' He hadn't mentioned it before.

'Oh?' She smiled lazily.

'You're good. You were beautiful on stage. Sexy, too.'

Ruth didn't reply. For reasons she hadn't had time to understand, his comment depressed her. She pondered on the remark, picturing herself in the *Blue Angel* costume, miming a knowing, humorous sexuality she didn't possess in real life. And she thought that all evening Owain must have been looking beyond her, beyond the simple reality of her, with her curiosity and her desire to talk, towards an imagined, alluring image. She was silent. He'd come prepared, too, with the discreet, cellophane-wrapped French letter. A short time ago the fact had seemed convenient and reassuring. Now, abruptly, the thought was distasteful to her. Her silence was not companionable, but had an unmistakable aura of hostility.

After a while he asked, 'You're all right, are you, Ruth? Not upset about anything?'

'No.' She disliked herself for the prevarication. It was so obvious she meant the opposite.

'Hey.' He raised himself on one elbow. 'You wanted to. You did, didn't you?'

She nodded. 'Yes.' She saw that the sky had begun to lighten. Dawn was coming on. For the first time that night she was cold, and shivered. She felt lank-haired and scruffy, her eyes hot and sore in their sockets.

Owain picked up his jacket from the ground next to him. 'Wear this.' She sat up and he placed it solicitously round her shoulders.

'I'd like to go home now.' For the life of her she couldn't have said whether this hostile mood was justified or sheer perversity.

'You're angry. I don't understand.'

'I'm tired.' She couldn't rouse herself to explain further.

As a trusted long-term resident, Ruth had a key of her own, though she rarely needed to use it. She had said goodbye to Owain perfunctorily, wishing bleakly that he'd find something to say to set the atmosphere right between them. But by then he had stopped trying too. Dog-tired, she went to bed, craving the oblivion of sleep.

The next day the sky was blue and optimistic. She felt slightly better. Rebecca was curious. 'You must have been awfully late. I didn't hear you come in. Was it that chap, the one from your mother's village?'

Ruth nodded. She'd missed breakfast. They stood talking in the downstairs hall with its clean smell of polish and its patchwork of carpets. She was still aware of a nagging depression, which she determined to ignore. A thought struck her. 'His father's quite well-known in trade unionism, apparently. And he's a journalist . . . Owain Roberts his name is.'

'Really!' Rebecca was impressed, animated. It was as if she'd mentioned Laurence Olivier or someone, Ruth thought. 'I read an article by him a little while ago, about the Marshall Plan. It was really shrewd. What an opportunity! Did he give you all the inside dirt on the armaments row?'

'No.' Ruth grinned, in spite of her dejection.

'Well, what *did* you talk about?'

Ruth shrugged, smiling. 'Ordinary stuff. Our hopes and fears.'

'Oh Ruth, you're such a . . .' Rebecca sighed disgustedly. 'God, what a waste!'

6

September arrived, the last month of Ruth's engagement at the Illyria Theatre. Nights came down earlier and the mornings were misty and soft, the air smelling of mushrooms and leaf-mould. There were fewer children on the beach. Rebecca spent her spare time closeted in her room – sitting cross-legged and tousle-haired on the bed – doggedly catching up on all the holiday homework she'd left until the last possible moment.

At the theatre there was an air of winding-down, a shifting, restless feeling, as the players lost the comfortable sense of permanence that had been with them earlier in the season. Now their eyes were on the next job, the next source of income.

Alice's immediate future was assured. In November, after a short break, she would begin rehearsals for *Cinderella*, at the Empress, Brixton, where she was playing the younger and less vindictive of the ugly sisters. Eric would be going to Wolverhampton for the pantomime season, by popular demand, reviving a previous season's success as Baron Stoneybroke. Which was about right, as he remarked with a jaundiced grin. Both were concerned about getting decent digs for the winter months, and their conversation centred almost obsessively around this subject.

'I remember some rat-hole in Dudley,' Eric reminisced lugubriously. 'Winter of Forty-six – you remember that winter?' Alice nodded and tightened her lips sagely. 'Ice on the water jug every morning. And the landlady had the nerve to tell me that the steam from my chamber pot was rusting the bed springs.'

60

Almost as soon as the season ended, Mr Murphy would be embarking on a tour with a girlie-show called Fenton's Follies. He was full of complacent, puffing innuendo at the prospect of his proximity to so many scantily dressed lovelies.

'Does he honestly think they're going to look at him with that great gut of his?' Sheila commented scathingly. She herself was going back to the mobile hairdressing business for the winter, living at home in Reading with her parents and helping out at a local dancing school. 'I like my home comforts come the cold weather,' she told Ruth, as she washed out her stockings in the dressing-room basin with the final sliver of a bar of Lux soap.

Len Street, Rebecca's father, had offered Ruth a temporary six-week job down at the Post Office. She was inclined to accept and keep her room at the top of the house. It would fill the gap nicely. That way she'd have time for a month or so with Sarah and Guy in France before confronting wintry Manchester and searching for somewhere to live.

Owain stood barefoot and shirtless in the tiny galley-like kitchen of his South London flat, making tea. A bare light bulb shone above his head. It wasn't yet seven o'clock. Recently he had been sleeping badly and waking early. He ignored the greasy stack of last night's supper dishes. Neither he nor Iris was averse to a homely touch of squalor. She was still in bed, her sturdy body huddled under the pink and red paisley eiderdown her father had given them. Only her short brown hair showed above the bedclothes, curling crisply on the rumpled pillow. She must have heard him getting up, but she hadn't muttered a greeting or asked for tea. Her drowsy shape had seemed unfriendly, as it often did. An indecisive hostility had lain between them for months. They no longer even discussed it.

The tea was probably brewed by now. He poured some into a blue and white china mug, topped it up with milk and sugar and passed through into the living room. The cold ashes of last night's fire lay, pale grey and powdery, in the grate. The mornings were getting chilly. A discarded black sweater lay across a chair. He pulled it on, crossed to the window with his mug of tea and stared out, his eyes still vague with an early-morning stupor. Below him a car and a couple of buses crawled along the Camberwell New Road, hazy in a white autumnal mist.

Nowadays he relished moments like these when he was alone, with no immediate task in hand. Self-indulgent moments when he allowed himself to contemplate the supple, erotic image of Ruth. He was still in a kind of shock. Outwardly his life ran as before, with meetings, briefings, and deadlines, a lunchtime drink in El Vino's, the haphazard domesticity of his life with Iris. But alongside the normalcy, this new presence pervaded his consciousness, compelling, taking different forms. Sometimes he imagined her on stage, incandescent amid the hackneyed bonhomie of the concert-party. Or he saw her questioning him about his life with an innocent middle-class eagerness he found amusing and intriguing. Or arching herself towards him in the throes of passion. Or stubborn or subdued, as she'd been finally, her uncombed hair and heavy eyes making her appear perversely young and desirable. His body reacted constantly to the pictures in his brain. At the same time he despised himself for the obsession. It was futile and adolescent, and accompanied by a dull ache, a nagging sense of failure, at the mishandling of an opportunity.

The truth was that Ruth had been mysterious to him. He'd never had dealings with anyone like her, though in all modesty he was popular with women. Owain had lived his life in political circles, and the women he'd encountered had generally been practical, energetic creatures, impatient of dreaminess, artiness, and other such decadent qualities. He hadn't known how to approach Ruth, and felt he'd cut a poor figure and finally offended her in some way he still didn't understand. He was only too aware that he and Ruth had almost nothing in common and that to compare childhoods was about the best they could hope for in terms of conversation. But she'd kindled in him at the time a simple exhilaration he'd almost forgotten, the feeling that life held boundless options and he had only to choose.

He laid his forehead against the cold glass of the window. A row of bombed-out houses across the road was being rebuilt. One of the labourers arrived on his bike, his overalls tucked into cycle clips above dust-caked boots. Owain drained the lukewarm dregs of his tea. Plenty of time for another cup before he woke Iris for work. As he turned, his eye was caught by the sight of his portable typewriter on the table and an untidy jumble of papers, reminding him of his own obligations. He grimaced dourly. An article on the US Control of Communists Bill for the *New Statesman*. God knows why they'd asked him to do it – he had no firsthand knowledge of the subject. At best it would only be a scissors-and-paste job.

As he returned, barefoot, to the kitchen, Owain reflected that he had only to wait and slowly his painful preoccupation with the memory of Ruth would fade and die and his life would again become all of a piece. But a part of him protested at the thought.

Iris appeared at the kitchen door, naked under an old blue shirt of his that she wore as a kind of dressing gown. It suited her, with her heavy breasts and smooth olive skin. She had a broad, well-modelled face, and pale, full lips. Her brown eyes had the sleepy, heavy-lidded look he always found arousing. He experienced a drift of desire, fanned by his thoughts of Ruth, but he made no move to touch her. There was a wariness between them that stifled spontaneity.

'What's the time?'

'Only a quarter past.' He poured her a mug of the stewed tea. No sugar. She accepted it expressionlessly. Both of them had always been vague and distant in the morning, so there, at least, their relationship remained the same.

Iris picked up the stacked crockery and placed it in the sink, running cold water on it to small effect. Hot water had to be brought from the bathroom, where an explosive, vengeful geyser was installed. She gave up and turned to him, 'Perhaps you'd do these later.'

'If I've got time,' he replied, keeping his voice neutral and non-committal. It was the pattern of their exchanges.

She cut herself a slice of bread and spread it with the remains of a jar of jam – the butter ration only lasted them two or three days. Then she took both tea and bread and headed silently towards the bathroom. Once his heart had ached dully at the continual subdued hostility of her attitude – and his – but gradually he was developing the habit of indifference.

He and Iris had met four years ago, give or take. She was a teacher. Both of them had been members of the same communist group. When he thought of those days he pictured a succession of frugal meeting rooms, sandwich suppers and pooled tea rations. Absurdly he remembered it as always being winter, though the usual summer months must obviously have intervened. He saw himself and Iris and the other comrades huddled in woollens and gloves in the teeth of a continual fuel crisis, rubbing their hands together and laughingly blowing out plumes of warm breath into icy rooms. Looking back, it had all been pretty spartan. And yet for a time there'd been a closeness among the group that he'd never experienced since. It came, probably, from their shared conviction that they

64

had a monopoly on the truth. Within the group certain basic assumptions were taken for granted. That couldn't be done in the outside world. It was wonderfully reassuring. Their passionately held beliefs survived rows, personality clashes and constant, niggling differences over detail. As a couple within the group he and Iris had felt blessed, and others had reinforced their view of themselves.

'You two ought to figure on a recruiting poster, looking into the future, all clear-eyed and idealistic,' Hugh, an older comrade, had told them more than once, with a wistful tinge of envy in his voice. Owain could still see his austere, rather handsome face and wire-rimmed glasses. At thirty-five he seemed middle-aged to them, and they used to laugh because he obviously lusted after Iris and couldn't hide the fact.

Another mental image recurred constantly from that time. Again it was a winter scene and it stood as a kind of shorthand for the whole period. He and Iris had been canvassing in a blizzard after a day's work – tenements in the snow, outlined by the glow of street lamps, the padded silence of their footsteps, the flakes stinging their cheeks. People standing in their doorways with mistrustful eyes. Himself and Iris hectoring and persuading, low and urgent. The elation when, against all the odds, one or other of their wary 'victims' professed interest, and they could write 'follow-up visit' on the damp reporter's notebook he carried in his pocket.

Then thawing out in the room in Muswell Hill, where they lived at the time. The gas pressure was so unreliable that the flames choked and spluttered continuously, changing colour in an alarming fashion. Iris had her cold hands cupped round a mug of cocoa, a tired, dazed, happy look in her eyes. The freezing sheets of their bed, and her warm, full body.

But already, it was clear to him now, they'd been living on borrowed time. It reached the stage where the horror tales of Stalinist repression could no longer be dismissed as mere inventions of the capitalist press. Acquaintances of theirs had visited the Soviet Union and implied guardedly that people in Britain didn't know the half of it. Then came the coup d'état in Czechoslovakia, the Berlin blockade, the denunciation of Tito. He and Iris became more and more torn. With all their hearts they longed to hold on to the dream, the hopeful, nurturing belief. At the same time they detested the evasiveness and bad faith of diehard friends who blandly ignored or denied what they didn't want to confront. Some people offered a stoic alternative; that of hanging on grimly until Stalin died or was ousted. Then perhaps it could all come right again . . .

For weeks he and Iris had talked about leaving. There were constant rows within the group, which became ugly and hurtful, trampling on past affections and shared good times. Owain remembered Hugh reduced to hard, body-rending sobs one evening by the onslaught of some of the younger members, himself included. The older man had taken his glasses off to wipe his eyes. The controlled severity of his face had disintegrated, leaving in its place a shocking, puffy vulnerability.

'You fucking little . . .' Hugh was sitting on an upright, rush-seated chair. He'd covered his face with one hand and bowed his head, almost as though in silent prayer. But he was shaking. They left him alone after that.

After similar meetings he and Iris would often stay up all night, going over the same ground time and time again. Iris had been a party member for longer than he had. For her the issue was even more shattering and emotional. Always afterwards he visualized her during that time, sitting on the edge of their unmade bed, wearing a pair of his thick climbing socks on her feet to keep warm, hair pushed back off her forehead and standing up in spikes, her face white, as though the colour had been bleached out with the strain and fatigue and intensity of her dilemma. Each time the memory induced in him a sharp wave of tenderness. Even now.

Perhaps without the strange euphoria of those early days the love between himself and Iris would never have come into being. Perhaps, like a tender plant, it needed that atmosphere to survive. Owain had gradually become convinced that the disintegration of their relationship dated from their leaving the party, though they hadn't noticed anything at first. The world outside seemed tepid and adult by comparison. But they were still together. The memory of those times was a potent and compelling fireside. They ought to leave it. One day they would.

Groggily Ruth opened her eyes. In front of her the rectangle of floral-curtained window shone dimly. Reluctantly, but automatically she withdrew one arm from its cocoon of warmth and squinted at her wristwatch. Half-past eight. She was sleeping late these days, and heavily.

Then the remembrance caught up with her and twisted her insides with a sick fear. It was a sensation which, in the last week, had become all too familiar to her. Still nothing. That made her ten days overdue. Alongside her everyday routine she was living a nightmare. Or a potential nightmare, for surely it couldn't be true. Still her innermost voice refused to admit to the possibility that she could be pregnant.

She shifted higher in the bed, leaning back on the pillows, clasping her hands behind her head, focusing drowsily on the familiarity of the room she'd woken to for weeks now. She had developed a proprietary affection for it, with the old-fashioned jug and basin on the washstand – though she used the bathroom downstairs when it was free – and the solid oak chest of drawers with its tarnished triple mirror. On top of it, in a tooth mug, was a pink carnation wired to a tuft of fern that Teddy had given her yesterday in mock-homage after some wedding he'd attended. The floor was covered with the usual mix of carpet offcuts and the wall lined with three different designs of paper. Marie and Len bought odd rolls at knock-down prices from a decorator friend.

On the wall facing the bed was a full-page photograph of Aneurin Bevan, Rebecca's hero, cut from a magazine and framed by Len. Opposite the window was a reproduction of a Van Gogh self-portrait. Over the years its colours had undergone a slow chemical change so that now the painting seemed to have been executed in minutely varying shades of an acid yellow-green.

There was no wardrobe, simply a rail, screened off by a long curtain in the same floral print as those at the window. By chance – since it must somehow have been obtained on the cheap – the fabric was unusual and attractive, a faded navy with pink and green flowers in the William Morris vein.

Everything was in its place. Blankly her eyes took in the details. Contemplating the homely bedroom she found it inconceivable that her life should not be running on its normal, trouble-free course.

Last night, though, before the show, she'd been violently sick, without apparent reason, and afterwards had retched drily into the lavatory bowl, as though the reflex action of her stomach could not be checked. Eventually she regained control and returned to the dressing room, pale and hollow-eyed, subsiding shakily on to one of the tall stools which were the only form of seating.

Sheila was applying sticky black mascara with poker-faced concentration, leaning forward to within a few inches of the mirror. She caught sight of Ruth's reflection. 'You look rough.'

'I've just thrown up.'

'Fancy.' The dancer gave her reflection a wry and knowing look. It didn't mean anything. It was merely

Sheila's teasing, automatic response to any mention of female sickness.

'No bright remarks, thank you.' Ruth knew that, given an iota of encouragement, Sheila would be talking about the pudding club and buns in the oven. She couldn't face it, not even as a joke.

Now, as she lay propped in bed, another memory came back to her. In her mind she saw herself sitting on the sunlit beach with Owain, ostensibly gazing out at the glittering sea and the azure sky, but in reality contemplating her own future, which seemed as wide and bright and beautiful as the horizons before her.

A baby. A child would put paid to everything she had planned. By January, when she was due to start the new job, her waistline would already have thickened. In March the company planned to mount its first production. By then she'd resemble a barrage balloon. Performances of Tennessee Williams's *The Glass Menagerie* were mooted for May. And it would be in May, she'd calculated, even while denying the possibility, that the child would be born.

If it existed.

And the foolish, shameful fact was that she didn't know who the father was – Paul or Owain. The situation was material for farce, and so ironic. It made her seem the kind of woman Paul admired, who conducted her love life with the freedom and insouciance of a man. And yet before Paul she'd only ever had one lover.

A knock came on the door. 'Come in!' she called.

It was Rebecca, scrubbed and spruce in her school uniform. 'Mum says are you coming down for breakfast?'

Ruth shook her head. 'Tell her no . . . I'm sorry.'

Rebecca pulled a face. 'You *are* okay?'

'Just lazy.' Ruth mustered a wry and shamefaced grin.

7

'That's the place.' Rebecca pointed to one in a row of tall, similarly proportioned Victorian houses. The front door had stained-glass panels depicting bluebirds in a frame of red and green arabesques. A spotted laurel bush flanked the arched portico.

Ruth nodded, looking waif-like. Her pale hair straggled across her face, which was white and peaky. Her hands were sunk deep in the pockets of her trenchcoat. She shivered, yet it wasn't all that cold. In the murky light of a late October evening the houses seemed to exude an air of sullen privacy.

'Like I said, the older sister of a girl I know went there. All very hush-hush. Well, her sister looks fine – healthy and happy enough – and she doesn't seem to be pregnant, so I suppose it all went according to plan.' Rebecca felt like the plain, sensible friend in a film. Ruth was the beautiful heroine, touched with tragedy, the one with star quality.

'Thanks for finding out, Becky. You're a pal.' Ruth touched her arm affectionately, her eyes wide and grave like in a close-up. Rebecca marvelled at the appropriateness of her every gesture, which unconsciously invested their exchange with an air of subdued drama. Rebecca felt warm inside, proud of her own role, practical and helpful.

Since the theatre season had closed Ruth had been working at the Post Office. She walked in with Len every morning. By all accounts she was already the star of her new workplace – a character, one of the boys – her down-to-earth good humour a piquant contrast to her aloof, classic looks. It was the same quality she'd brought to her job with the concert-party.

'Have you made up your mind?' Rebecca asked.

'I'll think about it.' There was a hint of fear in her eyes which Rebecca had never noticed before. 'I'm not keen, but what else can I do?'

There was a pained silence. Rebecca could think of no reply. 'Sure you won't come to the lecture?' She was on her way to a meeting to hear a crusading scientist talk about the sinister, undreamed of implications of the new nuclear bomb.

'No.' Ruth shook her head and tried to smile. 'I'm quite depressed enough without that.'

Dear Paul,

I don't know where you are, so I'm going to send this to your parents' address. Let's hope it catches up with you eventually. I wonder what you're up to. Becky and I have talked about it and tried to guess. I think you're in Paris – Down and Out, like your friend, Orwell. Becky reckons you've followed your heart and run away to become a quantity-surveyor or a bank clerk.

The thing is, Paul, I'm pregnant. I wish I could think of a more graceful way of putting it, but diplomacy never was my strong point. I just wanted to tell you. I'm not sure why I want you to know. Maybe it's because I've always been able to talk to you, and – even though I've confided in Becky – I seem to be living a very secretive sort of existence at the moment.

It's emphatically not because I want you to do anything about it. So don't come running with your Moss Bros wedding suit in your valise. I'd only send you packing. Perhaps I feel I can tell you just *because* I know you won't feel the need to make an honest woman of me.

The next bit will amuse you. You see, I don't even know if you're the dad. I was 'looked up' by a friend of a friend shortly after you left. He was merely fulfilling a duty. He was rather romantic-looking, like one of those freethinkers in Turgenev you used to talk about – your literary lessons aren't forgotten! Well, to cut a long story short, he could be the father too.

God, Paul, sometimes I'm certain I must be dreaming. Becky, needless to say, has been wonderfully practical. Someone she

71

knows has had an abortion and she's found out the address. We went and looked at the house this evening. It's one of those forbidding-looking Victorian mansions we used to think housed all sorts of secrets. Well, apparently some of them do.

Very soon I'll pluck up courage and knock on the door. I've got to. If I don't, a massive iron portcullis will clang down on my future. But, Paul, I'm scared. I haven't told Becky, but I'm scared, scared, scared.

The only thing that's keeping me sane at the moment is a temporary job I've got, down at the Post Office here. I use it as a kind of exercise in acting. I'm dying inside, but outwardly I'm chirpy, chatty, a real giggle. Becky says they all think I'm wonderfully unspoiled for an actress. Anyway, I focus on that. If I didn't I'd long ago have turned into a whimpering heap of jelly.

At school they used to have models of foetuses at every stage of development. They used to fascinate me. The eight-week-old one looked a bit like a mole I used to think. The trouble is I can't help thinking. And thinking. And I'm not sure if I can . . .

She laid down her pen and, perched sideways on the edge of her bed, looked at the pages of script. The writing was scrawly, febrile, as if her thoughts had come too fast. Vincent Van Gogh stared down at her enigmatically from his cracked black frame. On the end wall Nye Bevan smiled and waved with unabated cheeriness. What on earth had made her want to tell Paul all this? Ruth took the three sheets of the letter and ripped them through from top to bottom.

'Payment in cash, of course. Ordinary used pound notes. I charge fifty pounds . . .' The woman's voice died down momentarily as she watched for Ruth's response to her mention of the specific sum.

Ruth suppressed all visible reaction. But she nodded coldly, her hair hanging down like a curtain across her face.

'You *can* manage that?' A sharp note of enquiry.

'Yes,' Ruth replied tonelessly, not wanting to give her the satisfaction of a warmer reassurance.

'Bring it with you on the day. And don't call here again before that.' She was fortyish and rather smart, with coppery hair that looked like an advert for Pin-up home perms. She appeared ready to receive visitors in a draped afternoon dress of rust-coloured wool, her legs crossed in a conscious, elegant pose. She wore matching suede high heels. She had introduced herself as Audrey, though with an air that plainly stated that names were not important. The room had a tasteless luxury with swathed velvet curtains and artificial flowers on low, shiny tables.

Ruth had always pictured abortionists as aged crones with damp fag-ends drooping from their lips. Audrey smoked, but in a sophisticated, actressy fashion. Next to her was a heavy glass ashtray containing more lipstick-marked butts. Ruth felt her own hostility was misplaced. She needed this person. Audrey was going to be her salvation. 'When will you be able to see me?' Mentally she winced at the cautious euphemism.

'This Friday evening. Six-thirty,' Audrey stated flatly. 'Sooner the better.'

'I'm afraid you'll have to wait for a little while, love.' The woman who opened the door had a motherly air and a strong Welsh cadence to her voice. Audrey's accent was home counties, with a tinge of pretentious gentility.

She led Ruth past the living room where Audrey had received her the other day, and into an adjoining smaller room. 'Mrs Paget's been delayed. Nothing to worry about, though.' The woman was skinny and middle-aged, with rough, dark, greying hair and a thin, tired, well-modelled face that must have been beautiful in her youth. The pink overall she wore conferred a vaguely pro-fessional air upon her.

'Books.' She bent, with a smile, and touched a stack of magazines – *Illustrated* and *Everybody's* – on another of

73

Audrey's low, polished tables. Then she left. Ruth heard her muffled footsteps climbing the stairs.

On her own she had leisure to contemplate the implications of the woman's words. Nothing to worry about. If ever a phrase was guaranteed to raise suspicion and doubt. A picture flashed into her mind of a white, inert body on a couch, splayed legs, a river of blood. She closed her eyes as if that could shut out the image in her brain. Her flesh crawled.

She mustn't weaken now. Soon the whole thing would be over. Cling to that. In any case maybe the delay was due to something quite innocent. Perhaps Audrey had washed and set her hair and it wasn't yet dry. She shivered. The room was chilly and had the kind of unbending cleanliness she couldn't abide. Another fake flower arrangement, of tiger lilies and striped coleus leaves, flaunted its raw colours on a gingery whatnot in one corner.

Ruth reached for a magazine. She would read an article, any article, and absorb herself in it. There was a piece on the uninspired state of the West End theatre with its star system and safe, guaranteed hits. Ruth agreed with the premise in advance. The article would hardly serve to distract her.

She leafed further and confronted a two-page spread of baby photographs. A copywriter had added quotes that seemed appropriate to the expressions on the infants' faces. It was the sort of thing Ruth would normally have flicked over with total disinterest. Now she studied the round, immature faces with attention, and it struck her how each had a distinct personality, even at a year, even at a few months, and an undeniable, irrepressible life force.

'Laugh, you woulda died,' the writer had quipped ponderously under the portrait of one child, whose features seemed alive with gurgling delight. Ruth thought of

74

the creature growing in her body and couldn't equate it with this animated human being. The models in the school biology lab answered her imagination more closely. If anything, she thought of the foetus as a small alien tucked away inside her. A tiny, sexless, blank-faced mole inside her body, as she'd written in the ill-fated letter to Paul. But she realized that even for this almost abstract being she harboured a kind of tolerant affection and a sense of responsibility, as if her body was its refuge. And now she was about to betray it, like a priest delivering up a fugitive who'd taken sanctuary in his church. But she had to do it, or sacrifice herself. She must stop thinking. It was her right to put her own future first. Every woman had the right.

Again she heard footsteps on the stairs, descending this time, sounding positive and confident as they approached down the hall. Ruth guessed that they belonged to Audrey. It was the moment she'd both wanted and dreaded. The door opened briskly and Audrey entered with a bright smile that didn't reach her eyes. She wore a clean, white, knee-length smock, above which her hair and make-up were immaculate.

'I'm sorry you've been kept waiting, dear.' The voice contrived to sound simultaneously flat and genteel. 'We've had a little complication, nothing really, but it's all sorted out now.' Her manner was far more gracious than previously, the charm seeming forced and artificial, as though to compensate for the hint of disarray Ruth detected in her eyes.

'You're ready?'

Ruth nodded in what she felt was a reluctant and unconvinced manner. She would never be ready for this. She heard muted voices from the hall, and a baffling, gulping intake of breath like a sob. Audrey's eyes slid sideways, as though she'd been distracted in spite of herself. Then the front door slammed.

Ruth stood up, like Alice in Wonderland, tall and dizzy. An image of the sleeping, unsuspecting little mole flashed into her brain. She was about to accept its destruction. She felt a violent distaste for this house, with its cleanliness and secretiveness. Her legs were unsteady as she looked into Audrey's hard eyes.

'Perhaps we could sort out the finances first.' Audrey took a step towards her, smiling.

Ruth thought, if I hand over the fifty pounds, I've agreed. I'll be committed and I'll follow her upstairs like a lamb. Her fingers tightened round her bag, as though Audrey meant to wrest it from her.

The decision was taken. There was nothing she could do about it. Slowly and emphatically she shook her head. 'I'm sorry. I've changed my mind.' She experienced relief, coupled with a wave of despair.

8

Ruth sauntered down the darkening promenade with her hands in her pockets, enjoying the blue, windswept dusk and the lights coming on. Out of season, the town seemed more of a community. There was something comforting about it. She drew in deep breaths of the cold, salty air.

Since yesterday, when she'd walked away from Audrey's oppressive house and bridling indignation, she'd closed down her mind and her reactions. She felt numbed and peaceful. Very soon she would have to confront the enormity of what she'd done and plan for the future, but for the moment all that could wait.

Rebecca had been shocked and incredulous when Ruth arrived back at the Crow's Nest. She believed that abortion should be legal, women should control their own fertility. As far as she was concerned Ruth had thrown away her future on a simple whim.

'Do you think I don't know that, Becky?' She was weary, slumped in a wicker chair in Rebecca's room. She hadn't even taken off her coat.

'But *why* did you do it?' There was an expression almost of pain on Rebecca's thin face. She was sitting cross-legged on the bed, and raised her hands to her head in a gesture of bafflement.

Ruth shrugged. 'We're not the same. You think people should be logical. All of a piece.' She felt drained of emotion and energy, but roused herself to explain, while knowing in advance that explanations were useless. 'My head was like a roulette wheel. At that moment when she asked for the money it could've gone either way. The ball rattled around and settled in the groove marked no. It was instinct. It must've been right.'

'You're living in a dream world.' Rebecca shook her head. 'You need a keeper.'

'You're being arrogant.' Ruth spoke without rancour. 'Look, it's going to be like a knife twisting in my guts thinking of that job in Manchester, passing it up. But I did it. And now I know I just couldn't have done anything else.'

Before Rebecca could reply the telephone rang downstairs. Marie and Len were out. Rebecca dived out of the door and headlong down the four flights of stairs. It was a conditioned reflex. You had to move fast or the caller would ring off before you could get to the phone.

Left alone, Ruth closed her eyes and savoured her new feeling of peace. The more so, since she knew it would be temporary. She contemplated the small alien in her body with a kind of admiring resentment. In the last few days it had come into its own, making passive, imperious demands. And she'd given in to them. It sapped her energy too, making her easily tired and causing her to sleep like a log.

She wasn't sure how much time had passed before she heard Rebecca's nimble step on the stairs again. She burst into the room, her eyes full of an irrepressible animation. 'That was Paul!'

With her attention turned inward, Ruth hadn't reacted straight away. Paul seemed to belong to another life almost. To before.

'He rang to find your address. He was amazed to hear you were still with us.'

'You didn't let on about the baby?' The question seemed vital to her. If he was going to know, she must tell him herself.

'Course not. I offered to call you to the phone, but he wouldn't have it. He sounded a bit unsure. He's coming

78

'down, though, tomorrow, to see you . . . Whether you like it or not.' Her grin held a wry amusement at Paul's impulsiveness, and a trace of anxiety as to how Ruth would take the news.

'How does he know I'll see him?'

Rebecca shrugged. 'He doesn't, and he wouldn't ask. He said you might say no. He'll be in the Pied Bull at seven-thirty. And he hopes you'll come too.' She smiled. 'Ever so humble, he sounded.'

'Very convincing,' Ruth snorted. 'Moral blackmail, that's what it is. He thinks I can hardly refuse to see him after he's come all that way.'

That had been yesterday. And here she was on her way to meet him. She'd debated with herself abstractedly whether she shouldn't bear a grudge. He'd left very abruptly, after all. Then again, both of them were free agents, and she hadn't taken his departure personally. She'd never been any good at grudges anyway. In fact she was looking forward hugely to seeing him. Aside from Becky, she hadn't talked to anyone for ages who was on her wavelength.

It hadn't even occurred to her to arrive late. It was bang on seven-thirty when she pushed open the frosted-glass swing doors of the pub. She looked around, thinking that she should, after all, have planned things a little more carefully. It was uncomfortable arriving as a lone woman in a pub. You got ogled, and served with an insulting air, as though your reasons for being there could only be louche. Already some of the male customers were eyeing her. Some had even turned round to get a better view.

'Ruth!' A welcome and welcoming shout from one corner. It was Paul, scrambling to his feet as he waved to her, looking relieved and hugely pleased.

'Hallo Paul.' It was good to see his odd, wry face and familiar twisted grin. Even the decadent eyes.

He kissed her warmly, but circumspectly, on the cheek.

79

'I was so scared you wouldn't come. There's no hard feelings then?' A penitent air, assumed for her sake rather than his, Ruth guessed.

'I suppose there could be if I thought really hard about it,' she said with a mock-malicious smile. 'But I never have.'

Jubilantly he bought her a gin and tonic, which he knew she liked, though finances rarely ran to it. They had always drunk beer in the past and, when times were really hard, they'd been known to share a shandy.

'I'm a success story,' he claimed with a broad smile as he brought the drinks, depositing them on a table whose gloss was underscored with a pattern of inter-connecting circles, a legacy of years of wet-rimmed glasses.

'Why's that?' Ruth picked up her drink and raised it to him briefly. She took a largish sip and a glow spread through her body. She realized then that the calm she'd been experiencing was illusory. The last few days had left her tense. The alcohol began to warm and loosen her.

'I've got a band going,' he stated modestly, then lifted his glass, contained and enigmatic, leaving her to do the questioning. But before she could do so he proclaimed with a heartfelt emphasis, 'Oh God, it's good to see you again, Marlene.' An old lady at the next table in an uncompromising black felt hat glanced their way, startled. She smiled before turning back to her companion.

Ruth smiled too, at Paul, mentally echoing his sentiments. 'A band. That's wonderful. How did you do it?'

His simple elation was heartening to see. She remembered him at the theatre, always with a cynical cast to his face and voice, except when he was playing the piano. 'When I left here I swore to myself it was now or never. I'd keep plugging on and somehow I'd do it.' His voice was warm and confidential, as if he'd waited to tell *her*. She pictured the torn pieces of her letter flushed down the lavatory. 'I've got a friend in Soho, and I've been staying with him. I've been frequenting clubs' – he grinned with conscious rakishness – 'and getting to know musicians. Asking them outright if they were interested or knew anyone who was. Making a nuisance of myself. And gradually it came together. There's five of us . . . The Windmill Street Wailers,' he added drily.

'What?'

'That's us.'

'Oh, I see.' She smiled. 'And have you had much work?'

'A fair bit,' he said eagerly. 'And now we've got a regular spot in a club in Poland Street. They gave us some cash up front.' His eyes flashed with an amused, hang-dog look. 'But I spent it all coming down here. I had a sudden overwhelming urge to see you . . . But what are you still doing in Llandudno?'

'Working at the Post Office. Keeping the wolf from the door.'

'And when do you start in Manchester? The job that's going to make your reputation and get you noticed?' He quoted blithely from conversations they'd had earlier that summer.

Ruth said nothing. She picked up her glass quickly to hide her discomfiture and took a sip. His casual words expressed baldly what she'd thrown away, causing her mood to swing violently. She experienced a moment of total desolation.

Paul looked quizzical at her sudden silence. 'You're okay? It's still on, isn't it?'

She stared down into her gin, contemplating irrelevantly the floating piece of lemon among the sparkling bubbles, her pale hand clasping the glass stem, the textures sharp and clear, as she wondered how best to phrase what she had to say. 'I shan't be taking the job. I'm pregnant.' Her voice sounded sullen to her, rather

81

than stoic, or tragic or sombre, moods she'd have preferred to project.

He didn't reply. He was looking at her, curiously,
searchingly. She met his gaze. 'So no more theatre. Not
for some time.'

He took her hand. 'Why didn't you tell me?'

'I wrote a long letter. And I tore it up.'

'Why?'

She gave a tight shrug. 'I didn't like what I'd written.'

'Won't you have an abortion? Get rid of it? I could
probably lend you some money.'

'Money's not the problem. I had it all arranged. Then
at the last moment I backed out. I can't do it, I'm afraid.'

'Hell.' He spoke as if to himself, vehemently, under his
breath. Out loud he said, 'Let me get you another of
those. Then we'll talk about it.'

'There's nothing to say.' She resisted his assumption
that he should be involved in any discussion. And she
placed a hand over the top of her glass. 'I shouldn't drink.
Not now.' Though it occurred to her in passing how
convenient it would be if something should happen spontaneously, through no fault of her own.

Paul urged. 'Come on. You look as if you need one.'
He added pointedly, 'I know a woman who drank a whole
bottle of Scotch. And the baby was right as rain. It's not
that easy.'

She allowed herself to be persuaded. As he said, she
needed it. His breezy words about the theatre had really
struck home. Paul wove his way through the Saturday-
night crowd towards the dark, polished bar.

She watched him with an edge of amusement, wondering what it was that made him different from the other
men here. There was a carelessness in his walk, speech
and clothes, a kind of freedom. It was conscious and
based on his liberated literary heroes. He was well aware
that he put certain people's backs up, and not displeased

with the fact. Ruth noticed a middle-aged man with a long jaw and a handlebar moustache following Paul with his eyes, wearing an expression of unconscious distaste.

Other people were attracted. Paul must have passed some droll remark to the barmaid, because she grinned, quick and spontaneous, and spoke back. Paul replied to her. He was still smiling as he made his way back towards Ruth with the drinks. He bent to place them on the table, looking across at her at the same time and saying, 'I've had an idea.'

'What about?' She was suspicious. Pleased as she was to see him again, she didn't want him trying to sort out her life. She'd do that herself, in her own time.

'About you.' He looked her in the eye, deliberately provocative.

'Paul.' A warning note. 'This is my business.'

'Partly mine, I'd have thought,' he said mildly.

She experienced a surge of indignation at his presumption. This was her problem. He'd been out of touch for over two months and here he was preparing to make suggestions and involve himself in the situation. She said sharply, 'You're assuming you're the father, I take it.'

He appeared genuinely startled. 'Well yes, I was.'

'Hasty. Very hasty.' Their eyes met and locked, hers challenging, his confused and quizzical.

They were distracted by the click and hiss of a microphone. A florid-looking man was settling himself at the piano on a platform at the far end of the pub.

'Oh God.' Paul was rattled. 'I don't think I can take the floor show. Do you mind if we walk for a bit?'

The sea was black, but glittering with the shore lights, as they wandered along the sand. Paul ducked his head in the wind, his hands sunk in his pockets. A V of black polo-necked sweater showed between the lapels of his jacket. He looked bemused and non-committal and very

83

young as she told him about Owain. She had guessed that he wouldn't allow himself to show jealousy, if, indeed, he felt any. It ran contrary to his creed.

Afterwards he walked for a while in silence, then he remarked, with an engaging candour, 'I feel like a prat. I was so sure it was mine.' He hated to lose face, but managed to do so with a good grace. She warmed to him. 'Still, it doesn't affect the idea I had,' he added.

'Come on then.' She was reconciled to him. 'Let's hear it.'

'It's a brilliant plan, but I can't tell you about it without a string of warnings and qualifying remarks.' He looked unusually vulnerable. 'You've got to hear me out and not be hasty. It'll take some getting used to.'

She smiled at his hesitation. It didn't sound like him. By now she was intrigued. 'Come on, out with it.' She felt calm again, tolerant and slightly tipsy. 'I promise I won't laugh.'

Two teenaged girls passed them, up on the promenade, arm in arm, singing a current sentimental popular song in close harmony. Both were chubby, wearing heavy coats and ankle socks, but in the earnest, uninhibited blending of their voices there was a kind of rapture.

'Ah-h-h.' Paul watched the girls recede into the distance and turned to Ruth to share his reaction. 'Magic!' He was sincere in his emotion, but Ruth knew that he was also being perverse. He'd captured her interest and now he'd make her wait. She refused to chivvy him.

Then he caught her hand suddenly and pulled her close, kissing her with a slow and deliberate sensuality. She kissed him back, remembering how she liked the smoothness of his lips. They stood close, alone on the sand, and Paul said, 'I think you should marry me.'

'So that's it.' She was sceptical, her voice low and amused. She felt detached. His words meant nothing to her.

He was restless. 'Let's sit down. I can't persuade you like this.'

It was nicely incongruous to be lounging on the damp sand on this windy October night, with the black surf lapping ten feet in front of them, the sounds and lights of a Saturday night above them.

'I can't imagine what you're going to say.'

'First I'll put in the boot. Your kid's going to be a bastard. And there'll be plenty of people just waiting to make life hell for the poor little devil because of it.'

'Thanks, Paul.' Drily she acknowledged the truth of his statement.

'Just thought I'd mention it in passing. Not to influence you, you understand.'

'Of course not.'

'What I really want to do is persuade you to forget everything you've ever associated with marriage. Like G-Plan furniture and the man from the Prudential and serving up Batchelor's peas to the boss when he drops in for tea. That's nothing to do with us. We'll never be like that.' He leaned on one elbow, intense in the white haze of the street lighting. 'We can invent marriage. Our own kind. A new, improved form.' Grinning, he quoted an imaginary sales pitch.

'How do you mean?'

He was eager. 'We can make it anything we like. I mean you not knowing who you're pregnant by is perfect. A perfect starting point. Already we've got a different kind of family. And we won't cut ourselves off. We'll have other people living with us – like Becky, when she comes to London. We'll be flexible. Open . . .' He took her hand, raising it to his lips, kissing her palm as he scanned her face for a reaction. 'What do *you* think?'

Ruth was used to Paul's enthusiasms and generally viewed them with more than a grain of scepticism. In the dialogue between the two of them she'd assumed the role

85

of cynic. All the same, the image he offered of a shared life was intriguing, and surprisingly tempting. More tempting, she was forced to admit, than the austere future she'd envisaged for herself as a single mother in bedsitterland, with a variety of poorly paid, home-based jobs.

And there was that American paperback book she'd read years ago about an unmarried mother. There'd been a scene where the child came crying home from school and asked, 'What's a bastard, Mommy?' Sentimental rubbish, of course, and at the time she'd read it out to friends, mockingly, in a whining child-actor's voice . . . But in the last few days it had come back to haunt her.

Nonetheless, as far as Paul was concerned, her misgivings remained. 'You and me?' She gave him a look of amused complicity. 'We're not in love. We sorted that out ages ago.'

'Yes.' He shrugged. 'That's what we've always said.' There was a silence between them, broken by the swish of the waves. There was a timeless feeling to the sound. Paul looked out to sea. 'I'm not sure what "in love" is. I've always thought you were the most . . . desirable woman I've ever met in my life. I'm pissed. Not much, but a bit. And maybe that's why I'm telling you . . . I've never understood why you weren't way out of my reach . . .' His voice was flat and emotionless, as if he'd let slip a mask against his better judgement. She was impressed. He turned to look at her. 'I don't know about in love, but I really wish you'd say yes.' He reached out and spanned her wrist with his hand. She experienced the beginnings of a slide into compliance.

9

In mid-November Rebecca's older brother, Phil, visited from Liverpool with his wife and new baby daughter. Tickled with the novelty of being grandparents, Len and Marie used up the remains of a reel of film on snapshots of the sleepy child, with its wispy, spiky thatch of black hair.

It had been back in August that Rebecca had taken her picture of Ruth and Paul. Without Phil's visit it could have been another six months at least before she was able to release the photograph from the bowels of Len's camera.

With Ruth gone, Rebecca became a schoolgirl again, her life focused and simple. She moved down to her winter quarters on the second floor, next to the bathroom, where she had a wireless and an electric heater, which she shut off dutifully during peak hours to conserve fuel. She worked hard on her Maths, History and English, the subjects she was counting on to buy her a new spacious future the following autumn.

On her desk stood an enlarged, framed snap of Len and Marie, looking youthful, windswept and laughably old-fashioned as they sang 'The Red Flag' at the end of some socialist jamboree in the Twenties. Next to it she propped up the photograph of Ruth and Paul. Looking up from her text books and the smooth, lined sheets of paper covered with her small, forward-sloping hand-writing, she would stare at the picture, examining Ruth's broad, brilliant smile and Paul's slightly jaundiced grin, the bright sky and the sparkling water circling their ankles. It seemed an age ago, that summer day, almost a time of innocence.

In those days she'd admired them uncritically, dazzled by everything they said and did. They'd burst into her life, banishing its staleness, breathing an aura of glamour and disrespect. Now, back in her bookish, restricted world, Rebecca felt older, and her view of them had become harder. She was disappointed that Ruth had reneged on her plans for the future, so easily it seemed, almost without a struggle, and on top of that taken the easy option of marriage to Paul, whom she didn't love. She'd assured Rebecca of that countless times in the past.

'Thanks for everything, Beck. You're a friend. And you'll live with us, won't you, when you come up to university? We won't take no for an answer.' Ruth had given her a quick, tight hug as she left. Behind the drift of pale hair her grey eyes had seemed subdued, as though she were aware of Rebecca's feelings about the course she'd chosen, and in some way condoned them. Then she had smiled at Paul almost stealthily – a smile of solidarity – as if the two of them were wrong-doers up before some kind of judge.

In their three-sided relationship Rebecca felt herself an equal now, no longer the admiring onlooker. At the same time, the pair of them possessed a quality she coveted, a quality that was hard to put into words. But no one down here was quite like them.

She'd heard one of the neighbours down at the bus stop telling another woman about some relatives of her, recently moved back to Britain after a year in the States. 'But I don't see much of them, dear.' She'd shaken her head with an air of finicky distaste. 'They're a little bit *raffish*.'

Raffish. Rebecca smiled to herself. It seemed a Thirties word, and mildly ridiculous. But in a sense it described her view of Paul and Ruth to perfection. The prospect of living with them shone in the distance like a fire on the horizon. But the opportunity wouldn't just fall into her lap. She'd have to work for it. With an effort of will she turned back to her copy of *Land and People in Nineteenth-Century Wales*.

1951–2

10

They lived, so Ruth had written, above a secondhand book shop in Marshall Street. The proprietor, Ernest Broadbent, occupied the ground and first floors, and rented them the two upper storeys quite reasonably, since they'd offered to do all interior repairs themselves. Their flat could be reached direct by going through an arched passageway adjacent to the shop. It smelt of cat's pee and led to a skeletal black fire escape. In working hours it was simpler to come and go through the shop.

Ruth had sent a scrawled but accurate sketch-map and, after taking the tube to Oxford Circus, Rebecca had no difficulty in locating the street and the shop.

If Broadbent's had a heyday, it must have been back in an earlier decade. The sign and the legend 'Books Bought and Sold' were executed in decorative, squarish letters of black and gold, but the colours had faded and blended to an almost uniform nicotine brown. The windows, which displayed a number of single, dusty volumes, individually priced, had a yellowish tinge, and an Open sign attached to the door was discoloured round the edges with age. The façade above the shop front, of faded pink brick, was in a passable state of repair, but marked with irregular patches of damp. Still, she'd yearned for this place since last autumn, Rebecca reflected, with a flicker of self-mockery and here she was. She'd had to seek special permission from college to lodge here, and there'd been hesitation. But hostel rooms were over-subscribed and a dispensation had been given.

It was around four in the afternoon, so Broadbent's was open. Rebecca pushed the door and a bell rang loudly. The walls of the shop were covered with faded-looking volumes. An elderly man with rimless glasses and a brush of yellow-white hair sat reading behind the counter. He raised his eyes as she entered, but otherwise remained motionless.

'All right if I go up, is it?' Irrelevantly she held out her small suitcase. Marie had sent off the rest of her belongings in two brown-paper parcels. 'I'm a friend of Ruth and Paul.' He nodded indifferently and returned to his book.

She could see the staircase at the other end of the shop, through another book-lined room. The stairs were painted brown at their outer edges, the wood left plain in the middle, as if they'd once been carpeted. The wailing sound of a trumpet drifted faintly towards her, reassuring her that she'd come to the right place. Rebecca passed the first floor and carried on, coming to a landing laid with brown linoleum. Three doors led off it, all closed, but the music came from behind the central one.

She knocked, and after a second or two the door was opened. Paul stood there, looking crumpled and unshaven, brown curls dangling in his eyes. He smiled blearily at the sight of her.

'Becky! You got here.' As he opened the door wider to admit her, she became aware that he wasn't alone. Another male figure lounged in a tan corduroy chair near the window.

'How are you, Beck? It's great to see you.' Paul took her suitcase, depositing it on the floor, then enfolded her in an affectionate bear-hug. His manner was assertive and more familiar than she remembered it, perhaps for the benefit of his watching companion. Bristles rasped her cheek as he kissed her.

Then he turned towards the other man. 'Beck, this is Richard. He lives with us too.'

The stranger smiled. 'Glad you're here at last. Ruth's

94

been telling me about you non-stop for days.' He seemed easy and friendly. He was a large man. Fat actually, Rebecca thought, though the fat seemed sustained with a fair amount of muscle. He was bearded and looked as dishevelled as Paul.

Both men had striped mugs half-full of cooling tea. Richard sat in a reclining position. One arm hung loosely over the side of his chair. A half-smoked cigarette dangled from his fingers. Paul was on his feet, but she imagined that prior to her arrival he'd been similarly inert.

The record that had greeted her on the stairs – Louis Armstrong, she guessed – came to a short, fierce climax, then stopped. 'Brilliant stuff.' Paul crossed to the gramophone and removed the record, adding it to an untidy pile of discs without sleeves.

An earthenware teapot stood on a table near Richard. Paul took off the lid and peered inside. He grimaced. 'Stone cold. I'll make you some fresh, Becky. You could do with it, I bet.'

'I wouldn't mind.'

'Ruth'll be back soon. She's slipped out with the nipper to get some biscuits.' He went out, carrying the pot. He was barefoot, she noticed, and wore a darned navy pullover. Loose grey flannel trousers hung from his narrow hips.

She was left alone with Richard, who yawned hugely then apologized profusely. 'Late night.' Tersely he explained his torpor. 'I play with Paul – trombone. We did a party last night. It went on till gone three.'

'So the band's on the up and up?'

'We get by.' Richard looked dubious. 'But you do it for love, 'cause the money's terrible. Still.' He gave a short laugh. 'Our needs are minimal.'

'Paul does some plumbing on the side occasionally, so Ruth wrote.'

He nodded. 'And Ruth helps out in the shop. For

peanuts, naturally. My sideline's translation – German, Russian. But there's never enough of that.'

'Specially no Russian, I imagine.'

He grinned. 'Devils incarnate, the Russkis. I should know. My dad's one.'

She wanted to question him further on that, but was distracted by the sound of voices on the landing. Ruth's floating, laughing tones, then Paul's, more laconic, and alongside, vague, infantile noises.

Then Ruth burst into the room. 'Becky! You're here at last.' She was flushed and animated and carried a baby on her hip. Rebecca stood up. Awkwardly, because of the child, Ruth kissed her. Her swinging hair brushed Rebecca's face and neck. 'Now you've arrived the family's complete.'

She had changed in some respects. Oddly, now she was a mother, she appeared more of a student. Her straight hair was longer. She wore a black sweater and tight-ankled trousers in the manner of Left Bank Paris. Her face was pale with make-up but she wore no lipstick. Rebecca thought that Paul's influence had made itself felt. In some ways it seemed that Ruth had cultivated an image at the expense of her own native style.

'Becky, this is Ben.' She hoisted the child higher. He was about five months old, and had Ruth's clear grey eyes. He stared at Rebecca unblinkingly, and she found his solemn gaze a touch unnerving. She wasn't much used to babies – her brother's was the only one she'd come into close contact with – but the child's grave face was appealing.

'Hallo, Ben.' She touched his tiny, curled hand. He turned his face away.

'He's just learning to be shy. He never was before. But he'll get used to you.' Ruth held out a packet of digestive biscuits. 'We've killed the fatted calf for you, look.'

'Honoured, I'm sure.'

Paul brought a tray with tea, and while it was brewing he put on another record, a piano blues this time. Richard sang along in a husky undertone.

Rebecca found that she was mildly shocked by this afternoon idleness. It wasn't like a tea break, with a time limit pressing, but an end in itself. They chatted, Paul changed the records. Ben kicked his legs on the floor, and time was immaterial. It went against everything she was used to.

In Llandudno, holidaymakers apart, the only people who sat down in the afternoon were housewives, righteously savouring the peace and tidiness of their own creating before the children got home or it was time to get supper on. She was being unfair of course. Paul and Richard worked at night. Still this blithe inactivity made her uneasy.

'Ruth's got a baby-sitter,' Paul told her. 'And we're not working. So we're all going out on the tiles tonight.'

She smiled at him, warmed by the simple affection of their welcome. London was a lonely place, everyone had warned her, yet she had this ready-made family.

After a while Ben began to grizzle. 'Hungry, are you?' Ruth picked him off the floor. Unconcernedly she lifted her sweater and flipped open the fastening of her bra. Momentarily Rebecca glimpsed a voluptuously white and swollen breast before the baby's head obscured it from view.

'Have you noticed, Becky,' Ruth remarked out of the blue as the child suckled greedily, 'how everything in this flat is brown? The floors, the paintwork, the furniture, even the teapot. I'm working on it, though. If I buy anything it's always in some different colour. If I'm only here long enough I'll have the whole place looking like a Matisse.'

'I'll get my dad to send up some of his dog-ends of wallpaper.' Rebecca hoped her embarrassment didn't show. In theory she was all for a woman's right to nurse her child when and where she chose, yet in practice it made her nervous. It was the kind of small-town attitude she hoped to be rid of now she was in London at last.

'Ruth looks well, don't you think?' Paul asked later, as he and Rebecca sat together in a basement beneath Oxford Street, the premises of the London Jazz Club. The dregs of two cups of strong black coffee had been pushed aside – no alcohol was served – but she could smell a mixture of beer and Scotch on his breath, consumed earlier that evening at a pub.

Rebecca was mesmerized by the activity of the dancers. She glanced at Paul and nodded automatically, her brain connecting with the question only afterwards. She was a little surprised by it. 'Well' was a bland, all-embracing word and not one that would have occurred to her as she watched her friend perform a fast and complicated jive. Ruth danced with rapt concentration, and yet she seemed detached somehow from her twisting body and flying hair, the intricate manoeuvres of her feet.

Richard was dancing with the minimum of effort, his large frame lumbering from side to side and one hand extended as a sort of pivot for Ruth's whirling figure. He looked genial and restful in the surrounding frenzy, though he was sweating as much as anyone.

'She seems happy, don't you think, with the baby and everything?' Paul rephrased the question. He hadn't asked lightly, Rebecca realized. He really wanted her reassurance, as if he harboured doubts.

It wasn't that easy to give. 'I've only just arrived, Paul. How can I say?'

He appeared to think this over, then he smiled, slightly grudging. 'You seem so grown-up now, Becky.'

She shrugged. 'I'm *more* grown-up.'

'You used to look at us with such veneration.' He

sighed comically. 'It was good for the ego. Now you sum us up . . . judiciously. It's a bit unnerving.'

She laughed. 'You're still my idols. I've waited forever – to come up here.'

He took her hand. 'Dance?'

They joined the mêlée. The floor was packed with people cavorting energetically. You got jostled and bumped however careful you were, so there was little to be gained by caution. Rebecca had never danced with Paul. He had an eccentric, forward-leaning, knee-bending manner of dancing that she thought rather stylish. She was hesitant at first, feeling herself a country bumpkin, but soon lost her inhibitions.

The band performed on a small raised dais adjoining the dance floor. The leader, a tall man with subversive sideburns, played cornet. An Old Etonian, Paul told her slyly, knowing her distaste for the bastions of privilege. But the atmosphere here was egalitarian enough. It was every man for himself as the dancers struggled for room to manoeuvre. At the tables around the dance floor rows of solemn jazz students sat, listening gravely, giving the impression that they deplored the exuberance of the dancers.

The tempo slowed as the band slid into 'Careless Love'. The languour was welcome, and most of the couples subsided into an exhausted shuffle. Paul led Rebecca in a few steps of a slow jive, then held her loosely against him. She felt his hands moving across her back in a slow, caressing fashion and experienced a twinge of misgiving. But among the crowd she glimpsed Ruth briefly, closely entwined with Richard, her head on his shoulder, eyes closed, and she put her own unease down, once more, to her provincial ways. Tentatively she raised her hands to Paul's shoulders. He smiled and pulled her closer, but she was relieved when the next number brought a return to the faster tempo.

'Let's go, Becky.' He launched her like a spinning top into the thick of the dance. For Rebecca the evening became an exhilarating, hypnotic trance that excluded everything but the music and her own movements, which took on a kind of inevitability and a momentum of their own. Even Paul seemed almost superfluous, a home base to which she returned from time to time.

On the edge of her vision she was conscious of a woman with slicked-back hair and a loose red sweater who appeared to have entered a state of ecstasy, shaking and shimmying like a revivalist fanatic. Her partner, gaunt and black-clad, resembled a shadowy, intense acolyte. In a flash of amusement Rebecca remembered having read in history about the medieval dancing madness, and thought it must have been something like this.

She came back to reality as someone shook her by the shoulder. It was Ruth, shouting to be heard above the noise of the band. 'I've got to go. Ben'll be wanting his feed. Richard's walking me home.'

'What about you, Becky?' Paul asked. 'Do you want to stay?'

She noticed with surprise that she was soaked with sweat and physically exhausted. She lifted her damp hair away from her neck and had a sudden mental flash of the station that morning with Marie and Len kissing her goodbye. Only that morning? It seemed worlds away.

'I think I'll go too. To be honest I could do with some sleep.' She went with Ruth and Richard. As they left the noisy basement Rebecca noticed that Paul had already found himself another partner.

One of Rebecca's aims, before term began, was to visit the South Bank, where the Festival of Britain was in its last month. Soon after her arrival Paul declared that he would take charge of Ben for the day, so that Ruth could

100

go too. The indulgent air with which he made this offer made Rebecca think that such occasions were rare.

Ruth bustled anxiously before they left, making up a couple of emergency bottles for Ben, firing a barrage of instructions at Paul, then writing them all down in case he forgot.

It was a day of bright autumn sunshine. They caught a bus and climbed to the upper deck. Ruth seemed exhilarated at the outing, chatting nineteen to the dozen and pointing out places of interest at every turn. Away from Paul, Rebecca thought, she seemed more natural, dropping the bohemian *femme fatale* persona she unconsciously adopted when he was around.

'Look, Beck, there's the Skylon. Isn't it weird?' As the bus approached Waterloo Bridge the main landmark of the exhibition came into view, a tall and slender silver column shaped like an exclamation mark, with no visible means of support, shining futuristically against the blue of the sky.

Rebecca thought the exhibition wonderfully modern, with the colourful, geometric shapes of the pavilions. The exhibits themselves were duller. The portentously named Dome of Discovery was a po-faced hymn to scientific progress, but there was a fascinating film show, with animated shapes, colours and patterns that seemed to come out of the screen and hover in the air above your head. And everywhere there seemed a holiday feeling, a sense that the exhibition somehow marked the beginning of the end to the glum post-war austerity.

'They even have open-air dancing two nights a week,' Ruth laughed. 'Just like on the continent. But it's been such an awful summer that some evenings people have been dancing in trilbies and macs.' She was skittish and giggly, as if straining to extract as much fun from the outing as she could. 'It's so nice to get out of the flat for a day,' she sighed more than once during the afternoon.

101

They ate fish and chips, perched on the concrete rim of one of the raised flower-beds, and listened with shared glee to a pair of lovers who were conducting a vehement whispered row. 'You're a bloody blackguard, that's what you are,' the woman finally hissed to her spivvy-looking boyfriend, at the end of her tether, then looked visibly surprised by her own archaic phraseology. Ruth and Rebecca collapsed in muffled giggles.

Afterwards they strolled back across Waterloo Bridge in the late afternoon sun, reminiscing about the Illyria Theatre and sharing a bag of Sharps toffees.

'I feel like I did when I was single,' Ruth said. There was a plaintive note to her voice, which she probably hadn't intended, and which Rebecca chose to ignore.

11

Soon enough Rebecca had an alternative world of her own to distract her from the enjoyable, but somehow ambiguous, atmosphere of the flat in Marshall Street. On a damp and misty autumn morning, term began at King's College in the Strand, where she'd been accepted to study history. Suddenly her life was full of purpose again. She was energized. There were lectures to go to, reading lists and weekly essays. And the newcomers were wooed by the older students to join their clubs and societies. Rebecca took her work seriously and was cautious about committing herself too widely, but she was determined to follow up her political interests. She opted for the Labour Club, partly, she admitted to herself, because it might turn out to be a good way of meeting like-minded students.

By chance a general election loomed, and everyone knew that the position of the Labour Party was precarious. The socialists had held office since the end of the war. As well as being deeply divided among themselves, they'd become the scapegoats for all the country's ills, particularly the cost of living and the eternal shortages. Rebecca was secretly convinced that this particular election was a lost cause, but the newly recruited Labour Club members agreed that they'd make a concerted effort. They were small fry of course, just cogs in a huge wheel, but every little helped.

Three evenings a week they trekked to some outlying area to help the local network, knocking on doors and canvassing anyone from Bloomsbury intellectuals to dock workers. In this situation Rebecca was on familiar ground.

She'd been doing this kind of thing since her early teens, and had become confident and sure of her facts. Over the years she'd developed her own techniques and she shared her experience with the others. Apart from anything else, it was a handy way of coming to terms with her new environment.

The group of them would do the rounds until half-past nine or so, dividing the streets up between them, like brush-salesmen. After that it was considered anti-social to disturb people in their homes. Then they usually caught the bus or train back to Daphne's – a blonde, county sort of girl, who lived at home with her parents in Victoria. Her house was warm and comfortable, and her mother a cosy, accommodating person, who plied them with cocoa and fruit cake while they planned further sorties.

'Feeding time for the workers,' she would trill, as she entered triumphantly, her tray overflowing with bourgeois refinements, a lacy cloth, matching china and silver sugar tongs, while Daphne winced with embarrassment.

Rebecca was always tempted to exclaim, 'Gosh, Daphne, your mum's a brick,' like they did in the adverts for drinking chocolate, but it would have been churlish, and she had to admit the refreshment was welcome before the dull, damp journey back to Marshall Street.

The first friend Rebecca made in London was part of this group. His name was Carl and he came from Chorley. He was tall and fair, with gold-rimmed spectacles, quite handsome in a bony sort of way. His father worked on the railway and Carl was conscious of his working-class origins. He was energetic and ambitious, aware that university would open doors for him, and determined to grasp at opportunities. His singlemindedness riled some of the older students, who considered a period of humility in order for first-year newcomers.

He canvassed with an air of driving conviction. He was like a steamroller, but quick-witted and sure of his facts.

Women in general were impressed by his looks and seeming confidence, but he brought out a competitive edge in men that was sometimes counter-productive.

Rebecca thought his belligerence a front, a form of self-protection. When he was with her he showed a quieter, more thoughtful side. Like her, he was reading history, so in the early days they became a pair, meeting for lectures, eating lunch together, boosting one another's confidence in the vastness of London.

One evening they were waiting on Waterloo Bridge in the rush hour for a bus to take them canvassing in the Camberwell area. In the autumnal twilight the home-going workers seemed as numerous as milling ants. They felt provincial, anonymous, insignificant. 'We're two hicks in the big city,' Carl remarked conversationally.

Rebecca warmed to the uncharacteristic hint of insecurity and linked her arm through his. 'Yes. But two nonentities are better than one.'

In gratitude for their campaigning, the Camberwell socialists invited the King's group to an election-night party. Daphne borrowed her parents' Morris for the occasion. They drove down early, jammed in like sardines, so that she could help ferry apathetic – and sympathetic – voters to the polling station. Meanwhile the rest of them sat round on folding chairs in the cheerless committee rooms, drinking weak tea and discussing whether the first-time voters, who were rallying to the Conservatives in droves, would be numerous enough to tip the balance.

When the polls had closed they adjourned to a large and rather grim-looking house in a quiet crescent half a mile or so away. It belonged to Harry who'd been organizing the transport. He was bald, with a booming voice and a little moustache, like Mr Attlee's. They'd been told that he was big in local government. Each member of the King's contingent clutched a bottle, a

105

modest contribution towards the festivities. Harry stood in the hall in his shirtsleeves, greeting them and briskly commandeering their offerings. 'Time for a little redistribution of wealth,' he quipped.

'That means we bring light ale and get given Mouton Rothschild, does it?' Carl asked and Harry smiled thinly.

The party centred round the front room, where an imposing walnut-veneer wireless-set on a table in one corner had become the temporary household god. The guests clustered round it, on chairs or on the floor, drinking beer and eating sandwiches, and shushing one another when it seemed that a result was in the offing. Harry's wife, an efficient blonde woman, and two pretty, teenaged daughters, made mountains of fish-paste sandwiches, delivering them in batches like a relay team with cries of, 'Mind your backs!'

Most of the guests were a generation or so older than Rebecca, Carl and the other students. They circulated for a while, and were patted on the back and thanked all over again for their efforts, but then they drifted into an overflow room and formed a splinter group of their own. The room was carpeted and curtained, and cosily lit by a single standard lamp, but otherwise emptied of furniture. Were they expected to dance? The idea seemed frivolous, and anyway there was no music.

They settled themselves in a circle on the floor. In the mildly uneasy circumstances of this adult party it came home to Rebecca that they'd become a group. There were private jokes and references between them, even a kind of wry affection after their three weeks of combined effort.

Harry drifted in and topped up their glasses. 'Booze for the intelligentsia.' He used the word laughingly, but without hostility.

'Don't mind if I do.' Daphne held out her glass, cheerily feigning drunkenness. The party atmosphere had blurred the edges of her middle-class carefulness, and Rebecca found herself thinking that she wasn't a bad sort. She herself felt consciously happy sitting here in this strange house, elbow to elbow with Carl, mildly tipsy, and with a group of – if not friends exactly – congenial acquaintances.

The older guests amused themselves by bringing the students blow-by-blow bulletins on all the latest developments, which they greeted either with cheers or groans. The election was expected to be close-run, and it was far too early to jump to any kind of conclusion.

Suddenly their monopoly on the small back room was broken as another group – three men and a woman – came and took possession of the opposite corner. They must be new arrivals, Rebecca guessed. She hadn't noticed them before. But she was distracted by one of the benevolent messengers from the other room, a woman with a toothy smile and a shiny purple dress, who stuck her head round the door.

'Four more seats to us,' she announced, and beamed as they toasted her in lukewarm beer.

'How many does that make, Peg?' one of the other group called across.

'Let me see now.' She narrowed her eyes and began to tick off imaginary numbers on her fingers. Then she threw up her hands with engaging confusion. 'I couldn't tell you exactly, love. But we're ahead of the game right now. It's something like forty-three–forty.'

Rebecca felt Carl's elbow nudging her furtively in the ribs. 'See that chap over there – with the beard.' He indicated the man who'd questioned Peggy. 'That's Owain Roberts, the journalist.'

'Is it?' she asked sharply. 'How do you know?'

'I saw him once at a meeting. Talking about Tito and Yugoslavia.'

She studied the man with interest. In recent weeks she'd read two or three articles by him in the *New*

Statesman, but she was curious on Ruth's account rather than her own. The slim, bearded figure, with his hand on the shoulder of the female member of the group, could be the father of Ruth's son, Ben. And here he was in front of her, talking and drinking beer, unaware, unconcerned.

'So that's him.' She spoke without thinking, as if to herself. Carl looked at her, surprised. She offered him a token explanation. 'A friend of mine went out with him once.'

'Oh?' He showed interest, but she didn't expand on the comment. She didn't know him well enough for confidences.

From then on she gave only a corner of her mind to the conversation that buzzed around her. She was distracted. Owain Roberts became the object of her furtive and fascinated scrutiny. He was terribly different from Paul, she thought. When Paul talked he expended energy recklessly, constantly striving for effect – affectionate, cynical, funny, controversial in rapid succession. There looked to be a kind of stillness about Owain Roberts. He said less than his companions and yet in some way he seemed to be the focus of the group. When he did speak they paid him attention, though he kept his voice low and even.

No doubt about it, he was more handsome than Paul. Not that that signified. You either liked Paul's brand of ugliness or you didn't. Still, she was impressed with Owain Roberts's looks. In the muted light of the room, pulling on a foreign cigarette – she could smell it – he made her think of a moody black and white photograph. Ruth had joked that he resembled a Russian revolutionary. Rebecca thought he looked more French or Italian, in the dark, plain clothes that showed up his pale features. He looked serious, but his face lit up from time to time with a slow, ironic smile.

Her impression of him was in dumb show. She could hear nothing of what the four of them were saying, except that at one point the woman raised her voice and Rebecca heard her say, with an edge of vehemence, 'I don't see how you can say that, Owain,' but then her words were swallowed again in the general hubbub.

Rebecca experienced a vague, unreasoning distaste for the woman, though she immediately knew that it was because of Ruth and quite unjustified. Her friend didn't expect to see Owain Roberts ever again, nor did she want to. Still, illogically, Rebecca felt his possessive hand on the woman's shoulder as an affront. She was a totally different physical type from Ruth, sturdy and voluptuous, with smooth olive skin and short, brown curls. She wore trousers and a yellow sweater that emphasized her large breasts, and she gave an impression of energy and self-reliance. Rebecca pictured Ruth's dreamy eyes and impish smile, and thought that Owain Roberts had catholic tastes.

In spite of the physical contact, Rebecca could see no overt signs of affection between the two of them. The woman's expression as she looked at Owain seemed to be one of watchfulness. He stroked the back of her neck absentmindedly, but otherwise paid her scant attention. He got up suddenly. She saw him offering to refill his companion's glass, but she indicated that it was still half-full. Rebecca heard him say, 'Well, I've got some catching up to do,' as he went out, carrying his own tankard.

Almost simultaneously Carl stood up. 'Drink, Becky?' He smiled down at her from behind his spectacles, openly affectionate and slightly drunk.

She shook her head. 'Not for me, but I could do with a visit to the bathroom.' He took her hand, pulling her to her feet, and they left the room together.

She made her way up the thickly carpeted staircase and

was taken aback by the modish smartness of the bath-room. It was done up like a real room, with wallpaper that featured French cafés, and people sipping drinks under parasols. A glass shelf above the lavatory held bottles of bath salts, their stoppers shaped like glamour girls in strapless dresses. She thought of Harry and his brisk wife, and the luxury seemed faintly incongruous. In these surroundings Rebecca was tempted to linger and brush her hair and renew her lipstick. As she peered at herself in the mirror, she noticed that her eyes looked deeply shadowed. Her throat hurt too, the sign of a cold.

She remembered that there was a handkerchief in her coat pocket. Their outer garments had been whisked away to one of the bedrooms. But which? Standing in the upstairs corridor, she contemplated a number of possible doors, but was afraid of being thought nosy if she investigated them.

As she deliberated, a door opened at the far end of the passage, and Owain Roberts came out. With the unex-pectedness of his appearance she experienced something like panic. He didn't know it, but she'd been observing him minutely for the last half-hour, thinking about him, speculating. He had a significance for her of which he was totally unaware. Suddenly the space in which they found themselves seemed oppressively confined. He walked towards her, tall and unconcerned. For a brief, wild moment she imagined introducing herself, telling him the whole story about Ruth and Ben. In the couple of seconds it took for him to pace down the corridor time seemed suspended.

He was level with her now, a quizzical expression on his face, as though her embarrassment was obvious to him. They faced one another in the narrow passage.

She managed to ask, 'Which bedroom are the coats in?'

'That one.' He indicated the door he'd come out of, then smiled, cool and friendly. 'You're not leaving, are

110

you? With the excitement reaching fever pitch?' There was a hint of irony in his tone.

'Not yet. Just getting a handkerchief.' The reply struck her as ridiculously vapid. He continued on his way downstairs.

She got home just before dawn. The streets were damp and silent, and from somewhere there was a smell of malt in the air. The election result still hung in the balance.

'Your place, Becky.' Daphne drew up alongside the kerb. Steve, one of the King's students, sat next to her in the front seat. Rebecca dozed against Carl's dufflecoat. He'd taken the opportunity to place one arm tentatively round her shoulder. She stirred and yawned. It was hard to tear herself away from the rough warmth of Carl's coat. Mike, another member of the group, slept next to them in the cramped seat.

Outside it was raw and chill. Rebecca crept up the fire escape which led to the kitchen. Through the grey drizzle she could see a light shining in the glass panel of the door. Ruth was already up, giving Ben his early feed, sitting on one of the upright kitchen chairs, and wearing a pair of men's striped pyjamas. On the brown oilcloth in front of her she'd propped a well-thumbed school edition of *Measure for Measure*.

As Rebecca entered she looked up and smiled, her eyes glazed, lost in the poetry, hair hanging on her shoulders, tangled from sleep. 'This play,' she said sleepily, 'it's bloody brilliant, you know.' Ben suckled steadily, one small proprietary hand curved on her breast. A rush of affection for her friend caught Rebecca off guard and she didn't complicate the moment by mentioning Owain.

At final reckoning the election resulted in a win for the Conservatives. Though she'd armed herself against disappointment, Rebecca found that she was quite deeply depressed at the thought.

111

'Everything's going to be fairer now, Beck.' She'd never forgotten Len telling her that after the Labour victory in 1945. She was twelve at the time and felt proud that he was taking the trouble to explain things to her. It was a much-simplified prediction, aimed at a child, but somehow she'd hung on to those words. She remembered too a euphoria in the air, the feeling that this was progress with a kind of inevitability about it. And now here they were back at square one.

What made the situation doubly frustrating was the fact that the Labour Party had actually polled more votes than the Conservatives, and more than they had in '45. Their defeat was down to the vagaries of the British electoral system.

Ruth merely shrugged when Rebecca harangued her about the unfairness of it all, looking up from the floor where she was building up bricks and knocking them down for Ben's amusement. 'What difference does it make in the end, Becky? We'll go to bed and we'll wake up tomorrow, and we'll be the same people, and we won't see any difference in anything around us, no matter which of them's in power.'

Rebecca shook her head in weary exasperation. 'God, you're hopeless, Ruth.'

12

It was a sharp morning. Ben's nose was red as Ruth
pushed the pram up Brewer Street. She liked Soho at this
time of day, before the outsiders arrived, when the locals
ruled the streets, taking their children to school, cleaning
the windows and floors of their shops, greeting one
another in Italian, French, Greek, Chinese. She liked to
go out early to buy fresh croissants for breakfast. It was
one of the perks of living in Soho. Usually Paul was still
asleep when she got back, but Richard always dragged
himself from bed to linger with her over coffee. Sometimes Becky joined them, but more often than not she left
earlier to meet Carl in a caff for tea and toast before they
clocked in at the library to do an hour or so's work before
the first lecture.

Rebecca's energy left the rest of them standing. Richard
swore she lived forty-eight hours out of every twenty-
four. Without the restraining influence of home and
family, she seemed always on the go, with her university
work, her political interests and her dazzled exploration
of London's theatres, galleries and cinemas.

Ruth worried that because of all the activity she
crammed into her day Becky was losing weight, even
though she'd always been on the skinny side. Ruth was
vaguely anxious that Marie would hold her responsible.
But it suited her, she had to admit. Below the dark fringe
and shoulder-length bob Becky appeared all eyes, and her
small face blazed with animation. She wore trousers all
the time now, and they went well with her boyish figure.
Following Carl's example she'd bought herself a dufflecoat. In the rough, masculine garment she appeared

touchingly waif-like. Perhaps because she now had a child of her own, Ruth found herself viewing Becky at times with something akin to a maternal glow.

However, there were intervals, too, when she experienced a vivid stab of envy at the wealth of options open to her friend each day. She could make up her mind to stay in or go out at the drop of a hat, unhampered by responsibility and answerable to no one. She could stay out half the night or work in her room until the small hours. The decision was hers alone. At times, thoughts like these suffocated and tormented Ruth as she went about her daily tasks, like cooking, washing and caring for Ben. She suppressed them as best she could, but it was like stuffing the detritus of a room into a cupboard when visitors arrive, leaving a precarious, deceptive tidiness.

She would have liked to see more of Rebecca, but she was always passing through. Most days, though, they managed a coffee together, however brief and rushed. And there was the occasional rare evening when Paul and Richard weren't working and Becky had no essays to catch up on. Then they'd buy some cheap wine and play records, talk and laugh, and have a marvellous time.

'Hallo, Ruth. How's you?'

As she turned into Marshall Street she met Glenda, one of the army of streetwalkers that flourished in Soho. She was on her way to buy breakfast too, unmade-up, wearing fluffy slippers, her legs bare and goosefleshed, her hair a snarled mane. Glenda loved Ben and pounced, peering into the pram, calling him a little smasher and cooing at him until his small, blank face broke into a smile.

'Oh, he's lovely, Ruth.' She looked a sturdy, unpretentious country girl. On duty she seemed quite different, in her red patent high heels and mock-leopardskin coat, her honey-coloured hair set in deep finger waves and a sultry, calculating expression on her face.

'He doesn't like this weather much.'

'Oh,' Glenda gushed. 'He's got a little red nose.' She saw the paper bag on Ben's knitted coverlet and touched it. 'Warm rolls, mmm. I'm on my way to get some as well.' She waved to the baby with a little flicking, childish motion of the hand, and he smiled again, but he hadn't yet learned to wave back.

Unusually, Ernest was polishing the dusty windows of his bookshop as Ruth arrived home. He nodded good morning – a minimal movement of his head with its tufted grey hair. His greetings always had an air of surliness about them, but it was just his manner, people said.

Ruth manoeuvred the pram down the narrow side passage. There was a small shed where Ernest allowed her to leave it. She picked up Ben and the croissants and climbed the fire escape. She could smell coffee as she opened the door. As she'd expected, Paul was still sleeping, but Richard was up, standing by the square, scuffed sink and doing some washing-up from the previous night. He was tousled and unshaven, and had a staring, early-morning look about him. But she had known he'd be waiting. He seized on any chance to be alone with her.

'Coffee smells good. It's cold out there.' She propped Ben into his high chair. He'd had some cereal before they left, so he wasn't hungry. She got a plate down from the kitchen cabinet, which had been brown, in true Broadbent fashion, but Paul had painted it a bold turquoise blue. She still wasn't sure it had been an improvement. She emptied the four croissants on to the plate. 'We can be pigs. Two each, since there's no one else around.'

He smiled at her as he poured out the Nescafé and handed her a mug. 'Warm your hands on that.' He spoke cheerily, indifferently, but his eyes had an intensity that lent the mundane words a kind of significance. Sometimes she wondered if he was in love with her.

'How'd it go last night?' The band had been playing in the club in Poland Street.

'Same as ever.' A slow grin crossed his large, bearded features. 'The crowd went wild.'

'Big 'ead.' She bit into the warm flakiness of a croissant and handed Ben a little piece to play with or eat, as the fancy took him. Then she sipped the hot coffee. Sometimes she thought this was the best moment of the day, their cosy, communal breakfast in the steamy warmth of the kitchen, with nappies drying on the overhead airer, and the hot glow of the gas fire. Each morning she became more reluctant to end this interlude and take up her chores.

'Paul's fan was there again last night.' Richard had a mischievous expression on his face.

Ruth smiled grimly. 'Was she now?' In the club there were always women hanging round the musicians, making eyes at them, available. But this particular admirer was more persistent than most. She'd taken a shine to Paul and sent him notes that were whimsical, original and blatantly suggestive. Ruth had seen her on one of the odd nights she managed to make it to the club, a dark girl, handsome and, Ruth thought, slightly crazy-looking. But undeniably attractive.

'She waited for him afterwards, but he gave her the slip.'

'I'm glad to hear it.'

The situation caused her only the tiniest ripple of anxiety. Ruth was usually in bed when Paul got home. Often she'd been sleeping, warm, heavy and relaxed. Paul still had the exhilarating aura of his music, the club, the people, clinging to him like an invisible garment. He'd undress and warm himself against her, then make love to

116

her in the secret dark, fuelled by the energy of his evening and by whatever fantasies had drifted through his head.

Before, there had always been an element of tension – the fear of disapproving landladies and sudden interruptions. Now they had time, privacy and a huge, old-fashioned feather bed, which offered the opportunity for sexual exploration, a slow lingering sensuality. To Ruth it was a revelation. The memory of her nights stayed with her in the daylight hours, a voluptuous secret, imbuing her movements and gestures with retrospective languour.

A folded newspaper lay on the table. Richard reached for it, his brawny arm protruding from the rolled-up sleeve of his sweater.

Ruth darted her hand towards it. 'Can I have a quick look first?' She knew he'd let her.

They read the paper a day in arrears. Rebecca bought the *Manchester Guardian* each morning then left it on the kitchen table at night for the rest of them to peruse or not, as they chose. Ruth scanned the news pages with only the most cursory attention, but recently, with increasing frequency, she had come across references to the Manchester Experimental Theatre Company, and usually it was spoken of in terms of interest and warm approval.

She flicked through the arts pages. Today she'd hit the jackpot. There was an interview with Delia Rogers, a young female member of the company. Pretty and self-opinionated, she smiled above a column some six inches long.

Ruth lowered the page to show Richard. 'Look, that could've been me.'

He peered. 'She looks a stuck-up bitch.'

Ruth felt a quick rush of anger at the casual male insult. 'You'd have said that about me.' Adding coldly, 'She's just happy. She's got what she wants.'

117

He shrugged, surprised by her defensiveness. 'I don't like her face, but I do like yours.'

She turned her attention back to the paper. The young woman's opinions could have been articulated by herself. She deplored the static complacency of much of the current professional theatre and talked about the need for new approaches, a greater excitement and flexibility. She spoke glowingly of the stimulating, fulfilling atmosphere of the Experimental Company, and of her own wonderful role in *The Glass Menagerie*.

Ruth read, and was riveted as she tried to imagine herself in the actress's place, but it was becoming increasingly difficult. The makeshift domesticity of her own life was acquiring a kind of inevitability. It was humdrum in some respects, but relatively painless, and held the matchless consolation of Ben himself. The sight of him at any moment – awake or asleep, smiling or crying, absorbed or puzzled – filled her heart with a sharp tenderness that hurt like a knife. She viewed the world through his eyes, new and miraculous, as he saw clouds and birds, colours and movement for the first time. To be Delia Rogers would be to be without Ben.

And her life held other pleasures – the mildewed exoticism of Soho, her friendship with Becky, the richness of her sexual reconnaissance with Paul, Richard's unspoken, but all-too-obvious desire and admiration, which fuelled her vanity. She drained her mug and handed him the paper. Her life was congenial and familiar. Delia Rogers's was risky and demanding.

She smiled at Ben. 'Who's going to have a bath then? A bath.' She flattered herself that he was beginning to understand that word. She picked him up and he wriggled happily in her arms. A lock of her long hair fell forward, and he seized it in his soft little hands. He was altogether delicious. Still, after reading that interview, she couldn't shake off a certain heaviness of spirit.

13

In the summer of '52, during her third term at university, Rebecca ran into Owain Roberts again. Some of the more politically minded students, including herself, Carl and Daphne, had organized a forum on NATO and the European Defence Community. They invited a number of speakers, not all of whom were free or willing to come. Among those who accepted was Owain Roberts.

They'd been apprehensive about the meeting. There'd been all sorts of setbacks during the planning stages – problems over the venue and guests cancelling at the last minute. But in the event it turned out to be well-attended and lively, with plenty of honest debate which never degenerated into aggression.

Rebecca was impressed with Owain's contribution. He put the case for the Bevanite Left, with whom he identified, claiming that Britain was still crippling herself with excessive spending on rearmament. He spoke clearly and simply and received quite an ovation, which coincided with Daphne's entry with tea and biscuits. She blushed scarlet as Owain joined the applause, directing it towards her.

Afterwards, the students who'd had a hand in organizing the day were relieved and elated. Most of the speakers had to hurry away, but Owain was still there after they'd cleared up. Carl suggested that they go for a drink and invited Owain to come with them.

It was a soft, summery evening. They strolled to a pub off Piccadilly and found room at a large table near the open door. The pub was full and they were fairly cramped. Owain was sitting between Rebecca and

Daphne. He produced a packet of Gitanes and offered them round, taking one himself. The tobacco scent on the warm air struck Rebecca as sensuous and summery.

Daphne accepted a cigarette, inhaling deeply and sniffing the smoke like a Bisto kid. 'Ahh, Paris.' A beatific smile. 'An August evening in Paris.'

Rebecca noticed that Daphne's middle-class raptures caused the flicker of a smile to cross Owain's features. 'Funny, it makes me think of Cardiff,' he said, adding whimsically, 'For reasons too complicated to go into.'

Daphne blushed. She did so often, and it was a failing of which she despaired. Her friends thought it sweet and teased her, which made matters worse. That evening she had a bandbox neatness, in her pink shirtwaisted dress, with her blonde hair newly permed. Over the months Rebecca had grown fond of her. She was immensely good-natured, always willing to give lifts, make tea, wash up. So much so that Rebecca sometimes felt the necessity to protect her from herself.

Owain was modest, friendly and relaxed, and he seemed to enjoy their company, though he claimed they made him feel like some superannuated pundit. It was obvious that he hadn't recognized them, so Rebecca didn't remind him of the election-night party.

She mentioned her admiration for Aneurin Bevan, which Owain shared, and he told her some anecdotes about the battling politician that were new to her. Rebecca was struck by the affection in his voice, and she found herself liking him, almost against her will. Her view of him had always been coloured by her own relationship with Ruth. Her friend and Owain had parted on hostile terms. 'I didn't like his idea of me,' Ruth had told her once enigmatically. Then she'd shrugged. 'Maybe I was unfair. I don't know. It doesn't matter now anyway.'

Owain offered to buy a round of drinks. As he pushed his way through the bodies towards the bar, Rebecca thought how much more approachable he seemed tonight than at the party last autumn. Then she'd thought him watchful and ascetic. This evening he was almost affable, tanned and healthy-looking in a check shirt that gave him a casual, off-duty air. Returning with fistfuls of drinks, he shot her a wry, alarmed glance as a customer gestured expansively in mid-anecdote and almost sent the glasses flying. He gave a relieved grin as he set the tankards down safely on the table. 'What a vivacious chap.'

Knowing how much he admired Owain's articles, Rebecca tried to draw Carl into the conversation. But he was unfavourably positioned at the far side of the table and trapped between two third-year students. He made an effort, but he was defeated by the Saturday-night hubbub of the pub. She, Daphne and Owain went back to their private conversation. They'd all read a recent piece by Bertrand Russell on what was becoming known as the arms race, and they discussed it with gloomy relish.

At closing time Rebecca invited Carl and Daphne back to Marshall Street for coffee. They were standing on the Shaftesbury Avenue corner of Piccadilly Circus. 'You'd be very welcome as well, of course.' She looked up at Owain, feeling less bold than in the cramped conviviality of the pub. After all, they were students and he, in however small a way, was a celebrity.

'Love to.' His reply was instant and easy. He was staying the night up in town with friends. 'They're night birds and they're not expecting me at any particular time.'

As they strolled along Great Windmill Street it occurred to Rebecca to wonder how Ruth would react to Owain's unexpected appearance. Then she remembered that Ruth was taking Ben down to Paul's parents in Raynes Park for the night so that she could have a rare night out at the club. She was mildly relieved at the thought. It wasn't exactly that she expected their reunion to be traumatic, or dramatic or anything – Ruth seemed

121

pretty indifferent to the memory of Owain. It was just that the surprise of their meeting would probably jar the pleasant, passing camaraderie that had sprung up between the group.

Soho was lively and noisy. Although the pubs were closed there were clubs that catered for late-night drinkers. The air was warm and muggy, the sky turned velvety-mauve by the glare of the street lamps. Small gaggles of people lingered on street corners chatting in a rich variety of languages. The strangely nostalgic smell of foreign tobacco drifted on the air, making Rebecca think of Owain's French cigarettes. The general street-murmur was punctuated by bursts of good-natured laughter. Women in doorways smiled optimistically at likely clients.

Naturally the bookshop was closed at that time of night so they entered the flat via the fire escape. Rebecca put the kettle on, then led them straight upstairs to her bedroom on the top floor.

She loved this room. At home there'd always been a kind of impermanence about her sleeping quarters, which shifted from season to season. She had never been allowed to colonize the walls with posters and cuttings because of the imminent presence of the spring, summer and even Christmas visitors. Paul and Ruth had positively encouraged her to make the room her own. She'd pinned magazine cuttings to her walls, close-ups of Bogart and Bacall, Yves Montand, and a smouldering new American actor called Marlon Brando. At King's she'd inherited the job of painting posters for the Labour Club meetings. It was a task she'd warmed to, mixing unusual graphics with bold, telling images from newspapers and periodicals in a striking collage effect. She was pleased with her creations and brought them home afterwards to help conceal Mr Broadbent's dun-coloured wallpaper.

Even before he sat down Owain began to examine them with interest. 'Are these your handiwork?'

She nodded.

'I like them. They're eyecatching. Did you do one for today's meeting?'

'Four altogether, actually.'

'You couldn't let me have one of them. As a souvenir?'

'Yes, of course.' She was gratified. 'Give me your address and I'll send it to you.'

He smiled his thanks. 'How does it feel to be surrounded by your own propaganda?'

Rebecca shrugged. 'I'm a convert already, so it doesn't make much difference. Basically, I'm trying to hide the wallpaper.'

'I can understand that.' He eyed an area of wall where the mottled beige and brown were still visible.

There were only three chairs in her room, so after she'd brought the coffee Rebecca sat on the floor. Owain began to talk to them about his dreams of starting up a political review of his own. 'With no hard line. Everyone can say their bit.' A gleam of amusement. 'Even Hitler and Genghis Khan. And there'll be articles by unknown people. Intelligent, ordinary people with something to say. I definitely don't want the same old stable of political hacks all the time.' A smile. 'And that includes me.' He leaned forward earnestly in his chair, elbows on knees, his mug dangling from between his fingers. 'I'd like line illustrations by good, unknown artists – with the emphasis on unknown. We're not going to be able to pay anyone expensive.' He looked at Rebecca with a semi-apologetic smile on his bearded features. 'It's seeing your posters that made me start on about all this. I get obsessed and bore the pants off everyone in sight.'

But they were carried along by his fervour and wanted to know more. Carl was dubious. 'It's an interesting idea. Idealistic almost. But I'm not certain about the lack of a point of view. It seems to me that in theory you could

123

convince hoards of people on a policy you're personally totally against . . .'

'I'd like to take an issue in each edition and state the two opposing points of view. Then it's left to logic and reason – I hope – to carry the day.' He was talking, Rebecca reflected, as if no difference of age or experience existed between them. The proposed magazine, however remote a possibility, sounded intriguing. She sipped her coffee, feeling happy. It had been a stimulating day, and a successful one.

A knock came at her bedroom door. She pulled a face. 'Who can that be?' Puzzled, she got up and opened it. Ruth stood outside with Ben in her arms. 'I thought you were out.' Surprise made Rebecca sound curt, even rude.

Ruth shook her head. 'Ben's got a temperature. He's teething too. I wasn't going to dump him on anyone like that.' She placed her cheek against the child's. 'I've been sitting with him in the dark, downstairs in the living room. He's been sleeping. But now he's restless.' Then she grinned, suddenly provocative. 'Well, Beck, are you going to let me in?'

'Of course.' Rebecca could think of no possible words to warn her of Owain's presence.

Rebecca entered, carrying Ben. His cheeks were hectically flushed, and on one side there was a patch of skin even redder than the rest. He'd managed to force almost all of one hand into his mouth. He looked tired, but his grey eyes were wide and very bright. He stared at Carl, Daphne and Owain with expressionless curiosity.

Ruth brought a new dimension into the room immediately, fragmenting the temporary intimacy they'd been enjoying. Unconsciously, given an audience, she exuded drama and the effect was heightened by her pale make-up, long, straight hair, blood-red shirt and dark trousers, and by the child in her arms. She scanned the occupants of the room.

124

'Hallo there.' She smiled at Carl and Daphne, then turned back to Owain, waiting for Rebecca to introduce them. Almost at once, though, her face showed a startled recognition. But immediately she turned her disarray to a conscious, willed surprise. 'Goodness. It's a small world.'

Owain looked at her, puzzled at first, and then with a dawning incredulity. 'Ruth?'

I should have mentioned the possibility, Rebecca thought. At least Ruth knows about Owain and the meeting. He's got no idea. Owain turned again to Rebecca, nonplussed, as though any explanation must come from her.

'You two know each other, don't you?' To her own ears the attempted insouciance had a decidedly insincere ring. 'I lodge with Ruth and her husband. I didn't mention it because I thought they'd be out and it seemed . . .' she was floundering, '. . .an unnecessary complication.'

Ruth flashed a broad, affectionate smile, and patted her reassuringly on the back. 'Gosh, Becky, you sound so *guilty*!' The comment was admirably timed and made them all laugh, restoring a certain ease to the atmosphere.

'It's certainly good to see you again.' Owain suppressed his obvious discomfiture with a game display of conventional chitchat. He asked how long Ruth had been married and admired Ben as he sympathized with his teething troubles. The social equilibrium was restored. Ruth sat down on the bed and Ben snuggled into her body, still sucking several fingers. They made an attractive tableau, and Rebecca sensed that Ruth was not unaware of the fact. At a stroke Carl, Daphne and herself had all but vanished from Owain's consciousness, though moments earlier they'd been locked in animated conversation.

Now Rebecca's cosy room was filled with the tension between Owain and Ruth. Ostensibly they enquired dutifully about the people they had in common, however remotely – Sarah, Ruth's mother, and the friends she

125

knew from Owain's Welsh village. But their words were unimportant, just a means of making contact. What signified was their acute awareness of one another.

Her friend had adopted the persona that Rebecca least liked in her. The one she privately thought of as her *femme fatale* act. Ruth flaunted a kind of passive, implicit awareness of her own attraction and the effect it might have on others.

She talked in a husky, lazy fashion, that wasn't affected exactly but quite different from her usual impulsive speech. In the muted light of a corner lamp her eyes were deep with a hidden excitement, and a smile hovered on her lips that stated plainly that the conversation between them was merely to satisfy convention. She cradled Ben with slow, conscious movements.

Owain seemed almost painfully aware of her every word and gesture. His eyes were fixed on her face. From a sense of social responsibility he made an effort to move the conversation away, to include the others in the dialogue between himself and Ruth. There was a new brittleness in his manner of speaking and a kind of unease. The openness he'd shown them all evening was gone. Carl and Daphne did their best, offering polite interjections and little bursts of tepid laughter, but Rebecca sat silent, small and mutinous, watching them all with something akin to hostility.

14

A month or so later Owain found himself in the unlikely position of covering the Fifteenth Olympiad in Helsinki for the *New Statesman*. Rather late in the day, the idea had been mooted for a fairly lighthearted review of the Games and their political implications. In the thick of the Cold War it was, after all, rare for the East and West to meet with any degree of informality. Owain's name was put forward. He was known to be keen on sport and to play the occasional game of rugby. This, it seemed, was qualification enough.

Owain was not at all averse. Iris was spending a large part of the school holidays with her parents in Leicester. The assignment, with its leisurely deadline, struck him as something of a sinecure.

Helsinki appeared to him as a town of austere and functional skyscrapers, incongruously set down in a land of lakes and forests. The opening ceremony took place beneath heavy, slate-coloured skies and driving rain, which slackened to a fine drizzle for the athletes' parade. Anonymous in the huge stadium, Owain sensed a willingness, almost a hunger, among the spectators to show themselves free of the tensions and suspicions of the world political scene. They cheered the huge contingent of Russians with as much warmth as they offered the Americans. Owain found himself oddly touched by this almost defiant demonstration that people were more important than regimes.

After the Olympic torch was lit a young woman in flowing white robes mounted the rostrum and attempted to make a speech in favour of peace. For a time there was confusion, a questioning hubbub. Was this or was it not a scheduled attraction? A moment or so later the woman was led away between two straight-faced officials, but the ripple of comment that followed her seemed approving rather than otherwise.

During the following days the awareness stayed with him that politics were supremely irrelevant to the struggle between athletes, men and women stripped down to vest and shorts, reduced to their own strength, skill and courage, the rivalry between them intense and wholly personal. Owain knew that the thought was trite, yet the truth of it came home to him sharply again and again. And he saw that the rivalry was coupled with a kind of fellow-feeling, an instinctive comradeship which took no account of nationalities.

The British had small success and Owain soon tired of his fellow-journalists' obsessive discussions on the poor form of Bailey, Chataway, Bannister and the others. They worried at the problem like mongrels sharing a large, meaty bone, blaming everything, from the lack of indoor facilities for year-round training to the shortage of beef steak in the post-war British diet. In the evenings Owain felt he had to get away.

He discovered a congenial bar called the Tivoli, a darkish place with rustic carved furniture, wine-coloured velvet curtains and an imposing mahogany counter, which ran almost the length of the room. The clientele looked to be vaguely arty, and on his first night he got into conversation with a thin, ascetic-looking sculptor and his blonde wife, who reminded him of Ruth and stirred pleasurable ripples of nostalgic lust.

The second time he went there Owain sat on a high stool at the bar, and found himself next to a small, stocky man of about his own age, with owlish glasses and a rueful, likeable smile. They began to talk and Owain discovered that he was a Hungarian, a journalist like himself, covering the games for a paper back home.

His name was Janos Molnar and their conversation was halting at first. Owain spoke no Hungarian, and Janos's English was fractured and elliptical, but by mixing it with French they got along reasonably well and as the evening progressed their ears became attuned to the vagaries of one another's pronunciation.

Inevitably they started by discussing the Games. Both of them were admirers of the Czech runner Zatopek who was dominating the long-distance events. Owain got embroiled in an ambitious analysis of the athlete's technique, and found his French wasn't really up to the shades of meaning involved. But Janos showed great good will, nodding emphatically and commenting '*Oui, d'accord*' at every opportunity.

He bought them both a glass of some fiery local brandy and they moved across to a table where they could talk more comfortably. Owain offered Janos a Gitane and leaned forward to give him a light. At the same time he passed some remark about the success of the Russian team.

Janos drew dourly on the cigarette. When he was sure that it was lit he looked across the table at Owain with an expression of droll distaste and commented sagely, 'Stalin no good.'

Owain was intrigued by his frankness. It was terribly rare to meet a citizen from one of the Soviet satellite countries in such relaxed conditions, and he was keen to discover more about his companion's political outlook. By way of encouragement he began to confide haltingly to Janos the story of his own post-war involvement with communism and his gradual disenchantment.

Janos listened closely. In later years Owain retained a vivid impression of the way he appeared then, his face intent behind the owlish spectacles, the smoke from his

Gitane spiralling into the muted reddish lighting of the bar, his superficial air of amiable good humour replaced by a look of deep interest.

Afterwards he picked up his glass and casually downed the contents, poker-faced and stiff-wristed, as if taking medicine. He gave a crooked grin and said, 'We have similarities.'

As a schoolboy and a student Janos himself had favoured Marxism. During the war, when he was still in his teens, he'd resisted the Nazis and been imprisoned. Then the Russians had liberated Hungary. 'That liberation,' he commented, 'was like the embrace of a boa.'

'A what?' Owain was puzzled.

'A boa.' Janos made snake-like movements with one hand.

Owain understood. 'Ah. A boa constrictor.'

At present the Stalinists were all-powerful in Hungary. Opposition was silenced, hundreds imprisoned. 'I couldn't talk like this there.' Janos made a play of looking cautiously round the room as if suspecting eavesdroppers. He smiled. 'Even here I'm nervous.'

Owain bought two more glasses of brandy. 'To give you courage,' he said, placing the drinks on the table. Across the bar he noticed the blonde wife of the sculptor he'd been talking to the previous evening. He waved to her. She was wearing a blue dress and talking animatedly to some companions. She smiled and raised her glass to him.

'*Très chic*,' Janos said admiringly. He showed Owain a photograph of his wife, a dark, handsome woman with severely styled hair and perfectly arched eyebrows. 'My wife, Eva. She's a nurse,' he told Owain proudly. 'You're married?' he asked.

Owain shook his head, but he returned the compliment, extracting from his wallet a snapshot of Iris that he carried with him. She stood on a beach wearing shorts and a blouse that emphasized her tanned arms and full breasts,

130

smiling into the camera, open and happy, with none of the veiled hostility she so often showed him nowadays. Looking at it, Owain experienced the familiar pang of affection and regret.

'*Elle est belle*,' Janos said, with his likeable, wry smile, and Owain didn't feel inclined to embark on explanations.

They stayed talking for several hours longer. Owain lost track of time. They drank several more rounds of the fiery brandy. On this neutral ground there was an ease between them, and Owain found himself liking the stranger. It struck him that the air of artless amiability that he cultivated was deceptive. On closer acquaintance Janos came across as shrewd, and probably more deeply embroiled than he cared to admit in resisting the regime back home. He told Owain about a close friend of his who'd been imprisoned and tortured for some supposed ideological irregularity. 'The Avos, the secret police, they are . . .' He considered for a moment, turning down the corner of his mouth. 'They are *des salauds*,' he spat, the mildness of the insult contrasting comically with the venom of his contempt.

Owain offered him another cigarette and asked whether he thought things would be any different if Stalin were to die. Janos was optimistic: everything would be better then. Owain wasn't so sure. He couldn't see the Russians easing up – from the Kremlin's point of view the satellite states were an unruly bunch with inconvenient nationalistic tendencies.

'We'll have a bet,' Janos smiled, 'when it happens.'

It occurred to Owain, in his professional capacity, that Janos was a marvellous contact – a private citizen from an Iron Curtain country, who was intelligent, talkative and politically aware. He suggested they exchange addresses and keep in touch. Janos was enthusiastic. He would hand his letters to an Austrian journalist friend who visited Budapest often. 'That way I can tell the truth,' he said.

Just after midnight he stood up and took his leave. He was unsteady on his feet by then, and he wobbled his head from side to side like a drunk in a silent film. 'I'm a little bit . . .' Janos smiled expressively, leaving the sentence unfinished. He placed a flat corduroy cap squarely on his thick, brown hair and raised one hand in an awkward, decidedly unmilitary salute. 'Goodbye, Owain. You'll hear from me, I promise.'

15

Paul turned the sausages as they sizzled in their bath of melted lard. 'Shit, they're bursting. They always do.'

'It's the bread in them. They weren't like that before the war.' Sagely Rebecca echoed words of wisdom heard from Marie time without number.

A haze of pungent blue smoke rose from the frying pan and drifted towards the open fire-escape door. Bright, thin September sunshine filtered in through the window. As Paul prodded the sausages he swigged periodically from a bottle of brown ale that stood next to him on the draining board. Nowadays he seemed almost always to have a bottle of beer on the go. It made him playful and expansive. 'Hey, Becky, look at this. It's like science fiction.'

She peered, fascinated, as the pink innards of the sausages spilled out, coiling into twisted, tortured shapes. 'I like them like that.' The soft insides became edged with a delicious burned crust.

Paul was critical. 'They won't look right.'

Ruth had taken Ben to visit a friend of her mother's in Hertfordshire. She'd lived with Maggie for some years during the war, as an evacuee. They were still very close and Ruth regarded her almost as a surrogate grandmother for Ben. Richard was out too and Paul had offered to cook for himself and Rebecca, a mound of mash with sausages sticking out of it, like the ones in the comics that – next to modern novels – were his favourite reading. He'd laid the kitchen table in honour of the occasion with a check seersucker cloth and a candle stuck into an empty beer bottle, although it was only lunch time.

The mashed potato was ready, keeping warm in the oven. When the misshapen sausages were cooked to his satisfaction Paul attempted to stick them into the mash. The results were disappointing. The sausages flopped out, partially disintegrating in the process. He patted and kneaded the mash to achieve the desired effect.

Rebecca watched with growing misgiving. 'Paul, I think I'll eat mine now, while I've still got an appetite.'

He looked up with his twisted grin. 'Just let me get it looking right for one split second . . . There!' He stood back to admire it, head on one side.

She was dubious. 'It doesn't look quite like it does in the comics.'

His confection lacked the triumphant symmetry of the artists' originals. The deformed sausages sagged from an amorphous mass of cooling potato. But Paul ignored its shortcomings, waving his bottle of brown ale like a stage drunk. 'Looksh good to me.'

Rebecca was just back from the summer vacation. Over lunch Paul told her about the tour of dance halls the band had just completed. The money had been an advance on their usual, but apart from that the fortnight hadn't been a notable success. In many of the halls no one, not even the management, had expected or wanted a jazz band. The clientele was accustomed to gliding smoothly and somnolently around the floor under a revolving glass ball, and objected to the Wailers' upbeat tempo.

'We were booed in Bedford and hissed in Harlow.' There was an expression of sly amusement on his mobile face, suppressed laughter in his eyes. He didn't seem unduly cast down by the experience.

'Threatened in Thaxted? Stoned in St Albans?'

He smiled. 'How did you know?' He speared a sausage on his fork. The ends hung down limply on each side of it. 'Thank God we're playing the club tonight. At least they love us there.' He contemplated the sausage. 'In the

134

Beano they always pick them up whole on their forks, but they don't look so droopy. I suppose they must eat them by biting off chunks, just like my Mum always told me not to.' He gave a demonstration.

'You look like one of those people who eat doughnuts off a string with their hands tied behind their backs.' Rebecca was beginning to flag. 'You're a wonderful cook, Paul, but I can't finish this.'

'Honestly?' He scooped the food from her plate to his, adding a large dollop of brown sauce.

'How can you eat and drink so much and still be skinny as a rake?'

He looked down almost with surprise at his spare frame in the dark, polo-necked sweater, corduroy trousers and tennis shoes. 'I *try* to put on weight, but I can't.' He carried on eating, washing down the food with gulps of brown ale. 'Becky, what are you doing this afternoon?'

'Library probably.' Most of her friends weren't yet back from vacation.

Paul sighed. 'God, it's a crime. You're always working. You're like Faust, growing old and crabbed in the pursuit of knowledge. Come for a walk with me instead.'

She poured a couple of inches of his ale into a striped mug that stood on the table, took a sip and screwed up her face. 'I'm only nineteen, Paul.' She smiled at him, fit and tanned from the beaches of Llandudno. 'But crabbed, I'll admit. Still I'll come for a walk.'

It was only at Maggie's that Ruth had the experience of re-entering the world of her childhood. Since Sarah, her mother, had moved to Provence, visiting her was exciting, like going on holiday. Her surroundings there were intriguing and new, but harboured no associations. Alder, the Hertfordshire village where Maggie and her husband, Ilya, lived, was the only place where she still found a sense of her own past. Wheeling Ben's pushchair down the familiar High Street, she met people at every turn who called 'Ruth!' in tones of pleasure and affection, and cooed over Ben, shaking their heads over how time had flown. 'Fancy you with a big, bouncing toddler.'

The shops never seemed to change at all, for all everyone kept saying how modern and affluent the country was becoming in this new Elizabethan age. Along with Viyella nightgowns and Chilprufe vests, the draper still displayed the large pairs of fleecy *directoire* knickers that the children used to giggle over in her day. The leering statuette of a plaster pig in a boater and striped apron still dominated the butcher's window, along with a sinister strip of fly-paper, coated with black, immobilized corpses. The centrepiece of Maison Bernice, the hairdresser's, remained an inscrutable, elongated, almost featureless female head in a wig that seemed to be made of curly wood shavings.

Copse Hill was as leg-achingly steep as she remembered it, but the trek was made worthwhile by the looming prospect of Maggie's welcoming house at the summit, with its warm, coral brickwork and pointed windows. The front entrance was still flanked by the soft, pink, rambling New Dawn rose. The name had stuck in Ruth's mind, although she was no gardener.

The interior was a mosaic of natural textures and subtle, faded colours, homely and cluttered. Maggie had been at art school with Ruth's mother, and the house reflected her visual sense and hospitable personality. Staying with her you were cosseted and pampered. There was always strong, hot coffee on the go, homemade bread, tart, chilled wine, large delicious meals in spite of rationing, eiderdowns and hot water bottles. Ruth had always, in the back of her mind, carried the vague belief that one day she'd live in a house like this, with a rambling garden and the same spacious, warm-hearted atmosphere –

though the way things were it didn't seem terribly likely, she thought with a wry, inward smile.

Ilya Denisov was a theatrical designer, a Russian by birth, a small, compact man with humorous brown eyes and a moustache. Maggie was slim and beautiful, with black hair tied back from her face, always dressed according to her own mood, with little regard for current fashion. Both were about fifty now, their two boys away at university. Ruth saw that they had wrinkles, that their hair was streaked with grey, but she didn't believe it. Their smiles were as youthful and optimistic as she recalled them. 'Admit it, you're just actors made up to look middle-aged,' she remembered urging them on a previous visit, and the feeling remained.

They adored Ben and he loved coming here. He was walking now, and there was space and a host of unfamiliar toys to play with. Wooden trucks and bricks, child-sized chairs that Ilya had made for his own boys, and bright, soft toys sewed by Maggie and kept here to amuse him.

'He's like a little king, spoilt rotten,' Ruth told them, but she loved to see his pleasure in the house that had meant so much to her.

The Alder house was rich with memories, most of them happy, full of love and laughter. But there were others too. Black days that Maggie, Ilya and the boys had lived along with her, and which had left permanent scars. The remembrance of tragedy intensified and deepened the attachment she felt towards the mellow, expansive Denisov household.

During Ruth's time spent there as an evacuee, Maggie and Ilya had also given shelter to a young Londoner of about her age, a boy called Alan West. For a long time he was morose and hostile, moping around the house with reproachful eyes, like a forlorn mongrel. But as the months passed he gradually came to trust his substitute family, and finally to harbour a solid and affectionate loyalty towards them.

The friendship between Alan and Ruth grew slowly and cautiously, but eventually it blossomed into a fierce calf-love. Never since – except perhaps in her feelings for Ben – had Ruth experienced anything as total, painful and ecstatic.

Now, more than eight years later, she could no longer recapture the emotional nakedness of those days, but had to trust her own memory. Time and her own self-protective instincts had dulled the brightness, leaving her a legacy of wariness in matters of the heart. Still, there were pictures imprinted on her brain. She could see the two of them lying side by side in some dry, bleached grass by a stream, Alan seeming asleep. Then he had turned to her and said – the words spilling over from a dream, she imagined – 'I couldn't stand it if you loved someone else . . .' After all this time she could see him saying it, hair hanging across his forehead, his eyes, defenceless and intense, more expressive than the words.

She'd answered simply, 'Why would I do that?' At sixteen she had believed they'd last forever.

Now from the back doorstep she watched Maggie and Ilya playing with Ben in the garden. They were kneeling, and Ben was walking from one to another with his shambling, unsteady gait, practising his new skill. They clapped each time and he gave a loud, hiccupping laugh at their encouragement, his shorts drooping round his knees, and his soft, sturdy legs tightly encased in red knee-socks.

Her mind returned to the past. In the late summer of '44 Alan's father had been killed fighting in France. Alan had gone back to London to comfort his mother. She retained another image, the last. The two of them clinging together on the station platform, though they'd always been shy of kissing in public. She'd tried to transmit to him her strength and support, their bodies straining together. She never saw him again. In London he was killed by a bomb.

She had told Paul about it once, briefly, and hinted to Becky, but she had no desire to discuss Alan with people who hadn't known him. It was only here that she allowed herself to dwell on thoughts of him, as if there was a protection in this house, an immunity, no fear of glimpsing the ghost of her adolescent self.

Her mourning had been long and painful. She turned away from the living – her mother, friends – trying only to keep her memories of Alan alive and fresh. She pictured herself at that period, white and thin, hollow-eyed, always cold, her hair lank on her shoulders. It was all behind her now and had been for years. She'd relearned pleasure, made a career, had a child. But secretly she still thought of the events of that summer as the most significant of her life.

Ben looked about him, wanting her suddenly, needing to reassure himself that she was still there. Ruth knelt down on the flagstones outside the back door, and held out her arms. 'Here I am,' she called. 'I'm here, Ben!'

He turned and saw her. His fresh round face was wreathed in smiles. As he toddled precariously towards her across the sunlit lawn, she experienced a moment of pure love.

After lunch Ben had a rest and Ruth drank coffee with Maggie and Ilya on the lawn. In sheltered places the sun was beautifully warm. She leaned back luxuriously in her deck chair and watched a cluster of butterflies round a sturdy pinkish ice plant. Its squat shape was set off by the deep purple leaves of a shrub standing behind it.

'I love being spoilt like this.' She savoured the heartening warmth of the coffee. 'I feel like one of those Russian nobs with their dachas . . . Though I love Soho, and I don't think Paul'd want to live anywhere else.'

'How *is* that husband of yours?' There was still the hint of an accent in Ilya's speech, though he'd lived in England since the Twenties. 'And when are we going to see him again?' He looked exotic somehow, elegant and different, in spite of his hairy Harris tweed jacket with the leather elbow patches.

'Paul's fine.' Why did she feel just a touch evasive saying that? 'He's working tonight or he'd have come too. He's not at all averse to Maggie's home comforts.' Like almost everyone Paul relished the atmosphere of this house, so different from the cloying suburban neatness of his mother's.

'How does he feel about touring?' Maggie asked. 'He must miss Ben.' Both of them had pigeonholed Paul approvingly as a doting father.

'He loves getting back to him,' Ruth agreed. 'But the touring brings in a bit of money.' Again she had the uncomfortable impression that she was peddling bland half-truths. There was a new evasiveness about Paul nowadays that she didn't understand. Yesterday the two of them had quarrelled with a bitterness that had surprised her.

'What earthly good is it you earning more when all you do is spend it on beer!' she'd shouted. And immediately she was reminded of a part she'd played once, at Bedford Rep, as a wronged Victorian wife in a spoof melodrama. Perhaps that was what marriage did to you. But the reproach was beside the point. It wasn't a question of money. They weren't well off, God knew, but she had enough for her needs. It was the constant swigging that bothered her. And something else that she couldn't pin down. Sarcastically she taunted him with trying to be Scott Fitzgerald or Hemingway or someone, though that wasn't fair either, not really. It was only beer that he

140

drank. And it made him pleasant, funny, not brutal like her mustachioed husband in the play. Still, a nagging unease remained.

'You're not worried about money?' Maggie asked gently, misinterpreting Ruth's pensiveness. She harboured a guilt complex about being comfortably off and was always ready to help less privileged friends.

Ruth shook her head and grinned at her, affectionately amused. 'No need to reach for your cheque book, Maggie. I'm not on my beam-ends yet.'

A walk with Paul invariably took in a visit to Dobell's Jazz Shop in the Charing Cross Road, a dark and dusty emporium filled from basement to roof with new and secondhand records of specialist interest. While customers browsed, tantalizing snatches of music were played, awakening their interest in new directions and prolonging their stay.

Paul riffled through the racks, frowning and intent. He turned to Rebecca and groaned. 'God, I could spend a fortune here, no sweat.'

In the event he bought her a present, a record by Jimmy Yancey, a pioneer of boogie-woogie piano and a hero of Paul's. She liked his sound and Paul had remembered. He was always pleased when outsiders showed an interest in his music.

She smiled at him, touched. 'You're a gent.' They strolled onward in the direction of Trafalgar Square. He asked her how she'd found Llandudno during the summer vacation.

'It was all right. I did my waitressing, and sat on the beach, and swam, like old times. I felt different, though.'

'How do you mean?'

She shrugged her shoulders. 'Like a city slicker, I suppose. Just that nothing's changed. Mum and Dad still worry over the same old things. And they have their little habits and routines, so set. And it all seems so important to them. It's endearing in a way, but infuriating too.'

Outside the Portrait Gallery they passed a pavement artist, surrounded by his own technicolour views of mountains, lakes and sunsets. He was bearded and wore a long, belted mackintosh, and an oddly distant and abstracted expression. Rebecca dropped a coin into his cap, but didn't meet his eye. He made her feel uneasy.

Paul glanced at the chalked pictures with perfunctory interest, then turned away, seeming to give the artist no thought. 'I've got excellent memories of Llandudno,' he said.

'Oh yes.' She was sceptical. 'I seem to remember you shook the dust from your feet at your earliest convenience.'

He gave her a push, rough and friendly at the same time. 'You're too quick, Becky. You've got little piggy gimlet eyes on the lookout for hypocrisy.' As he glanced sideways at her she was, for an instant, sharply aware of his strange, likeable ugliness – the mane of curly hair, the knowing brown eyes, long nose, crooked smile. 'What I mean is, it's where I met my lady wife.'

As they wandered along the Victoria Embankment the Thames glittered in the sun. It was good to be back, Rebecca thought. London was looking its best in the lazy glow of this September afternoon. She was aware of a feeling of belonging. Last autumn she'd felt strange and over-awed.

They made their way home via a tangle of minor streets. Paul was talkative and entertaining, and he seemed to know the area like the back of his hand. By the time they reached Soho it was opening time and their feet ached. They dropped into the French Pub in Dean Street for a drink, flopping down at a table in a secluded corner below a collection of framed photographs of celebrated customers. Rebecca lingered over a glass of cold, white wine, but Paul downed three drinks quite quickly. They seemed to affect him. He leaned forward, resting his elbows on the table, and began to talk softly and compulsively about Ruth, telling Rebecca how beautiful he thought her, how much he loved her, how all his friends envied him. He spoke with a kind of self-fuelling intensity, holding her gaze. His brown eyes had a fixed, bright, watery look.

'I don't deserve her,' he declared in a maudlin fashion, coming back to this conclusion again and again.

She was taken aback by his change of mood. He wasn't given to confidences, favouring instead a flippant, throw-away manner of speaking. His earnestness seemed somehow irrational, and she was ill at ease, falling back on a listening role, staring at the table, fiddling with her glass, finding herself unable to contribute. Luckily it was almost time for him to go to the Poland Street club to begin his evening's work and she reminded him of the fact.

Outside in the street, his surprising burst of vehemence seemed as quickly forgotten. He flashed a quick, casual smile over his shoulder as he turned to go. 'You'll come along later, will you, Beck? We haven't seen you there for ages.'

She thought about it. 'I might,' she said.

Now it was September the nights came down early. Ruth sat on the back doorstep, clasping her knees, watching the twilight fall. Natasha, the Denisov's elderly Labrador, lay close by on the flagstones. The sky darkened rapidly, almost visibly, shade by shade, until the shrubs became patches of shadowy grey, the lawn almost black, though a lamp in an upstairs window cast a homely splash of light across the grass.

From inside she could hear whoops of pleasure as Ben

143

enjoyed his bath under Maggie's supervision. Alone like this she felt a kind of oneness with the girl she'd been, as if for a moment she'd re-entered her younger skin and looked out through adolescent eyes. In the old days she'd sat here times without number, blankly staring, chin cradled in her arms, allowing thoughts to drift into her head, random and unwilled. There was a kind of melancholy in the remembrance, a sense of time passing.

She'd had the feeling then of waiting for life to begin, the conviction that fulfilment and excitement were waiting for her, just around the corner. But now she supposed life *had* begun, and it held limitations and imperfections she hadn't foreseen. She shivered. Tonight she felt old and obscurely cheated, though she couldn't have explained why. A cold sliver of moon was visible now above the black trees at the end of the garden. There was silence apart from the rustle of leaves. Ruth put out one hand to touch Natasha's warm, dark, glossy coat.

She heard Maggie calling her from upstairs. 'Ben's all ready for bed now. Are you coming up to kiss him goodnight?' The dog pricked up her ears at the sound.

Ruth stood up. 'Come on inside, Natasha. It's cold out here now.'

16

Recently Paul had started to sing as well as play the piano. Most evenings he performed two or three numbers, though Sid, the clarinet player, was the band's official vocalist. Rebecca arrived as his first song was being announced. She was curious. She hadn't been to the Left Bank Club for months and hadn't heard him yet. She slipped into a seat at a table with Sid's girlfriend, Anita, a fat redhead who grinned at her arrival, revealing large front teeth that made her look like an amiable Disney rabbit.

'Just in time for the star turn.' A breath of sarcasm in her tone. Rebecca knew that Sid was none too pleased with this new development.

As it happened Paul was singing 'Death Letter Blues', the Yancey number he'd bought for her at the record shop that afternoon. He looked small and undistinguished in the white spotlight. Rebecca was aware of a little edge of concern for him, like a mother getting ready to watch her child in the school play.

It was a solo. Paul accompanied himself, like his hero, Yancey, while the rest of the band took a breather. He began to sing with confidence and conviction. Immediately she was impressed with the authentic blues sound to his voice. I should've known he'd be all right, she thought. Both tune and words were stark and sincere, with a lyrical sadness. There was a rough-sweet intensity to his singing as he followed the spare rise and fall of the melody. She hung on the sound. Her arms were goosefleshed. As he sang and played, his skinny frame radiated a sensuous power.

'Wow, he's not bad,' she whispered to Anita, smiling innocently, wanting to shame her a little for that brief display of ill-nature.

The dancing couples – silhouettes from Rebecca's vantage point – moved slowly, clinging. At the tables people were silent, their heads turned towards Paul. Momentarily he'd cast a spell. He looked distant as he sang, as if he were transported and had become someone else. There was a shadow of a smile on his lips at the ends of lines, or when the plangent piano took over. The simple strength of the blues lent him a dignity she found seductive. It was a side of him she hadn't seen before. It was strange to equate this person with the companion who'd joked and teased her all day, and cooked sausages and mash like in the comics. When the song was finished the applause was enthusiastic. He smiled whimsically, raising an eyebrow in negligent acknowledgement. That was all. Then the band swung into the next number.

'Yes. He's okay,' Anita agreed, conciliatory now. 'Not a bad crowd here tonight.' She wore a black jersey top with a deep V that revealed a great deal of mottled, pinkish-white cleavage. 'How you doing, Becky? Long time no see. Been busy with the studying?' Among the band, Rebecca guessed, Paul characterized her as a pious young swot who would one day discover what life was really all about.

Like many of the early Fifties shrines to revivalist jazz, the Left Bank Club was housed in a large basement. In honour of its name the cellar was perfunctorily decorated with strings of raffia onions and candles stuck in wine bottles. The employees wore striped fishermen's sweaters, which were vaguely French, though hardly Parisian. Round the perimeter of the room were small tables laid with red check cloths, which were anchored in place by metal clips. A heavy, square, white china ashtray stood on each. Only coffee and soft drinks were served, though

146

some regulars smuggled in their own discreet supplies of the hard stuff, and the band tippled openly from beer bottles as they played a rousing version of 'Jazz Band Ball'.

Side by side Rebecca and Anita watched the dancers. Just in front of them an attractive, dark-haired girl swirled her floral skirt with provocative abandon.

Anita pointed. 'That's Paul's paramour.' Her front teeth showed in a mischievous smile.

'The famous fan.' She'd heard Richard joke about her lots of times.

'A bit more than that, I'd say.' Anita gave a knowing sidelong glance. Rebecca was sharply curious, but made no comment.

She watched the woman though. She was a good dancer, she had to admit. Her partner was a blond boy who seemed younger. They made a handsome couple and seemed conscious of the fact. Instinctively, because of what Anita had said, Rebecca disliked them, the woman shaking her shoulders and showing her stocking tops with a sultry, self-congratulatory look on her face, the man grinning with equal self-satisfaction as he whirled her round, his limbs long and loose, his shirt open to the waist.

She glanced at the bandstand and caught Richard's eye. He made a little movement with his shoulder by way of welcome. His trombone interweaved with Sid's clarinet in an intricate counterpoint. Sid was red-haired like Anita, tall and good-looking, though a bit sheep-like in Rebecca's opinion. But when he sang it was with surprising verve. His voice was loud and raucous and seemed at odds with his decorous appearance.

When 'Jazz Band Ball' was finished, the musicians took a break for five minutes. The dark woman went over to them, and Rebecca and Anita followed. As Rebecca approached she saw that the woman was talking to Paul.

He was standing, and she faced him, leaning back, braced against the piano, a provocative set to her body and an amused, pixie smile on her face. Paul didn't notice Rebecca. She saw him tweak the girl's hair which was hanging over her shoulders. She grabbed his hand and squeezed it, half-petulant, half-flirtatious. She held it as she made some remark to him – a witticism, from her expression and Paul's abrupt laughter. Remembering Anita's earlier remark and the knowing smile, Rebecca was suspicious of their exchange, indignant for Ruth.

She stayed away from Paul and joined Richard, who was with Joe, the drummer, an aggressive Scot – older than the rest of them – with bad teeth. She said hallo, but gave only half her attention to their conversation, strongly aware of Paul's animated dialogue with the woman.

Joe flicked his eyes stealthily sideways in their direction and remarked *sotto voce* to Richard, 'I see Paul's bit of stuff's here tonight.' His thick accent made the comment difficult to grasp. There was a short delay while Rebecca worked it out in her mind.

Richard looked at him in a warning fashion, indicating Rebecca with an almost imperceptible movement of the head.

'Don't mind me,' she said.

But Paul noticed her and waved. 'Hi, Becky!' Taking hold of the woman's hand, he waved it at her, casual and unembarrassed. 'This is Marion.'

'Hallo, Becky.' The woman gave her a friendly smile. Rebecca smiled back. The two of them seemed unconcerned. Maybe their friendship was nothing.

Back at their table she and Anita were joined by two male colleagues of Anita's from the film-distribution company where she worked as a secretary. One of them asked Rebecca to dance. He was deeply tanned from a foreign holiday and sported sunglasses even in this twilight basement. She thought him pretentious, but they danced

148

well together, with a smooth, easy style, and they stayed on the floor, with short breaks, for the rest of the evening. Afterwards he asked to walk her home. Rebecca debated with herself how best to refuse. She had no particular desire to see him again. By chance, as she stood deliberating, Paul walked by.

'Paul'll walk me home,' she said brightly. 'We live in the same block.'

He came to her rescue, reading the situation. 'Don't worry, old boy, I'll take care of Becky.' She smiled inwardly. Paul never called anyone old boy. He was ready to leave. There was no sign of Marion.

Back at Marshall Street, in the kitchen, Paul had another beer. 'The adrenalin's still racing round my system,' he explained. 'I'll never sleep without it.' Unusually, he poured it into a glass. About a third was left in the bottle. He offered it to Rebecca with a questioning lift of the eyebrow.

She shrugged. 'Why not?'

They drank the beer standing up, almost like medicine. Paul leaned against the draining board. The electric light was harsh in the confined kitchen. The black night sky, at the window and the glass door panels, showed like blank eyes.

'Not your type then? The bloke with the sunglasses.' He regarded her with a teasing, man-of-the-world expression, but she sensed an interest that was sharper than he pretended.

'Not really.' She left a judicious pause. 'Bit of a prick.' Ruth would have admired her timing. Paul let out a bark of laughter. Since she had been in London, she'd begun to use words that would have scandalized the neighbours in Llandudno. There were times when they seemed right. The *mot juste* as her French teacher used to say.

He was still grinning, seeming to relish the obscenity in

149

her mouth. 'You make me laugh, Beck. Like butter wouldn't melt . . . But you don't miss a thing.' He added, 'I enjoyed today. Our walk.'

'Me too.' She upended her glass, swallowing the last of the beer, then rinsed it under the tap and placed it upside down on the draining board. 'I'm dead beat now though. I'm off to bed.'

Paul moved sideways, insinuating himself between Rebecca and the sink. 'Hey, Becky.' He raised a hand to touch her cheek.

'What is it?'

There was a pause, while he said nothing, and she became aware of creeping, unworthy suspicions, a muffled incredulity.

He came closer, so that his body was touching hers. His hand moved back, caressing her hair. 'Can't I come with you? To bed, I mean?' His voice was low, deliberately seductive, though with a trace of diffidence too. His face was very close, serious and intimate. A sensuous downward curve to his lips, which were full and alluring.

She was mesmerized, aroused, realizing perhaps for the first time how attracted she was, how easy it would be to fall in with this bold new suggestion, but never for a second forgetting the taboo.

'Of course not,' she replied in a normal, reasoning tone. 'There's Ruth.'

He tipped her head gently backward so that he was staring her full in the face, his eyes inviting honesty. 'Wouldn't you like to?' The pressure of his body affected her as much as the soft, persuasive voice. She could clearly feel his arousal, and was weak with her own.

But the veto was stronger. 'You don't really think I'd do that to Ruth?'

They faced one another for a long moment, then he released her, taking her by the shoulders and standing her away from him in a kind of symbolic acquiescence. Briefly

150

he held her there like that. 'It's not simple black and white. I thought you'd see that.' He let go of her shoulders. 'But it's your decision, Beck. Shame, though.'

Rebecca found it hard to sleep after that, although with the long walk and all that dancing she was more than ready. She was conscious of Paul lying in the bedroom next to hers, and wondered if he was awake like herself . . . but decided that he probably wasn't. She'd been wrongfooted by his suggestion, but, on second thoughts, she was not as surprised as all that. There was something about Paul that made you expect . . . She thought again about the dark woman, Marion, at the club.

It was somehow galling to admit to herself that the idea of sleeping with Paul interested and excited her. After all, she had a lover of her own. Carl. A lover who was handsome and wonderfully well-built, and she knew a lot of girls envied her. The two of them had so much in common that it had been almost inevitable that they'd become a couple . . . And yet sometimes she had the unworthy thought that making love with Carl was like a game of tennis. Good, healthy exercise at the time, but something you forgot about until it happened again. With Paul there seemed an awareness of sexuality in everything he did . . .

Ruth was due back early the next evening. At about six o'clock Sid, the Wailers' red-haired clarinettist and singer, dropped by with his girlfriend, Anita, who'd come straight from Sunday lunch with relatives. She looked most unlike her Left Bank self and was wearing a black and white hound's-tooth-check frock with a white, piqué collar and a black bow at the neck. She was shod in black patent shoes with high heels.

'God, you look masterful in that outfit, Nita.' Paul mimed admiring dazzlement, but Anita was in no mood

151

to respond to his banter. She and Sid had come with serious intentions. They wanted to discuss another tour that the Wailers had planned. They found Paul and Richard sitting cross-legged on the floor with the gramophone between them, replaying the last half-minute of a Bix Beiderbecke solo over and over, mesmerized by the lyrical finale. Rebecca lounged in a nearby chair reading a book about the Weimar Republic. A pot of tea, a half-full milk bottle and three empty mugs stood dotted on the carpet. She could detect no strain today in the atmosphere between herself and Paul. It was as though his almost cursory midnight proposition had been a dream.

'Listen to this, Sid.' Paul put the record on for the umpteenth time and the cornet solo soared again, pure and golden, with the minute, heartbreaking hesitations.

As the sound died away Sid nodded briefly. 'Smashing, Paul,' but he resisted the atmosphere of time-wasting relaxation. His pale face was unresponsive as he stared down at the carpet with lashless eyes.

His hair was a kind of coral colour, straight and brushed smoothly back. Anita's was exuberant, curly, and frankly ginger. She crossed large legs in pinkish nylons. 'Let's face it, Paul, that last tour was a pig's breakfast,' she said in a straight-talking tone not calculated to bring out the best in him. She mooted that they take the proposed venues one by one, and plan a strategy for each. Where the dance hall was unknown, Paul would telephone and ask for the advice of the manager. 'Then we can work out what's wanted in advance, and aim at a specific public. Compromise a little.' Her patient, explanatory tones seemed more suited to a class of eight-year-olds.

Listening, Rebecca had sympathy with Anita and Sid. Paul was hopelessly vague. But she knew they'd get nowhere like this. Thoughts of organization ran counter to his freewheeling view of himself, and Richard allowed himself to be carried along by Paul's airy contempt for specifics. The more Anita tried to pin them down, the more evasive they would become.

Paul smiled at her, amused and urbane, a gleam of good-natured malice in his eye. 'Compromise, Thumper! Don't mention that word in my presence.'

The band had christened her Thumper, after the Disney rabbit, because of her prominent front teeth. In the right mood she wasn't averse, but now she flushed angrily at the flippant tone of his reply. Rebecca heard the click of the front door. Ruth must be back.

'Nita's right, Paul. We've got to be systematic about this tour,' Sid urged glumly. Rebecca had never been able to equate his lugubrious personality with his gut-bucket vocals.

'We're home!' Suddenly Ruth stood framed in the living-room doorway holding Ben, smiling, out of breath and slightly pink, her hair streaming on her shoulders, full of a mischievous vitality. 'Quick, Paul, Ben needs to pee!'

Paul leapt up and located the child's potty behind a chair, while Ruth dealt deftly with Ben's underpinnings. He was bundled on to the china receptacle, his feet hardly touching the ground. Almost immediately they heard the muted tinkle of urine.

'Good boy!' Ruth exclaimed admiringly. Then she lifted him up to give him a smacking kiss while Paul removed the pot. 'Look, Becky's here,' she told her son happily. 'We haven't seen her for a long time.' She began to question Rebecca about Llandudno, her parents, the Post Office, the theatre. Anita sat by with a thin smile, all hope of constructive discussion banished now Ruth was back, stirring the air like a breathless whirlwind. Rebecca hadn't seen her since July, and it was almost a shock to rediscover her friend's quick radiance, the compelling quality that made her instantly the focus of the room.

Paul came back in, carrying the empty chamber pot. Now Ruth rummaged in a paper carrier bag she'd brought in with her. 'Look, Paul, what Maggie's made for Ben.' She held up two small, bright Fair Isle sweaters. 'Aren't they great? But this is the best.' She searched again and produced a tiny jerkin made of soft denim. 'Isn't it wonderful? He'll be a little rebel. A mini-Marlon Brando. Paul's mum always buys him things with ducks on them and scalloped edges that make him look like Little Lord Fauntleroy,' she explained to the others.

'I don't suppose he notices the difference,' Rebecca said drily.

'Becky, such a cynic,' Ruth laughed. Then she leaned across and touched her arm. 'I expect that's why I've missed you.'

Thoroughly sidetracked, Anita and Sid resignedly admired Ben and the new clothes. Ruth asked after Joe, the band's Scottish drummer, whose family had arrived *en masse* recently to visit him and check up on his life-style down south. In their honour, he'd taken it into his head to springclean the down-at-heel room where he lodged. She and Paul had chanced by as he was taking down the limp, floral curtains that had hung in his window from time immemorial.

'He boiled them up in a great galvanized iron bucket on his gas ring.' Ruth laughed with gleeful incredulity at the memory of it. 'They just disintegrated, and there was this awful smell. Joe couldn't believe it. He kept dipping a ladle into the bucket and stirring it and bringing out spoonfuls of this disgusting gunge.' She mimicked the drummer's anguished cry. 'Ma curtains, Ruth, they've turned to sludge soup!' Her impersonation of Joe's bewildered distress and his heavy accent were spot on, so that even Sid and Anita were cajoled out of their sulks and into laughter.

As Ruth related the story Rebecca happened to glance at Paul. He was watching his wife with an unconscious, absorbed smile, and an expression of such naked love in his eyes that she felt like an intruder for having intercepted it.

17

It took Owain ten minutes or so to feel his way into the game. The cold drizzle and driving wind made handling the ball difficult. The pitch was heavy and muddy and sometimes it was hard to keep his feet. Even so, he couldn't deny a leaping exhilaration at being there, playing. He had missed it, he realized.

Stepping in as fly-half for an injured teammate, he was the hero of the hour, welcomed in the dressing room by men he'd known forever, with whom he had rugby in common, and a childhood, but little since. Pulling on the familiar yellow and blue Carreg-Brân jersey, he'd been warmed by their laconic acceptance. In the last six years he'd played here intermittently, to say the least.

Their opponents scored first after the Carreg-Brân full-back fumbled a long kick near his own line, and Tŷ-Gwyn's scrum-half scrambled over for a try. Standing behind the line, waiting for the attempted conversion, Owain was aware of a ragged line of supporters strung out along the far edge of the field. He could make out the white hair of his father, Ianto, and Iris's red jacket, reminding him momentarily of the real world, with its tensions and ambiguities. But he forgot them as the ball soared, seeming to hang against the grey-white sky, falling in a slow arc between the posts.

'Sodding good start.' He recognized the flat, sarcastic tones of John Williams, the team's squat, fair-haired scrum-half, Owain's cousin.

The autumn afternoon was damp and blustery. For the rest of the first half the game was scrappy, but just before half-time Owain was able to take advantage of a loose

155

ball and run, weaving and dodging, miraculously avoiding interception, to touch down between the uprights.

'Good one, boy!' Terse, hoarse calls of approval floated on the misty air. Owain was exultant – absurdly so – at his success, at his body's effort. It felt good, and even better when his try was successfully converted. At half-time the teams were level.

The second half of the match was hard fought, inconclusive, frustrating, each team's manoeuvres constantly checked by the other. The grey, inert afternoon was jangled by the jagged shouts of the spectators, the players' yelped instructions, the thudding squelch of their feet, the occasional blunt collision of flesh on flesh. Owain was coated in mud, but felt his body hot and alive, immune to the blanketing drizzle.

Close to the end of the match, with the scores still tied, Owain attempted a drop goal from outside the opponents' twenty-five, but it skidded off the muddy toe of his boot and went careening and bobbing towards the touchline. One of the Tŷ-Gwyn forwards picked it up and started to charge back up the field. Owain was the nearest of his team and he hurled himself at the larger, fatter man, hitting him in the stomach with his shoulder. The force of the tackle flattened the player. The ball was dislodged and went spinning into the void. Owain's cousin, John, the scrum-half, was following up. He plucked the ball from the air and scampered over in the corner for what proved to be the winning score.

A short time later the whistle blew. After the regulation sporting cheers, Owain began to walk from the field with the other players, panting, elated, at peace.

'Come back, boy, any time.' A teammate touched him briefly on the shoulder.

At the edge of the field Ianto stood, white-haired and patriarchal, blocking his path. 'Good game, son.' The words were undemonstrative, but his father wore a look of secret pride that Owain saw as predatory and gloating, and his calm was ruffled by an age-old resentment: that his father valued him only as far as he displayed masculine courage, prowess, hardness. Then his pride was unforced and fierce, with an almost primitive quality that touched some spring of revulsion in his son.

Next to him Iris stood silent, a boldly defined figure in red jacket and black trousers, attracting interested glances from Owain's teammates, with her olive skin and well-shaped face, framed becomingly by short, brown curls. But as she observed Owain's muddied exhilaration her eyes were cold and joyless.

Owain's mother, Jo, presided over the Saturday supper table. He could remember, as a boy, thinking her prettier and more free and easy than the other mothers, and still a dark handsomeness showed through the style she'd adopted as appropriate for middle age – a loose chignon, a plain wine-coloured wool dress, a hand-knitted cardigan. The table was set with the good linen cloth, embroidered by some aunt in satin stitch and lazy daisy. On it was spread sliced spam, salad, bread and marge, a pot of tea. A glass bowl of pickle offered a hint of flavouring. A luxurious, hoarded tin of salmon between the six of them provided the *pièce de résistance*. Owain's younger brother, William, had come for tea, with his wife, Nancy, who was heavily pregnant.

Owain savoured the bland, wholesome meal without interest. Since leaving home he'd discovered a taste for foreign fare, herbs and spices, but his parents detested the thought of food that had been mucked about with.

'More salad, Iris love?' Jo offered the plate of quartered tomatoes, cucumber and tough, wet lettuce. Iris flashed her an easy, self-contained smile. She liked his parents and they liked her. She was wearing the yellow sweater that set off her olive complexion and shapely figure.

157

She accepted a second helping. 'The lettuce is grand, Ianto. So fresh. We can't get them like that in London.'

He was gratified, the stern immobility of his expression melting into a pleased smile. 'I keep us going clear into November with the cold frame.' Ianto approved of Iris, with her political awareness, and her sensuous, but sensible good looks. And she treated him with affection and respect, tactfully sidestepping his moments of bitterness and anger. At such moments Owain reflected, time and again, how much easier it was to treat strangers with equanimity than your own family.

Until a year or so ago his parents had viewed his relationship with Iris simply. Owain's found himself a nice girl – suitable too, a teacher, he could imagine them telling relatives, with the blithe implication that their marriage was only a matter of time. But, though Jo and Ianto still prized Iris, there was a wariness now when she and Owain visited, and a kind of bewilderment, as if his parents felt cheated somehow out of a future they'd seen as inevitable.

'You young people nowadays, you take your time,' Jo muttered occasionally, though as far as Owain could see, that wasn't the case at all. Most of the teammates he drank with were fathers several times over.

'Owain's got it right,' they joshed him, claiming to envy his freedom, admiring Iris's voluptuous poise, but he sensed that in truth the two of them were considered more than a touch eccentric for not having tied the knot.

Ianto never broached the matter. His relationship with his son was sticky enough without that. 'Tell us about Morecambe, then, Owain,' he said suddenly. Often he sat silent for minutes while the rest of them chatted and bantered. Then his still, unemphatic voice would stop them in their tracks, demanding instant attention. Ianto sat forward, his elbows on the cloth, in shirtsleeves and braces, his shoulders and arms still powerful. Always his

158

skin looked slightly tanned. His hair was thick and had been white for some years now, although he was only about fifty, and this added to the imposing weight of his appearance.

'You should've come, Dad.' The annual Labour Party Conference had been held the previous week at Morecambe. It had been a stormy affair. Owain had been covering it, in a freelance capacity, for an international socialist review, which was based in Paris and published in four or five languages.

'They asked him,' his brother, William, put in, holding his cup out to Jo for more tea. He was a younger, clean-shaven version of Owain, thin and dark, with a brooding look. The brothers themselves admitted the resemblance. But William was the practical one, people said, a whizz with machinery. He worked in a local garage.

Owain looked at his father. 'Why didn't you?'

'Bloody circus.' Ianto shook his head with heavy distaste. 'Snapping and snarling like a pack of dogs.' He'd finished eating and pushed his plate away. He spoke with a bitterness that saddened Owain, though in a sense he understood it. Increasingly he had the feeling that his father had lost his way.

In spite of their edgy relationship, Owain was fiercely proud of Ianto's past. Through the Twenties and Thirties he'd been in the vanguard of the trade union movement, leading the village through grim, protracted strikes, fighting tirelessly for his fellow miners' rights. Owain had magazine cuttings from the Thirties showing his father, young and savage, speaking at Miners' Federation rallies, proposing motions at Labour Party Conferences, a fearless, undeviating personality, with no doubts about his mission in life. The culmination of his struggle had come five years ago, when the coal mines had been officially nationalized, and a life-long dream had come true.

However, the promised land hadn't materialized overnight. There were new problems, different ones, and Ianto had lost his clear-cut sense of direction. 'Them and us' had been his creed and motivation, but it wasn't as simple as that now. He was increasingly frustrated in a bureaucratic world, and he reacted with moodiness, rejecting subtler shades of meaning.

'Nye was on good form,' Owain ventured. From way back Ianto had admired and identified with Aneurin Bevan. He had that, at least, in common with his son.

Jo began to clear the plates. Ianto handed his over, smiling at her briefly. 'Tasty, love, tasty.'

Iris got up to help, considerate and practical. 'I'll bring these, Jo.' Owain was appreciative of her pleasantness towards his family.

Ianto turned back to his son. 'Nye's all right,' he said gruffly, 'but I've not time for those hangers-on of his.'

Owain experienced a quick, hot rush of anger, as he did frequently at his father's casual judgements. He could only construe the remark as personal. It struck at the root of the tension between them. Ianto subscribed to the body of opinion that held that Nye was bedevilled by a gang of unscrupulous intellectuals, jumping aboard his bandwagon. Owain felt implicated, provoked, but he swallowed his indignation. It was the only way.

'There's a lot of people'd disagree with you,' he replied evenly. In fact the Bevanite faction had received a massive vote of confidence from the rank and file of the Labour Movement. On the other hand, the Mineworkers' Union had their knives out for Bevan. The situation was becoming ever more involved. It wasn't fair, Owain told himself, to blame Ianto, a straightforward man, for his snap verdicts.

'Blackberry and apple?' Iris brought in a large pie. Without further ado she began to serve it out with neat, dexterous movements, distracting them momentarily. The

160

chink of pots could be heard from the kitchen as Jo began the washing-up.

'Owain?' There was an intimacy in Iris's questioning look, but no warmth. From him she withheld what she gave so easily to others.

He nodded. 'A small piece.' Then, turning back to Ianto, 'You should've heard the speech he made on the Wednesday night. Reaching out, wanting unity. It's so false this idea of a scheming bastard just waiting to grab power. That's not what it's all about . . .'

'It's the hangers-on,' Ianto repeated. 'And the bloody journalists.' This time the intention to hurt was unequivocal.

Owain bit his lip. For Jo's sake he wouldn't be riled. He'd made a resolution to ignore his father's needling. Over the years they'd had so many violent disagreements that had turned vicious, personal, and proved nothing. And Jo was caught in the middle, sick with loving them both and being forced to witness the antagonism lurking just below the surface, ready at any moment to leap into violent life. He closed his mind and ate his pie.

Nancy, William's wife broke the charged silence. 'We're thinking of getting a television, Iris.' Above her pregnant, distended body her face seemed callow, fresh and unformed, like a child's, her long hair pulled tightly back into a ponytail.

Iris smiled. 'Posh,' she commented admiringly.

'Well, with the baby, we won't be able to get out much and William thought . . .'

She was interrupted by the scraping of Ianto's chair. He stood up, leaving the rest of them eating, crossed the room, settled himself in the green wing chair by the window and lit up a Woodbine. An age-old tradition. His privilege as head of the family. He drew on the cigarette with a kind of restful arrogance, then coughed with a

161

rattling of phlegm. The cough had been part of him for so long that they scarcely noticed it, let alone commented.

Jo came in to clear whatever crockery was available. Ianto told her casually, 'We'll be slipping down to the Travellers', love, in a minute. Me and the boys.' He never consulted his sons. It was taken for granted that they'd go. The pub was their unquestioned male prerogative.

In the Travellers' Rest were friends of Ianto's, and gradually his father became involved in conversation with them, distracted temporarily from his sons. Owain found himself alone with William on the far side of the room from the bar, standing face to face – it was Saturday night and crowded – leaning against the whitewashed brick wall. Under normal circumstances William was shy, a little in awe of his older brother, but tonight, emboldened by the beer, he became expansive, offering opinions and advice.

'You won't find many like Iris, with looks and brains, and down-to-earth with it. Not stuck up like some . . .' He took a long gulp of his beer and added boldly, 'When are you going to make an honest woman of her, then?' He used a jokey, self-conscious turn of speech, feeling his own lack of education.

'It's not that simple . . .' Owain hesitated, debating whether to be frank about himself and Iris, drop the bland, non-committal mask they wore for the family's benefit.

But he had no time to reach a decision. William was off again, full of missionary fervour. 'It *is* simple, boy, it *is* simple. You just have to decide. They joke about marriage – you know, tying the noose and all that nonsense. But it's not like that, Owain. I've never been happier . . .' He was garrulous, tipsy, his eyes below a black fringe of hair were dark, liquid, fevered almost. For Owain it was like looking into a mirror, seeing his earnest younger self before his life became hedged about by compromise. He was touched by his brother's artless openness, and briefly, irrelevantly, he was reminded of that young student he'd met in the summer. Rebecca, her name had been. The same thin, eager face beneath a similar fringe of hair.

'You're scared. You think you're giving up something valuable.' William rattled on, flushed and animated, one hand curled round his tankard, holding it against his chest. 'But you're gaining far more. A friend. Someone to share everything with. A kid . . .'

The dissatisfaction that had been with Owain all day, to a greater or lesser extent, resurfaced. A buried exasperation at the sham of this communal visit. In his head there was an image of Iris, hostile and closed to him after the rugby match, rejecting his pleasure and exhilaration, surrounding herself with a cold, smooth glass wall.

But – almost in the same split second – came another memory. He'd visited her school in Brixton once to collect impressions for an article on the new spate of immigration. Iris had been with a small group of pupils with reading difficulties. For them her smile was playful and encouraging, an unconscious radiance shining from her eyes. She was that person too.

It had become habit for both of them to show one another the worst of themselves, hurting and snubbing each other, the good memories becoming unreal, no longer sufficient to warm them. It was hopeless. They'd gone too far. This moment of privacy with William was opportune, a chance to get things out into the open.

'Bloody brilliant tackle this afternoon, Owain.' His cousin John pushed towards them through the crowd, beery, pink and genial. Owain reflected that the truth, after all, would have to wait.

Iris woke with a start. She must have fallen asleep almost the moment she got into bed. Awareness returned slowly.

163

Groggily she registered the dim strip of light across the ceiling from a chink in the curtain and the inhospitable gusting of the wind outside. It had been strong like that all day. At the same time she became conscious of a sense of desolation inside herself, black and frightening, and remembered her dream.

She'd been trapped, injured at the bottom of a ravine. Small, helpless, a dot, she lay looking up at its towering sides, the narrow patch of gloomy sky far, far above her. Then Owain came, starting down the rocky wall of the gorge, slowly and painfully, coming to her aid. The descent took a long time. At first his figure was tiny, ant-like. But minute by minute he came closer, feeling for foot- and hand-holds, getting larger, more visible, until she could see his face sharply, pale and concerned and wonderfully familiar. She'd loved him as he struggled towards her, reaching the floor of the ravine, wanting only to help her. But when he came near she laughed like a crazy woman, writhed on the ground, clawed at him, so that he couldn't touch her. He'd stared at her, sad and uncomprehending.

Iris lay between the smooth, laundered sheets, panicking and alone, wishing she could turn to Owain and bury her head in his shoulder, his warmth, have him comfort her. But he wasn't there and if he had been she would probably have lain stiff and hostile on her own side of the bed.

She thought back to that afternoon, when Owain had walked off the rugby field, sweating and panting, full of a private physical elation. She'd loved him then, like before, with a kind of bleak yearning for the past. But it seemed a weakness that she must hide, that she must punish him for.

She lay with her eyes open in the dark. It must be late, well past midnight, surely. The pub would have shut ages ago. Owain should be here, lying next to her. Jo allowed them to share the bed in the small back bedroom. 'Ianto and I were no saints when we were younger,' she'd confided once, briskly. Iris knew that Owain's birth had followed hard on his parents' wedding. The bed was brass, inherited from some relative, and jingled at the slightest movement. A self-censoring device, Owain had called it laughingly when they were younger and used to make love stealthily, cautiously, trying not to wake Ianto and Jo, stifling their hilarity beneath the bedclothes. She lay and waited, then drifted into a tense, troubled sleep.

Owain lifted the latch on the back door, let himself into the kitchen and switched on the light. On the scrubbed table Jo had laid out the breakfast things for the next day. The only sound was the loud, regular ticking of the wood-framed wall clock. It was almost one o'clock. He was tired, Owain realized, what with the game that afternoon, and the long, solitary walk after the pub, across Avon Meadows, through the wood. At the same time he felt calm and invigorated. The cold and the wind had been cleansing. The silent darkness had focused his mind.

He locked the door with the heavy iron key and dropped it into the green vase on the mantelpiece, next to the supercilious china angel that had watched over his boyhood. In the hall he took off his shoes. The stairs creaked as he climbed them, sounding loud in the silent house.

He opened the door to the back bedroom and went inside. Iris didn't stir. If she was asleep he'd wait until tomorrow to tell her. He began to undress. The room was cold – he could feel it on his skin – but the core of him was warm from walking. He lifted one corner of the washed-out mauve and grey coverlet, which had been on his bed throughout his childhood. Slipping between the sheets, he tried to keep to his own side of the bed, away from Iris's naked body, trying not to wake her, but she

165

stirred and turned towards him, reaching for him with blind instinct. Her body was smooth and warm, and he could feel her face against his shoulder. In reflex he became aroused. Automatically he stroked her shoulder. It would be easy in this unusual truce to put off the hour again, postpone their parting, as they'd been doing for so long, until it had become a habit.

'It's no good, Iris, is it?' Paradoxically he was holding her like a lover. 'We're no good together. We've known it for ages.'

She lay still and inert against him, not contradicting. Her silence was a confirmation.

'I'm moving out when we get back. You can keep the flat on if you want to. I should've gone ages ago. Or you should.' It seemed easy to say the words, natural, and yet they'd found them impossible for so long. Owain felt calm and cold. He held Iris close, and laid a hand against her cheek, but the movement was precise and willed.

Sometime in the early hours he surfaced momentarily into consciousness. Iris was still in his arms. She was crying silently, her grief controlled, reined in, so that Owain wouldn't wake and hear her.

1953—4

18

On 2 June 1953, Coronation Day, Ruth and Paul went down to Raynes Park to leave Ben with his grandparents for the night. In spite of his declared republican beliefs Paul was keen to hold a party in the Marshall Street flat and seized on the pretext. They stayed with the Macdonalds for the day, watching the ceremony on their television, though Ben got bored quite quickly with the flickering, grey, nine-inch square and Ruth found that the endless procession of dispossessed European royalty soon palled.

There were modest decanters of both sherry and port on the sideboard in honour of the occasion. Quite early in the day Paul began to make inroads into the port. He became flushed and frisky, amusing Ben by clowning with a pair of red-and-green-lensed cardboard spectacles – a new fad for viewing three-dimensional photographs in magazines – until the child was helpless with laughter.

'You *are* a naughty boy, Paul,' his mother chided him fondly, as he refilled his glass for the third time. Permed, powdered and innocent, she was obviously under the impression that this was a patriotic aberration. You don't know the half of it, Ruth thought, watching. Paul's drinking had crept way beyond the stage where she could simply laugh it off.

Nevertheless, the day passed quite painlessly. At lunch time they sat down to a huge shepherd's pie. It had been Paul's favourite dish as a child, and his mother cooked it unfailingly when they visited. It seemed to Ruth that she'd eaten hundreds of them. Dessert was a spectacular Bird's custard and jelly-baby recipe her mother-in-law had clipped from a magazine, thinking it would appeal to Ben.

'Look, Ben,' Ruth urged. 'Isn't it lovely?'

The sponge and custard were in the shape of a house, while jelly-babies clustered at windows and doors. Ben looked at it, pensive and inscrutable. He ate some of the custard that was served to him, but spat out his allotted jelly-baby with a suspicious air that was almost adult. Ruth was too full of mash and mince to manage any.

Paul tucked into second helpings. 'This is wonderful, Mum.' She glowed at her son's praise, pink and proud, like a housewife in an advert.

'A loyal toast, I think.' Mr Macdonald had a small moustache and a sparkiness that the rigid respectability of life in Raynes Park hadn't managed to extinguish. There were times when Ruth could see Paul in him. He went to the sideboard and poured them all a sherry in little stemmed goblets. He handed them out ceremonially, then lifted his own glass high. 'To our new young Queen, God bless 'er.'

'God bless her,' Mrs Macdonald repeated dutifully.

'And all who sail in her.' Paul drained his glass.

'Oh, Paul.' His mother giggled guiltily at the slight joke.

Outside in the road, between the rows of neat gardens and clipped privet hedges, overlooked by picture-windows with draped net curtains, two long trestle tables had been set up under a threatening sky. Teams of women bustled about with plates of jam tarts and jellies and jugs of orange squash, preparing a coronation tea for the children. The houses were decorated with flags and bunting. The children – in improvised red, white and blue outfits – hung about, getting in the way of their benefactors, impatient and excited, showing off, trying to sample the piles of cakes and sandwiches prematurely, being shooed

170

off by the harassed helpers. Ben was fascinated by the colour and activity.

Some men were erecting a net with balloons, to be released later. Paul's father joined them, genial and bossy, pointing emphatically with the stem of his pipe, calling instructions to a man up a ladder.

Paul and Ruth watched from the sidelines, while Mrs Macdonald sauntered among the neighbours in her blue nylon blouse and Sunray pleated skirt, passing the time of day and flaunting her grandson. There was consternation as a tentative shower began to spit.

'I reckon they'll manage without us,' Paul said. 'We might as well push off home.'

'We'll invite anyone who doesn't give a bugger about the New Elizabethan Age,' Paul had declared expansively when he first had the idea for the party. That meant the band, for a start, and selected members of the Left Bank Club, various Soho regulars, including Ruth's streetwalking friend, Glenda, and Becky's left-wing pals. 'Though they're a bit earnest,' Paul said. 'but their hearts are in the right place.'

As they pushed the furniture against the wall with the help of Richard and Rebecca, put away the breakables, and decorated the flat with balloons and some of Becky's posters, they became skittish and elated, dipping into the stock of beer and cheap wine in the kitchen and looking out the best records for dancing. In the back of a cupboard they found a large and baleful-eyed clown doll that someone had given Ben and he'd taken against. Rebecca draped it with a string of small union jacks and hung it from the ceiling in the hall.

Ernest Broadbent was spending the day and night with his daughter in Tottenham so, with Ben taken care of, they had the place to themselves. 'We can have an orgy if we want to,' Paul declared, 'and no one can say us nay.'

171

Ruth put on her party clothes, a man's tartan shirt and black toreador pants. Her blonde hair hung loose on her shoulders, she was barefoot, and wore the hoop earrings that Paul loved because, so he said, they were common. As she came down again from their bedroom to the main body of the flat, Richard was in the hall, attaching some recalcitrant balloons to the wall. He stopped and watched as she walked towards him down the staircase.

'You look knockout,' he said. It was a statement of fact rather than a compliment, but she could see in his eyes the secret and vulnerable gleam that betrayed the strength of his feelings for her. She found it reassuring, fortifying. It was one of the consolations her current life was built on.

As she came abreast, she reached up, ruffled his hair, and grinned, complacent and come-hither, in momentary satire of a celluloid sex goddess. 'Flatterer.'

Richard smiled at her with affection, but somewhere behind the smile lay a hurt. He made her think suddenly of a captive bear, with his large body and his guilelessness.

Soon after eight, people began to arrive. Anita was among the first of the guests, tubby but exuberant in red trousers and a patriotic red, white and blue ruched off-the-shoulder blouse, a white rose tucked precariously into her shock of red hair. She had her fiancé, Sid, the clarinettist, with her, and a bottle, which she put with the others.

'I've plonked my plonk on the table,' she told Paul, stridently facetious, as he kissed her cheek with simulated old-world courtesy. 'Doesn't Sid look good?' she demanded of the company at large. The clarinettist seemed a touch sheepish in a striped shirt with elasticated armbands, a bow tie and a jaunty bowler, in imitation of an old-style New Orleans jazzman. His pale ginger hair was slicked straight back off his forehead.

'Pretty damn dashing,' Ruth agreed.

'Devilish striking couple, Thumper.' Paul smiled slyly.

'Sarcastic swine.' Anita gave him a shove that wasn't altogether playful.

Glenda struggled up the fire escape with two enormous bottles of champagne.

'You flash thing!' Ruth was taken aback.

'If you don't mind the wages of sin.' A dry challenge behind her smile.

Ruth hugged one of the bottles to her. 'I'm easily corrupted.'

When she'd invited her to come along, during one of their early-morning encounters in the street, Glenda had seemed pleased. She was dressed for the occasion in a demure, rose-splashed summer dress, her honey-coloured hair caught back loosely with a ribbon as if – what a strange thought – their planned anarchic party was for her the equivalent of an invitation to tea at the vicar's.

'Don't you look nice,' Ruth said brightly.

'This old thing,' Glenda replied with an odd edge of sarcasm. She seemed ill-at-ease, as if unsure what to expect. Ruth poured her a large drink.

Vincent, the Wailers' dark-haired trumpeter, considered himself the group's heart-throb. Not without reason, for he cut a swathe – Sid's glumly envious terminology – through the young women who clustered round the band night after night at the Left Bank Club.

Ruth regarded him with secret amusement. The studied, unsmiling, sinuous glances he bestowed on his victims made her think of Rudolf Valentino, though she suspected he'd have been mortified by the comparison. Robert Mitchum was his hero and, more recently, Brando. In his lighter moments he could recite whole scenes from their films by heart. He sidled moodily through the fire-escape door in jeans and a black top, a cigarette drooping from his mouth and a comma of greased hair dangling across his brow. Silently he placed a quart bottle of ale on the kitchen table.

'All right then, Ruth?' He greeted her laconically.

'Fine. And you?'

'Can't complain. Got a Double Diamond anywhere among this lot?' There was a conscious carelessness in his speech to her that bordered on the brusque. Once Richard had revealed slyly that Vincent, in a drunken moment, had referred to Ruth as a moonlight woman, all pale and untouchable, and the incongruous and vaguely ridiculous image flashed into her mind whenever she met him.

She poured him a drink. Inexplicably he winked as he accepted the glass. 'How's the nipper?' He adored Ben, and had a stock line of patter with him about the pub crawls they'd go on together when Ben was a big boy. The child would listen, open-mouthed and uncomprehending, but fascinated by the hypnotic good humour of Vincent's voice.

'He's very taken with all the flags and things and celebrations,' Ruth said. 'Hallo, Daphne, glad you could make it,' she added, distracted by the arrival of Rebecca's college friend.

Vincent grimaced dourly. 'Yeah, your Ben's about the right age for all this malarkey.' He saw himself as something of a revolutionary, though as far as Ruth knew, his opinions had never been translated into the slightest hint of action.

'I got quite sentimental watching the television,' Daphne volunteered. 'Quite choked up at the solemnity and the Englishness . . . I wouldn't have thought . . .'

'A-a-ah.' Vincent shook his head disgustedly. Though he softened his response with an indulgent masculine smile at Daphne's female soft-heartedness.

Later on they watched as the distant South Bank firework display lit up the night sky in arcs and whorls, and constellations of silver-red, green and gold, followed by erratic trails of weirdly coloured smoke. They turned off the lights, opened the windows and drank Glenda's champagne. The festive party sounds were stilled for a time as they leaned out into the fresh damp evening air.

'Now this is something like,' Vincent breathed. Already his hand rested on Glenda's shoulder as if it belonged there.

Ruth thought it magical, this sudden quiet and dark. She found herself next to Paul, his uncompromising profile black against the street lighting and the fitful brightness of the sky. He put his arm round her shoulder and she nestled into his side. A particularly spectacular configuration showered against the purple horizon, hanging there, spreading like a stain, poetry in motion.

'You could almost imagine they were heralding in a new age,' she said softly, turning towards him. Their stillness and the fireworks supplied a frisson that she hadn't found in the daylight pageantry or the surburban bustle of the street party. 'Suppose they could. Supposing it was as easy as that.'

Paul looked at her. 'Let's wait and see. Maybe we're in for some surprises. Shake us up a bit.' There was a vehemence in his tone that startled her, that she suspected owed something to alcohol. But it seemed more than that somehow, his words heavy with unspoken meaning.

But she had no chance to question him, for Anita came up behind them and laid a plump, white arm across each of their shoulders.

'I'm having a marvellous time,' she confided, leaning forward to push her head in between theirs. Her red curls tickled Ruth's cheek. 'Aren't they bloody wonderful?' she added as a new burst of colours flowered above the dark roof tops.

* * *

175

When the fireworks were over, the party regained its momentum. Paul had looked out a pile of records that were suitable for dancing to, and he put them on Sid's auto-change machine, borrowed for the occasion. People began to dance with renewed vigour. The floor shook until Ruth feared for the stability of the building.

She was still pensive after the pause for the fireworks, and chose not to dance, but sat on the sofa, which had been pushed against the wall, with her feet curled under her, watching the dancers abstractedly.

Richard came across to her. 'You look all introspective. Would you like to dance?'

She shook her head. 'No, I'll just sit here for a while.' But she felt a rush of warmth for him, for his clumsiness, for the broad, good-natured, bearded face, and his awareness of her mood. She grinned. 'I'm feeling a bit alienated.' It was a word they'd adopted recently in the Marshall Street flat, thinking it rather modish, and they used it often like a private password. She patted the brown plush cushion next to her. 'You could stay and talk to me.'

He sat down beside her, his large body peaceable and comforting. 'How were the grandparents?'

She pulled a face. 'Okay, but I always get the impression that they disapprove of me vaguely. They'd rather Paul had married someone plump and capable with a perm and large breasts . . . and an apron.'

He laughed softly. 'Sounds so healthy it's perverted.'

Close by them Rebecca danced with Carl. She was lithe as a cat, tanned, in a black sleeveless shirt and trousers, her dark hair flying. Below the fringe her small, smooth face was vivid with life, her dark eyes deep and shining. Ruth watched her as she twirled expertly, then turned to Richard, for all the world like a proud mother. 'Look at Becky . . . Full to bursting with life. She's so beautiful.'

She paused, and added, 'But she doesn't know it, and if she did, she wouldn't care.'

Carl looked handsome and healthy, his sunburned skin contrasting with the white shirt he wore. There was an air of competence in his dancing, as in everything he did, but his movements appeared mechanical, as though this was a necessary social skill that he'd mastered. Secretly Ruth thought him rather prosaic, unworthy of her friend. He was the perfect companion for her, of course, a fellow campaigner. At present the newly acquired British A-Bomb was the target of their particular concern. Both of them deplored their country's enthusiastic participation in the arms race.

Richard watched Rebecca with a similar, almost proprietary fondness. 'Becky's funny. She changes the whole dynamic of this household. The four of us.' He bent down and picked up a beer bottle that stood by the sofa leg and refilled his glass. 'Maybe she's our conscience,' he said musingly. 'What do you think?'

'It's a point of view.' She laughed. 'But I'm not sure the idea would go down well with Becky.'

As they danced, Ruth considered Rebecca and Carl as a couple. They were having an affair, she knew, but to Ruth it appeared an unromantic, fraternal relationship, almost an affair of convenience. Still, you shouldn't judge . . . Though once Becky had been talking to her about Carl and remarked unguardedly, thinking aloud, 'Sometimes I think there must be more . . .' Then she'd checked herself and immediately changed the subject.

'Look at Vince.' Richard nudged Ruth surreptitiously. The Wailers' trumpet player had backed Glenda into a corner and stood talking to her, one hand braced against the wall behind her, so that she was trapped inside the predatory circle formed by his body. It was impossible to tell what Glenda thought of the situation.

Anita danced past them with Joe, the Scottish drummer, rolling her large hips and shaking plump shoulders. Joe squired her gamely, countering her exuberance with a solemn style of his own. As she passed by, Anita smacked Vincent playfully on the bottom. He jumped and glowered, none too pleased at the interruption of his tête-à-tête. She laughed at his wrath, displaying her prominent teeth.

But Ruth was distracted by the sight of Paul on the opposite side of the room. He was jiving with Marion, his fan, as Richard had dubbed her. As they moved, the two of them laughed and talked with pleasure and a sort of tension that betrayed their mutual attraction. Paul wore a smile that Ruth knew well, a kind of turning down of the lips, a suppressed amusement, at something Marion must have said, and abruptly she perceived his pleasure in the woman's company as threatening. Marion was wearing a wine-coloured summer dress and her dark hair looked soft and clean. She seemed fully conscious of her own seductive powers.

They performed a particularly flashy manoeuvre in their dance. Paul spun Marion round in a kind of spiral, then caught her to him round the waist, sideways on. Momentarily she relaxed against him, laughing over her shoulder, her eyes bold and provocative, and in that moment he kissed her on the lips.

Ruth's reaction was intense and physical. At once she was hot, breathless, sick. She'd seen Paul flirt many times. He did so instinctively, almost without thought, and with a style that amused her. She viewed it with a mental shrug as part of his personality, his head-on approach to life. But there was something about the complicity of these two that disturbed her, and in a hot, painful flash of knowledge she understood that they were lovers. She watched them with a hypnotized fascination. They twisted and cavorted with a seamless smoothness that now – to her mesmerized gaze – appeared cruel, as if they were flaunting themselves for her benefit.

'Richard,' she said in a low voice. He looked towards her questioningly. 'Paul sleeps with her, doesn't he? That Marion.'

He turned on her a long, lingering, troubled look, then nodded. 'Yes.'

'His fan,' she said, with a kind of wondering bitterness, and realized then that Richard hadn't talked about her for ages. He used to give reports on her progress, jokingly, at breakfast time. He hadn't mentioned her, Ruth supposed, since she stopped being a joke.

Richard put his arm gently across her shoulder. The quiet compassion of the gesture roused her out of her passivity. She moved away from him, not disposed to accept a victim's role.

'Don't feel sorry for me, Richard,' she said sharply. He withdrew his arm at once, as if she'd slapped him. They looked at one another. Ruth gathered all the strength at her disposal not to show weakness and hurt, though there was a pain inside her as if someone had hacked away a chunk of her heart like a section of masonry. 'We always said we'd have a marriage that was different. We agreed on that. And we have. And this is just another way . . .' Ruth had the impression she must look like a death's head, drained of colour, a *memento mori* to the surrounding revels. The sound of music, laughter and chatter echoed about her, ebbing, fluctuating.

'Can we go up to your room?' she asked Richard. 'It'll be cooler. Quiet.'

He got to his feet. 'Come on.'

Crossing the room, she felt like Medea or someone, wild-eyed and tragic, hideously visible. But people seemed not to notice. As she passed, Sid was trying to inflict his bowler hat on Daphne and she was laughing and protesting.

Paul and Marion were in her line of vision. Again, Ruth had the illusion that they were aware of her, disporting themselves for her sake. Marion wore a feline smile, it seemed to Ruth, as though inflicting pain were part of her pleasure.

Paul saw her approaching the door with Richard. Inconsequentially, a fragment of memory came to her from months back. Paul urging her – teasingly it had seemed then – to sleep with Richard '. . . and put the poor bugger out of his misery.' Now, overwrought, she fancied she saw the satisfaction in his eye, as if a situation he'd willed were on the point of coming into being. But she was probably imagining that too.

Upstairs Richard removed people's jackets and bags from his bed and piled them roughly outside in the hall. Then he closed the door and locked it.

Ruth stood to one side. In her suspended, emotional state, odd details of the room presented themselves to her with a vivid, empty significance – scattered records, a Fair Isle sweater hanging over the back of a chair, Richard's desk with some translation work in progress, a couple of technical dictionaries. She said irrelevantly, 'You're getting a fair bit of work, aren't you, from that printing firm . . .' And then a new wave of pain hit her, spinning her senses, and she buried her face in her hands.

'Hey, Ruth.' Richard came and put his arms round her. She stayed clenched, face hidden, refusing to relax against him and indulge herself in his sympathy.

She steeled herself. The wave passed. She moved away from him and straightened up, breathing deeply. 'I'm okay.' She found that she was able to muster a coldness, a self-possession. She wouldn't be taken by surprise again.

'D'you want a cup of tea? There's water in the kettle.' He had a gas ring in his room.

'Why not? Thanks.' She sat down on the edge of his

bed, with its beige and brown tartan blanket. Her composure was still holding. She looked down, concentrating on her bare feet, lightly tanned, the nails painted pink. Paul had done them the other day, while she was lounging in the sun on the fire escape. He'd been clowning, pretending to bite her feet to make Ben laugh. She hardened herself against the memory.

'We all talk as if sexual freedom was a good thing,' she said in a toneless, neutral voice.

'Yes.' Richard knelt to extract two white china mugs from a low cupboard. 'That's the theory.'

She sat and waited, and in time he handed her a mug of strong tea. She looked up at him. 'It's like stained boot polish,' she said. Then, 'I've been meaning to tell you. You're like Pierre in *War and Peace*. Have you read it?' Though why that should occur to her now . . .

He gave her a quizzical glance. ''Fraid not.'

She drank the tea, then placed the mug on the bedside rug, realizing suddenly that she felt exhausted, emotionally and physically drained. 'I'm really tired.' Music and laughter shook the floor. She nodded towards the source of the sound. 'That lot'll be here for ages yet.'

'Lie on my bed. I'll sit over here.' He had a sagging brown easy chair that went with the sofa downstairs.

'Thanks.' She turned sideways and stretched out on the plaid blanket, then raised herself on one elbow. 'Thanks for everything, Richard.'

He stood up and drew the limp blue curtains. Ruth lay on the bed, coldly wakeful, armed against the painful thoughts that might catch her unawares. She felt like ice, but hadn't the energy to crawl under the blanket. Tense and watchful, she had no awareness of the passing of time.

Some time later – an hour, hours, she didn't know – Richard came and lay down beside her, putting his arms round her. The warmth of his large body was a boon. She

181

lay still and let him hold her, in some state between sleep and consciousness, out of time and place.

He whispered, 'Ruth . . .' over and over and kissed her cheek. She became aware of his hand on her back under the tartan shirt she was wearing. She could imagine it, his large hand on her smooth, tanned back. The image aroused her. She could stop him if she wanted. He was waiting to see if she would. She did nothing. The hand shifted slowly to her breast. She kissed him softly on the mouth and moved against him. He was warmth, comfort, oblivion. He turned on the bed, covering her body with his own. She pictured Paul's face with its secret gleam of satisfaction.

19

Four days later Ruth sat minding Ernest Broadbent's shop. He'd gone to some house-clearance sale in St Albans. 'Good, big library,' he'd informed her, with a gloomy sort of relish. 'Should be some tasty items.' He'd taken a roll of grubby notes from the till and wouldn't return until late.

The door to the shop was propped open, and the bright June sun penetrated to shelves that she'd cleaned earlier, even getting out a ladder to reach the cobwebby heights near the ceiling. Not that Ernest would be grateful. He seemed to prefer a protective patina of dust clinging to his surroundings. But occasionally – partly to justify her salary – Ruth took matters into her own hands.

A solitary, grey-haired customer browsed silently in one corner. A defensive set to his shoulders stated that he'd rather be left undisturbed. Ben played quietly with some cars on the floor, vibrating his lips to make a continual low, soothing engine sound. Ruth read peaceably behind the counter. The Wailers were in the Midlands for three days, playing at local jazz clubs.

Since the morning after the party Ruth had felt strangely invigorated, almost light-headed. She had come to regard the redefining of her relationship with Paul with a kind of relief. It was though layers of misapprehension and unease had been burned away, leaving a core that was harder, clearer. She refused to mope or look into the future. Her present exhilaration was sufficient for her. There was a sense of lawlessness, of danger almost, at living with both husband and lover, that compensated, at

183

least temporarily, for the enforced inactivity of her present way of living. As she sat and read and watched over Ben and the shop, the routineness of these occupations was overlaid by a feeling of well-being and suppressed excitement.

A shadow partially obscured the rectangle of brightness that shone in through the shop's open door. Another customer. She looked up.

'Hallo, Ruth.' It was Owain Roberts, looking relaxed, brown and summery in a white shirt, trailing his jacket over one shoulder.

'Hallo!' She greeted him with pleasure, her cheerfulness spilling over into a welcome. 'What a surprise.'

He smiled. 'I was passing. To be honest, I wondered whether Rebecca was in.' They'd been in correspondence recently, Ruth knew. Something about a new magazine he was trying to get off the ground. She was vague about the details.

'Sorry. You've missed her. Lectures, I imagine. You know what a worker Becky is.'

'Never mind.' He lingered. 'It's good to see you. You're looking well.'

Simultaneously the grey-haired browser approached the counter with a pile of books. She took them and totted up the prices on a piece of paper. Ernest had a till, but he didn't trust it to do sums.

'That'll be eighteen and six.' She waited as the man prodded and poked in a multi-compartmented purse for the correct money. Another of Ernest's vagaries was to wrap customers' purchases with brown paper and string. It took ages, but when she'd finished Owain was still there.

'Would you like a coffee?' she offered. 'I usually make something for me and Ben around this time.'

'Yes, please.' He seemed enthusiastic.

'Keep an eye on the shop for a sec, then . . . Ben, shall we get you some milk?'

The child shook his head with an air of sturdy imperturbability. 'No.' At just two years old it was his favourite word. But he stood up readily enough, holding a car in each hand, to follow her upstairs.

Owain seemed struck by his looks. 'He's become so like you. It's almost uncanny.'

'He is, isn't he? Even I can see it.' She could observe nothing about Ben that clarified the riddle of his paternity. He was blond and grey-eyed like she was. The shape of his mouth, the line of his eyebrows were hers. A tinge of incredulity at the thought that Owain might be . . . But they'd agreed, she and Paul, that they wouldn't investigate.

'It's irrelevant, anyway,' Paul said. 'He's mine.'

When she came back with coffee, and milk for Ben, Owain had settled himself in the chair provided for customers, his long legs stretched out in front of him, his feet on a pair of low steps that Ernest used to gain access to the higher shelves. He was glancing through the book she'd been reading, an ancient brown volume, whose forbidding-looking cover was at odds with its hilarious contents. He looked up, smiling. 'This is brilliant.'

'Isn't it?' she enthused. She'd happened on the book while browsing the other day. It was early nineteenth-century, and consisted of a list of social annoyances, detailed with a sort of lugubrious resignation. It made her laugh out loud. 'I keep getting the urge to read bits out to customers.'

'I like this one.' He quoted: '"Hot curling irons in the hand of an operator, who, when he twirls them up to your skull, there keeps them, obsequiously waiting every time for your roar, as his warrant for untwisting them."'

'I know,' she laughed. 'And there's another one I love. About olives. Wait a minute.' She leafed energetically

185

through the book. 'Ah. Here it is . . . "The long and painful apprenticeship which you serve to the business of learning to like olives – without being master of your trade at last."' She grinned at him. 'That one hits home. I really *hate* olives.'

It seemed that they were suddenly at ease together, as if, since their last awkward meeting in Becky's room, time had worked for them in their absence, giving each an illusion of closer acquaintance.

Owain began to ask Ben about his cars, squatting at the child's level and picking them up one by one. As she watched the two of them it occurred to Ruth how different he was from Paul. There was a reserve about Owain, a containment, where Paul's responses were quick and close to the surface. Owain approached people and events with an innate gravity, so that when he smiled and laughed it seemed to come from some well deep inside, and the sincerity of it was like a present.

He talked to Ben attentively, patiently, so that the child became trustful, straining at the limits of his vocabulary to explain himself, while Owain listened and encouraged. Ruth wondered where he could have learned his manner with children.

'Are you married now, Owain?' she asked impulsively, and thought immediately that the question could be construed as prying.

But he answered easily. 'I lived with someone for a long time. But . . . it died. What there was between us. It took us a long time to admit it. Far too long.'

She was surprised by the honesty of his reply, and the fullness. He seemed almost to invite further conversation on the subject. 'What went wrong?' she asked softly, still half-expecting him to clam up.

'We were both communists for a time. It was important to us.' He shrugged and gave a half-smile. 'We lost our faith. And resented each other because of it, I suppose.'

186

Ruth knelt by Ben as he drank his milk, hovering. Sometimes he got distracted and spilt it. Owain's reply had no reality for her. She couldn't imagine two people letting politics come between them. It seemed so abstract – although Becky, no doubt, would understand. But she was determined not to lose the new flow of communication between them. 'Do you miss her?' she asked.

'Yes. In odd ways. But it wasn't working. More than anything I think we feel relief at having finally cut our losses.' He'd seated himself in the chair again, and lounged with one elbow across its curved back. 'In March, though, when Stalin died, I suddenly had the urge to talk to her. She was the only person I wanted to discuss it with – the implications, the way we felt about it. I phoned her. And when I got through she told me she was on the point of phoning me . . .' Owain let the sentence trail away. He looked across at Ruth. 'What about you then? Living happily ever after?'

Ben finished his milk, and she replaced his Rupert Bear mug on the tray, then sat down behind the counter again to drink her coffee. Ben climbed on to her knee, his boldness giving way to a sudden attack of shyness. He leaned his head against Ruth's white tee shirt and from this position of security, thumb in mouth, he watched Owain with calm, wide eyes.

'Happy ever after?' She picked up her own cup and grinned at him provocatively. 'What a silly question.'

'Is it?' He gave an answering smile.

'No one's totally happy, are they? There's good and bad.'

'What's the good?'

She gave a humorous shrug. 'All sorts of things. Ben, of course. And being young. And friends . . .' She pictured Becky, Richard . . . Paul? In all honesty could she include him? 'Paul sometimes,' she said guardedly.

'Only sometimes?'

Ruth felt disloyal. She never discussed Paul with anyone, not Becky, not Richard. This conversation with Owain was strange, so unexpected, so outside any usual context. There might be a certain relief in putting her mixed feelings into words . . .

'Paul's fun,' she began musingly. 'And very loving to Ben. And to me in his own way. But . . .' She considered, laying her lips momentarily against the crown of Ben's blond head. '. . . It's hard to explain. He always seems to be chasing something. As if he were frightened of dullness, ordinariness. There's got to be new excitement all the time . . .' That was enough. She wouldn't mention Marion, or Paul's drinking, or Richard. 'Dylan Thomas is a hero of his. And Henry Miller.' She grinned, breaking the solemnity. 'Says it all, doesn't it?'

'You love him though?'

'Yes, I do. More so since we've been married. But he's a perverse little bugger . . .'

'What about acting? D'you miss that?'

'Yes.' The old tug of muffled sadness at the reminder. A figure filled the open doorway, broad and stocky. One of Ernest's regulars. 'Morning, Mr Quinn.'

'Mind if I have a browse?' He sidled roguishly towards the topography section, as if to indulge a forbidden vice.

'We've got some new Baedekers in.'

Owain stood up. 'I must go.' He held out the small brown volume they'd laughed over. 'I'll take this one if you can spare it.'

'It's expensive – a guinea,' she warned.

'Worth every penny.' He felt in his pocket for the change. 'No, don't bother to wrap it.' He made as if to go. 'Goodbye, Ruth.' He had a vaguely indecisive air as if he would have liked to say something more.

'Goodbye.' There was a similar hesitation on Ruth's part. She added impulsively, 'Drop in again. Thursdays are good.'

'I will,' he said.

20

Rebecca sat on top of the 196 bus, travelling towards the Elephant and Castle. Outside, the early evening sun coaxed warm yellow-grey and ochre tones from the brickwork of the passing buildings. She felt alone, was alone for the first time in ages, venturing outside the comfortable sphere of King's with the easy companionship she now took for granted, and the strangely cosy ambiguities of the household in Marshall Street. She was dressed uncharacteristically demurely in a pleated grey skirt and sweater, her dark hair tied low in the nape of her neck. She'd been requested to look neat. It wouldn't do to have her confused with the actual members of the youth club. After all, she wasn't that much older than they. She felt nervous, and there was a tightness in the pit of her stomach. At the same time she was determined. It was her own choice after all to go and help, to do something practical.

It had been Owain who'd put her in touch. She'd run into him by chance one day in Broadbent's shop where he'd come to see Ruth, as he did almost weekly now.

'How's life?' he greeted her. He looked happy and energetic. She knew that plans for his magazine were advancing. Some sort of co-operative, Ruth had told her, but with possible backing from an MP. No names to be mentioned yet, though.

Rebecca, on the other hand, was feeling stale. She was just back from Llandudno for her third and final year at university, and its familiarity was beginning to pall. At present she saw the small world, with distaste, as a round of incestuous political arguments and petitions that changed little, a busy, cloistered self-importance. 'I wish I had some other outlet,' she told Owain. 'Something way outside that'd put all this lot into perspective.'

He'd mentioned a woman he knew. An ex-lover of his, so Ruth informed her later. 'She does a lot of community work, if you're interested,' he told her. 'Specially with kids and teenagers. Would something like that interest you?'

Rebecca wasn't sure, but she kept an open mind and telephoned the number he gave her. The woman's name was Iris. The voice at the other end of the line was cool, and not overly welcoming. Still, she knew of a youth club starting up at the Elephant where they needed helpers. Her tone suggested that well-meaning students with a social conscience weren't exactly what they were looking for. Nonetheless, she offered to arrange a meeting with Val Green, the vicar who was in charge.

Rebecca had been dubious. Never in her life had she had any dealings with purveyors of organized religion. On the other hand she was keen to break out of the restricting mould that encased her. She agreed to the interview.

Val – short for Valentine – radiated enthusiasm and waved aside her doubts. 'It's energy I'm after. Plenty of time to save your soul later.' He seemed keen to take her on – whether out of desperation or because he'd spotted some suitable quality in her, Rebecca wasn't sure. She suspected the former.

As she talked to him, the phrase 'muscular Christian' leaped to mind. He was youngish, with a broad, blunt, English face topped by fair curls that recalled Millais's portrait, *Bubbles*. But a barrel chest and short, stocky legs lurked under the tweed jacket and flannels that he wore with his dog collar.

This was her stop. The bus drew up opposite the bomb-site that still dominated the Elephant and Castle. Drifts of fireweed gleamed, warm and rosy, in the evening sun among the ragged piles of brick and concrete. Many of the weeds had gone to seed, so that each breath of wind released drifting fragments into the air, like feathers.

Rebecca scrambled hastily down the stairs of the bus. Outside, she took the road leading to the Nissen hut that was to house the club. She had only been here once before, and the streets seemed vaguely inhospitable to her. She had the sudden strong awareness that this wasn't her part of town. A group of children were engaged in a rowdy, ferocious game of French cricket, and as she passed their hard rubber ball missed her by inches, her narrow escape raising a chorus of muffled giggles. A group of teenage lads – some no older than thirteen, she guessed – stood smoking on a street corner. They called suggestively after her, and the absurdity of the situation reinforced her sense of isolation, of being conspicuous.

Val had already arrived when Rebecca reached the corrugated iron hut opposite a small garment factory that had one dusty, cap-sleeved red dress hanging limply at the window. He looked up with a broad smile from his task of fixing a net to a full-sized ping-pong table. 'Ready for the invading hordes?' he asked brightly. He seemed dressed for action in gym shoes which, combined with his dog collar, suggested a clean-living vigour.

'Ready as I'll ever be.' Rebecca envied him his confidence, his apparent lack of self-doubt. She still had Paul's Lady Bountiful taunts ringing in her ears. He disapproved of this kind of enterprise on principle as patronizing and Edwardian, and even Ruth referred to her plans slightingly as 'your do-gooding scheme'. Their doubts had made her all the more determined to go ahead.

The hall was bare apart from a couple of tables pushed against walls that were painted brown up to waist level and institutional yellow above this demarcation line. The windows were small and high up, hung with curtains obviously run up from some of the leftover blackout

191

material that popped up everywhere. At the far end was a small kitchen with a scratched sink, a gas geyser, a cupboard, and two crumpled tea towels hanging from a precarious aluminium rail. Over everything hung the dispiriting smell of Jeyes fluid.

Some new metal and canvas chairs, Val's pride and joy, were stacked at one end of the hall.

'Shall we get some of them out?' she said. 'Make it look a bit more welcoming.'

'Good idea, Rebecca!' He seemed to think her modest suggestion a brainwave, or perhaps it was just his manner.

A few minutes later two girls' faces appeared round the open door. One gave a shrill, hysterical giggle, and both disappeared.

Val walked to the doorway. 'We're open, ladies,' Rebecca heard him say. But there was no reply. She assumed that the girls preferred to wait for reinforcements before venturing into the off-putting void of the hall.

Soon a group of about eight came in. 'This the club?' one asked. She was plump, with a slight sneer, dressed in a tight pinstriped skirt, a white top and down-at-heel suede ballerina slippers.

Rebecca hastened to welcome them and to demonstrate the club's attractions, such as they were – the ping-pong table, the dart board, a shove-ha'penny board, a game of snakes and ladders that someone had donated. She felt like a secondhand car salesman, desperately vaunting the desirability of his mediocre wares, and the girls responded with an appropriate air of sceptical reserve.

The hall was beginning to fill up. Another group of girls arrived and some boys. In the main they seemed aged between thirteen and fifteen. The sexes kept to themselves. Mostly they stood in small clusters looking wary, or laughing among themselves with an air that was both defensive, and defiant. None showed any immediate interest in the activities on offer.

Val moved from group to group, blond, amiable, rather officious, introducing himself in his open, hearty manner, shaking hands, asking names. At one point he glanced towards the door and exclaimed with satisfaction, 'Ah, here's Tony!' There was almost a note of relief in his voice.

An older boy had just arrived. He must have been about seventeen, Rebecca guessed. He was tall and slim with a slightly pock-marked complexion and a fashionable Tony Curtis haircut, which she imagined he'd touched up with a pocket comb just prior to walking in. The boy had a straight nose, strongly marked eyebrows above knowing brown eyes, and thinnish but well-modelled lips. He displayed an air of quiet, subversive amusement at the scene in front of him.

'I've prevailed on Tony to come and help as well,' Val boomed. Then, to the boy, 'This is Rebecca, our other helper. From King's College, London,' he added proudly. Rebecca shrank inwardly, embarrassed at having her credentials so publicly announced. She and Tony nodded to one another non-committally.

Impatient with preliminaries, Rebecca challenged a group of girls to a game of table tennis. They eyed her blankly for a long moment then, to her relief, a girl called Heather stepped forward. She was round-faced and curly-haired and wore the uniform of straight, dark skirt and flat ballerina slippers. 'I'll play you, Miss.'

Years of living in a guesthouse had given Rebecca a deal of practice at the game. Len had converted their cellar into a kind of games room and its focus had been the ping-pong table. As a child she'd played there for hours, with friends or her brother in the off-season, with visiting offspring during the summer.

It soon became obvious that she was going to beat Heather with ludicrous ease. She became conscience-stricken. Her challenge had the air of a put-up job, though she'd issued the invitation merely to get things going. She tried to play badly, but to no avail. The final score was a rout. Heather returned, giggling, to the taunts of her friends. They'd collected quite an audience.

A boy piped up, 'My mate wants to play you.' A fifteen-year-old with close-cropped hair and cold, grey eyes stepped forwards.

'You'd be better off playing one another,' Rebecca protested. 'I'm supposed to be helping.'

'No, I want to play *you*,' the lad declared unsmilingly.

She shrugged. 'All right then.'

The boy presented a greater challenge than Heather. His reflexes were razor sharp, but his back-hand was suspect. This time Rebecca was ruthless, and she never doubted that she'd win. The lad became sullen and a couple of times claimed sulkily that he hadn't been ready for her serve. He threw down his bat disgustedly when the game was over.

'Poor sportsmanship, Harris,' Val remonstrated. The boy gave him a brief, baleful, sidelong glance.

'Miss, why don't you play Tony?' Heather piped up. 'He's good.'

'No.' Rebecca waved the suggestion away. 'I've hogged the table enough for one night.'

'Oh go on, Miss.'

'Show him, Miss.'

A hubbub from among the girls. The two games and the prospect of a third had succeeded beyond belief in dispelling their apathy.

'You're chicken, Miss,' a red-haired boy remarked cheekily. She ignored him but the clamour continued.

Val appeared in her line of vision, smiling, flushed, a genial master of ceremonies. 'I think, Rebecca, you may have to give way to popular feeling.'

Tony stood by the table saying nothing, his narrow face

inscrutable. But eventually he picked up a bat and tested it casually. 'Let's get it over with,' he said.

Reluctantly Rebecca confronted him at the opposite end of the table. They began to play. Tony badly wanted to win, she realized, and he had the killer instinct. To begin with, his vehemence worked against him. Some of his vicious, unanswerable smashes were wild and uncontrolled, but gradually he gained a sense of pace and length. Their eyes met often across the table. His expressed nothing, seeming not to see her. His blind involvement raised her game, so that she too began to play with incisiveness and inspiration.

Between points she was aware of ragged cries of 'Come on, Tone' and of Val shushing the watching teenagers. And, to her surprise, she had her own small group of partisans, a cluster of girls, including Heather, who'd rallied to her cause.

'You can do it, Miss,' they hissed furtively, whenever Val's attention was otherwise engaged.

The game was exhilarating, Rebecca had to admit, once she'd laid aside her guilt at monopolizing the club's best amenity. They'd agreed on one set only. She and Tony reached deuce, and battled for the advantage. They staged some impressive rallies that had the children gasping, as both of them retrieved shots that were seemingly unreachable. The score mounted. Each time one player took the advantage, the other fought, doggedly, to cancel it out.

'Real drama here.' A stage whisper from Val.

The score mounted to twenty-eight all. Then Tony served what should have been an ace, a rocket that skimmed the net by less than half an inch, carrying a fiendish spin, so that it exploded in a totally unforeseen direction. With wolfish triumph Tony watched it go. But impossibly, miraculously Rebecca got to it, turning its force and spin to her own advantage. It had passed him before he realized she'd returned it.

Now it was Rebecca's serve. A riveted hush. He'd be expecting a killer. Instead she served a long, slow, spinning ball that seemed to hang in the air, unfurling lazily like a yoyo. It unnerved Tony. He was wrongfooted. Attempting a stylish and leisurely chop, he missed completely. There was incredulous silence then uproar, with disgusted cries of 'Bloody hell, Tone' and, intermingled, the shrill jubilation of Rebecca's supporters.

Slowly Tony replaced his bat on the table and faced her across the net. As the hubbub died away he proclaimed, 'Jolly well played,' in a stagy, satirical upper-class accent, and was rewarded by the raucous laughter of his cohorts.

Later Val broached the serious part of the evening's programme, chivvying some of the boys to line up the canvas chairs in rows, and drawing the blackout curtains with the aid of something that looked like a boat-hook. Meanwhile, he and Tony set up a rickety epidiascope, which took some time and involved turning the lights off a score or more times and making minute adjustments to the positioning of the machine to achieve the best possible focus. The youngsters became restless and Peter – a red-haired lad, obviously destined to be the club's self-appointed joker – began to sing 'Why Are We Waiting?' in a provoking undertone.

Val, a convinced socialist, was determined to broaden his charges' minds as well as entertain them. He'd prepared a talk, with illustrations, on the new towns that were mushrooming round London – Basildon, Hemel Hempstead, Stevenage and the like. There was a muffled groan as he announced his intention, but no outright mutiny. Rebecca was dubious about Val's educational zeal, but in a sense she respected him for not taking the easy option.

While he held forth, she and Tony retreated to the grim little kitchen and Rebecca poured mugs of orange squash and laid out biscuits. Through the open door they could hear Val burbling on about overspill and green spaces to the accompaniment of scufflings and gigglings, his fair curls haloed in the light of the epidiascope. He spoke with enthusiasm, but was less than deft with the projector. The drawings and photographs sidled jerkily on to the screen at odd angles, even upside down, sending the watching youngsters into ecstasies of laughter. At one point Val was forced to stop the show and call them to order with a good-natured steeliness that Rebecca envied.

'Why does he bother?' Tony asked suddenly, looking sideways at her, warily, as if waiting to see her reaction before he said more. Rebecca didn't answer. Privately she was inclined to ask herself the same question, but she didn't think it would be fitting for her to admit as much to this youth. She smiled at him in a neutral fashion.

He leaned on the draining board, watching her, one hand in his pocket, the attitude negligent, suggesting buried provocation. 'Why d'you come here?' he asked. 'All the way out from London?' A pause. 'Your good deed, is it?'

The enquiry seemed to her covertly hostile, and no convincing answer sprang to mind. 'Why do *you*?' she asked. The question really interested her. His attitude intrigued her. He'd seemed involved in the table tennis, but apart from that his attitude that evening had been one of vaguely languid amusement.

He shrugged. 'It's something to do.'

'What do your friends think about it?' She didn't know what made her ask that.

'I don't care what they think.'

Rebecca recalled Paul's sarcasms on the subject of her prospective youth work, and decided that she felt the same.

* * *

197

A week later, before the next session, Tony came up to Marshall Street. Paul had offered to donate his old gramophone to the Club. His parents had acquired a new, modern machine, and passed on their old radiogram to him and Ruth. It was a massive, walnut-encased piece of furniture that transformed any record it played into a throbbing heartbeat that shook the flat. To Rebecca's surprise Tony had offered to travel up and help her carry Paul's discarded machine on the bus.

It was early evening, cold and wet, when she let him in. He looked different, slightly intimidated away from his home ground, his stylish haircut rumpled by the wind and rain, his cheeks childishly fresh.

'Would you like some tea?' she offered.

He shook his head. 'That's all right,' he said flatly. There was a constraint about him. He approached the flat as an outsider, as if he were entering alien territory, reserving judgement. His attitude had an effect on her, so that she saw the familiar surroundings as they might appear to the lad's cool eyes.

Leading him into the living room she was aware of its scruffiness, the homeliness seeming tinged with a certain squalor. The room was stuffy and the magnificent radiogram was festooned with the usual array of empty tea mugs. The montage of moody jazz photographs Paul had cut from some American magazines and arranged above the fireplace was beginning to peel away from the walls and curl at the edges.

Ruth lay on the floor with Ben, building a huge castle out of his bricks. The child's potty stood against one wall – empty fortunately – and a plate of sardine sandwiches, Ben's tea, had somehow become incorporated into the game. Ruth was barefoot and wore a pair of patched trousers and one of Richard's huge pullovers. Paul was back from a plumbing job he'd been doing for a restaurant in Greek Street, and he sat with a bottle of brown ale

198

beside him and his feet on a chair, reading a *Superman* comic. The smell of beer hung sourly in the air.

'This is Tony from the Club,' Rebecca said. 'Tony – meet Ruth, Paul, Ben.' She indicated each in turn.

Paul and Ruth smiled and nodded perfunctorily in his direction. By a stranger, Rebecca reflected, their casual informality might be mistaken for arrogance. Tony sat stiffly on the edge of the sofa, silent, waiting. Ben toddled across and solemnly offered him a couple of bricks. The youth accepted them awkwardly. 'Yeah, very nice.'

'Paul, could you get the gramophone down for us?' Rebecca asked. 'We ought to be going.'

Reluctantly Paul laid aside his comic and stood up. He was unshaven and wore a closely fitting grey sweater. In spite of his thinness, Rebecca noticed to her surprise the beginnings of a beer belly. Tony's slim youthfulness was a touchstone. She became aware of a puffiness round Paul's eyes, a general air almost of seediness which – since they lived in such close proximity – normally escaped her notice. Momentarily Rebecca was saddened by this new and unflattering view of him.

Later, in the bus queue, as he stood with his arms round Paul's record player, Tony remarked to her, in an oddly impersonal fashion, 'You look better like that.'

Rebecca had returned to her trousers and dufflecoat, hair straggling on her shoulders, rejecting the neat, anonymous clothes she'd worn the week before, which had made her feel like someone else. She'd do a better job this way, and Val could like it or not, as he pleased.

The rain had petered away to a misty drizzle. Now they were on their own Tony had regained his confidence. 'They're arty, your friends,' he remarked. There was a tinge of accusation in his voice, mixed with curiosity.

'I suppose so,' Rebecca said. 'I don't think about it. They're just friends.' She added, 'Look, here's the bus. We'll try and get the seat just inside.'

The vehicle glided to a halt. Tony stowed the gramophone under the stairs and they sat on the adjacent seat, which was open to the soft evening drizzle.

'*He* looks a bit of a piss artist.' The boy returned to his verdict on Rebecca's household, casting a sidelong glance at her to check whether he'd gone too far. The hint of a conspiratorial grin.

Rebecca was torn, not liking his simplified view of Paul, though recognizing the truth in it. Tony was being impertinent, but she felt disinclined to stand on her adult dignity and bluster, or register icy disapproval.

'Does he?' She took refuge in a show of indifference.

21

As the autumn of '53 passed into winter, Rebecca became more and more involved in her work at the Club, thinking about it and planning in spare moments during the week. The spartan, but now familiar Nissen hut was like an island of light and activity somewhere on the outer edge of the world she normally inhabited, and on each visit she rediscovered its inhabitants with pleasure. Gradually the children became individuals to her, their faces and personalities imprinting themselves with increasing clarity on her thoughts and feelings. Over the months the meetings took on their own particular flavour, a slowly evolving compromise between the different ideas and personalities involved.

The children themselves preferred to use the Club as an informal meeting house, where they could talk and laugh and play the Dickie Valentine or Johnny Ray records they brought in. By and large, they weren't too bothered about table tennis or seminars on road safety by the local bobby. But Val was all for a structured evening, with each member taking part in some organized activity and an improving official lecture or discussion to round the whole thing off. Sometimes he hijacked the gramophone and called for silence while he played the popular works of Tchaikovsky and Beethoven. He introduced his ideas with a reasonably light touch, but with determination. Rebecca was secretly impressed by his successful combination of banter and firmness, like that of a seasoned schoolmaster. The teenagers submitted to Val's pressure with a fairly good grace, but behind his back they splintered easily into their own gossiping groups.

Rebecca's loyalties were divided. She liked Val and had a certain sympathy with his drive to – as he saw it – improve and educate, though she felt strongly that his methods lacked subtlety. More and more often she found herself siding instinctively with the children.

However, there was give and take on both sides and gradually a truce emerged. Influenced by hints, arguments and outright harangues from Rebecca and Tony, Val began to be less rigid and concede that the Club was basically there for the children's enjoyment. At the same time he managed to salve his conscience by slotting some unmistakably worthy item into the programme of each meeting.

Rebecca's approach was stealthier. She relaxed with the children and chatted to them about everything under the sun. Then she would mention some current event and ask what they thought about it. The response was easy and natural. There was no need to push. The children enjoyed giving their views on national or political questions. They were honest and more perceptive than she, in her student arrogance, might have expected. Sometimes their arguments became heated. Val overheard them one evening discussing the rearmament of Germany. He stopped to listen and was impressed.

'Quite a little debate,' he remarked approvingly to the embattled children. 'Food for thought there.' Noticing him for the first time, they looked up, surprised by his warmth. As far as they were concerned they'd only been talking. Rebecca was convinced that if the discussion had been advertised in advance, and labelled with the grand title of Debate, the response would have been far less forthcoming.

Her interest in things political became well known, and individual children would seek her out to talk about public events that had caught their attention and ask her what she thought.

With some of the girls particularly, the conversation spilled over into personal matters and they confided in her about parents, school and boyfriends. Rebecca was quietly proud at this evidence of their trust. In time she even prevailed on the children to call her Becky instead of Miss.

She'd never really quite understood how or why it was that Tony got involved in the Club. The personality he presented was stolidly anti-authority, anti-organization, and his attitude to Val seemed one of sly amusement. Yet he was always there doing the heavy lifting, a whiz with electrical repairs, and dealing out his own rough justice to the kids when necessary. Although he was only two or three years their senior, the boys respected the strong but silent image he projected and his dry, taciturn humour; the girls were taken with his self-contained good looks.

With Rebecca he was guarded. He twitted her often about being an intellectual and a do-gooder and teased her about her arty friends. At the same time they gravitated naturally towards one another to form a kind of popular front against Val's officiousness.

As the months passed, Rebecca began to feel that, in spite of the differences between Val and herself, the Club worked. Out of the initial flatness, uncertainty and groping, an atmosphere had evolved that was unique and welcoming. New members joined and they came regularly.

'Bugger it – I can't come next week,' Heather said daringly to her one evening, and Rebecca saw in the throwaway remark a small measure of their success.

One evening Tony paid her a casual, unexpected compliment that pleased her absurdly. During the meeting two boys had been troublesome, and afterwards, as she and Tony cleared up, Val dealt with them in his brisk, firm, fair fashion.

'I must admit he's a good teller-off,' Rebecca remarked

to Tony as together they tackled the three-dimensional puzzle of fitting the Club's equipment into the inadequate cupboard provided. 'He's human, but rather formidable. And he looks so angelic with his curls.'

'Val's all right,' the boy said grudgingly, as he rolled the flex of the gramophone and jammed it into a tiny gap between the two ping-pong bats. 'But he's not on our wavelength.' Experimentally he tried to close the cupboard doors. There was resistance. He bent to adjust the contents, then tried again. 'We wouldn't get so many kids coming if it wasn't for you.'

At about eleven o'clock Ruth heard the fire-escape door in the kitchen open and shut. She laid aside her article on the Berliner Ensemble. Nowadays she was able to read all the bumph on theatre that she never had time for when she was actually involved in it. She knew chapter and verse. All the theory.

'Who's that?' she called. Was it Paul at last?

'It's me!' Rebecca's voice sounded enviably bright and exhilarated. She always was when she got home from the Club. It would be the last session before Christmas, Ruth guessed.

'The kids gave me a present,' Rebecca said happily as she entered the living room. Her eyes were bright, cheeks pink from the cold outside air, her hair dark against a red sweater that set off her colouring. 'Look!' She held up a rag doll with button eyes and black wool hair cut in a fringe. 'Look, it's me!' The doll wore trousers and a miniature facsimile of a dufflecoat. A small cardboard ping-pong bat was attached to one stumpy hand. 'Isn't it brilliant? One of the girls made it.'

Ruth was dazzled by Becky's breathless, windswept radiance. She felt stuffy and stay-at-home, with her book by the gas fire. 'It's lovely.' Her voice sounded forced and hollow to her. She didn't feel up to sharing in her friend's raptures.

But Rebecca seemed not to notice. She prattled on. '. . . And Tony gave me some chocs . . . I was rather touched. And bath salts from Val. Not very imaginative, but it's the thought that counts.' She dumped the gifts carelessly on a chair. 'It was a lovely evening. We had carols and one of the girls played a guitar. It was really quite moving.' A wry grin. 'I haven't felt that way about Christmas since I was in primary school.' A thought struck her. 'Where's Paul?'

'Not home yet,' Ruth said dully. 'He's been gone since two-ish. To meet a bloke called Dunbar, an agent. In one of those clubs – the Caves de France or somewhere.'

'You look worried.'

'I am a bit. He's had an awful lot of drinking time . . . God, I feel like a nagging wife nowadays. He can't go on . . . But you know him, bloody perverse. The more I get on to him about it . . . He won't let anyone else have a say in what he does.'

'It's just another night. Probably no worse than any other.' Rebecca's reassurance lacked conviction.

Ruth shrugged. 'Probably not. But the nights add up. And the days.'

Rebecca sat down by the fire opposite her. 'He's a happy drinker,' she said, attempting comfort. 'Not some Victorian heavy.'

'A barrel of laughs,' Ruth agreed drily.

They heard the click of the door. 'That's got to be him,' Ruth said. Richard was staying the night with his family. They heard footsteps and a loud slamming, then a tap running.

A minute or so later Paul stood framed in the doorway. The two women turned to look at him. He was flushed and rather tousled. His eyes had a bright, swimming look. His lower lip drooped a little. Almost subconsciously

Ruth registered all the symptoms, but at first glance he seemed no further gone than usual.

'Hiya, Marlene.' His amused smile had a sardonic and somehow restless quality. 'Waiting up for your reprobate hubby?'

Ruth shook her head coldly. 'I just haven't gone to bed yet.'

Paul eyed them quizzically. 'You two look like a reception committee. A disapproving one.'

Ruth ignored the remark. Paul crossed the room towards them. There was something marionette-like in his walk, reflecting a jaunty, disconnected state of mind. He came to the chair that held Rebecca's presents, noticing and moving them just in time before he sat down.

He held the doll out at arm's length. 'What's this?' Then he saw what it was supposed to represent and gave a sharp, staccato laugh. 'It's a flattering likeness, Beck.' He studied the toy with his strange, restless, drunken amusement. 'Give us a kiss, you tantalizing bitch!' he said, clasping the doll fiercely to his chest.

'Paul!' Rebecca reached out to rescue her gift. 'Watch it! You'll crush the bat.' She was indignant. He handed the doll to her casually, as if he'd already forgotten it.

'Any luck with Dunbar?' Ruth asked.

'He's a prat,' Paul said. 'All wind and piss.'

'So no luck.'

'He can't do anything for me. His connections are just . . . wrong. In the wrong area.'

'It took you a long time to find that out.' Ruth spoke with bland sarcasm.

'A long time and a lot of booze, you mean.' A demure and neutral challenge.

'That's right.'

Paul shrugged. 'Dunbar was paying. Set your mind at rest.' He gave a provoking grin. 'We went to some Caribbean place. John Minton was there. One of your

206

mum's pals.' He mentioned a painter-about-Soho, well-known in drinking clubs and jazz cellars. He had the irritating habit of promoting Sarah's most distant acquaintances to bosom friends. 'Pissed as a newt, he was.'

'You were in good company then.'

He nodded with a crooked smile. 'I had an agreeable day, thank you, my love.'

Rebecca stood up. 'I've got some reading to do. I'll leave you to it.' Gathering up her little pile of presents.

'Leave us to what?' Paul asked with a feline innocence.

She gestured vaguely. 'To whatever.'

'You're looking damnably lovely tonight, Becky.'

She paused briefly with her hand on the door knob. 'So I've been told.'

The silence she left behind was tense, somehow expectant. Ruth couldn't imagine that they would simply get up and go to bed. Paul's restlessness was catching. She wanted to provoke him, provoke something.

'Why do you do it, Paul?' she said. 'Why do you drink so much? Drink all the time. What's lacking?' She spoke with a quiet, false calm, as if opening a rational discussion. But she knew it was just a ploy. It was confrontation she was after.

He gave a short, derisive laugh. 'Christ, Ruth, you sound like someone's probation officer.' An amicable, informative tone, which was just as false as hers.

'I'm interested, though.'

He sat forward on his chair and looked at her for a minute. His eyes seemed dark, all pupil, with a liquid, unfocused quality. In spite of his stillness he seemed not quite in control. He wore his odd, almost bitter smile. She was struck, as ever, by the unconscious air of certainty he exuded. He seemed rooted in it, and it made him difficult to argue with. She had to remind herself not to take him at his own face value. His conviction didn't

207

necessarily make him right. He said suddenly, 'Suppose I ask you why you *don't* drink?'

'I find life satisfactory without it.' Even before she'd finished the sentence Ruth thought the reply weak, beside the point – and untruthful. Both of them knew that.

'No, you don't.' His comment had the conclusive ring of honesty. 'You don't at all.' A shadow of triumph in his grin. He was on safe ground. 'You've got a kid and you love him. But you're beached, immobilized here, with an unsatisfactory husband . . .' he gave her a mocking look, 'and a lover you don't give two hoots for. You had something that lit up your existence. Your acting. And you haven't got it any more.' He seemed to take satisfaction in this bald devaluation of her life.

'What's that got to do with *your* drinking?' she asked heatedly, wondering how it had come about that she was on the defensive.

He swept on with a drunken, self-absorbed fluency. 'Now if you drank – this is hypothetical, you understand – all this mediocrity would be lit up. You'd see the pleasure in each separate moment. You'd be witty and the people around you would seem witty. You'd respond to them spontaneously with all of yourself. You'd see things bright and beautiful and full of possibilities.' He paused, quietly theatrical. 'And in answer to your question, that's why I drink.'

Now he seemed to her to be posturing, seeing himself yet again as the hero of a novel. There had been times when she'd liked that about him. Now it seemed absurd. She had the cold urge to cut him down to size. 'Grow up, Paul,' she said. 'It's a weakness, your drinking. Don't try and make it into some kind of philosophy.'

He seemed unmoved and leaned back in his chair, linking his hands behind his head, watching her with calm hostility. 'Do you know what you're turning into, Ruth?'

She was ironic. 'Tell me.'

'You're like the schoolmarm in a Western. With a monopoly on all the decent values. Trying to foist them on the cowhands who are doing all right without them . . . You have an affair and you don't get any pleasure from it . . .' He grinned at her, foxily complacent. 'I enjoy *my* life. Don't try and make me feel guilty about it.'

'Impossible,' she said, with smiling venom. 'You're too entrenched in your own smug dreamworld. You can't see how shabby it is.'

He spoke suddenly, loudly. 'You're going back on it!' There was a threat in his tone, a slow, drunken emphasis. 'Our agreement . . . Don't you remember? We were going to be different. You agreed to it . . .' He framed the words with difficulty, and with a heavy, dangerous sarcasm.

She was pleased and went forward recklessly to meet the danger. 'I didn't agree to your sleeping with all and sundry and drinking yourself silly . . . You're ridiculous, a joke, with your bloody Dylan Thomas act.'

He leaned forward and deliberately slapped her twice across the face, with the flat and then the back of his hand. The blows landed hard and crisp. Ruth felt a rush of secret exultation. This was one argument she'd won.

Ruth couldn't get to sleep. She lay alone in Richard's empty bed. The sheets were rucked and ridged, but she couldn't make the effort to do anything about them. She was cold. Richard used fewer blankets than she was accustomed to. Still a kind of inertia prevented her from getting up, finding a sweater, or boiling up the kettle for a hot water bottle. She could smell Richard faintly on the sheets and the pillow case. His large body would have been welcome beside her. Warming, inducing drowsiness and sleep. Maybe that was what he was for her. Comfort. A kind of live teddy bear. Someone to make love to when she needed to blot out reality. In the dark, enveloped by his heavy body, she could feel weightless, anonymous, sensation and nothing else.

From somewhere below, Ernest Broadbent's grandfather clock struck three. This was the worst time for introspection, disaffection. As she lay there Ruth heartily despised her triumph at provoking Paul to strike her and so place himself demonstrably, unarguably in the wrong. He'd been remorseful, shed tears she saw as maudlin, told her he loved her. It had been easy somehow, the whole scene meaningless. At that moment his emotions were genuine, but ultimately the situation was a game. Nothing would change. Paul would continue to live his life to his own satisfaction, and she to remain confused that the pact they'd made that autumn evening on the beach had turned out so much to his taste and somehow so little to hers.

While Paul relished his various affairs wholeheartedly, she and Richard had remained, after the first euphoric days, locked in an uneasy, unsatisfying relationship. Once they'd had simple friendship, and she looked back on that time with nostalgia. They'd been tender and supportive of each other. And carefree. Richard lusted after her, but they'd allowed for that, known what was what.

Now he was abashed at the reality of being free to sleep with his friend's wife, at having the friend's blessing. Ruth remembered teasing him, 'You make love to me as if you'd sold your soul to the devil.'

He smiled, vaguely regretful. 'Paul's been my mate from way back . . .' He pulled her close and kissed her with a dazed, subdued air.

Her own scruples were different. She harboured the uncomfortable suspicion that in her affair with Richard she was merely dancing to Paul's tune.

'Mummy.' Ben stirred in his curtained alcove on the

landing. She lay quiet, listening. Sometimes he called out in his sleep, then settled again. She heard no more.

There was a bright spot outside these claustrophobic complications. Her growing friendship with Owain Roberts was pure pleasure, investing her Thursdays in the shop with anticipation, making them a private red-letter day. He came almost every week, commandeering the shop's chair for a couple of hours or so, with his long legs stretched out in front of him, drinking coffee with her, chatting to Ben who loved him, talking with Ruth in a relaxed, inconsequential fashion. In the leisurely world of antiquarian bookselling such behaviour was possible. Often a browsing customer would join in their conversation for a time, then return to studying the shelves.

He made a considerable detour to see her, en route from his present rooms in Bloomsbury to Fleet Street. Lying in the cold, black room, eyes closed, Ruth could picture his slim, sombrely clad figure viewed through the glass panel of the shop door, the short Roman haircut and clipped beard. She loved to see him enter the shop, reliable somehow, though their meetings were a casual arrangement, and wearing a smile that she prized, since it wasn't offered to everyone.

'Hallo, Ruth.' His greeting was always restrained, yet given weight by the steadiness of his greenish-brown eyes, conveying warmth, a genuine pleasure at seeing her again. Without the slightest flattery he made her feel that the relationship between them was special. It was straightforward too. Neither made demands on the other. She relished the simplicity. Often her life seemed far too complicated.

In the early days he used to say, 'You're sure it's okay my coming so often? I'm not going to get you the sack?' But Ruth knew that he was sounding out *her* reaction, not Ernest's. Soon, though, they took it for granted that both of them relished these oddly peripheral meetings. Ruth found it strange and wonderful that this kindness and friendship should have grown out of the misunderstandings and tensions, the over-hasty attraction of their early encounters.

She liked to see Owain with Ben, leaning forward on his chair and listening with grave attention while Ben, his grey eyes open wide with the effort of marshalling his limited store of words, talked earnestly about his small life, his toys, his parents, Becky, a visit to the zoo. Strangely, the thought that Owain could be the child's father hardly ever occurred to her. But once, as Ben toddled from Owain to herself and back again, holding out his furry blue teddy bear, Owain had caught her eye above his head and grinned with adult complicity. Then she'd had the sudden quick illusion that the two of them were parents, smiling together over their child's boisterous energy.

To Ben's delight, Owain had named him Stanley Kowalski, because he was stocky and punch-drunk, like the character played by Marlon Brando in a film he'd seen. When Owain arrived, the child would greet him by shouting 'I'm Ben!', provoking him to use the hilarious, unpronounceable nickname, and hiccuping with laughter when he succeeded. Ruth smiled to herself at the memory of it.

She and Owain talked about friends, books, radio programmes, the news, anything. Usually Ruth sat perched on a high stool behind the counter, resting her elbows on her knees, hair tucked out of the way behind her ears and straggling down her back. Owain propped his feet on the low steps Ernest used to reach some of the upper shelves. With the fan heater going, their mugs of Nescafé, the aroma of Owain's French cigarettes in the air, the winter mornings were cosy and timeless. Ruth could picture him in her mind, a look of private amusement flickering in his eyes as he spoke.

But they talked seriously too. He often mentioned a Hungarian journalist called Janos he'd met more than a year ago in Helsinki and drunk with one evening in a bar. They'd kept in touch, smuggling letters to one another via a journalist they both knew who was based in Vienna. Since the death of Stalin, Janos's letters had filled gradually with a controlled optimism. Things were freer nowadays in Hungary, he wrote, life was looking up, reforms were being made, and the Kremlin, it seemed, was letting it happen.

'We had a bet that night,' Owain smiled. 'He predicted things would change if Stalin popped his clogs. I wasn't so sure. Now he reckons he's won and he keeps inviting me to Budapest to pay my debt.'

'Will you go?' Ruth asked.

'Maybe one day. I still think it's too early to tell.'

She lent Owain a book on Bertolt Brecht. To Ruth's surprise he was fascinated by it and questioned her in detail about her own attitude to the theatre and acting. She began by answering vaguely, but he seemed to be genuinely interested, in a way neither Paul nor Becky had ever been. She began to discuss her ideas with him in detail – almost as she had with her fellow students at RADA, but rarely since – discovering opinions that she hadn't consciously expressed before, arising probably from all the books she was now at leisure to devour.

Ruth never talked to him about Paul, except in the most casual terms, and she knew nothing about Owain's current love life. It was as if they had a kind of tacit agreement. This pleased her, emphasizing, in a sense, that their friendship was a luxury, something set apart from the mainstream of their lives.

She heard Ben murmur again. Behind the thin curtains the oblong of Richard's window now showed a shade lighter than the surrounding gloom. She lay quiet, but

Ben remained restless. Ruth crept on to the landing and pulled aside a corner of the curtain that screened his bed.

'Is it morning?' he asked drowsily. If she took him into bed he might doze again.

'Not quite,' she said. 'Put your arms up. I'll carry you.' She picked him up. It was cold on the landing, but he was warm and heavy with sleep. She laid her cheek against his.

'Where's Richard?' he showed no disquiet at being taken into the strange bedroom.

'He's not here.' She climbed into bed. His small body, alongside hers, was beautifully warm. 'Go to sleep, Ben.'

He lay for a while with his eyes wide open, gazing blankly at the shadows and dim shapes of the room. She could remember Owain saying once, with wondering affection, 'Ben never looks surprised. His eyes just accept everything they see.'

It was Thursday, she recalled. Her regular day in the shop. She would see Owain. The thought gave her a solid and sleepy pleasure.

22

The sky was an outlandish mauve-red. Below, the Battersea fairground had a kind of intimacy – only the people closest to you were clearly visible, lit up with a flattering amber glow. Those further off were dark and shadowy. It was a soft night, the air like warm, blue velvet. Loud, sentimental music wheezed from the carousel and the big wheel. A cheerful, nostalgic smell of sausages and fried onions drifted in the air. Rebecca queued for the Big Dipper with Heather and red-haired Pete and a big lad called Charlie from the Club. She felt happy. It was their night out. They'd saved for it, held a jumble sale, done odd jobs.

'I'm scared, Becky!'

Heather hid her eyes against Rebecca's arm. She liked to put on a show of fluttery panic, though it was sheer perversity. She was a sturdy, self-willed character.

Rebecca gave her an ironic, affectionate smile. 'Wait for us by the exit then, Heather.' She had small patience with the little screams, vapours and protestations of fear that most of the girls at the Club saw as appropriate female behaviour. She knew perfectly well that wild horses couldn't have dragged Heather from her imminent ride on the Big Dipper.

'No, I've got to go through with it. I'd never forgive myself.' Their conversation was conducted against the rise and fall of the pleasurable screams that washed down from the roller coaster. Heather had got dolled up, as she'd told Rebecca, for the outing in a wide red skirt held out by stiff petticoats and a tight white top. She looked expectant, flushed and pretty, short curls framing her round, childish face. She held hands with Charlie, but turned towards Pete often with smiles and giggles.

'I'll look after you.' Daringly Charlie placed one arm round her shoulder. He was a tall, raw-boned boy, with greased blond hair, a beaky nose, and a vaguely bemused smile. It was rare for him to be so demonstrative in front of his fellows or Rebecca. The outing freed him, making him a little reckless.

'Get off. I'll manage.' Heather shook free from his arm, but she seemed pleased by his boldness.

'She'll manage,' Pete repeated provokingly. Apple-cheeked and ginger-haired, he looked twelve rather than fifteen, Rebecca thought.

'And *you* can mind your own business.' Heather spiked him with a pale, dimpled elbow.

'Stop squabbling, for goodness' sake.' Rebecca watched the strangely quarrelsome teenage flirtation with an inward smile, feeling as if there were decades rather than a few years between herself and these three children. 'Move up, look. There's a space in front of you.'

In time they reached the front of the queue. Seen from close to, the roller coaster looked sordid and shabby. A bare concrete passage led to the vehicles. They settled themselves in the rear car. Rebecca found herself next to Pete behind the other two. Charlie leaned back in a lordly fashion. His arm crept along the back of the seat behind Heather.

But his negligent airs didn't last once they got going. The cars trundled up a narrow track that seemed disturbingly rickety and gathered speed almost at once. Charlie withdrew his arm and gripped the rail in front of him. Rebecca did the same. She was momentarily aware of Pete grinning at her with a mixture of bravado and apprehension, then she concentrated on the ride.

The car rattled up a steep incline. Breasting the peak she had the quick impression that the carriage had taken flight into thin air, then it swooped into a drop that must surely be almost sheer, before careening into a hairpin bend. Rebecca screamed and heard screaming all around her and wondered if she was enjoying herself. There were more drops, more gyrations, and all the time they were jolted half to death. It wasn't until they slowed for the final stage that she became aware of the others again. Pete was making relieved, gulping faces and Charlie was regaining his poise, sliding his arm along the back of the seat once more.

Pete poked him in the back. 'Saw you looking after Heather.'

Heather turned round. 'He was screaming so hard,' she said scornfully, 'I reckon he's pooed his pants.'

'No, I haven't.' On the spur of the moment Charlie could think of nothing more crushing to say.

'Let's go shooting,' he said, when they stood, rather shakily, on solid ground again. Rebecca remembered him telling her once that his father had an air rifle and that he fancied himself as a shot.

'Why not?' she agreed. No doubt it was a means by which he hoped to raise himself again in Heather's estimation.

'There's Tony,' she said, noticing out of the corner of her eye a group of three older boys. Tony had come with a couple of mates of his own age.

'Hey, Tone!' Pete called.

He turned and saw them and waved, then came towards them with his friends. Wryly Rebecca reflected that they could have stepped out of a photograph above one of the alarmist articles that appeared almost daily in the press nowadays bemoaning the rise of the Edwardians, as the papers tended to dub them prissily, though the rest of the country called them Teddy Boys.

All three had hair greased artfully into a high quiff in front, sideburns, and a collar-length duck's arse behind.

They wore long jackets, narrow trousers and crepe-soled shoes known as brothel-creepers, and they walked with a quiet, deliberate swagger like bad boys in a film.

'Hallo, Danny,' Charlie said to the smallest of them, a freckled lad with sandy hair, cold, lashless eyes, and a smart-aleck expression. Charlie's tone held a barely perceptible trace of nervous respect, although he was head and shoulders taller than the older boy.

Tony introduced Rebecca. 'Danny, Phil. This is Becky. Our scout mistress.' He gave a tongue-in-cheek grin for her benefit.

'Hallo,' she said with vague, generalized good nature.

They nodded, eyeing her with smiles that held just a hint of defensive insolence.

Phil addressed Pete. He was black-haired, handsome and foreign-looking. 'We just seen Val. On the coconut shy. He was going berserk. Talk about the Dam Busters.'

'We're going shooting,' Charlie said.

'You coming?' Rebecca asked Tony.

'Okay.' He nodded with a quick grin, a compromise between his liking for her and the nonchalance dictated by the presence of his friends.

On the shooting gallery inscrutably smiling ducks passed by on an endless conveyor belt. The poker-faced proprietor distributed the guns with bored impatience, as if his customers were a slow, bumbling lot. He wore a striped shirt and braces, and his sour-looking mouth gripped the damp, compressed stub of a cigarette.

Rebecca stood back to let the kids go first. Pete aimed his rifle in a hurried, perfunctory fashion, and managed to shoot down three of the ducks. Not enough for a prize.

'Could've been worse.' Heather ruffled his red curls consolingly.

Charlie held the gun and examined it with an air of sage masculinity, weighing it in his hands.

'Get on with it, lad,' the proprietor urged.

The boy raised the rifle and aimed with slow, consummate care. He fired, missed, and blushed faintly.

Heather nudged Pete and said *sotto voce*, 'He'll shoot *himself* if he don't do better than you.'

'Elbow higher,' Tony advised. Charlie gave him a sidelong look of quiet venom. Tony grinned. 'Only trying to help.'

Charlie's next two shots went wide as well. Pete and Heather raised ragged, sarcastic cheers.

Charlie glared. 'Pack it in, can't you? You're putting me off.'

They clamped their hands to their mouths in mock guilt. Charlie managed to hit the next duck, but his last two shots were duds.

'They twist the sights,' he proclaimed sulkily, as he turned away, 'to stop people winning.'

'I 'eard that!' the proprietor called. Charlie stepped quickly out of range, not looking back.

Heather had a try, all giggles and cheeky sideways glances, and managed to bag one duck. Tony went next.

Rebecca's attention wandered. She scanned the display of prizes ranged to the far left of the stall. Giant pastel plush teddy bears dominated, behind curlicued glass vases in cyclamen pink and peacock blue. For five ducks down you won a modest glass ash tray with a groove at each corner to rest your cigarette. These goodies were separated from the public by a foot or so of space behind the barrier, which ran the whole length of the front of the stall. You could probably reach them, Rebecca speculated vaguely, if you leaned forward across the barrier in an absurdly obvious manner.

She heard Pete say, 'Good shot, Tone!' He was holding hands with Heather now, she noticed, while Charlie stared moodily ahead of him.

Tony's two Teddy Boy pals lurked – somehow the word sprang to mind – with their elbows resting on the barrier.

Surprisingly, they seemed unconcerned about Tony's performance. She would have expected them to be egging him on. Covertly Rebecca watched the one called Danny. At first sight she didn't take to him. There was something self-satisfied about him, yet ferrety. It wasn't his looks that brought the description to mind. He had a round, freckled face. Rather there was something sinuous in his manner, sly almost.

'Two more and you've got an ash tray!' she heard Heather squeak. Sour and watchful, the stallholder looked on.

Rebecca saw Danny make some brief remark to Phil, a quick, knowing smile lighting up his face. Then, nonchalantly, he leaned all the way forward and in one furtive, elegant movement he swiped the nearest ash tray and slipped it into his pocket. It was done so quickly that the next moment Rebecca could almost have imagined that she'd dreamed it.

'You've won, you flash bugger,' Pete was saying. The proprietor crossed to the display stand and picked up one of the cheap ash trays. He handed it to Tony in a swift, stiff, poker-faced gesture, as if it were ransom money.

Rebecca stood by in a kind of trance. She had the vague feeling that she should raise some kind of a hue and cry, but for a glass ash tray it seemed an overreaction.

'Hey, Beck,' Tony was calling. 'Let's see you make a fool of yourself.' He held out a rifle to her.

'Should be good for a laugh.' Pete pulled Heather closer to him, circling her elbow with his hand. He looked rosy and pleased with himself, and younger than ever.

Best keep what she'd seen to herself, Rebecca decided. She could talk to Tony about it some other time.

She liked shooting and wasn't a bad shot. 'I'll show you,' she said.

* * *

Rebecca wasn't sure she'd describe Tony as a friend, but over the months a certain closeness had developed between them. There were times when the two of them allied naturally against Val, though both were fond of him. At thirty or so, the priest seemed to belong to an older and more rigid generation.

In some ways – with his unthreatening good looks, tweed jacket and plimsolls, his nice wife and two friendly young children – Val was the very image of an enterprising young vicar, pioneering without condescension among the working classes. But in certain situations Rebecca became aware that, beneath the informality, there lurked the remains of a Victorian inflexibility, almost a streak of ruthlessness. Right was right. He'd expelled a lad called Martin from the club for scribbling some naïve obscenity in the men's toilets. Rebecca and Tony had intervened. The boy had been ashamed and hangdog. The words were cleaned off with one whisk of a dampened cloth. But Val had been immovable.

After the session Rebecca and Tony had seethed companionably. 'My gran used to have a picture on her wall,' Tony said, 'of this old-fashioned dad turning his daughter and her bastard kid out into the snow. Sometimes I reckon Val could do that.'

But their alliance was edgy. Tony could be prickly, and suspicious of Rebecca's motives in working at the club. He was constantly on the lookout for any hint of a patronizing attitude on her part. Sometimes he'd repeat her words in the diamond-cutting accent of a J. Arthur Rank starlet – she could never fathom out quite why, since the supposed imitation bore no relation whatever to her own idiosyncratic mix of Lancashire and Welsh.

He'd tease her for using long words, or he'd make remarks that pointed up the difference in their education. ''Course, we're all thick round here,' he'd say, with a smiling, searching look at Rebecca to see how she was taking it. Comments like these irritated her as insincere and unworthy of him.

At other times they relaxed and talked candidly, laying aside their antagonisms. The two of them liked a lot of the same films and radio programmes. Tony had no great opinion of politicians, but he was fascinated by personalities, and had a nose for hypocrisy and sham. He could mimic Churchill, Attlee and Eisenhower to perfection, down to their turns of phrase and quirks of pronunciation.

Tony worked as a building labourer, and for a time he was employed on a site fairly close to where Rebecca lived. They used to meet quite often for a cup of tea when he'd finished work, or else he'd drop into the Marshall Street flat for an hour or so.

He was intrigued, but rather shocked by the homely squalor of their household. 'It's like living in a gerbil's cage,' he said. 'With cosy bits of torn-up paper all over the floor.'

'Just a few toys,' Rebecca protested. 'Some books, a newspaper or two.' She'd visited him at home a couple of times. He lived with his family on the upper floor of a terraced house in a street off the Walworth Road. Privately she thought their flat too neat, lacking in warmth.

Tony remained wary of Paul, uneasy with his odd sense of humour, the shameless way he lounged about the house when other people were at work, his habit of drinking outside pub hours. But he approved of Ruth. She was a good mother, he commented approvingly to Rebecca, though it was obvious that he wasn't oblivious to her slim good looks and blonde hair.

Coming back to the flat one day, they'd surprised her dancing with Ben to some foolish Carmen Miranda record borrowed from Paul's parents. Dressed in jeans and a garish Hawaiian shirt Paul had bought for her in Old Compton Street, Ruth was swaying her hips with satirical relish, while Ben gurgled with delight and tried to copy her. The sudden appearance of Tony and Becky spurred her on to greater efforts. With sultry arm movements and a vampish rolling of the eyes, she played to her audience of three. Her clowning reminded Becky fleetingly of the spoof dance numbers she used to perform at the Illyria Theatre. She noticed that Tony was grinning broadly and had turned quite pink.

A few days after the outing to Battersea Funfair Rebecca found herself alone with Tony after a club meeting. Val had had to rush off to visit a parishioner who was worried about her elderly mother. Rebecca was in a hurry to get home as well and Tony came with her to the bus stop. He walked with his hands in his pockets, head down against the soft summer drizzle that had begun to bead their clothes and their hair. He seemed quiet.

Rebecca decided to mention what she'd seen at the fair. 'The other night, your friend Danny. He took something off the shooting gallery – pinched it. Did you know?'

He didn't answer right away, but gave her a sidelong glance stating clearly that it was none of her business. Then he shrugged, an impatient, dismissive movement of the body. It came to her that she'd made the same gesture to her parents time without number, and the realization brought home to her that, in asking the question, she was assuming the adult, authoritarian role to Tony's youthful rebel.

He said coldly, 'He showed it to me after. An ash tray. Big deal.'

'So why pinch it?'

'Don't ask me. It was Danny, remember?'

They walked on for a minute in silence. Then Rebecca asked, 'Does he do that sort of thing often?'

Tony stopped short and turned to face her in the damp twilight, head to one side, calm and sure of his ground. Not displeased with his tearaway image, the stylish hair-cut, the muted challenge in his brown eyes, he said amicably, 'Mind your own business, Becky.'

She made a deprecating gesture. 'Okay, I will. But don't forget – that kind of thing can lead to . . .' She left the sentence unfinished. 'I think you'd be crazy to get involved.'

23

'We're becoming sleek and prosperous,' Paul had said one evening in March, looking up from his umpteenth re-reading of *The Catcher in the Rye*, his current favourite novel. He could quote chunks of it by heart.

'Bourgeois lackeys,' Ruth agreed. It was a phrase of Becky's that had caught her imagination.

But it was true. Their life had seemed more settled for two or three months, ever since the night just before Christmas when they'd quarrelled over Paul's drinking. Paul had been shocked and mortified at having raised his hand to Ruth, and since then he'd made a determined effort to cut down on alcohol. So far he'd been successful and Ruth was cheered by the sincerity of his attempts.

At the same time the Wailers were gathering a sizeable following, both locally and in their increasingly regular sorties to jazz clubs in the provinces. In fact the *Melody Maker* had devoted a whole page to them recently, with a large photograph. The reporter had described Paul as the brains of the outfit, 'a quizzical existentialist, with a whisky voice and a Yancey touch on the keys'.

'He didn't realize it, but *I* fed him that line,' Paul said when he read it, adding regretfully, 'The whisky's all in the past, though.'

During the daytime he was getting a fair amount of plumbing work, boosted by the seasonal bonus of burst pipes. Ruth had had a modest increase in salary too. Ernest Broadbent was expanding into mail order, and she handled that department, wrapping and invoicing a score or so of books each morning on the kitchen table while Ben played on the floor with crayons and the off-cuts of brown paper. She still worked every Thursday and other odd times in the shop.

Her affair with Richard had ended. They'd talked about it for the whole of one cold and windy January night while Paul was away visiting his parents, and they'd agreed to call it a day. There was a shade of sentimental regret in the decision, but Ruth's overwhelming reaction was one of relief. It was good and peaceful to have a friend around the house again, though the communication between them was no longer spiced, as in the past, with the hint of unfulfilled possibilities.

As Paul read by the gas fire Ruth sat across from him knitting a striped sweater for Ben. How domesticated we look, she thought, faintly incredulous.

Her meetings with Owain continued, slotting agreeably into the present calm of her life. She could see that he was fond of her, as she was of him, but he always respected her married status. Wryly she'd told Becky a few days ago, 'With Owain I feel like someone out of *Brief Encounter*. Frightfully decent and restrained. . .' She could mock herself gently – and him – but she would have found it hard to admit how intensely important his friendship was to her.

'You know what, Ruthie?' Paul looked up from his book again. 'I'm thinking of buying myself a pair of check carpet slippers. I feel they'd be right for me at this point in my life.'

However, the tranquillity was not to last. Spring brought a restlessness. In May Paul and the Wailers spent a weekend in Coventry at a jazz festival. When Paul came home he was high-spirited and perverse, with an unspoken, half-guilty defiance in his manner. Neither of them said anything. The current of understanding between them was instinctive. She guessed that he'd been drinking, that he'd probably spent the night with someone. Richard seemed quiet, as if in confirmation of her suspicions.

The weekend was a catalyst. Paul's attitude changed. As the days brightened and the evenings lengthened he began to drink at home again. The first few times he wore a bland and challenging grin, like a schoolboy flouting his teacher, knowing that, in the end, not much could be done about it.

'So you're not a reformed character after all,' Ruth said, as he sat bare-chested by the open window one afternoon in early June, with Ben dozing on his lap and a bottle of lukewarm wine at his elbow. She spoke in a neutral voice, unwilling to give him the satisfaction of her anger. She'd nagged and raged enough in the past. Now she was almost indifferent.

'No, I suppose not.' He looked at her from behind dark, inscrutable sunglasses. Ben woke for a second, then his head fell forward again in sleep. 'It wasn't really us, though, was it, Marlene?'

'I don't know.' She shrugged. 'It might have been. If you'd *really* wanted it.' But as she spoke there was the thought that she'd never quite believed in their precarious domesticity. She turned away with a hardening of the heart.

'How are things?' Owain asked breezily a day or so later in the shop.

Then, for the first time, she talked to him about her fears for Paul, about his drinking and their marriage. She spoke hesitantly, disjointedly, mentioning things as they occurred to her, in no kind of order. Owain said little, but listened closely, asking the odd question. Ben played on the floor, immersed in his cars, paying them no attention.

'. . . It's the future that worries me more than the present. Paul's health if he goes on like this . . . What

227

he'll become . . .' It was a relief to talk to someone outside their tight household.

Owain offered no advice, but said that if ever she wanted to leave, he could find her work and somewhere to stay . . .

'No.' She was adamant. 'I'm not thinking of that. Paul stood by me when . . .' She broke off. It was a subject she didn't care to pursue with Owain.

He was tight on time that morning and a few minutes later he stood up, ready to go. 'Take care,' he said. There was concern in his eyes. Then, quickly, as though he'd taken a decision, he leaned forward and kissed her softly on the cheek.

24

The day they both finished their finals Carl bought a bottle of champagne. He was sheepish about it, as though in doing so he'd somehow betrayed his side in the class war. They'd expected to feel elated, but both were numbed, a little dazed. He and Rebecca chose not to join in the noisy general celebration, but walked back to Marshall Street hand in hand, through the humid, late-afternoon streets. Ruth was home when they arrived, writing out invoices for Ernest Broadbent. Paul was out, unblocking someone's drains. Tony looked in for a few minutes after work.

Carl opened the champagne in a clumsy, unpractised fashion, spilling some of it on the kitchen floor. 'It's a bit lively,' he said apologetically, as he redirected its flow into some waiting glasses.

The champagne was sparkly but warm. There was no fridge in the flat. The four of them sat round on the living-room floor, sipping it gamely. Rebecca still lacked a sense of occasion, though she drank dutifully to Carl's toast.

'You'll be a worker now, Beck, like the rest of us,' Tony said, with a soft edge of malice. Students had it easy, he'd told her that often in the past.

'She can't wait,' Carl said defensively. Rebecca could see he felt a little embarrassed in his white shirt and tie. Tony was dusty and hot from work.

'Yes I can,' Rebecca laughed. 'I'm not in any hurry.'

'What's it to be then, Becky? Teacher? Probation officer?' Tony poked gentle fun at her social conscience.

'Let's wait and see what results I get.'

'Bound to be brilliant,' Ruth said confidently. She was

the only one of them, Rebecca thought, who seemed at home with the champagne, holding it up to the light so that the glass sparkled, and drinking it as though she enjoyed it. Ben was curious. Ruth dipped her finger into the drink and let him suck it. He closed his eyes and made a face.

'At least he's honest,' Tony laughed. He drained his glass and grimaced. 'It's like sour lemonade . . . I've got to go, Becky. Got a night out with the lads.' There was a touch of satire in the phrase.

'Stay out of trouble,' she said. But the words didn't sound as light-hearted as she'd intended.

He gave her a withering look. 'Do me a favour.'

Rebecca became aware of Carl nudging her insistently. 'Can you hear something?' he whispered. 'A knocking. Listen . . . from downstairs.' She was warm and drowsy, unwilling to surface. Carl sat up. 'It's someone at the kitchen door.' Clumsily, in the dark, he began to feel for his clothes piled by the side of the bed.

'I'll go,' Rebecca said groggily. 'I've got a dressing gown.' Heavy with sleep, she hoisted herself into a sitting position. The dressing gown hung at the head of the bed, a man's garment in sensible blue flannel. 'Maybe Paul forgot his key.' She got out of bed and pulled the gown on around her.

As she tiptoed downstairs, the knocking continued, over-loud and abrasive in the silent house. Above her, Richard's door opened and she called softly, 'It's okay. I'll go.'

Entering the kitchen, she switched on the light, and blinked in the harsh electric glare. Three in the morning almost, according to the wall clock. At night there was always the thought that it could be a murderer on the run or something similar, who'd chosen your house to shelter in out of all of London. But it never was, she told herself soothingly, as she bent and pulled the bolt, then turned the key in the lock.

'Tony!'

He entered the kitchen, white-faced, with a vagueness about him, deathly serious. He swayed as if he might faint. 'God, Becky . . .' He sat down heavily on a kitchen chair, looking as if he might be sick.

'D'you want a bowl?' The first words that came to mind.

He shook his head, making a vague, dismissive gesture.

'For God's sake, Tony, what is it?'

He didn't reply, but sat with his head slumped forward, one hand braced against the edge of the table. He shivered. He seemed young, a boy, without his usual assurance, his self-protective grin. His breathing was fast and shallow.

She touched his shoulder, speaking gently. 'Are you ill, Tony? Have you had some kind of accident?'

'Danny stabbed some bloke.' The statement, hoarse and unvarnished, cut across her questions.

'You're joking.' The cold, freckled face and sharp expression of Tony's pal, Danny, flicked across her mind. The sinuous movement with which he'd swiped the cheap ash tray.

'I walked all the way here.' He turned and looked up at her, blank-faced.

'How bad was . . .?' What should she say? 'I mean, he's not dead?'

Tony shook his head. 'Leg. But bad . . .' Unconsciously he touched his own thigh. In the harsh light Rebecca saw stains on the dark cloth of his trousers. Surely it couldn't be . . . She touched one of the patches, drew her finger across it. It was damp still. She turned her hand upward and saw the red-brown smear.

'That's blood.' She spoke as though to herself, hardly believing. 'Look.' She showed Tony.

231

He nodded, pale as death. 'He was bleeding like a . . . I was trying to help him . . . Then his mate came and took over.'

'What . . . How on earth did it happen?' She filled the kettle. The boy was in shock. A drink might help.

'I know him, the bloke. And he knows us.' His voice was cracked with an edge of quiet hysteria. But his manner was fatalistic. They'd been recognized. The outcome was inevitable.

As the kettle heated Rebecca tried to calm him down and to extract some kind of logical sequence from his disjointed statements. As she eventually understood it, a neighbourhood greengrocer had left a small window open round the back of his shop. Danny, with Tony and Phil, had investigated, trying to get in, more out of curiosity – boredom even – than in the hope of finding anything worth stealing. It was known that the proprietor was careful with his takings, banking them regularly, emptying the till at night. They'd managed to force a window when they were disturbed by a local man, a trader on the market, who ran an electrical goods stall.

'Bloody nosey parker,' Tony remarked sourly. 'Everyone hates him. Trust him to be wandering round people's backyards . . .'

His name was Nat Henwood. He'd challenged them and laid hold of Danny who had his arm and half his shoulder in the window. He'd been rough, and the physical manhandling, coupled with the man's self-righteous busybody delight at catching them, had enraged the boy and he'd pulled out a flick knife.

'Stupid bloody thing his brother gave him. Danny always carries it. Makes him feel big, but he never used it before . . .'

There'd been a clumsy, scrappy scuffle. Nat had tried to grab the knife and Danny had lunged at him, hard, with wild instinct, catching the leg Nat had raised in a graceless movement of self-defence.

'He went down, making a noise like a bleeding elephant. I tried to help him. There was blood like . . . Stuck my handkerchief over the hole, but it didn't do much . . .' The boy smiled in grim amusement at the memory. 'Danny scarpered. I said I'd call an ambulance. Phil was hanging around like a spare . . . Then Nat's mate appeared. Don't know where he'd been up till then. He must've heard the racket. He said he'd look after things. I went and phoned an ambulance. Then me and Phil got scared over the police. Phil went home and I came here . . .' A note of surprise in his voice at the thought.

Rebecca handed him a cup of sweet tea. He nodded. 'Cheers.' Holding it between his hands as if to warm them, he said, 'He knows us all, Nat does, so it won't be long . . .'

'What on earth are you doing, Becky?' Carl entered the kitchen, barefoot, wearing just a pair of grey trousers. Tony looked up sharply. Rebecca saw a speculative, disconcerted expression cross his face. She imagined he'd never viewed her as a person with a sex life.

But Carl was doubly taken aback at the unexpected twosome they formed. 'Tony's in a bit of trouble,' Rebecca said quickly.

It was five o'clock before they could persuade Tony to bed down on the sofa in the living room. He was dog tired, almost asleep at the kitchen table, but talked compulsively, seeming to need to cover the same ground time and time again, to relive the night's experience.

In the end Rebecca pointed out that she and Carl needed their sleep, even if he didn't, and he allowed himself to be left, curled up in a sleeping bag, his drawn young face incongruously framed by a frilly floral cushion.

'I want to join the army, Becky,' were his last, enigmatic, mumbled words before he fell into an almost immediate sleep.

The next morning Carl set out in search of a lawyer he'd met via a friend who was studying law. The man worked for a foundation that specialized in the defence of young, impecunious first offenders. Carl seemed energized by the challenge, fresh and focused, freed from the anti-climactic apathy of the previous day. He had a cause to get his teeth into, Rebecca thought. It was the kind of situation Carl relished. He looked handsome, blond and purposeful behind his metal-rimmed glasses, like the idealistic young attorney in a Hollywood movie.

Tony telephoned his parents first thing to let them know where he was, but he didn't say why. He wanted to explain the situation to them face to face. Then Rebecca went with him to his local police station.

She'd spent a good hour during the night persuading, haranguing, convincing. Tony wasn't deeply involved, she reasoned. The worst he'd done was to help force a window. He'd shown concern for the victim, tried to help him, phoned an ambulance. It must be in his favour to turn himself in of his own accord. Tony was dubious. Apart from anything else, there was Danny to consider. A mate.

Rebecca bit back the scathing words that came to mind. She pointed out reasonably, 'You're not giving Danny away. You said yourself he's been recognized. You all have.' Watching his closed, stubborn face, she wanted to shake him. Eventually Tony backed down, though he wasn't keen. Going to the police smacked of collaboration, crawling.

'Good God, Tony!' Rebecca had exploded. 'You've only got one life. And you're in trouble. You'd be crazy not to do what you can to make things better!'

He was subdued and taciturn when they presented

234

themselves at the station. Ungracious. And Rebecca, with her youth and her student appearance, commanded small respect from the red-faced, red-haired officer on duty. Things looked up when Val arrived to stand bail and to confer weight and gravity on the proceedings. Rebecca was grateful for his air of competence, his boyish handsomeness, his face set and stern above his dog collar. He did his bit, but was cold with Tony.

'I'm bitterly disappointed in you,' he told him with clipped formality. Tony said nothing, staring down at his blood-stained trousers, pale, with a dark smudge under each eye. Rebecca felt sad for the laying low of his youthful arrogance. She had the sudden urge to cuddle and comfort him, and wished that Val could be more forgiving. But he'd come, that was the main thing; and given his moral backing, if not his warmth.

She sat outside on a heavy, polished bench in the tiled waiting area while Tony was being questioned. Afterwards the red-haired officer questioned her briefly. He seemed pleasanter this time. Rebecca stressed Tony's role at the youth club, his helpfulness and reliability.

'He's a young idiot, that's all,' the officer said as he dismissed her. She thought his weary tolerance was perhaps an encouraging sign.

Much later that day, after Tony's parents had been informed and all formalities observed, he was allowed to go. He and Rebecca wandered aimlessly through the streets round the Elephant. It was nearly five o'clock. The children were out of school and playing. A mellow sun shone, striping the pavements with long shadows. Fireweed and ragwort glowed, rosy and yellow, from broken walls, the remaining pockets of bomb rubble. Rebecca was aware of a slow sense of unreality. She felt dazed and light-headed from the events of the last hours and the lack of sleep.

Tony was quiet, as he'd been all that day. They sat down on a wall outside his old primary school, a classic London double-decker in red-brown brick, with a tarred playground marked out with white lines for football and netball. He stared ahead of him. Then he turned towards Rebecca and repeated the words he'd mumbled the previous night, before sinking into sleep. 'I'm going to join the army. If they'll have me.' He spoke more to himself than to her.

Rebecca's immediate reaction was negative, a reflex distaste. 'What on earth for?' It was an instinctive right-eous recoiling from a profession she regarded with ingrained hostility.

'It means I can get away.'

'Why bother? You'll be doing your National Service soon enough.'

He shook his head. 'That's not the point. I want to sign on. Be a professional.'

'Why the army? Why don't you go to night school? You're great with electrics.'

'Come on, Becky.' He looked at her with impatience. 'I'd still be hanging round in this dump.'

She was unconvinced, but thought it would be mean and discouraging of her – for the moment at least – to belittle his plan further.

They sat for a while in silence. Two girls passed with fruit lollies on sticks. 'Look, they've sucked all the colour out of them,' Tony remarked inconsequentially. 'I hate it when that happens.'

A thought occurred to Rebecca. 'Tony,' she said.

'What is it?'

'Have you ever stolen before?' She faced him levelly. 'It could come out, you know.'

He met her gaze. 'No, I never have,' he replied blandly. Searchingly she held his eyes, willing the words to be the truth, and knowing she'd have to be content with the denial.

Abruptly he seemed to tire of talking about himself. He gave Rebecca a curious sidelong glance. 'He's your

236

boyfriend, then, that Carl . . . Your lover,' he added
daringly. In his mouth the word sounded oddly Victorian.

'Sort of.' She caught from him an air of slight
embarrassment.

'Sort of,' he mocked. 'Are you going to marry him?'

She shrugged. 'Who knows?' Carl wanted it, expected
it perhaps.

He looked amused. 'You don't sound very passionate,'
he said in a teasing, accusing tone.

'We're very compatible,' she said cautiously. 'We
believe in the same things.' The last twelve hours or so
had lowered barriers between herself and Tony. In relation to him she no longer felt like a scout mistress, as he'd
called her once. 'I don't think I could go to bed with
someone who didn't think the same as me politically . . .'
But he was right. She didn't sound very passionate.

It was her turn to change the subject. 'About the army,'
she said. 'It might sound good in court. Your wanting to
join.' She thought with regret that her dislike of the idea
was probably naïve.

'Yes, it might.' Tony brightened at her tentative
approval. He stood up and stretched. 'I'd better go home
and face the music. I'll take you to the bus stop.' As they
walked side by side along the dusty pavement he said
shyly, 'You've been a pal, Becky.'

With characteristic efficiency Carl arranged for the lawyer
to take on Tony's case, and Rebecca and Val agreed to
be character witnesses. All they could do now was wait.

Carl planned to spend the summer working on an Israeli
kibbutz. Rebecca was deeply envious, but her parents
were finding things hard – Marie was suffering badly with
varicose veins – and they couldn't manage without her
help for the summer.

'You'll *have* to soon enough,' she pointed out on the
phone. Then she felt mean. They'd worked hard all their

lives and always encouraged her with her studies. She resigned herself to the usual season of waitressing and chambermaiding.

She saw Carl off at the airport. With his backpack and khaki trousers he looked fit and workmanlike. It was easy to imagine him digging and hoeing in the glare of the sun, muscular in shorts, with his cropped fair hair and utilitarian spectacles. He was the type.

'Take care of yourself, Becky,' he said, kissing her, his lips dry and smooth. 'I'll miss you,' he added with a gleam of sincerity that seemed to her somehow dutiful.

'You won't have time.' She hated his freedom. 'Write. Tell me everything.'

When he'd gone she felt flat and glum. As she drank a cup of bitter espresso at the airport, Tony's half-joking words came back to her. 'You don't sound very passionate.' Low as she was, they disturbed her. She could dismiss them of course – he was just a boy talking from ignorance. But, then again, what if his was the voice of truth?

She thought of Ruth, of the look she had sometimes. Sultry, languorous, knowing. Would she ever feel like that or was she differently made? Rebecca was rarely bothered by this kind of questioning. She was busy and active where Ruth was housebound, had an air always of waiting. Another flash of memory occurred. Paul caressing her hair, inviting himself to her bed, and she experienced a passing pang of regret at the lost opportunity.

Looking into her empty Pyrex coffee cup, she imagined Carl with some bronzed Israeli girl. At that moment, the prospect of his having some kind of affair appeared pretty inevitable to her. And what if he married and stayed? He seemed to her made for the grinding idealism of the life. Would she mind? Rebecca pushed her cup away and didn't pursue the question.

In Llandudno she made beds, washed up, served at

table and waited for her exam results with a dull sense of anti-climax. At night, in her room, she began to write. The subject that interested her was the youth club. From this distant perspective she seemed to glimpse a significance in Val's role, her own, Tony's, the children's, as though they had some relevance to the way society was shaping. Her jottings proliferated, and gradually took shape into a long article.

Carl wrote letters to her. She read them eagerly, but what they described remained unreal to her, abstract. He sent a photograph of himself eating at a long trestle table with a crowd of healthy, smiling strangers, and as she looked at the picture he seemed to her to be merely one of them.

25

In the late summer of '54 Ruth decided that she'd take Ben to Provence that autumn for an extended visit to Sarah, her mother, and her husband, Guy. When she mentioned the fact to Owain one morning in August, he revealed that he, too, was planning to go to France in late September with a couple of friends from his university days – they went walking together for a week or so every year.

'Come and see us,' Ruth invited him impulsively. 'My mother'd love to see someone from her old village. She'll never stop asking you questions about all the people she knew and what's changed. All that sort of thing.'

Owain was keener than she would have expected. 'It might be possible. If I can I'll arrange to stay on for a day or two.' His interest seemed positive and realistic. Somehow she had the feeling that he'd manage it.

Ruth and Ben arrived as the heavy, blackish-purple grapes were being harvested. Lorries laden to the axles with fruit bounced along the uneven roads, and the vineyards bustled with casual workers of all ages and both sexes. On the low vines the leaves were splashed with yellow and red, and the air had a sharp, golden, autumnal clarity.

Ruth had always loved the area, but as Guy drove her in his *deux chevaux* via winding backroads from the station in Avignon, she experienced an almost physical relief at being there. Away from Paul. She suddenly realized, almost with surprise, how oppressive their recent life together had been. She drank in like a reviving

240

draught the peace of the landscape, the blue of the sky, the russets, ochres and deep, intense reds.

Guy parked his car in Lacoste, a small village perched dizzily on the steep flank of a hill, one of many in the area. 'Sarah asked me to bring home a *tarte aux pommes*,' he told her. 'So I must visit the lady in the *boulangerie*. She likes to talk. I'll be ten minutes . . . More.' He shrugged his shoulders with a rueful, peculiarly Gallic resignation.

Ruth got out with Ben, glad of the opportunity to rediscover her surroundings. For her, the steep, terraced villages of the Lubéron area had an effortless elegance, with their narrow streets and steps and low archways. She loved the crumbling, textured façades, and the faded paintwork, the walls swathed in dark, reddening vines and creeper, the earthenware pots on windowsills and steps, filled with tumbling geraniums.

Sarah and Guy lived a couple of miles outside the village in a square, solid farmhouse with walls of honey-coloured stone and a low, pitched roof with curved, coral slates. They'd bought the place outright eight or so years ago, moving from rented premises near Avignon. A single-storey extension with large, south-facing windows had been added as a studio.

The house was surrounded by a low stone wall, against which grew rosemary, lavender, and a spreading pyracantha bush, smothered in orange-red berries. Behind the house was a large area of ground where the walls were higher and where Guy cultivated a flourishing kitchen garden.

From her very first visit there, Ruth had always had the impression that, wherever you looked, the surroundings composed themselves automatically into a still life or a post-impressionist landscape. So, in a sense, it seemed natural that Sarah, with her passionate visual awareness, should come to rest in this part of the world. And yet

241

Ruth still found it strange. She was used to imagining her mother against the prosaic backdrop of her childhood, their unremarkable ground-floor flat in the Fulham Road. She couldn't help being impressed all over again, and surprised, each time she encountered Sarah at home in this exotic and extremely foreign location.

'You're an imposter,' she'd teased her once. 'A show-off. You don't belong here.'

'No,' her mother had agreed. 'I don't really. But even if Guy died, or ran off and left me tomorrow, I'd stay here now. It suits me. I don't belong, no. But I'm happy as a permanent outsider.'

Sarah was in her early fifties now, and her career had reached a stable and gratifying plateau. She had a solid reputation in art circles in both England and France, but remained an individual figure, isolated from fashions and influences. Years ago, when living with her second husband, Ruth's father, in New Mexico, she'd made the decision to paint only for herself. From then on she would be the sole judge of her success. It had been for her a moment of truth. There had been times since when the going had been hard – during the war years she'd barely painted at all – but she'd never been seriously tempted to swerve from this principle.

Her life with Guy in Provence was profoundly satisfying to her. She worked hard, endlessly fascinated with the small, but visually stimulating, world she inhabited. Her canvases showed a direct and sensuous appreciation of the gardens, buildings, food, plants, landscapes that surrounded her. A visiting critic had written, with Parisian portentousness, that her paintings were 'a perpetual hymn of thanks for the physical world'. She'd read the review out to Guy with a mocking solemnity, but a corner of her mind admitted that the man had a point.

Ever since Ruth could remember, her mother had looked the same. She was small, slight and compact, always dressed in a black shirt and trousers, keeping her appearance deliberately simple, leaving her visual energy free for her painting.

'I used to love colourful clothes once upon a time when I was young,' she'd told Ruth once in passing. Then she shrugged. 'Later on I just lost interest.'

Her hair was strong and dark, curling round her face, which was tanned from the Provençal sun. From close to, Ruth saw, with a momentary surprise, a significant sprinkling of grey that wasn't noticeable from a distance. Her face was spare and well-shaped, the defining bones clearly visible, though with the passing of time the lines were becoming more deeply etched in the smoothness of her skin.

Ruth always had the impression that, more than most daughters, she could view her mother dispassionately, as a separate person, and she assumed that this objectivity dated from the war years when they'd lived apart. After the bombing started, Ruth had been evacuated to Maggie's house in Hertfordshire, while Sarah stayed in London to do her war work. Their separation bred tensions. Sarah, she knew, had felt that her daughter was increasingly becoming a stranger to her. Meanwhile Ruth, rebellious and hostile, had clung to her surrogate family – Maggie and her two young sons, and Alan, the young evacuee with whom she'd fallen in love. But when Alan was killed by a V2 rocket, some primitive, undeniable instinct had prompted Ruth to turn to Sarah for comfort and go back to London with her in spite of the danger from bombs.

The following year was difficult; Ruth was confused, griefstricken and withdrawn. Sarah alternated between moods of impatience and overwhelming pity. But eventually they'd found a balance, a tentative, affectionate peace.

Soon afterwards, though, they separated again. Ruth

left home to begin her acting career. Sarah married Guy and came to live in France. She remained a constant in Ruth's life, a focus, the person she admired and trusted more than any other. Yet rarely, since Ruth had been twelve or so, had they shared an easy intimacy based on the trivial day-to-day minutiae of a close family life.

It was hugely pleasurable for Ruth to rediscover her mother's familiar quick grin, to see her at home among the clutter of this house that was so natural to her now. It was good and warming to share in the contentment she radiated, to watch her talking to Ben, gravely, like an equal, teaching him French words which he mimicked delightedly and made him giggle.

'He gets always more like you,' Guy said, as they sat outside in the shade of the hanging vines. 'Nothing of Paul in him at all.'

For perhaps the thousandth time, Ruth experienced a twinge of guilt at the world's bland, benevolent assumption that her child was Paul's. And a frisson of incredulity at the thought that Owain would be here next week – and all of them would talk and laugh and eat together, and only she would possess the quiet knowledge of the possibility that he was Ben's father.

Meeting Sarah and Guy for the first time, Paul had been bemused. 'It's like marrying into a family of Berbers or gypsies,' he remarked. He was deeply impressed by their bold, unconventional looks. At the wedding they'd contrasted oddly with his own parents, pale and tame in their Marks and Spencer's finery. Even on a January day of bluster and drizzle, Guy and Sarah had looked swarthy and striking, like members of a different and less domesticated race. Ruth had felt a secret glow of love and pride in them, and thought it strange that she – tall, slim and blonde like her father – should be represented by these exotic beings.

In his mid-fifties, Guy remained hawk-like and imposing, with his high cheekbones, jutting nose and steady, brown, deepset eyes. His appearance seemed fixed, eternal. Though his hair would become greyer and his skin more wrinkled, Ruth could see that he'd look almost the same in his eighties as he did now.

Like Sarah, he was a painter, but his family had always lived off the land, and Guy divided his time between painting, and creating his kitchen garden on the tract of land behind the house. It was decorative as well as useful, with hollyhocks and sunflowers alongside the tomatoes, aubergines and salad vegetables. He'd built trellises for shade, where a vine mingled with climbing beans and squash, clematis and wisteria.

'It's my kingdom,' he told Ruth, with smiling pride as he showed her the latest developments. Usually when she got up at around seven or eight he'd have been working out there for an hour or more. He grew too much for his own and Sarah's immediate needs and sold the surplus to bolster their joint income.

He was less single-minded about his art than Sarah. The two of them lived happily from hand to mouth. 'Guy's more of a winter painter,' Sarah had told Ruth once, unconcernedly. He favoured the bleaker, subtler colours of that season. Sometimes he worked flat out for months at a time. His work sold well locally and, in the wake of a healthy influx of money, he would stop painting for a while.

'I have to breathe and think and serenade my muse,' he explained drily to Ruth, adding with a grin, 'Sarah's not so *névrosée* . . . neurotic. She works always with no problem.'

Ruth was touched by his pride in Sarah. Whenever she arrived he'd take her aside and ask conspiratorially, 'Don't you think Sarah looks well?' He took huge pleasure in the way his wife had flourished in his world.

Just occasionally Ruth found herself tempted to point out crisply that her mother had prospered for many years in her own native country, but she bit her tongue, feeling that it would be churlish of her to voice any such thought.

Ben took a great shine to Guy and enjoyed going out with him to work in the garden. 'Come on, Guy, we'll dig,' he'd plead, pulling at his hand.

Ruth took a photograph of them from behind as they walked towards Guy's plot, the upright, swarthy Frenchman hand in hand with her fair child, his small, muscular legs trotting to keep up, the two figures haloed by the luminous early-morning Provençal light. Later, she enlarged and framed the snap, finding it powerfully evocative. Guy found Ben a trowel and a watering can, offering him a patch of bare earth to dig in, and they spent hours in one another's company, content and totally absorbed.

As the visit progressed, Sarah experienced vague flashes of unease with regard to Ruth, though she'd have found it hard to explain exactly why. On the surface she was bubbly, thoroughly enjoying her visit, and their company, revelling in the opportunity of displaying Ben to his grandmother and step-grandfather, as she teasingly referred to Guy. But below the seeming liveliness Sarah sensed a listlessness, a lack of . . . harmony, for want of a better word.

When, on the first day, they'd asked after Paul, a quick, disconcerting grimace had crossed Ruth's face – Sarah could still visualize it – a fleeting hardness. They'd been sitting outside the house, drinking wine in the late afternoon sun. Ruth had seemed off-balance for a moment. She'd taken a slow sip of her drink before replying, 'Happy enough. Going on in his own sweet way.' Her voice held an edge of cynicism that fell heavily into the careless conversation.

The awkwardness hadn't recurred, but Sarah sensed that Ruth had imposed an unspoken taboo on that particular line of enquiry. When she referred to her life in England, it was friends she talked of – Rebecca, Richard, and this Owain who was about to visit them.

Sarah had met Paul four or five times, on each occasion for a period of several days, and always in England – he'd never visited them in France. She found him easy company and liked his rather louche sense of humour and his funny, affectionate way with Ben. Yet, like a wild animal scenting unspecified danger, she sensed something about him that made her wary. He seemed driven, fearful and suspicious of conventional happiness, destructive almost. He conjured up a picture in her mind of a boy shooting with an air rifle at his own toy soldiers, making them useless to play with. But she dismissed the image as uncharitable and over-dramatic, at a loss to understand why she'd imagined him like that.

Perversely, Sarah was worried by Ruth's obvious delight in her visit. It was almost as if their peaceful, picturesque world were a refuge, a haven from a life she found vaguely unsatisfactory. Ruefully she recalled the way Ruth used to be when she visited in her RADA and acting days. Exhilarated and artlessly self-centred. Talking non-stop about every aspect of her own world, its trials and successes. And by the end of the visit, she was visibly impatient to be gone and plunge again into her life's vital challenge. This time there was a reticence about her and she sighed languidly that she could happily spend forever in the blue and gold of a Provençal autumn.

26

As Owain approached in the late-afternoon warmth, Ruth appeared by chance round the side of the house. It came almost as a shock to him to see her suddenly like that in these far-flung surroundings. Their arrangement had been vague and fluid. In this new context her familiar beauty appeared to him a revelation. She moved with an unhurried holiday languour. Her skin reminded him of a sunwarmed apricot, the cliché seeming new-minted and shining with truth. Her slim, rounded shoulders emerged from a sleeveless pale green shirt, and were brushed by her hair, which was blonder and finer than he remembered it. She wore calf-length jeans and backless flat sandals. She seemed lost in thought and didn't notice him. There was a basket on her arm, as if she might be on her way to the local shops. Briefly she looked down the road, away from him.

He called her name. With an air of sharp enquiry she turned her head, then saw him.

'Owain!' There was a note of delight in her voice. 'You made it then.'

As she walked towards him, smiling, her eyes seemed to shine with a radiant vulnerability. He was conscious that his own must hold a similar nakedness, more like a lover's than a friend's.

Ruth watched Owain as he lay propped on one elbow in the pale, dry grass, with a glass of red wine, talking to Sarah and Guy. She experienced a kind of proprietary pride in him. Viewing her guest through their eyes, she saw someone who was his own person, intelligent and somehow . . . decent, with a private gleam of amusement in his eye. Paul aroused a complex array of feelings in the people he encountered. He stimulated interest, but also antagonism. Owain, she'd noticed before, commanded simple respect and liking. As he discussed the labyrinthine complexities of French politics with his hosts, Ruth was impressed by his knowledge. Though, of course, politics was his stock-in-trade. Guy leaned forward on his wooden bench, his hawk-like face eager and animated, wholly absorbed in their conversation.

Ruth sat cross-legged on the grass, cradling her drink between her hands. She said little, but between herself and Owain she sensed a passive current of awareness, as if the fact of their reunion in these distant surroundings had freed them in some way to acknowledge the depth and pleasure of their friendship.

Ben was sitting among them, playing with a wooden jigsaw, his brow beetled, tongue protruding from between his teeth. But suddenly he turned to Owain and remarked conversationally, 'I'm Ben.' His grey eyes shone, alive with anticipation.

Owain grinned. 'You're Stanley Kowalski,' he riposted. It was their joke and Ben gurgled with satisfied laughter. Carelessly Owain reached out and ruffled the child's hair. His forearm was deeply tanned and stippled with dark hairs, his face thin and bearded like an El Greco. The casual-affectionate gesture touched a sudden spring of sensuality in Ruth. She was disconcerted by the force of her response to it and had the uncomfortable impression that her feelings must show on her face.

The week's outdoor exercise had served to bring Owain's physical presence into sharp relief. He looked fit and somehow larger than life. Lounging at ease in the grass, he wore a bleached-looking blue shirt, open at the neck, the sleeves rolled, that emphasized the bronzed torso beneath it. A brief, disturbing, incongruous image flickered in her mind. Ruth imagined herself stretched out next to him here in the grass and running her hands along the toned muscles of his body. She felt hot and foolish and focused her attention on a trellis beyond him, swathed in the ruby coils of a vine, like the backdrop to some classical painting.

Sarah prepared a buffet meal, with bread and salads, cold, spiced meat and wine, and chalky goat's cheese. She laid it out on the long, sturdy table Guy had made for her, in the whitewashed main room of the house. They helped themselves and sat round talking on the long, low divan, or on cushions on the floor. The house had electricity, but often, like tonight, they preferred the light of an oil lamp, which gave the room a shadowy intimacy.

Sarah examined Owain Roberts with interest. It was odd to think that the two of them, strangers, had in common a youth spent in the confined world of her native village of Carreg-Brân. Not that it showed, she thought. Laying aside the Welsh cadence of their speech, they seemed citizens of the world, well used to a wider stage. Yet buried in the consciousness of both of them lay an intimate knowledge of the same landmarks – the looming winding-house of the colliery, the parched summery grass of Avon Meadows, the stained-glass, bluebird door panels in the more affluent of the upright rows of grey cottages, the corroded gilt sunburst of the Travellers' Rest inn sign. All shared images from the landscape of their childhood.

How unreal it seemed to think that this personable adult was the son of Ianto Roberts, the bugbear of her youth, with his taunting eyes and sly hostility. As children, the two of them had been sharply aware of one another, with a mixture of antagonism and attraction. But Sarah had always considered her own family – with its grocer's shop, its respect for education – to be a cut above Ianto's. He'd been dirty, often barefoot in summer.

The First War had changed her own father. He'd become drunken, unshaven, savagely tempered. And Ianto had risen. He was active in the Miners' Federation, respected, a vigorous fighter for his co-workers' rights.

'I remember hearing your dad speak at a trade union meeting once,' she told Owain impulsively. 'He was electrifying. Convincing everyone that things could change. You felt drained after hearing him, and so sure.'

Owain smiled. 'He knew what he was fighting for in those days.'

'Not now?' Sarah was surprised. She thought he sounded as if he were pronouncing an obituary.

'Oh . . . you know.' He shrugged, as though mildly embarrassed by her picking up of his statement. 'The issues aren't so clear-cut nowadays.'

'How *is* Ianto?' she asked.

He gave a wry grimace. 'Not too good. Trouble with his breathing. It's partly the pit, and he's always smoked heavily, and I can't see him stopping.' Sarah sensed again a reservation in his attitude to his father.

'And Jo?'

'She's fine.' There was warmth in his voice. No holding back there. 'She's the glue that holds us all together.'

'I remember her when we were children. She was a bit older than me. Sometimes she'd come out to play, with her hair in curling-rags. She used to shake them back over her shoulder and say they were ringlets. We younger kids were ever so impressed . . .' Sarah smiled at the sudden memory.

'There was a bench at the end of Crymlyn Road. Jo got this game up once. All of us kids were acrobats and we were doing handsprings over the back of it.' Pictures flashed into her brain. It must have been forty years since she'd thought of the incident. 'But the old men were scandalized. They always sat there. They said it was their bench and they chased us off. Jo was so indignant she put

251

her tongue out at this one old chap. She didn't half catch it later.'

'She's told *me* that!' Owain's grin was bright with bemused recognition. 'That bench is still there, you know. And the old buffers still congregate every afternoon . . .'

As he conversed with Sarah and Guy, Owain was aware of operating on two distinct levels. A part of him enjoyed the piquant food, relished the company of amusing, civilized people, felt stimulated and at home. But always inside him crouched the boy from a working-class family, casting a watchful, critical eye over the spaciousness of their lives.

The room they were in symbolized somehow the way he felt. It was largish, not opulent, but furnished with a kind of . . . arrogance. The walls were plain white. The shortcomings of a battered low divan were hidden by a casually draped coverlet, printed with a bold cubist design in strong shades of saxe-blue, ochre and black. There were cushions, strikingly coloured and patterned, the fabrics seeming chosen for their own sake, and not because they harmonized with one another. Carved dark wooden chairs stood here and there, the scuffed varnish adding in a sense to their quality, like aristocrats serene in shabby clothes. In one corner lay the severed burl of a sizeable tree, plain and unpolished, its intricate markings thrown into relief by the white walls. The surface of a large vase seemed scraped and scratched with pigments of grey and ochre. It held the skeletal, blackened seed heads of some sculptural, unfamiliar plant. There was texture and design at every turn. The oil lamp threw a soft, warm light. The room was untidy, with a makeshift quality, and yet it proclaimed unmistakably the confident style of its owners.

Mentally he contrasted Jo's cramped living room, neat and highly polished, the furnishings in timid shades of beige and brown, everything in its place. Sarah remembered Jo as a bold, hoydenish girl with spirit, yet nothing of this showed in her surroundings. It wasn't just poverty, so it seemed to him – they were quite reasonably off nowadays – but a fundamental narrowness, a drabness in her expectations of life, and he experienced a flash of resentment on her behalf, an undirected anger.

'Owain, help yourself.' Sarah was smilingly hospitable. 'If you don't, the gannets'll get it.' She indicated Guy and Ruth.

He shook his head. 'No, I'm fine. It was wonderful though.' Summoning up a deliberate, bourgeois politeness.

Ruth crossed to the table, barefoot, to refill her plate. 'God, I'm such a pig.'

She grinned at him over her shoulder, graceful and quick, seeming to him to embody the instinctive style he'd been contemplating. It made her mysterious to him, opaque. And desirable, like something to be conquered.

On the following day, Guy and Sarah left before dawn to catch the train for Paris, where they were spending a couple of days. A friend had an exhibition opening, and he'd invited them to stay. As she made Ben his breakfast in the red-tiled kitchen, Ruth was conscious of a bubble of anticipation inside her at the prospect of two days alone here with Owain.

He appeared around nine, yawning, in jeans and a grey American sweatshirt, his feet bare. She marvelled at this rare opportunity for close, unhurried communication.

'Coffee?' She took in his casual appearance with pleasure.

'Don't mind if I do.'

Ruth savoured a luxurious awareness of the options that lay open to them. The day could unfurl in any manner of ways. She felt lazily receptive, with no sense of responsibility or anxiety.

Owain sat himself down at the scrubbed wooden table. 'Hallo, Ben.'

The child dug his spoon into the boiled egg in front of him, and offered a precariously brimming mouthful of yolk. Owain snapped it down like a wolf, to Ben's huge delight.

'You encourage him wickedly,' Ruth said.

'That's because he's not my responsibility.'

He spoke with an air of certainty, and Ruth experienced the unnervingly vivid temptation to reveal to him the ambiguities of her son's parentage and so jolt him out of his ignorance. She crushed the impulse instantly. It was mischievous and could only lead to trouble. Impassively she poured black coffee into a thick china mug and handed it to him. As she did so their eyes met. His seemed to her somehow speculative, as though he had plans for the two of them. She met the look blandly.

Owain said, 'There's a portrait in the hall. Of a woman. You know the one I mean? Who is it?'

'I know the one. Guy painted it.' The picture had been hanging in the same position ever since she'd first come to this house. It showed a young woman staring from the canvas with a direct and challenging gaze. She had long, red hair, tied behind, and wore a shapeless man's sweater. The depiction was unglamorous but entirely arresting. The woman's face had a bold sexual assertiveness. 'It's Dominique David, the singer. She's a friend of Guy's and my mother's. Or was. She spends most of her time in America nowadays. She and Guy were in the Resistance together during the war. They killed someone. A high-up German. They had to go into hiding for months.'

'Good God! Small world.' Owain was interested and impressed. 'I saw her once in some Left Bank dive just after I was demobbed. She was bloody good. Incredible

254

magnetism. And someone told me a bit about her wartime activities.'

'Guy says she was brilliant in those days. Really strong and original. But she toured America and some movie bigwig got hold of her. I saw a piece on her last year in the *Illustrated*. She's living with him in Hollywood in some Spanish-style ranch with a swimming pool.' Ruth grinned. 'My mother and Guy disapprove . . . But then they're awful puritans at heart.'

'I admire them,' he said. 'There's a kind of life force about them. They make you think growing old might be bearable after all . . .' Ruth had a sudden flashback. Herself and Owain that night in Llandudno, peering in at the geriatric old-time dancers. Owain's distaste for the spectacle that she and Paul had found touching and likeable. She felt a momentary tenderness for Paul.

Owain couldn't relax. It was now or never, he thought. There'd never be an opportunity like this again. If he let it slip they'd be back to the restrained Thursday mornings in Broadbent's dusty shop. Nothing would have changed and that would be that. Ruth seemed to him overwhelmingly desirable in this setting. He saw the picturesque household, with its paintings and unconventional charm, as the natural element for her spirited grace.

A buried seam of lust ran alongside their easy conversation. He was sure it must show in his eyes, dark and hot, searingly obvious. He felt like a hunting animal, stalking his prey, ready to pounce, his friendship turning, under pressure, to opportunism.

She was wearing a thin black cotton dress, full and gypsyish, with a scooped and gathered neckline. A silver chain drew his eyes to the column of her neck, which arched as she threw her head back to laugh. He longed to touch it with his fingertips, stoop and lay his lips to hers in a declaration of intent. There was a flush beneath her skin, a kind of incandescence. He remembered kissing her once in the shop, out of concern and friendship, but that had been something else entirely.

Ruth made sandwiches, splitting a *baguette* into long sections and filling them with goat's cheese, tomatoes and onions. She wrapped the bread and stowed it in a basket behind Ben's pushchair. They walked along a footpath that wound past a field of clipped lavender bushes, the neat long rows gleaming in the sun with a metallic grey-mauve sheen. The lane wound upwards, bordered by tough shrubs of live oak.

Both of them focused on Ben, chatting to him and making him laugh, pointing out things of interest. In this way they distracted themselves from the tension that had become almost palpable between them.

'We look like a family party,' Ruth said suddenly. 'The local people probably think you're my husband. Paul's never been here, you know.'

Owain said nothing, turning eyes on her which seemed eloquent with the implications of her blurted statement. She felt herself blush foolishly, like a teenager. She ruffled Ben's hair as he sat in front of her in the pushchair, in an attempt to cover her awkwardness.

'Don't, Mummy.' The child raised one hand to his head, his tone the very essence of patience and pure reason.

They reached the hilltop. Below them the valley spread, fertile and cultivated, marked off into geometrical enclosures of low vineyards, orchards, lavender fields. They picnicked by a group of gnarled olive trees. When they'd eaten, Ben seemed sleepy. Ruth laid him on a small cot blanket and he dozed, partly shadowed by the overhead leaves. His soft, childish mouth was open a little and his hands loosely curled. She watched him silently, her love raw as a wound.

Owain lay back in the dried grass, his hands linked behind his head. The afternoon was still and golden, with just the hint of a breeze. He stretched luxuriously. 'God, London in three days' time. And the dock strike's still there waiting for me. I'm down to write a probing analysis the moment I arrive.'

'I don't much want to go back either.' The remark sounded more bleakly heartfelt than she intended.

He looked at her quizzically. 'Bad as that?' There was a note of concern in his voice.

She shook her head and smiled at him. 'Not really. I didn't mean to sound so tragic.' She shrugged her shoulders. 'It's just that, well, I've always thought of autumn as a time of change and making resolutions. Starting something . . .' She stroked the fine, fair hair away from Ben's face. He hardly stirred. The sun filtered, hot and mellow, through the screen of leaves. 'But I know that until Ben's old enough . . . Well, nothing's going to change . . .' Abruptly Ruth disliked the wistful tone to her voice. 'Oh . . . forget it.' She looked up at the cloudless sky, narrowing her eyes against the golden glare.

There was a silence between them. It was protracted and seemed to hold a significance, as though Owain had deliberately rejected any easy comment he might make, and was searching for words. She turned to look at him. He was sitting up now, elbows resting on his drawn-up knees, forearms hanging loosely. He appeared thoughtful. 'I know what you mean about a change,' he said slowly. 'I feel the same.' His eyes met hers steadily, showing greenish depths. 'I think I've reached the end . . .' He hesitated. 'I might as well be honest . . . Look, Ruth, I don't want to be . . . just any friend. I need more. I want to be close to you. Love you, even. Sleep with you.' There was a pause. The words hung between them, suspended, unexpected, but somehow inevitable. Then his expression lightened a little. He said wryly, 'You see, if a few hours' chat a week among the mouldering tomes is all you can give me, I'd just as soon bow out.'

Having slept after lunch, Ben was lively and talkative that evening. There was no question of putting him to bed much before ten. He had the toddler's instinctive knack of seeming extra winsome while living on borrowed time, heading off any attempt at rigid adult discipline.

Ruth concentrated on him, on his smiling face and saucy eyes, avoiding contact with Owain and his hot, buried, questioning look, his expectations. He was oppressive to her, something she'd apply her mind to when there was leisure. At the same time excitement knotted the pit of her stomach. Once she shivered involuntarily, as though her body sought to release the clenched muscles.

'Spaghetti.' Perfunctorily she placed three dishes on the bare kitchen table, hardly aware of the processes that had been involved in cooking it. She performed the tasks like an automaton, while the adrenalin pumped inside her. Privately she marvelled that the food looked as it always did, as though she'd sliced and stirred and strained in full awareness.

Currently it was Ben's favourite meal. He liked to suck the long strands into his mouth one by one. Owain imitated him, making her son laugh in a way that boded ill for bedtime, ignoring Ruth, the question mark hovering above them precluded small-talk.

'There's some wine,' she remembered halfway through the meal. The remains of a bottle of rough red stood on a shelf.

'Okay.' He glanced at her, unable to do so casually. Always the insistence showed behind his eyes. The urgency. She filled a glass and handed it to him with simulated negligence.

As they'd wandered home that afternoon through the

bleached, end-of-summer landscape, Ruth had felt dazed but somehow peaceful, as though, if she wanted it, she could bring into being a new era in her life. In a sense, Owain's words had barely surprised her. Simply – like a photograph in its bath of chemicals darkening, developing – they'd brought into focus what until now had been hazy and implicit. Their meetings, so pleasurable at first, had become repetitive, a stalemate situation. And yet to do without them was unthinkable. At the same time she understood that accepting Owain's ultimatum would change everything. It wouldn't be like her bungled fling with Richard. She glanced at him walking silently next to her. He was desirable, with a quiet determination. He would be demanding, want commitment. He'd occupy her thoughts and fill her senses. Glibly she'd talked about new beginnings, but . . .

After the meal, with the dishes still on the table, Ruth began to play a game with Ben, one of his favourites. She laid one hand on the table, and he put his small, soft mitt on hers. She covered it with her other hand. Happily he placed his on top. She withdrew her hand from the bottom of the pile and placed it on his. Ben did the same. The process was repeated, starting slowly and getting faster. Ben became giggly and confused. Suddenly Owain reached out, placing his hand heavily over Ruth's, grasping her wrist in his sinewy warmth.

'Cheat!' She laughed, slightly breathless.

'Cheat!' Ben echoed.

'Can't I play?' He held her wrist circled in his hand for a long moment before releasing it.

When she eventually got Ben upstairs it took time to settle him. At Sarah's he slept in a small, sloping-ceilinged boxroom that had been cleared out and decorated for him, and furnished with two small chairs Guy had knocked together out of odd bits of wood and painted in a rainbow mixture of colours. Ben was proud of the room and usually went to bed like a lamb. Tonight Ruth read him three stories and chatted quietly for a quarter of an hour or more before his eyelids began to droop. Finally he raised no objection when she kissed him and tiptoed from the room.

Downstairs Owain had laid a fire, raiding the pile of cut timber that Guy had stacked ready for the winter. The new flames licked palely, casting large, hazy shadows on the white walls of the living room.

'Sleeping now, is he?' He was bent over the fire, placing smallish pieces of wood strategically to encourage the blaze.

Ruth nodded and sat down by the hearth. Now it was early October the evenings were becoming chill.

'We'll talk now,' he said.

'Yes,' she agreed warily.

'I've got you cornered.'

She grinned faintly. 'Yes.'

'What's it to be?' He looked at her, simple and single-minded, now that Ben's inhibiting presence no longer came between them.

'God, Owain.' She shrugged her shoulders. 'You make it sound as if I'm choosing between brands of washing powder. It's a bit more complicated than that . . .'

'No, it's not.' An air of certainty.

'There are other people to think of.'

Owain stood upright, a piece of kindling wood dangling from his right hand. 'You mean Paul?'

'Of course.'

His expression was dismissive. 'Paul's your problem. I've only met him a couple of times in passing. And nothing I've heard about him has made me want to know him better . . . He's your problem,' Owain repeated. 'He's nothing to me.'

The atmosphere between them had shifted towards a

subtle hostility. Ruth turned towards the fire and said nothing. She felt disinclined to leap to Paul's defence, although she disagreed with Owain's simplified view of him.

Owain crouched on one knee, placing the final piece of timber on the fire, and monitored the blaze for a moment. His attitude suggested to her a contained energy, reawakening a sexual interest.

'I'll miss you if you stop coming to the shop,' she said.

He turned towards her. 'A clean break, as they say. It's better than stalemate. I can't take that any more.'

She looked at him, approving for the thousandth time the thin, bearded features. The shadowy firelight was flattering to him. A brooding nihilist. With a gleam of self-mockery she recalled describing him so. Years ago, when she'd been young. She shook her head. 'I'd miss you.' Her tone measured and merely factual.

Owain reached out towards her. Through the thickness of her hair she felt the warm weight of his hand at the back of her neck. 'I've been wanting you all day,' he said.

'Yes.' She met his gaze with a glint of friendly malice. 'You've been wearing your seducer's eyes.'

Fleetingly he parodied a look of theatrical lust. Then he kissed her with slow deliberation. Ruth let it happen, closing her eyes. When it came down to it maybe this was the best way. Talking could send you round in ever-decreasing circles.

1956

27

That evening there was a stuffy, timeless quality about the offices of *Red Lion* magazine – based in Red Lion Square – that made Owain think of an Edward Hopper painting. He and Rebecca sat at their typewriters at opposite ends of the room, each in the cone-shaped pool of light thrown by their respective anglepoise lamps. Wider, fainter circles of illumination spread across the cream-painted walls and the dull, swirly pattern of the lino on the floor. The ceiling and the corners of the room had receded into outer darkness.

It was January. Two bars of an electric fire glowed. The small heater was democratically placed between the two of them, at the full extent of its flex. Beyond the uncurtained windows a wet and windy night blustered. Between two buildings the moon showed, silvering a horizontal drift of cloud. Owain relished the atmosphere of quiet and concentration. In the evening you could get so much done without the phone ringing or contributing writers dropping by, drinking tea, as if you, like they, had all the time in the world.

Rebecca glanced up from her typing momentarily, caught his eye and grinned before returning to her work. Becky was a find, no doubt about that, bringing to his newly founded magazine an imaginative maturity that frequently surprised him, as well as an impressive capacity for sheer hard work. He'd become hugely fond of her, with her engaging personality and wry, practical outlook on life. She made him think of some small, quick animal – shrewd, amused, brown eyes below the dark fringe of hair, the compact, tenacious little body. It was amazing that Ruth's closest friend should have turned out to be such an ideal candidate for the job.

With a kind of inevitability his mind drifted from Becky to Ruth. He'd be seeing her tomorrow – she'd be staying the night. The thought summoned up a kaleidoscope of pleasurable images, bringing in its wake the habitual sense of wondering happiness, that after the false start and the long months of hopeful friendship he'd become her lover, on terms of intimacy with her graceful body, her smile, her quick, bright glamour. The fifteen months or so since their stay in Provence had been filled with a constant, conscious feeling of fulfilment, the exhilaration of his affair with Ruth paralleled by professional satisfaction, as his brainchild, the *Red Lion* review, went from strength to strength. With a sense of his own good fortune, Owain went back to the leader he was writing.

Rebecca was transcribing an interview she'd done last week with Tony Taylor, her former companion from the youth club. He'd been on leave from a tour of duty in the British zone of Germany and – with his anonymity guaranteed – had some quotably salty comments to make about the British Army. Rebecca had been relieved to find that his old irreverence was still alive and kicking. At the same time, he seemed pleased with life, older and more confident, and convinced that, in opting for the military, he'd made the right decision.

It had been good to see him. They'd spent the evening in a pub near where he lived. It was a freezing, foggy Monday night, and they had the place – and a cheerful coal-fire – pretty well to themselves. They reminisced about old times at the youth club and talked about Tony's trial. Now, more than a year later, they were able to laugh about it. Some of it.

'You know, Nat and his mate were so keen to see Danny go down that they made me out a bleeding saint,' he recalled wryly. 'And what with you and Val saying

how great I was, and that smart lawyer your boyfriend got
hold of . . .' He gave her a sudden, quick look of enquiry.
'You still with him? The boyfriend?'

She shook her head.

'Got someone else?'

'Don't really have time at the moment, with my job.'
She spoke proudly, truthfully.

'You know what, Beck?' His grin was uncharacteristically sheepish in the taut, alert face. 'Back then I sometimes used to imagine you and me . . . But you were
older, and I never had the guts. Now if it'd been the other
way round . . .'

Rebecca typed on. She was getting quite fast. Owain
was right. You only needed two fingers.

'. . . Chinless wonders. They bark at you like strangulated mongrels. There's one in particular – we call him
Towser . . .' She could almost hear Tony's flat accent, the
edge of hoarseness.

'Much more to go?' Owain spoke suddenly, bringing
her back to the present.

'Couple of pages.'

'Fancy a pie and a pint over the road in ten minutes?'

She nodded, smiling. 'Yes, I think I do.'

Owain had finally got his *Red Lion* review – mooted since
'52 – off the ground a year ago. In that time Rebecca's
weekly interview on the back page had become something
of an institution. It generated a reliable amount of mail
each issue, some enthusiastic, some frankly venomous,
and was the bit she liked best about her job on the
magazine.

It had come about almost by accident. One day – ages
ago, shortly after Ruth had come back from France where
her affair proper with Owain had begun – Ruth had
mentioned, in the maddeningly casual way she had, that
the *Red Lion* review was a mere couple of months away

from coming into being. Rebecca decided to send Owain the piece she'd written during the summer in Llandudno about the ups and downs of her year with Val's youth club and the light it shed on certain aspects of the post-war welfare state. He thought it lively and penetrating and accepted it for use in a forthcoming issue. He was intrigued too by her portrait of Val as a young, socialist vicar coping with a tough, urban parish. 'Why don't you interview him for us?' Owain wrote back. 'I think he'd make good copy.'

The encounter was an eye-opener for Rebecca. The Saturday she went to see him, Val was on his own, his wife and children away visiting his in-laws in Surrey. She found him in a cynical mood, ready to be frank with her about his doubts and frustrations. She never did find out what had provoked his singular bout of pessimism.

He prepared tinned spaghetti on toast, which they ate in the kitchen, washed down with some warmish beer he'd got in. Presumably he didn't drink often, because he soon became flushed and talkative, his blond curls dangling in his eyes, making her think of Leslie Howard playing some whisky-priest. She was startled. Val was always so controlled, bland almost.

'It's like a ball and chain sometimes, my faith. A handicap I have to drag around with me, falsifying all my relationships,' he confessed. 'This,' he pointed to his dog collar, 'makes everyone nervous, unnatural in some way. People get pop-eyed with politeness or else they run away, put up a wall against me before I've even opened my mouth . . .'

It was something Rebecca had never thought of, and she was struck by the disillusionment of his tone.

He'd not lost his personal belief, he insisted, but, 'Sometimes I feel like the guardian of some dinosaur, some huge and lumbering anachronism . . .'

There were other heresies. He admitted that recently

he had been torn in his socialist faith as well. 'We're richer, more equal – and more confused. Sometimes I'm convinced we were happier when we were all peasants. Ignorant and brutish. Is education really all good . . .?'

'Such talk, Val.' Rebecca was shocked. And yet, on reflection, she'd always seen in him something old-fashioned and authoritarian.

'You're sure I can use this?' she asked as she left.

He nodded, standing in the doorway of his modest vicarage, wearing a black cassock and looking every inch the photogenic young vicar. In any case, the magazine had promised him anonymity.

'Maybe people should know that a priest can be a "crazy mixed-up kid".' The fashionable cliché sounded out of place in his mouth, but oddly endearing.

Val had surprised her, but Rebecca thought the interview harmless enough. So both she and Owain were caught off guard by the furore it aroused. For a few days Val's words stirred up a national storm-in-a-teacup, ensuring that every copy of *Red Lion* was snapped up from magazine booths nationwide. The dinosaur tag, particularly, caught the imagination of the tabloid press. Rebecca even heard a comedian on the Light Programme work it into his act.

The interview was brought to the attention of a prominent bishop, who thundered that the traitor who'd given the interview should be unmasked and unfrocked. Owain received several unpleasant phone calls demanding that he reveal the identity of the clergyman involved. He refused point-blank, remaining calm and stubborn in the face of considerable pressure.

'Everyone's always saying how advanced and unshock-able we are nowadays,' Rebecca marvelled. 'Something like this proves that nothing's changed at all.' She was concerned for Val, who was privately terribly embarrassed by his *faux pas*. He'd imagined that he was merely talking off the cuff to some obscure little publication that would probably fold after a couple of issues. And now his own words confronted him at every turn, splashed across newspapers that he refused to have in the house.

'It's so unfair,' Rebecca said to Ruth and Paul, who were fascinated by the whole rumpus. 'Val really cares. He works hard and does a damn good job. But because he's honest about his doubts he's seen as some kind of anti-Christ.'

With a bad conscience, Val lay low, remaining anonymous. The fuss died down. For Owain, it had served a purpose. *Red Lion* had become notorious. A whiff of excitement hung about it, and sales rose dramatically.

It was bought, in the main, by youngish, left-wing, vaguely rebellious people who saw themselves as impatient with the fossilized conformity of their society. And yet its standpoint wasn't wildly revolutionary. Owain's aim was open-mindedness, irreverence certainly, but chiefly a complete independence from any kind of party line.

At the height of the Val controversy Owain's assistant – a young woman who combined editorial work with some feature-writing – left suddenly, to go with her husband to Australia. With almost indecent haste, Owain offered Rebecca her job. She accepted equally readily.

'If I'd dreamed a job, it would probably've been this one,' she confided to Ruth. 'Don't tell Owain I said so, though, I wouldn't want him to feel too much of a benefactor.' For Rebecca this was the start of a period of intense and conscious professional happiness. Almost all her waking thoughts were directed towards the task in hand, and her energetic nature revelled in this brand of single-mindedness.

There were four permanent members of staff: Rebecca and Owain, a secretary called Ella – a phlegmatic, carroty-haired vegetarian from Balham – and Bobby, their production assistant. Fresh from Camberwell art school, he was Irish, with burning eyes in a pale face, and hair that fell arrestingly in a tumble of Brylcreemed waves. Over the months there were moments of friction between the four of them, but basically they were welded by the passionate conviction that *Red Lion* was God's gift to Britain's open minds.

The demarcation between their separate functions was blurred. In an emergency – and there were plenty of those – all of them would turn their hand to anything. On Thursdays, for instance, when the magazine appeared, all four of them would combine to become the subscriptions department, stuffing endless envelopes for their postal subscribers and carrying them to the Post Office in relays in a variety of bags and satchels.

All of them were enthusiastically committed and delved inside themselves for skills to bring to the job. In addition to her hastily learned editorial techniques, Rebecca revived her interest in graphics that she'd discovered while producing Labour Club posters at university. She designed column breakers and her own style of cartoon, using topical photographs and formal, stylized lettering.

But the interviews were her first love. She came to admit to herself that she had a talent for approaching people and drawing them out. 'Becky talks to you with such . . . respect and intelligence and genuine warmth that you don't hold anything back. You come out with thoughts that you hadn't realized were there until she drew your attention to them.' This was Val's rueful verdict to Owain over the telephone a week or two after the sensational little flurry over his own interview had died down. 'She was the same at the youth club,' he added. 'She had the children talking about themselves and thinking about world affairs completely unselfconsciously. I must say I admired her skill.'

For each issue Rebecca found a new subject. She chose ordinary, private people, not celebrities, never naming them, though mentioning the jobs they did. But almost always she produced something sharp and extraordinary, mining the seam of obsession, humour, anger and innate irreverence that nestled richly in the kind of people everyone took for granted.

A pundit reviewing the magazine called her page 'a vivid gallery of contemporary types'. A fan wrote, 'I always open *Red Lion* at the back page. I have to read your piece first. It's one of life's little treats . . .' Rebecca was heartened by such tokens of appreciation, but she'd have loved her work even without them.

Ella, the other female member of the *Red Lion* staff, had a distinctly unpromising air. 'She never smiles!' Rebecca exclaimed wonderingly to Ruth after the first week. Ella was pasty-faced, aged around thirty, with straight, lank hair and an offhand way of speaking. But there was more to her than met the eye.

For one thing she was hugely reliable and got through impressive amounts of work each day, handling *Red Lion*'s copious correspondence, itemizing all expenditure minutely and accurately in readiness for the accountant's monthly visit, answering the phone, dealing with legitimate enquiries, cutting off time-wasters with a quietly-spoken steeliness.

Ella never took a lunch hour. She simply laid out a square of greaseproof paper on the desk beside her and carried on working, munching at the hard-boiled eggs and cold hazelnut rissoles that seemed to form her staple diet. Rebecca discovered eventually, when she got to know her, that she lived at home with her mother, studied Eastern religions in her spare time and wrote verse. About once a month she would produce a new poem. They were spare, stark and much reworked, and they read rather well. She showed them round the office in her usual undemonstrative fashion.

Once Owain included one of them, more to fill a column than for any other reason. It was about the hurly-burly of life and the need to cultivate a still inner core. Ella had letters from several readers who found it inspiring. From then on she became a regular contributor, though she seemed unimpressed by the honour. Rebecca developed an affection for Ella and her dry, lizard-like outlook on the world. 'You can get used to almost anyone,' she admitted to Ruth a few months later.

Bobby was different. Ruth arrived at the offices in Red Lion Square one day when he was throwing a fit of the vapours.

'He has ze, 'ow you say, artistic temperament,' she commented sardonically to Rebecca in a stage French accent.

Rebecca was sanguine. 'He's worth a few wobblers. He's bloody good.'

Bobby was Rebecca's age and he had boundless self-confidence and undeniable flair. With the limited resources at his disposal he made *Red Lion* look somehow modern, approachable, different from worthy weeklies like the *Spectator* or the *New Statesman* that rivalled it in the field.

He had a way with page layout that gave an illusion of space, without in fact wasting it. His father was a printer, and he understood the business, knew what could and couldn't be done. At the same time he was keenly aware of trends in painting and graphics, and the knowledge spilled over almost subconsciously into his work.

One day he'd be poached. There was no getting away from that. In fact people had already tried. One of the glossy magazines had offered him twice what he was getting now.

'But I'd rather have the say,' he remarked, 'like I have here.' At twenty-three he was given an almost free hand. And he was emotionally committed to *Red Lion*. Every

Thursday lunch time he'd walk through the surrounding area, touring the bookstalls and smiling fondly at his handiwork, discreetly rearranging the display sometimes to give the review a more prominent position.

He had another talent. He drew strange little distorted, spidery cartoons with a mapping pen in Indian ink, signing them simply 'Bobby'. They were surreal and wholly personal, though sometimes a political message could be deduced. Rebecca thought them brilliant, though she couldn't have said why. But it seemed that the public at large shared her admiration. The weekly Bobby cartoon became yet another reason for buying *Red Lion*.

Until she worked on the magazine Rebecca had met Owain only in passing. If she thought about him at all, her impressions were positive. He seemed clever, modest, interesting . . . And then suddenly she was spending more time with him than with anyone else in her life.

'He's very much respected,' Ruth had told her breathlessly in the early days of their romance. 'It doesn't matter who he's talking to. He behaves the same with everyone.' The actress in Ruth led her to present a subtly altered persona, depending on whom she was with, and she marvelled at someone who seemed so sure of his own identity.

For some reason her words had stayed with Rebecca, and her early experience on *Red Lion* bore out the truth of them. From his years in political journalism Owain had a host of contacts he could call on for contributions to the magazine. To begin with Rebecca had been dazzled when political lions like Dick Crossman and Michael Foot telephoned to speak to him, though Ella put them through with her usual bored composure.

Owain's office consisted merely of a desk at the far end of the room, so Rebecca was able to bear witness to the fact that he treated these celebrities with the same mildly distant, rather amused amiability as he did his employees. She came to realize, though, that the seeming distance was deceptive. Owain was very much aware of them, their talents and their potential. He constantly encouraged them to break new ground and take risks, dismissing their own self-doubts.

'I've every confidence in you,' was the phrase he trotted out with a maddening calm, accompanied by a quirky, challenging grin.

'You'd say that if you packed me off to climb Everest in my underwear,' Ella retorted glumly once, as he sent her on a complicated trek to a variety of private libraries to research what she could find out about an obscure American political sect. But what he said was the truth. He believed in them. The knowledge was invaluable and Ella's mission was successful. They might not have been as stretched in another job, but neither would they have learned half as much.

With the reputation he'd already established Owain was able to attract a pool of established names to add lustre to the magazine. But he was always keen to give deserving new talent a chance, welcoming young hopefuls who came by with articles, ideas or artwork, offering them time and attention, staying late sometimes to make up for the working hours lost.

He had his faults of course. He could be curt, particularly when preoccupied. And Rebecca felt that he would always be handicapped by a secret, ingrained class consciousness, a legacy of his boyhood. He mistrusted money and posh accents and public school breeding. They made him wary and hostile in a way he could never quite hide. It was a weakness for someone in his profession, where it was important to get along with people, and where, anyway, appearances could be deceptive. Owain wasn't smooth enough, Rebecca thought. But sneakingly she liked him for it.

'You spend so much time with Owain. What's he like to work with?' Rebecca remembered Ruth asking her curiously one Sunday morning the previous summer, as they lounged in the living room of the Marshall Street flat with coffee and the papers. It was the most relaxing moment of Becky's week. Paul was still asleep and Ben was spending the weekend with his grandparents in Raynes Park. Richard had moved out some time earlier to set up home in Maida Vale with a girlfriend, a nurse. A Mozart horn concerto tootled upliftingly from the radiogram. Ruth had taken to borrowing classical records from the library recently. It was one of the many small ways in which she signalled her separateness from Paul.

Rebecca was engrossed in reading about the current Cyprus question. She looked up from the *Observer* and shrugged. 'Like working for Clark Kent and Superman rolled into one. With a little of Vladimir Ilyich Lenin thrown in for good measure.' Her reply had been brisk and mildly hostile – unfairly perhaps.

Ruth's question touched her on the raw. It assigned her to the old familiar role – that of the heroine's friend, the confidante. She had played it often since she'd known Ruth, accepted it with fairly good grace. But recently it had grated on her, probably because Owain showed signs of regarding her in the same light: asking her things about Ruth, fanning his passion by talking about her. Rebecca had experienced the same kind of irritation with him. She was caught in the middle. Her function, she supposed, was to smile on their love in a benevolent fashion. But no one had ever thought to ask her whether the role was to her liking.

In spite of her fondness for both of them, Rebecca was finding their mutual raptures a strain. In particular she found Owain's view of Ruth as the gallant little wife of an out-and-out bastard hard to take. The other night in the pub, after they'd been working late, Owain had referred slightingly to some recent misdemeanour of Paul's and Rebecca's patience had snapped.

'It's too easy,' she'd declared sharply, 'to dismiss Paul as a dyed-in-the-wool villain without one redeeming feature. If that was true, why on earth would Ruth have married him in the first place?' The force of her protest had startled her, and him, but she heard her voice continue, with a wealth of feeling. 'They're both alike, you know. Heads in the clouds. Contemptuous of anything practical. If it weren't for Paul's drinking they're actually very well suited.'

28

The night before Owain left for Wales, he and Ruth went to see a film called *Occupying Power*. It was the kind of unremarkable Hollywood movie they wouldn't normally have bothered with, but this film starred Dominique David, the French singer who'd been in the Resistance with Guy, Ruth's stepfather.

'I just know it's going to be awful,' Ruth said to Owain as they queued in the frosty February night. But she was highly curious. Her memories of Dominique were hazy but vivid at the same time. When she was a child, Ruth had known her for a time as a friend of her mother's. She recalled wild red hair, an exuberant grin, and an air of recklessness.

'Nothing wrong with a bit of good, honest corn.' Owain smiled, with an effort. He looked strained in the bleached fluorescent light of the cinema frontage. His thoughts were elsewhere. Tomorrow he'd be going home to where his father was lying gravely ill. Over the last year Ianto's cough had changed rapidly, from a thing so familiar that they barely noticed it to something sinister – a protracted, painful clearing of the throat, an inability to swallow. He'd lost weight and been persuaded, finally to seek medical advice. Cancer had been diagnosed and since then the illness had accelerated.

The visit to the cinema was partly an attempt to distract Owain. Ruth held his arm more tightly. She felt separated from him by the gloves, sweaters and wool coats that they wore against the cold, so that the love and support she wanted to communicate seemed somehow muffled.

Inside, they had to sit through the inevitable stodgy British B-movie, with its pipe-smoking detective in his mac, its urbane lawyer, the starlet with her crisp elocution, her sweater smoothed over firmly corseted breasts.

'I dreamed I was grilled by the prosecution in my Maidenform bra,' Owain whispered to Ruth, drily parodying a current advertising slogan.

The main feature was, unashamedly, a vehicle for Dominique, produced by the mogul with whom she was currently living. In his press photographs Ruth had thought him handsome in a foxy, gangsterish way, and the articles always stressed, with a quiver of titillation, his air of power and menace. At any rate he'd cashed in unabashedly on Dominique's Resistance legend, and in the process it had become monstrously Hollywoodized.

Dominique herself appeared to have been groomed for stardom, as they phrased it in *Moviegoer* magazine. Her vital, luxuriant hair had been tamed into a carefully pretty, feathery, face-framing style, and her complexion given a high, pink Technicolor blush. *Her* Maidenform bra was worn under a well-cut black dress, in order to defy a coldly sarcastic Nazi officer played by Klaus Netzen, an imported German actor who specialized in this kind of part.

'What a shame,' Ruth gasped, genuinely shocked by the suppression of Dominique's flamboyant individuality.

The character she played was spunky and fiery. All the same, Dominique spent an awful lot of the film gazing admiringly at the hero, Lloyd Bradford – a smoothie, smirky actor Ruth had always thought – as he despatched an unlikely number of sneering Nazis.

'In real life she's the one who killed . . .' Ruth shook her head unbelievingly.

There was a bewildering mixture of accents. Some of the Nazis were German and some American. And the discrepancy between Dominique's French vowels and Bradford's mid-Western tones was puzzling, since they were supposed to be the same nationality. The roles were undemanding stereotypes, but Dominique brought an unsettling sincerity to her part which upset the balance of the film. Ruth thought she was touching, with a truth and intensity that the bland material hardly merited, but her performance threw the movie out of kilter, causing some of the audience to titter nervously. In the dark, Ruth flushed with mortification at their reaction.

'What a waste!' Owain had carried a torch for Dominique since he'd seen her in Paris as a young soldier shortly after the end of the war.

'What on earth made her do it?' Ruth wondered aloud, as she and Owain walked arm in arm towards Soho in the cold, clear night. Guy had always stressed what a sure instinct Dominique had for choosing material that suited her. Ruth could only speculate wildly. Could it be that the legendary menace of her powerful lover had been brought to bear, causing Dominique to abandon her own native good sense?

'It was the money,' Owain said. 'What else?'

Ruth shook her head. 'I doubt it. According to Mum and Guy she was never much bothered about that.'

The film had temporarily succeeded in distracting Owain from his preoccupations, but now they came surging back like clouds passing across a sunlit landscape. He knew that in a matter of weeks his father would die.

A day or so ago he had asked Ruth how she would feel in the equivalent situation. She'd thought for a moment, then said slowly, 'I'd feel grief. Overwhelmingly. I'll miss my mother terribly. There'll be a . . . desolation at knowing she's not in the world any more.' Then she'd given the small shrug that he'd come to know as a mannerism of hers. 'But when it happens, I'll cope. It'll be sort of full circle. I love my mother, and I'm at peace with her. I don't think I'll feel guilt or regret.'

Owain hadn't replied. He'd been impressed by her sober realism. Ruth who was so quick and vivid, so . . . flighty, his mother, Jo, would have said. But in this she was sure and strong. Owain, whom she held to be the steady one, his own man, had no such ease. In his relationship with Ianto he was as resentful and confused as a boy.

Each time he hated to say goodnight to Ruth. When she left him she returned to a husband of sorts, a child, people who needed her, though they trapped her too. He'd be going back to his empty flat off Russell Square, and tomorrow to the bedside of a father who, even approaching death, would look at him with wary, evaluating eyes.

'I'll be thinking of you,' Ruth said. 'Every moment.' She was so beautiful, her blonde hair spilling over the shoulders of her coat. He loved her, and held her against him with a sort of violence.

'How was Abe Lincoln tonight?' Paul asked. He'd assigned to Owain the role of prig, bearded reformer, in an effort to cut him down to size. His speech was a little slurred but he appeared to be in reasonable shape. The room smelled of Scotch, but he'd cleared away the evidence.

'He was fine.' Ruth was distant and serene. Nowadays she hardly noticed her husband's jibes. He buzzed like a fly in a corner of her world. 'We saw a film . . . Ben's been okay, has he?'

'A little lamb.' Paul mimicked his own mother's fond phrase.

'I think I'll go to bed.' She made for the living-room door, still wearing her coat.

'Not a moment to pass the time of day with your hubby? I've been waiting up for you.' He raised an eyebrow. The harsh electric light showed brutally the alcoholic puffiness of his eyes. Each time the sight filled her with pain.

'I'm tired, Paul.'

Even before the advent of her affair with Owain they'd almost stopped sleeping together. It had been more Paul's choice than Ruth's. She could still see, bitingly clear, his apologetic grimace as he told her one night, with casual honesty, 'I've never fancied anyone as much as you, Marlene. But it's all become a bit predictable.'

She'd finally realized then that he hankered after the nervous tension of the first encounters, when Shirl, his landlady, could have walked in on them at any moment. His words had cut deep and devastating. For her, the slow, sensuous sexual exploration of the first years of their marriage had been a revelation. She found it almost inconceivable that Paul would seek out quick, shallow couplings in preference, craving the risky urgency she found so unsatisfying.

Now she was numbed against this particular pain. As she'd guessed on that October afternoon in France, more than a year ago, Owain's shrewd and thoughtful presence, his smile, green eyes and wiry body would absorb most of her interest and energy, and her awareness of Paul receded accordingly. Ben apart, Owain had become the focus of her life.

She loved and admired him almost without reserve. And Owain's infatuation with her was like a mirror, reflecting back a flattering, enhanced self-image, restoring a confidence eroded by years of passivity. She became assertive and organized herself.

With the co-operation of Becky as babysitter, she had enrolled in a once-a-week drama workshop in Bethnal Green. Coincidentally it was run by an ex-member of the Manchester Experimental Company. His name was Ryan

Jaquier and he was a bull-necked, shock-haired actor in his late thirties.

'He's a bit of a bully, actually,' she told Becky. 'But he packs punch.'

Now, when she pictured her week, Thursday night was ringed with a luminous halo. Ruth travelled to Bethnal Green on the Central Line, then walked through inhospitable streets to a dark, Dickensian pub. They met in a large upstairs room.

'It's a bit like a secret society,' Ruth claimed, laughing. 'Never seeing one another outside the community room of the White Horse.'

Many of the other actors were younger than herself, a few barely out of drama school. There were aspiring James Deans, and hopeful Juliette Grecos with long hair and black-rimmed eyes. At first Ruth had felt abashed. She was twenty-eight now, and felt positively matronly in this company. But her embarrassment quickly evaporated. Age and sex were supremely unimportant as they screamed like banshees or mimed a herd of buffaloes stampeding over a cliff, or performed other exercises that any layperson would have found ludicrous and inexplicable.

Between them they devised and improvised their own material, drawing recklessly on their personal experiences and emotions. To do this you had to trust your fellow actors. Ryan, for all his boisterousness, his lumbering bulk, was miraculously able to foster an atmosphere where this was possible. Over the months they learned to jettison their inhibitions, expose their feelings and take risks without the fear of being sniggered at. Ruth realized then how much she'd missed this joint experimentation during the last homebound years.

'It's probably better than psychoanalysis,' she told Owain. After the sessions she was drained and at peace, but exhilarated, with a sort of heightened affection for the other members of the group who, like her, had shown themselves vulnerable and figuratively naked. 'There gets to be such a bond between you, though if I met them in real life I might not even like them.'

She found, too, that the intervening years had changed her, deepened her knowledge and awareness of life. Things no longer seemed as black or white as they once had, and this added a dimension of thoughtfulness to her youthful panache, which she hadn't lost. The change had made her in some way more original. She no longer opted for the first impetuous idea that occurred, but looked further into herself for truth and nuance.

'You really surprise me at times,' Ryan said to her one evening. 'Sometimes I think I'm jaded, I've seen everything, then some nights you find a reaction that's totally unexpected, but so true . . .' He wasn't one for personal praise so the remark pleased her. She recalled the joy of performing and felt that she'd made a small but decisive step towards regaining a career. With the class, and Owain, and Ben growing up – he went to nursery school twice a week – Ruth had the impression that her life was becoming full and hopeful again.

However, the place in her life occupied by Paul had shifted radically. In some ways now he seemed to her like a wayward, exasperating brother, a permanent but often worrying fixture. His drinking had gained momentum, though he was still in control up to a point. Ruth knew that if she left him in charge of Ben he'd limit his intake to a safe level. He still led the Wailers – though the upturn in their fortunes had somewhat dissipated – and did the plumbing jobs that had become their major source of income, eked out by his share of a legacy from relations of his mother's and a part-time job Ruth had found in a nearby restaurant.

Still, there were times when Paul was brought home incapable, carried almost bodily from a taxi by some old friend like Richard, or Vince, the Wailers' sultry-eyed trumpeter. At such times, while they helped Ruth manoeuvre him up the fire escape and into bed, they made it clear that they saw her as some kind of saintly, wronged wife.

She knew now, though, with an absolute certainty, that nothing she could do or say would deter Paul from his self-destructive bouts of drinking, so she accepted them. All she could do was be there until inevitably, sooner or later, his health cracked. Frequently Owain urged her to leave Paul to his own devices, almost pleading with her to bring Ben and come and live with him. He was earnest and impatient by turns, but Ruth was adamant. In the foreseeable future she was going to stay.

'I remember Mum saying that she waited six years for Guy during the war, without even knowing whether he was dead or alive.' She'd given Owain the vulnerable grin he found hard to resist. 'So I think my stubbornness must be inborn.' She never for a moment forgot Paul's open-hearted acceptance of what was possibly another man's child. That moment on dark, windy Llandudno beach had been more decisive for him than he would ever realize.

In spite of his own philandering, she knew that Paul found her affair with Owain painfully hard to accept. It was too important. The bargain that he'd flaunted at her a thousand times in their disputes had rebounded on him.

Once, lying in a semi-stupor across their bed, he'd said to her, 'I hate that priggish bastard. He's filled your head so there's no room for me, and it hurts . . .' His voice was thick as if he were talking through sleep. She was surprised. Such self-revelation was rare from Paul nowadays. 'I need you, Ruth,' he mumbled. 'God, I need you.'

He was hot, possibly feverish. She laid cool hands on his forehead. 'You've got me.'

29

Owain watched his father as he slept in the dim bedroom. His parents' bedroom. It had been the same all his life, with the upright iron bedstead and the framed print of the Swallow Falls at Betws-y-Coed, tinted in faded ochres, blues and greens. Jo had made a few changes recently, though. The walls had been re-papered with a design of small, brownish flowers, and the useless pink curtains, which admitted every ray of dawn light, had finally crumbled away to nothing and been replaced by a more serviceable maroon pair.

Ianto lay beneath the much-laundered floral cotton spread that had always been on the bed he shared with Jo. His face was passive and earth-coloured, and shockingly thin. He lay like that for much of the day. The hospital had sent him home, saying there was nothing further they could do for him. The last operation had stemmed the advance of the cancer in his throat for only a short time. It had been explained to Jo that further surgery would probably be ineffective as well as hugely distressing. She'd accepted the news with resigned courage. The end could come at any time – in days or weeks.

Owain had urged his mother to take a day off, go and see Nancy, her daughter-in-law, and the children. She appeared worn out with looking after Ianto day and night, and he was on her mind constantly. Not that she'd have had it any other way, but a break could only do her good.

'Just tell me what to do,' Owain said, though there wasn't much in the short run. Ianto had to be turned every so often to prevent bedsores, taken to the toilet, and offered drinks and soup, but he hadn't much appetite.

Preoccupied with the launching of the magazine, Owain knew he hadn't been home as often as he should have during the last year. He'd followed the course of his father's illness largely from a distance. On the rare occasions he'd visited Ianto, both in the hospital and at home, his father had looked older and thinner, but nothing like this. It had been a physical shock to see his present emaciation. Ianto's condition left him unable to swallow anything more substantial than milk or soup, and over the weeks and months his limbs had wasted to little more than bones covered by skin, and his cheeks had become shrunken, bringing his teeth and eyes into painful prominence. Immediately Owain had been put in mind of the archetypal victim of a Nazi concentration camp . . . He still found difficulty in equating this wraith with the hale, powerful figure he remembered.

As he watched by the bedside, Owain's mind wandered. He had arrived the previous day and was still imbued with his London life. It was Thursday, and Ruth would be attending her acting workshop that evening. He smiled. He'd never seen her there but it pleased him to imagine her, trim and workmanlike in sweater and trousers, among anonymous others, and to visualize their earnest discussions, the ritualized exercises and heightened emotions, and Ruth with her playful radiance brightening the drab, echoing room.

He knew with calm certainty that since they'd been together Ruth had been happier and more purposeful. And that she loved him. She showed that all the time, in so many ways. He had believed that therefore he could persuade her to leave that bastard of a Paul . . . But some quixotic, misplaced loyalty made her as immovable as stone – at least for now. If he thought that it would always be so . . . He coveted her incandescent glow fiercely for his own life.

Ianto stirred.

287

'Can I do something for you, Dad?' His voice seemed to ruffle the air in the silent room. But his father's feeble movements stilled themselves.

'Don't bother him if he's sleeping,' Jo had said.

Ianto relapsed into immobility and Owain returned to his thoughts. The magazine was always on his mind. It was hard for him to absent himself from something he was so involved in. But he'd phoned Rebecca from the pub at lunch time – his parents didn't have a phone – and she'd assured him that everything was fine. 'Couldn't be better.' There'd been a laugh in her voice when she teased him, saying, 'So you see, Owain, you're not indispensable . . .'

She always made it sound as if her responsibilities sat lightly on her, but he knew from his own experience how thorough she was, and capable. The combination of qualities set his mind at rest. He placed enormous trust in her. She was cordial but self-contained – her own person. Unguardedly in the early days he'd talked to Rebecca about Ruth, and about his hopes that she would come and live with him. But he'd understood gradually that Becky was reluctant to discuss such things. Presumably she preferred to keep her work and her private life in separate compartments. With a quiet stubbornness she'd refused the role of go-between. Owain had come to respect her for it.

He heard the sudden intake of breath that heralded Ianto's speaking. His voice was variable now, sometimes a dry, almost soundless whisper, at other times some of the volume returned, coupled with a thick roughness like a stage drunk's.

'Do you want something, Dad?'

'Want a piss.' The words sounded like a death rattle.

Ianto was still capable, with help, of taking himself to the lavatory. When Owain had been a boy there'd been an outside privy, the stone floor smelling harshly of disinfectant. Since those days an inside toilet had been installed downstairs, but Ianto was too weak even for that trek. A sombrely gleaming item of furniture had been borrowed from somewhere and installed in the bedroom. It bore the oddly genteel name of a commode.

Owain struggled to help his father from the bed. There was a method, he knew, but he was clumsy and unpractised. Ianto became impatient. Jo had the knack. He didn't like her going out. He'd become dependent and tyrannical.

Owain supported his father's frail body. With his job, Ianto had been muscled and fit into middle age – until the illness. Now he was light as a child, a bag of bones. Owain experienced a moment of shamefaced revulsion.

Ianto could barely stand at the commode, and his head drooped as if with blank apathy. Owain loosened the striped pyjama trousers and they fell in a heap at his feet. The skin of his father's bottom and legs hung in folds from his shrunken frame, as if he were wearing a suit grotesquely too large. He looked defenceless, ridiculous. Without warning Owain felt the pricking of tears. It was as if there had been some kind of macabre role reversal, so that abruptly Ianto became the child, and Owain his protector.

He swallowed, regaining his self-control, and stood hovering, ready to step in if his father's legs buckled. Out of nowhere a sudden memory surfaced. Himself, aged perhaps fourteen, arriving home late from the house of a teacher friend, Holman Hughes. He'd gone to borrow books for a history essay. They'd got talking and hadn't noticed the time passing.

'It's so late.' Holman was mortified. 'Apologize to your parents for me.'

Owain had let himself in the back door. The kitchen was in darkness. Jo was out, he knew. He switched on the light. Ianto was waiting. Without a word he'd struck his son across the face, sending him sprawling on the tiled floor. 'Can't wait to get away from us, can you!' Ianto snarled, a twisted, passionate look on his face. A look of hatred, Owain thought. 'Can't even be bothered to get home on time. Too busy hobnobbing with that bloody . . .'

Owain had loathed his father's brute strength and loathed him even more for insulting courteous, gentle Mr Hughes. He pulled himself slowly to his feet. 'He's better than you . . .' His voice was sullen. He'd wanted to sound controlled, contemptuous.

'We're your family!' Ianto had seized him by the shoulders and shaken him in a frenzy of anger. 'We're the ones that go without so you can waste your time at school.' His face, close to Owain's, had been red, uncontrolled, ugly. Ever after, when he remembered that moment, Owain experienced a cold, still fury.

He'd not thought of the incident in years. Yet now, picturing Ianto's expression at the time, he read into it a new dimension – a vulnerability, a deep, unspoken hurt. Seeing the episode abruptly in an altered light. In any case, it was hard to equate the powerful tyrant of his memory with this wrecked being.

Owain stooped, pulling up and tying his father's baggy pyjama trousers as he might have done for Ben. Ianto showed no emotion at the indignity and allowed himself to be shuffled back to bed.

Jo insisted on being home for tea time so she could cook some fresh soup to tempt her husband. She came downstairs, wry and disappointed, to where Owain sat by the stove in the kitchen. 'Two mouthfuls,' she said with a resigned grimace. 'He's given up.'

'It's got to be faced,' Owain said gently.

Jo turned down her mouth at such defeatist talk. She'd made a panful of the soup and now shared it out between the two of them, cutting bread and cheese to go with it. They sat silently eating at opposite ends of the bare table. There didn't seem much point in bothering with cloths and things at the moment, Jo said. The wall clock ticked loudly in the hushed room.

'He's pleased you're here, Owain,' she remarked, out of the blue.

He looked up, wearing the closed, sardonic expression that had become his automatic reaction to any talk of himself and Ianto.

'Don't look like that.' Jo studied him and shook her head. 'He's been hard on you, God knows. But, Owain, you should've understood him better.' She pushed her empty soup plate a little way to the side and pulled the plate with the bread and cheese towards her. 'You're supposed to be the clever one.' Her voice faltered. She looked down at the table, sudden tears blurring her eyes. 'You should've understood him better.'

In bed that night Owain was restless. His day had been inactive. He had energy and nothing to do with it. He lay, turning impressions of the past hours over in his mind, visualizing his mother's tired, puffy features, Ianto's skull-like face on the pillow. The visions recalled contrasting images. He was reminded of one New Year's holiday shortly after the war – it must have been ten or eleven years ago. He'd been in his early twenties, studying in London on a serviceman's scholarship and home briefly for the festive season.

No, it must have been '47. New Year's Day. The day the Labour Government had passed the Bill nationalizing the coalmines. The Bill Ianto and his like had been fighting for all their working lives. In mining villages up and down the country there were dances, marches, bonfires and socials. Carreg-Brân was no exception. He remembered seeing Jo and Ianto dressed up ready for the fun, and thinking, with a flash of pride, how youthful they looked, how full of life. Jo had on a red dress. Her hair was still glossy and dark, and waved like a Hollywood filmstar's. Ianto's powerful body was encased in a blue suit, with a striped shirt and a tie; his hair, already white, had been thick and alive round his ruddy face.

There'd been a dance. Everyone in the village was there and Ianto was the hero of the hour, kissed and clapped on the shoulder at every turn. They all knew how hard he'd fought from the age of eighteen. Ianto had been expansive, with a smile and a joke for everyone. Owain thought that night was probably the high spot of his father's life. Nothing since had ever been as clear-cut, as straightforwardly pleasurable.

He could remember standing with his brother, William, by the makeshift bar, and watching Ianto clowning as he danced with the sexy, fat wife of a colleague.

'Look at Dad. What a villain.' William had grinned, his face shining with affection.

But for years Owain had been incapable of simple, open feeling towards his father. 'He deserves tonight,' he'd replied stiffly, with an effort, and he meant it. But the spring of love was dammed up. That night, and now, Owain experienced a dull, spreading pang of regret.

Ianto got used to his son's presence over the next three days and Owain became accustomed to his father's invalid routine, confining his horizons to the four walls of the house. He became skilful at feeding, lifting and washing Ianto, and came to notice, as Jo did, the small signs indicating that he was thirsty, too hot or uncomfortable.

He rang Rebecca daily to discuss the progress of the magazine. She asked sympathetically after his father, but there was no mistaking the happy confidence in her voice. She was enjoying being in charge. She urged him not to worry about work. There was no need; they were coping. 'If you want to stay, or feel you should, then go ahead.'

Owain found that he did want to. It was obvious that Jo was comforted by his presence. And a dying man, a dying father – however estranged – had rights.

He came to realize with surprise that Jo had spoken the truth. Ianto *was* glad to have him there. Although he seemed already half in another world, there was the shadow of a smile when Owain offered him water, straightened the pillow, or drew the curtains to let in the weak February sunshine. Owain found it difficult to harden his heart against this frail, dependent being. Ianto spoke little now, and any conversation they did have was purely functional, but the old antagonism seemed somehow absent.

'You should have understood him better,' Jo had said. It occurred to Owain that perhaps Ianto had suffered too because of their hostility. Since Owain had been a boy his father had been closed to him. Ianto would have considered it weakness to discuss his feelings or show hurt. The past couldn't be undone, but Owain found himself regarding his father with a new kindness.

On the fifth day of Owain's stay Ianto became restless and seemed troubled, plucking at the bedclothes and reaching with his stick-like arms into the air for something that wasn't there. That night he left his bed and stumbled on to the landing. Jo was sleeping downstairs on a Put-U-Up. Owain heard his father moving about and came and found him, a disconcerting, almost nightmarish figure in the half-darkness with his wild-eyed emaciation. He led his father back to bed and spent an hour trying to calm him.

The next day Jo phoned the doctor. She was frightened Ianto would hurt himself if he started to sleepwalk. He was so weak.

The doctor prescribed morphine. 'It won't be long now,' he told them. 'A matter of days.'

The medicine calmed him but reduced communication. There were no more smiles, no hoarse, terse instructions. Ianto lay seemingly in a state of suspension, neither sleeping nor waking. Every so often the restlessness returned, but their voices reassured him.

'Keep talking to him,' the visiting nurse told them. 'He can hear you. Hearing's the last thing to go.'

At night Owain sat up with him. He was better able than Jo to cope with the lack of sleep. For him those nights had their own kind of peace, with the silent street outside and the small reading lamp burning in a corner of the room.

On Friday, in the small hours, Ianto was restless again. Owain pulled his chair up close to the bed and talked to him soothingly. 'It's okay, Dad,' he kept saying. 'It's okay. I'm here. It's Owain.' He took his father's hand. It lay in his, dry and cool. By and by, Ianto drifted back into passivity. Owain watched him with a calm, quiet affection that was new to him.

His father died the following afternoon. He and Jo sat by while Ianto's breathing slowed until it was barely perceptible, then stopped with a soft shudder. Owain could tell the very moment of his death. Afterwards he held his mother as she sobbed passionately against him. His own tears came, unforeseen and miraculous, welling slowly, like blood from a stone.

'The funeral's Thursday. And he'll be coming back the following day.' Rebecca passed on the information to Ruth. Under the circumstances she could hardly stick to her rule not to act as messenger. Owain and Ruth had a pact that he'd never phone her at home.

'Wonderful!' Ruth was flushed with pleasure, looking up from the table where she and Ben sat eating a tea of garlic mushrooms on toast. The recipe was her latest craze and Ben had a strangely sophisticated passion for it.

'Thanks for telling me, Becky.' Ruth, too, had come to respect her friend's determination not to be caught in the crossfire between herself and Owain. She added with comical ruefulness, 'I don't half miss him.'

'I expect you do.' Rebecca thought her own voice sounded dry and ungiving.

'Come and sit down,' Ruth invited. 'There are more mushrooms. I'll do some for you.'

Rebecca shook her head. 'No, I'm only passing through. I'm going to the pictures.'

'Oh, Becky.' Ruth gave a breathy laugh. 'Such a social whirl.' She was teasing, but Rebecca saw a shadow of disappointment in her eyes. She always felt a bit mean when she hadn't time for Ruth. In spite of everything, her friend was still a restricted young mother. All the same, Rebecca told herself, she'd been steadfast in offering Ruth her Thursday nights so that she could get out to her drama group.

She went upstairs to find clean clothes and brush her hair. Bobby from work had asked her to go with him to a film club in Bayswater to see a movie by some Swedish director he thought was God. She found a high-necked sweater and warm trousers and put them on. It was cold, a night for her dufflecoat, though she didn't wear it as often as she had as a student.

Rebecca looked into the long mirror to brush her hair. She was thin again. Quite often, absorbed in some task at work, she forgot to eat lunch. I ought to take sandwiches, she resolved vaguely.

A pair of small silver snakes hung from her ears. They'd been left in her predecessor's desk after she went to Australia. Owain had found them one morning and fastened them on her. 'They're a badge of office,' he joked. Rebecca had worn them ever since. She wasn't one for vanity, but she thought them unusual, and liked the way they gleamed sombrely against her shoulder-length dark hair.

In the last days an uneasiness had crept into her relationship with Ruth, though she didn't think Ruth was aware of it yet. Owain was the trouble. Rebecca experienced a pang of despondency, a disagreeable feeling that she'd rarely encountered in her active young life. Finally she could no longer ignore thoughts that for months she'd sublimated, buried and denied. Owain was the trouble. Talking to him on the phone had made that clear to her. He had sounded drained and emotional, unable to summon up the ironic distance he put between himself and others. The laughter and pub chat she could hear in the background seemed to her to emphasize his private disarray. Listening, she had the futile longing to comfort him physically, hold him close against her, with her arms round him. The image had given her such pleasure that she allowed her mind to linger on it, even while she reported on the progress of a long-running dispute with the printer, forcing herself to sound cheerful and in control.

'Everything's fine,' she assured him repeatedly. And it was. The challenge of running the magazine was meat and drink to her. On the surface all was as it should be. But simultaneously Rebecca found herself bewildered and disorientated by feelings which had taken her by surprise, and which – now she'd admitted their existence – seemed to expand and fill her head. Stupid, useless feelings, since Owain was Ruth's to love and not hers.

'Beck! Look at this!' From downstairs Ruth whooped with excitement.

Rebecca grabbed her dufflecoat and went to join her. Ruth and Ben were watching their new acquisition – a television set with a nine-inch screen, the gift, predictably, of Paul's parents, who'd invested in a larger model for themselves.

A small, grey figure capered on the screen. '. . . Look at me, boys and girls, you wouldn't think I was a married man . . .' The sound quality was a bit crackly, but there was something in the tone of the voice that struck a chord.

'Look who it is!' Ruth was ecstatic.

'Watch it! Watch it!' The performer stuck both hands on his hips, shifting his pelvis with a slight, petulant movement. 'I'm not having you on . . .'

'Oh, my God!' Realization dawned on Rebecca. 'I don't believe it!'

On the tiny screen Eric King pouted, postured and bridled as he used to on the stage of the Illyria Theatre. They watched, entranced. For television his jokes were less suggestive, but apart from that his act hadn't changed.

'Well, you're a rum lot!' He still had the same catch-phrase. Satirically the two women chanted it along with him, echoing perfectly his timing and inflexion.

Ruth was bright-eyed with nostalgia. 'Gosh, Becky, doesn't it take you back?'

Rebecca was caught off-guard by a sentimental tug of friendship for her. Hastily she looked at her watch. 'Is that the time? I must rush.'

'Enjoy yourself.' Ruth stood up and gave her a quick kiss. 'Cheerio, me old beauty,' she added, in a lightning, spot-on imitation of Walter Gabriel from *The Archers*.

Rebecca was dubious. 'Bobby's tastes are a bit more avant-garde than mine.' She bustled to dispel a twinge of conscience at Ruth's show of affection.

30

'I've an idea. Why don't we have a little game? Let's pretend that we're human beings and that we're actually alive . . .' On stage a young actor harangued two others. He was eloquent and abrasive, with a raw, bullying power and he seemed drunk on the words that poured from his mouth. Ruth was on the edge of her seat, rapt with a kind of recognition.

Look Back in Anger at the Royal Court Theatre had caused a bigger stir than any play she could remember. People claimed that here at last was a true warts-and-all picture of post-war youth. Jimmy Porter, the hero, was hostile, voluble and passionate, both cruel and tender to his beautiful, passive, middle-class wife. A male friend was trapped in the middle, loving them both and valiantly trying to defuse the grinding conflict between them with his own stubborn good humour.

The critics had been sharply divided in their verdict on the play. Some had loathed and detested the hero and everything they thought he stood for, suggesting that a stiff upper lip was the proper solution to his self-obsessed anger. Others stated that the play had a truth and intensity which shamed the sterile good taste that had bedevilled the British theatre for years. One reviewer exulted that the author had managed to contain both the class war and the sex war in the same powerful package. At every performance a proportion of the audience walked out in high dudgeon and went home to write outraged letters to the newspapers. The rest stayed to cheer.

Watching, Ruth reflected with a glimmer of amusement that the Porter household held definite echoes of her own home life in Marshall Street. And, as the hero inveighed against a whole range of targets, his style was oddly familiar to her. He talked like Paul or Owain or Becky – like other people they knew – with a haphazard mixture of anger and dark humour, earnestness and irreverence. Real people spoke like that, but you didn't expect to hear it on the stage. She observed the actors like a hawk, identifying with them – both male and female – actively, passionately. They seemed exhilarated by the play and liberated by the aggressive language, performing their roles with total conviction. She watched with envy and a kind of hunger, narrow-eyed, forgetting herself.

Owain observed her covertly, dividing his attention between Ruth and the stage. He was intrigued by her total, rapacious attention. Normally during a film or play they touched and exchanged glances. Here he was excluded. Ruth was transfixed by the performance. In the dim light her profile was rapt and unmoving, her gaze fixed, lips slightly parted.

'What d'you think then?' As the lights went up for the first interval Owain touched her arm. It was like attracting the attention of a sleepwalker. Ruth turned to him with glazed, absent eyes.

'It's brilliant.' She shook her head, rousing herself. 'Brilliant. Don't you think?'

He smiled and agreed. Owain admired the vitriol of the language, though he had a sneaking sympathy with the blimps who labelled Jimmy Porter a gutless whiner. But Ruth was spellbound. He was touched by her fervour and didn't want to quibble.

'I haven't seen anything in . . .' – she gave the small shrug he knew so well – '. . . years that made me want to be in it so badly.'

During the rest of the play her absorption never flagged for a second. Owain thought how they both approached it from their own point of view. The play made Ruth ache to flex her acting muscles. As far as he was concerned, his interest had been aroused by the critic of *Home Counties* magazine – reputedly senile – who declared damningly that Jimmy Porter was the type of wretched, pseudo-intellectual scruff who read *Red Lion* each week, and that he resembled one of the babbling malcontents who railed endlessly in Miss Rebecca Street's weekly interview.

'Can we quote him?' Rebecca had been charmed by the accolade. 'What an advert!'

After the wary, disturbing ending there was a silence before the audience began to clap. Then the applause went on and on. People stood and cheered. There was more to it, Ruth reflected, than the heralding of an arresting new play. It was as if an honest blow had been struck, in real life, against hypocrisy and stifling good taste. There was a sense of liberation in the shouting. Paul would have loved this, Ruth thought. She sensed that Owain was sceptical of the mass raptures. Paul would have gone along with them, suspending cynicism.

She always loved the moment when, at the end of a play, the actors stepped out of character and became themselves, life-sized and smiling. Tonight she almost felt as if she were one of them, so fierce was her identification. She could sense the knowledge, behind their eyes, of the weeks of hope, doubt and discouragement, leading up to this minute that justified it all.

As they left the theatre Owain had his arm tight around her. It was as if he were aware of the strength of her feelings and wanted to enter into her mind and become a part of them. But tonight Ruth was closed and cautious. For her, the experience had been so personal that she was scared to share it. Talk could dissipate the magic. If she kept silent, the memory of it could be held inside her, whole and untouched.

Outside, in the miraculously light May evening, she

looked at him, half-apologetic. 'We won't talk about the play, Owain, if you don't mind. Not tonight. It's one of those things . . . I need time to sort out my thoughts about it.'

He shrugged. 'As you like.' There was an almost imperceptible flicker of hurt in his eyes, as though her withdrawal had wider implications.

'Don't be cross.' Ruth offered him the oblique smile she knew from experience he couldn't resist.

On the way home they discussed Paul instead. Having denied Owain her thoughts on one subject, Ruth compensated by taking him into her confidence on another. There was plenty of time for them to talk. After they'd been out, both of them liked to walk home, prolonging the evening, relishing the precious time alone together.

Ruth rarely spoke to Owain about her husband. In a sense it seemed disloyal. And she found it increasingly hard to justify to Owain her determination to stay with him. Even to justify it to herself. But the stubborn gut reaction remained.

'You know, I left Ben with his grandparents tonight,' she said, as they wandered down Piccadilly under the starry, navy-blue sky. 'I've stopped leaving him with Paul.'

'Why's that?' Owain was sharply curious.

'To be absolutely honest, I'm not sure I trust him any more . . .' She backpedalled hastily. 'Don't get me wrong. I've no thoughts of his harming Ben. He loves him . . . But his drinking's getting uncontrolled. He's getting more and more unpredictable.'

They walked on in silence for a while. Owain didn't question her. She'd accused him in the past of being too eager to hear bad things about Paul.

'He's pretty depressed,' Ruth mused. 'The band's not going well.' His brand of traditional jazz was taking a knocking from the dynamic American novelty, rock 'n' roll. Paul and the others had seen themselves as lawless trailblazers, but the young were beginning to look elsewhere, and they could now see themselves being relegated gradually to a fringe position as guardians of a quaint but limited branch of popular music. Bookings were falling off. 'Paul's coming up to thirty,' Ruth added drily, 'and he's not taking it very well.'

Another pause, then Ruth said, 'We went to see his parents a couple of Sundays ago. He's ever so fond of them and he's always on his best behaviour . . . But he was strange and unsteady before we left, though I hadn't seen him drinking. I wanted to cancel, but he wouldn't.' He'd looked awful that day. She could see him still, glassy-eyed, careful in his movements like an old man. 'They only have sherry in the house. He drank a couple of smallish glasses, then he had a sort of blackout. I and his father helped him upstairs to lie down. I went up to see him after an hour or so, and he was talking nonsense, just babbling.' He'd recovered later and made light of the incident, but it had scared her. She'd talked to him for ages the following day, urging him, begging him to see a doctor, seek professional help, but he refused point blank.

They crossed into Regent Street, its lights mellow under the velvety sky. There were still plenty of people about this spring evening. Ruth glanced at Owain walking beside her. He was withdrawn, shoulders hunched, hands deep in the pockets of his jacket. She felt a kind of bleeding in her heart. She loved him and she hurt him. That was the position, the way it was. He said nothing, but she knew that silently he was crying out for her to quit the wreckage of her marriage, come to him, take the step.

Why didn't she?

Ruth imagined Ben's confusion at the change, Paul's desolation . . . Would it be selfish or brave to make the decision? She no longer felt capable of judging.

* * *

I hope he's asleep. I do hope so, Ruth thought. Sometimes now she actually dreaded her encounters with Paul. Recently, each time she saw him he seemed to be someone different. Infrequently he displayed the charm and odd humour that she used to love in him. She could almost imagine that nothing had changed. But more often he would flaunt a maudlin cynicism, seeming red-faced and coarse-looking. The other night he'd grabbed her by the upper arms and shaken her with a bullying air she didn't recognize. Ben had been in bed, luckily, and knew nothing about it. In any case, she didn't think it would happen again. Paul wasn't violent . . .

However, Ben had begun to notice his changes of mood. 'Daddy's nasty today,' he'd said matter of factly the previous week, with no more emphasis than if he was commenting on the weather. That worried her. Up till then she'd clung to the thought that their father-son relationship was unaffected.

A square of light shone in the kitchen window at the top of the fire escape. That didn't mean anything. Paul left it on as a matter of course to light her way up the skeletal black steps. The door was open. She went in, remembering that Richard had been coming over. There was some jazz programme on the television that they were planning to watch and have a few beers at the same time. It was quiet in the flat. Paul must have gone to bed. He'd have locked up if he were going out.

Passing through the kitchen and into the hall, Ruth noticed a slit of reddish light in the living-room doorway. The corner lamp must be on, the one with the red shade. A split second later she heard a quiet, scuffling noise and started. Paul must be up after all. Ruth pushed open the door and entered the room.

'What on earth . . .?'

Paul lay face down on the carpet. He was conscious, moving, and yet, even at first glance, he appeared to be in an oblivious world of his own. He didn't look up as she came in, but seemed preoccupied with the pattern on the carpet, scratching and tracing it obsessively with the fingers of one hand.

'Paul, what's happened?' She was horribly shaken by his strangeness.

He didn't acknowledge her in any way, but remained scrabbling, like some dying insect . . . The room stank of stale Scotch and vomit. There was no sign of Richard.

Ruth knelt beside her husband. 'I'll get you to bed, Paul. Can you walk?'

He turned to look at her, but his eyes seemed sightless and there was no flicker of recognition on his face. The emptiness was shocking. She experienced a chill of fear. Placing her arms round his body, Ruth tried to lift him. Recently he hardly ate and seemed malnourished, but his inertia made him a dead weight, too awkward for her to shift.

Becky. Ruth went upstairs to find her, but she wasn't home. She couldn't face the long-drawn-out process of rousing Ernest Broadbent and explaining . . . There was Richard. She could try phoning him.

Ruth sat down in a chair and watched with a clenched horror as he lay plucking at the carpet. Her vital, abrasive Paul looked like a senile old man. She closed her eyes momentarily to blot out the degraded image.

'I'll phone for an ambulance.'

The resolution came to her with an abrupt clarity, though she saw the idea as a betrayal – to let strangers come and take him away. Her husband. He trusted her. But there was relief in the prospect. Involving the authorities would mean that the problem was out in the open. He'd be taken care of, saved from himself. And she would no longer have to struggle with the knowledge of her own impotence.

304

She might feel like a traitor, but the world would approve her action as right and responsible. She sat for a moment longer, delaying the finality of it, then roused herself. Best get it over with.

31

Just when everyone was telling her how complicated her life had become, Ruth was finding everything far simpler. Ben was one priority. Earning money was another. Everything else fitted in round the edges.

When Paul was taken into hospital Sarah had begged her to bring Ben and come and live in Provence for a while. Alternatively she herself would come over to Marshall Street and stay, bringing practical help and moral support. Ruth had been grateful and touched, but almost surprised by her offer. Now that Paul was in good hands she felt that her worries were ending rather than beginning. But she accepted her mother's offer of a loan to tide her over, and used most of it to pay her rent for the next six months. On top of the other upheavals in his life she had no desire to confuse Ben further by moving him into some strange bedsitter.

He went to nursery school each morning now. And Ruth had found a baby-minder, a Mrs Francioli, who would pick him up at lunch time and look after him until three, when Ruth returned from her waitressing job in Old Compton Street. Ruth wasn't mad on the woman. Her curiosity about Paul struck her as prurient and lip-smacking, but Ben seemed to get on with her all right, and that was the main thing. Ruth was aware that she was not now entitled to the luxury of agonizing over what was right for Ben. It was quite simple. She, Ruth, had to earn their living and he had to be looked after. She found a certain peace in the lack of choice.

There were days when he wasn't keen to go to nursery school, but she had to leave him anyway. Invariably later on he'd forgotten his morning tantrums. Children were tougher than you thought, and by and large Ben seemed to accept the new regime quite philosophically. Her main worry was paying for the nursery school and the baby-minder, which made large inroads into the far from princely sum she earned waitressing. But in September Ben would be starting school proper, so that would sort itself out. Becky had always said Ruth had her head in the clouds. Maybe that was why such practical problems seemed hardly to touch her. You did what you had to do and that was an end to it.

The first time Ruth went to visit Paul in the Middlesex Hospital she walked right past him. She carried on across the gleaming floor to the end of the ward, glancing to right and left at figures stretched out passively on beds or wanly upright in chairs, whiling away the long hospital afternoon. No Paul. She was puzzled. This was definitely the right place. She retraced her steps, examining the charts hanging on the bed-rails.

She found his name, Paul Macdonald, and glanced towards the occupant of the bay. Gooseflesh broke out on her body as she recognized her husband in a figure she'd scanned briefly and dismissed as too ill and too old. Perhaps because – as she later realized – he was sedated, Paul looked to her far worse even than when she'd last seen him, inert on the floor of their home. He was somnolent. His head lay at an angle against the grey leatherette of his upright chair. His eyes were heavy and almost closed, the skin around them the colour of dry earth. All the muscles of his face seemed slack and he wore a pair of striped hospital pyjamas that were several sizes too large. All the time she'd known him Paul had never worn pyjamas. A blanket lay across his knees. His hands traced the weave of it, plucking at threads, never still. This last detail shocked her more than any other.

She bent towards him and said softly, 'Paul.'

His eyes flickered open, gazing at her for what seemed minutes before they lit into an expression of wan recognition.

'Hallo.' A vague attempt at a smile.

Ruth sat down on a footstool opposite him. All she could think of was to frame the vapid question, 'How are you?'

Even drugged, there was a black, distant humour in his grin. 'Just great.' His voice was thick and his eyes stared dully at her from under drooping lids. 'Jus' great, darlin'.'

She took his hand, trapped it rather, to hold it still. 'God, you scared me the other night. You really did.'

He said nothing, but looked at her and nodded just perceptibly, as though it were his last reaction before falling into a profound sleep.

'They wouldn't let me see you before.'

This time there was just blankness. Not even the flicker of an eye. Talking to him was like throwing stones down a bottomless well.

Ruth had been expecting him to reproach her for letting him go, delivering him up to the experts, but he was way beyond that. His drugged, incurious acceptance of the situation was far worse. He reminded her painfully of a brain-washing victim in some rabble-rousing, anti-Russian film she'd seen once.

'Ben's been asking after you. I said you were ill. You'd gone for a rest in hospital.'

Paul seemed not to hear. He was concentrating on his blanket again, with the small, obsessive, plucking movement. Her heart ached as she watched him. Yet she knew, beyond a shadow of a doubt, that she'd been right to make the phone call. Enforced or otherwise, Paul needed help, professional help, and now he was going to get it.

* * *

'You've been a good boy at school?' Frank, the stall-holder, asked Ben as he weighed out potatoes for Ruth. He grinned at her foxily, revealing a flash of gold teeth.

'I played the drum,' Ben told him, large-eyed and earnest.

'Did yer?' said Frank admiringly. 'Just like your Uncle Joe.' He drank with the Wailers' Scottish drummer.

'Yes.' Ben nodded, delighted at the thought.

'Here. Don't tell your mum.' With ostentatious secrecy Frank slipped him an apple.

'Frank!' Ruth protested. 'I've told you not to.'

'He's my mate.' Frank lowered his stately bulk to nudge Ben conspiratorially and wink hugely. A wide, irresistible grin spread across the child's face.

When Ruth picked him up from the baby-minder, the two of them generally walked home via Berwick Street market. Ben had always loved to see the piles of bright fruit and vegetables. For Ruth there was another bonus at this time of day. The market was beginning to pack up and certain of the more perishable goods were cheaper. Some of the stallholders had known Ben since he was a baby, so it was like visiting a procession of tough, genial uncles. Since the two of them had been on their own, small pleasures like shopping had seemed sharper and fresher to Ruth, as though she'd emerged, like the sun, from behind a gathering cloud of anxiety.

Back at the flat Ruth would make them both a cup of tea. Then she set about the other job that brought in a little extra cash – the mail-order side of Ernest Broadbent's book business. The month of June was turning out to be glorious, so she opened the windows and let the sun pour in along with the summer street sounds, as she parcelled and invoiced.

Ben would sit with her, drawing and playing while he chatted about his day. He was growing and changing so fast now, with his widened horizons, and learning new words and phrases all the time that she hadn't taught him. To Ruth's secret enjoyment, the turns of speech he picked up from Mrs Francioli rang with a sharp Italian assertiveness.

'You crazy, no?' she heard him taunt his teddy bear one evening. He developed a philosophical Mediterranean shrug, an incongruously adult movement, and continually parroted his baby-minder's most characteristic phrase, 'You kidding?'

At nursery school he had made a new friend, a Chinese boy called Chat, with dark, thoughtful eyes and a fringe of black hair. His father was a cook at a nearby restaurant. Both boys were serious and capable of sustained concentration. They made up long, complicated games together, spreading out Ben's bricks, soldiers and toy animals over a widening area of carpet, lying on the floor, deep in their fantasy world, oblivious to Ruth working on the other side of the room.

She derived an enormous quiet happiness from watching them and listening. Suddenly life seemed spacious to her, full of unexpected pleasures. She was busy, but her time was her own. Until she was free of it Ruth had never quite understood how oppressive and constant her anxiety about Paul had become: whether he'd be brought home incapable and incoherent; whether he'd disrupt the day with the sardonic, destructive mood he couldn't keep to himself but must spread to everyone he met, needling and provoking.

In the last months, too, she realized that he'd exuded a continual sour aura of alcohol. It had hung in the rooms, a permanent, almost unnoticed fixture. Now the air around her seemed new and sweet. She noticed it afresh every day, unconsciously breathing in deep draughts.

There was guilt, though, at the totality of her relief, the joy of being her own mistress again. She talked to Rebecca about it. But Becky was scornful. 'I've always

310

been fond of Paul, but he'd become impossible to live with. A hopelessly lost cause. You tried, God knows, but there was nothing anyone could do.' She grinned at Ruth with sly amusement. 'The boys in the band are calling you a bloody saint.'

A dumpy, middle-aged auxiliary nurse stopped by with a trolley of tea. 'All right, Paul?'

Reaching for the cup she held out, he gave a twisted smile that was more like a grimace. 'Mustn't grumble, Joyce.' Ruth detected a note of satire in the reply. It was a phrase he'd always thought typified a bleak acceptance of the mediocre. 'How's that son of yours?' he asked.

'Blooming layabout.' She grinned with a sort of pride. 'Doesn't get up till lunch time. Says he's tired after all those exams.' She glanced at Ruth. 'That the missis?'

Casually he introduced them. 'Ruth, meet Joyce.'

'How do you do?' Ruth said stiffly, with the feeling of being an outsider at some breezy social club.

Joyce nodded. 'He's told us a lot about you.' She stared at Ruth momentarily with a look of not unfriendly curiosity, then added, 'Can't stand here gossiping. No rest for the wicked. Bye, Paul.'

'Cheerio, Joyce.'

'You seem chummy,' Ruth said, when the nurse had trundled to a safe distance.

He shrugged. 'There are some nice people in here.'

With the vitamins the hospital pumped into him, the rest and regular meals, Paul's health improved with every passing week. He acquired the almost ethereal look of someone whose body is free from toxins, who lives a quiet and regular life. Outside, in the real world, the fine summer had lent everyone a touch of the gypsy – brown faces, flashing eyes and teeth. But, sequestered in his hospital ward, Paul's skin was smooth and white, his eyes clear, his haggard jawline filled out and slightly rounded.

311

To Ruth's relief, the obsessive plucking movement of his hands had stilled.

However, she felt out of touch with him. Apart from asking after Ben he seemed to shy away from talking about the outside world, his own life. His future. It seemed to her that Paul had narrowed down his horizons to the comings and goings of the ward, his fellow patients, the nurses. Ruth guessed it was a form of self-protection. Outside, in the eyes of friends and acquaintances, he'd failed. Here he was a member of the gang, and a popular one at that. The nurses all liked him and told Ruth indulgently that he was 'a case'. He knew what part of the country each of them hailed from and the names of all their boyfriends. In fact, Ruth reflected ruefully, he seemed a lot more interested in their private lives than in hers. When she tried to tell him about work, or what Richard or Becky had said, his eyes would glaze over and his attention would wander.

Paul's parents travelled up every day to see him. Sometimes their visits would coincide with Ruth's. They were cautiously pleasant to her, but there was the suggestion in everything they said that Paul's raffish lifestyle had been at the root of his troubles.

'I just know they blame me,' Ruth told Becky wryly. 'They've always thought he should've married someone who wore an apron.'

Shortly before the end of June Paul was discharged. Two days earlier his mother had telephoned Ruth. She and his father wanted to take their son to Bournemouth for at least a month. 'We're retired, dear, so we've got time for him. We know how busy you are, working.' There was a note of anxiety in her voice, as if she expected her daughter-in-law to make a fuss, press her own superior claim, stand on her wifely dignity.

To Ruth the suggestion was a godsend. 'I think that's an excellent idea,' she said gravely. Though she couldn't imagine what Paul, even in his present fragile condition, would do with himself for a month in the super-genteel atmosphere of Bournemouth.

'I'm *so* glad you're in favour.' Perversely, now that she *had* agreed, Mrs Macdonald's tone suggested that Ruth was somehow hard and neglectful for having done so.

'Let me know where you're staying when it's all sorted out, so that I can keep in touch.'

'Of course, dear.'

That evening Ruth, Ben and Chat sat by the open window with ice-cream cones, talking and peering down at the sunny street below. Across the road an old Italian they knew well by sight played some slow, wheezily sentimental tune on his accordion. The boys imitated him, dragging on imaginary instruments, waving their cornets with dangerous abandon.

Ruth was conscious of an almost painful sense of well-being. The muddied waters of her life looked clear and calm to her, as they hadn't in years. And she understood, in a flash of self-knowledge, that a decision had been taken, simply and almost without her awareness, and that there was no going back on it.

She would never lose touch with Paul. They'd be friends and she'd help him all she could to beat his drinking. She'd share Ben's upbringing with him – the lines of communication between them must stay open and uncomplicated. But she wasn't going to live with him. Not ever again.

32

It was a Sunday afternoon in Hyde Park. A dream of a day; warm, with a tender blue sky and a slight breeze. Women lolled in deck chairs, their skirts hitched up above their knees, faces turned blankly to the sun. Men sported bare chests and knotted handkerchiefs. Lovers lay full length, sensuously entwined. Dogs and children were everywhere, romping idyllically. Rebecca and Owain strolled across the dappled shade beneath the trees. They'd come to hear a speaker Rebecca had interviewed a couple of weeks ago and been impressed by. It had been an impulsive decision made last thing on a Friday afternoon.

'We could meet a bit early,' Owain had suggested. 'Have some lunch at a pub.'

'Sounds nice.' She smiled, with the casual fake breeziness she'd perfected over the months. It had become second nature, camouflaging the rawness of her feelings for him. All over the world people must be doing the same thing, she thought. Unrequited love was hardly a rare phenomenon.

'Twelvish then? Green Park Station?'

'Fine.'

It seemed a luxury to have him to herself. She looked at him with pleasure. He was casually dressed, like her, in jeans and a loose shirt, that made him look younger and more relaxed. Meeting him off duty shifted the nature of their relationship in some small way.

'Ruth got off all right?' he asked. She'd gone to Bournemouth for the weekend with Ben, visiting Paul and his parents.

314

'Yes.' Rebecca nodded. 'She's not looking forward to it, though. Paul's Mum and Dad seem to have closed ranks in a rather . . . accusing manner.'

'The mealy-mouthed . . .' He gave a sideways look of disgust. They were kin to Paul. That was enough for him. The two of them could have spent hours discussing the rights and wrongs of the situation, but they stuck to their tacit agreement to let the matter lie.

The pub they went to had a small garden, its fences trellised and hung with heavy swathes of unpruned pink roses. The food was unusually enterprising, tasty and French. There was garlic bread and bowls of cassoulet, and the beer was cold. They carried their lunch outside to an agreeably rustic-looking bench and table. The hum of the traffic was ever-present and tall buildings dotted the skyline, but, these apart, they could have imagined themselves in some welcoming country pub. A small ginger cat came and sat close by, looking enquiringly up at their bowls of food.

Rebecca and Owain began to discuss a titillating piece of current Fleet Street scandal, involving the editor of a national daily and a handful of politicians from both sides of the House. It occurred to Rebecca suddenly that she was passingly acquainted with most of the protagonists and she marvelled at the way her job on *Red Lion* had widened her horizons.

Inevitably they began to talk about the magazine. There'd been a noticeable rise in circulation over the past two months and Owain had taken on a new man, Max, on the editorial side. He was an ex-public schoolboy turned radical, and Owain had an edgy, abrasive relationship with him, fraught at times, but somehow understood and enjoyed by both.

'He's bloody efficient in his effete way,' Owain said. 'Between them, he and Bobby and Ella can manage all the basics. With Max there you and I could have a lot more freedom.' His elbows rested on the rough wood table as he leaned confidentially towards her.

'So it's trips to Europe, is it? All expenses paid?' Rebecca was aware of a lazy contentment. She could have leaned across and touched his full, smooth lips. But, for now, she'd settle for this easy companionship, the beer and the sunshine.

He said suddenly, 'What would you say to a visit to Hungary?'

'Make it Biarritz and you're on.'

There was a glint of quizzical amusement in his eye. 'I'm not talking fun, Rebecca.'

'You've heard from Janos.'

He grinned. 'I admit it.'

'What did he have to say?'

'Lots. There's a lot going on there. We only hear the basics in the press. But people are coming out into the open. The atmosphere's changing. There's chaos bubbling just below the surface . . .'

Since Hungary's first heady flirtation with freedom three years ago, in the wake of Stalin's death, the forces of reaction had made themselves felt. Janos's early euphoric letters had become increasingly despondent. Things were going backward again, he stated gloomily. There were renewed restrictions and imprisonments. However, last February Khrushchev, the Soviet leader, had publicly denounced Stalin and his policies, reviving hope in the satellite states of a return to more liberal times.

'I'd like to see for myself,' Owain said. 'Maybe do a series of articles. That's what we could do with now – more on-the-spot investigation.' The cat jumped up beside him. Absently he rubbed its ears. 'It's just a thought, may not come off. But what do you think, Becky? Would you be interested?'

His eyes looked steadily into hers, enquiring. Her spirits soared. Would she be interested? In instant reflex

Rebecca crushed her eagerness ruthlessly. It was hypothetical as yet. A thousand things could go wrong. She answered with a firm neutrality. 'I'd like to very much, if it comes to that . . . Actually, I'd be fascinated,' she added, in case he should think her response lacking in enthusiasm.

'Good.' He held her gaze for a second, then drained his beer. 'It's pie in the sky at the moment, but it could come off . . . Finished your drink, Beck? Shall we be getting along?'

The speaker that Rebecca had interviewed, a man named Curtis, was slight, grey-haired and grey-bearded, and rather dignified. He had a practical, portable platform that he'd made himself. His voice was surprisingly rich and sonorous, so that he had no need to resort to the strangulated yelping that was the hallmark of some of the other speakers. His theme was the hydrogen bomb as collective lunacy, and he spoke in Hyde Park every Sunday.

'But don't you get discouraged at not making any difference?' Rebecca had asked him during the course of their interview.

He'd given a thin smile. 'Naturally. But I keep on plugging. You never know. One Sunday Eisenhower might walk past. Or Khrushchev. And be converted and save the world.'

His tone was reasonable rather than hectoring. He appealed to his listeners' sense of the ridiculous. As Rebecca and Owain approached he was courteously inviting some doubting Thomas to explain the point of a weapon which, if it were used, would ensure that the user lost everything that a war was supposed to win. In the face of this simple absurdity his victim's lame blustering about deterrence and tactical weaponry was falling decidedly flat. With his droll, round-eyed civility Curtis held

317

his audience in the palm of his hand. His gentle questioning sent ripples of laughter through the crowd.

'Now if he was our man at the United Nations . . .' Rebecca mused out loud. She was half-convinced that, with his childlike shrewdness he'd do more to debunk the arms race than all the expert debate in the world.

Almost immediately they were distracted by a hubbub from the next stand.

'You've got a bloody nerve . . .!' A voice from the crowd, raucous and threatening, sliced through the sunny good humour of the afternoon.

'You misunderstand . . .' The speaker was a well-groomed man of Eastern appearance, and his voice held a tone of polite reason.

'Oh I do, do I?' the voice hectored derisively. Rebecca couldn't see its owner, but his note of protest was taken up by others.

The speaker, raised up on his box, was visible to her, his clothing formal for a summer Sunday. He wore a navy blazer with silver buttons and what looked like an old school tie. His hair, smoothed back from a high forehead, lay in neat, corrugated ridges. The expression on his face was not unduly anxious. A banner next to him at head height read 'Fair Deal for Nasser'.

'Why doesn't he just commit suicide and have done with it?' Owain was grimly amused at the speaker's foolhardiness. Nasser was the man above all others that the national press – and a majority of the British public – currently loved to hate. Only a few days ago he'd had the almost unbelievable effrontery to nationalize the Suez Canal, to a chorus of incredulous, jingoistic abuse from the British and French, whose particular preserve it had been for a century.

In spite of the increasing brouhaha, the man kept talking. Rebecca and Owain approached his stand. His lips were moving, the expression on his face was earnest and placatory, but they couldn't hear what he was saying until, through a freak break in the shouting, an audible phrase blundered. '. . . At the right time – like your Churchill . . .'

There was a silence, monstrous and damning. The words seemed to hang in the air.

'Churchill!' The note of shocked mortification was almost comic. 'Why, you bloody little . . .'

Now they could see the owner of the voice. He looked to be in his mid-thirties, balding and stocky, his face burned lobster-colour by the sun. A solid-looking belly hung over his belt and strained the buttons of his check shirt. His short, muscular legs were braced in a pugnacious stance. As he shouted he retracted his chin self-righteously into his fleshy neck.

'Come down here and say that!'

'I intended no insult.' The speaker held his ground, apparently still confident that reason would prevail.

'Come down here, you little wog!'

The rest of the crowd had gone quiet, though a minute earlier a number of them had been heckling. The stocky man had appropriated the quarrel, made it his own, and they were spectators.

'That's damned offensive.' On his box, the speaker – an Egyptian national, Rebecca supposed – was abruptly rattled. Suddenly he was vulnerable and Rebecca felt the gooseflesh break out on her arms and body as she watched.

'What you going to do about it?' jeered his assailant. 'You and Nasser,' he added, seeming pleased by his wit, raising a snigger or two from the crowd.

'I'll get you . . .!' With a kind of despairing roar the Egyptian launched himself headlong from his box and rushed for the other man, stopping short immediately in front of him, his fists clenched, his face working with a passion that was both awe-inspiring and ridiculous.

Rebecca experienced a flash of shame at witnessing his loss of control. The speaker's grey trousers were incongruously smart, expensive and immaculately creased, his hair still sleek and unruffled.

The stocky man lashed out, catching him a blow on the nose with a movement that was cramped and amateurish, like that of a scrapping boy. Blood sprang to the Egyptian's upper lip and dripped, shockingly bright, on to his white shirt. The bystanders stared stupidly, mesmerized by the sudden violence.

The Egyptian retaliated, rushing at his opponent with an incoherent cry, catching him off balance, knocking him to the ground with a hefty, clumsy shove. Suddenly the man was sprawled ignominiously in the dust, looking foolish and laughably surprised. The Egyptian stood above him, staring, paralysed by the shock of what he'd done.

'You bastard.' Almost at once his opponent raised himself to one knee, then stood up in a single, agile movement that was strangely at odds with his bulk. And when he was upright they saw that in his right hand he held a knife.

'Oh my God.' A woman clutched at Rebecca's arm.

Holding the weapon at an angle, the man began to circle the Egyptian, half-crouched and beckoning him on with his left hand like they did in the movies about New York hoodlums. There was a deathly hush. The crowd was frozen. The Egyptian stared with more amazement than fear, as though the situation was unreal to him. Rebecca, too, had the illusion that the stocky man was playing a role. But the knife was real.

Somehow the spectators had formed into a ring. 'Come on then, wog.' The man smiled wolfishly like a middle-aged Wild One, still circling slowly.

Then, without warning, his knife hand was grabbed from behind and bent backward. Bemused, Rebecca saw, over the man's shoulder, the blur of Owain's face and beard. In dream-like dumb show he relieved the man of his knife with deft and practical movements. The crowd watched him silently. From a little way off children's voices floated shrilly on the warm air. The man was caught unawares, and offered only a token resistance. The incident was over before the spectators had rallied sufficiently to offer Owain any support.

33

Owain opened the street door. Outside, Ruth stood in a diffused halo of neon lighting, her face and hair palely luminous above a dark dress. She was home to him, everything he wanted. He took her in his arms, circling her slim body almost violently and pulling it to his own. His patience was already stretched. It was gone ten. Since Paul wasn't there Ruth waited until Ben was asleep before she'd come and spend the night. And she left around five in the morning.

'Give us a chance.' She laughed at his eagerness, pushing him gently away. 'Let's get in the door.'

He followed her up the staircase to his second-floor flat.

'Becky baby-sitting?'

'Yes.' Ruth turned as they climbed. 'She was telling me about yesterday. That thing in the park. Wow, Owain, what a hero.' Laughing down at him with teasing admiration, her hair falling forward across her face.

'Baloney.' He still found the incident strangely inconsequential. 'Just that everyone was standing there gawping as if they'd been turned to stone. As if they were watching the telly . . .' He held open the door of his flat. 'Anyway two coppers came along a couple of minutes later and made it all official.'

'You had a nice day, though, excitement apart?'

'Yes.' He smiled. 'I love Becky. She's like Tweety-pie. Wide-eyed and hard-headed.'

The hall was small and dim. Stacks of books and papers were ranged against a side wall. One of Becky's political posters was tacked above them. Ruth sat on a low chair and took off her shoes. It was always the first thing she did.

'She likes you too.' There was something in the tone of her voice that lent her words a deeper significance. Owain glanced towards her quizzically, but Ruth appeared to check herself. She stood up and laid her two hands on his shoulders, kissing him lightly. 'Let's go to bed.'

It was a hot and humid night, but the sash window in Owain's bedroom was open, admitting little wafts of agreeably cool air which stirred the red curtains. The bedside lamp was on, casting a low, intimate light. A striped blanket lay rumpled on the floor.

'I did it,' Ruth said, crossing to the bed where Owain already sat leaning on the pillow, hands linked behind his head, bare-chested above the sheet. Ruth still wore her white bra and pants. He liked to take them off her. Owain laughed about the plainness of her underwear, teased her, saying, 'Why don't you lead me on with that stuff from the small ads?'

'What did you do?' he asked idly now, taking her hand, pulling her down. They'd been together for almost two years, and there were touches of domesticity in their shared nights. But she never got over this. Lying down beside him and re-encountering all the textures of his skin, the smoothness, the rough dark hair, the ridges of muscle, the engorging penis. It was a kaleidoscope of sensations which remained as new and pleasurable however often she experienced them. Ruth stretched out luxuriously against him while his arms pulled her closer.

She laid her head against his chest. 'I told Paul.'

At once he was alert, subtly relaxing his hold on her. 'Told him what?'

'That I wasn't going to live with him any more.'

They'd left Ben with his grandparents and strolled down the Bournemouth front. It had been a blue, luminous day with the kind of clear light that reminded Ruth of an impressionist painting, lending an ethereal, timeless quality to the distant figures on the beach.

'It makes me think of Llandudno a bit,' she said.

Paul gave a wry grin. 'That's water under the bridge.' He had more colour now, but had retained the smooth, clear-eyed look that she found so strangely unsettling in her errant husband. Like a vegan, she thought, or her idea of one.

On the front they passed old, retired couples, walking slowly, concerned for one another's health and mobility, and Ruth had the impression that, arm in arm, the two of them formed a similar pair. Paul still had the slow carefulness about him of someone who had survived a crisis, someone who was husbanding his strength.

'It seems aeons ago, doesn't it, Llandudno,' Ruth commented. They'd been so young and quick and carefree in those days.

'Young blades we were then.'

Ruth had an overwhelming sense of their belonging together – an old married couple who'd come through a difficult time, sobered and realistic about their expectations of life and of each other. It would be horrifyingly easy to succumb to such a feeling. Tempting even. But she mustn't let herself. Ruth was convinced that the self-evident simplicity of the decision she'd taken in Marshall Street was the truth. She must hang on to that. She and Paul had no future together.

If she was going to tell him, now was the time, while they were away from his parents. This could be her only chance. Still she hung back, liking the atmosphere of elegiac friendship between them and not wanting to spoil it.

'The Wailers have got a new pianist, you know,' Paul said suddenly. He was aiming at a simple statement of fact, with no overtones of emotion, but his voice was not quite steady.

'You're joking.' Ruth was shocked. She'd seen Vince and Richard a few days ago and they'd asked concernedly after Paul, but they hadn't mentioned this.

'Had a letter from Richard. All tactful and apologetic.' His sang-froid cracked a little further. 'Didn't sound like him at all.' A flash of murky amusement.

'I'm so sorry. Really sorry.'

'Can't blame them,' he said. 'I haven't exactly pulled my weight recently. But I thought they might . . .' She could see in his eyes how deep the hurt went. And now she was proposing to tell him that their marriage was at an end. How bloody callous that was going to sound. Kick a man when he's down . . .

A fat, wispy-haired toddler in a short, pink dress came running adventurously ahead of her parents and almost collided with them.

'Watch it, sweetheart.' Paul bent to steady her. She stared at him with startled, round eyes. The child's parents caught up with her, fussing and smiling apologetically, scooping her up.

'You *must* look where you're going, Melanie,' her mother said, flustered and slightly pink.

From her arms the child stared at Paul. 'Man,' she said in a wondering voice, gesturing vaguely towards him.

'That's me.' Paul waved to her and turned to grin at Ruth.

But she didn't smile back. 'Paul, I'm leaving you,' she said, gazing into his sherry-brown eyes, half-wary, half-defiant.

There was a silence between them. She was aware of the holiday sounds from the beach. Shouts, laughter, the barking of dogs.

'Yeah.' He breathed rather than spoke the word.

Another hush. They stood awkwardly, face to face, while the passers-by skirted them.

'It's not that we won't see each other . . .' Ruth felt the need to leap in with explanations. 'We'll stay friends . . .'

'Christ,' he interrupted harshly and shook his head, looking pained. 'I'm a Hemingway man, a Mailer man. Don't give me Barbara Cartland.'

'Fair enough.' A certain posturing weariness in his manner grated on her, and she answered sharply, 'That's not important anyway. Not just now.'

He shrugged and took her arm. They walked on without speaking. After a while he said, 'I'm not reacting right, am I? I know that. But, to be honest, Ruth, as far as I'm concerned, I've been living on borrowed time for . . . a year? Two? I've always known this was coming.' He glanced at her. 'I didn't want it to. Don't get me wrong. But it's like I've been robbing you for ages, and getting away with it . . . for longer than I expected. And now I've been caught and it's almost a relief.'

She was struck. 'What a strange way to see it.'

'Remember our bargain?' He gave a self-mocking grin. 'What a farce. We were such innocents then.'

Ahead of them, on the beach, Ruth made out the small figures of Paul's parents and Ben. They had him by the hand in the shallows of the sea and he jumped the sparkling waves as they washed across the shingle.

'I've had a kind of death-wish ever since we've been married. It's as if, even then, I thought you should've been out of my reach, and I thought you'd leave me one day. So I pushed my luck more and more, so you'd have a reason, and it'd look as if it was my doing.' He shrugged again, with a glint of black humour. 'And I'd look less of a berk.'

Ruth turned towards him. She thought he appeared demoralized, in spite of his breezy words. He was slight and pale under the light tan. He looked blank, as though the effort of mustering a facial expression was temporarily beyond him. 'Well, I've told you,' she said. 'We both know where we are. That's the main thing.'

'And I've taken it like a brick.' He was satirical and made an unsuccessful attempt at his old, twisted smile. It petered out into a wan grimace. 'I've been pretty damned mature, haven't I? But Christ knows how I'm going to get through the night, and tomorrow, and all the nights after that.'

Owain was attentive as Ruth recounted their conversation, lying back with her head resting on his shoulder. There was a murmuring intimacy in their voices, a warmth where their bodies touched. The muted light dimly revealed objects grown familiar to her over the months. A Lowry industrial landscape and a framed Vicky cartoon, hung on the wall, and on the chest of drawers there was a photograph he'd taken of her in Provence. Next to it was the bold red splash of a silk poppy she'd found one evening – bizarrely abandoned halfway up the Marshall Street fire escape – and laughingly presented to him. She was fond of this room with its associations for her of escape and sexual passion.

'I've burned my boats,' she told him. 'And it's a relief more than anything.'

'Better late than never.' His tone was meaningful, holding shades of many past arguments. He'd been scornful of Paul's shaky attempts at bravado as reported by Ruth. She'd expected that. Owain had never had any time for him. But now he let the subject drop. Paul was a sore point between them, which they'd learned from experience it was wiser not to press.

Owain turned towards her, leaning on one elbow. His free hand brushed her leg and came to rest between her thighs. Slowly he began to caress her.

'That's so good.' She smiled at him with lazy complicity in the lamplight.

Around half-past four Ruth surfaced from a languorous half-sleep. Owain was shaking her by the shoulder. There was an aroma of fresh coffee. He always made some before she left. She opened an eye. A greyish dawn light was beginning to show at the window. She was warm and wonderfully relaxed.

'Oh, God.' With an effort she hoisted herself to lean on the pillow, pushing her hair back out of her eyes. This was the worst bit of staying the night. The reckoning.

'Your drug, madame.' He handed her a mug of hot, strong coffee. She wrapped her hands round it. Even the steam that rose from it was heartening. It was hard to wake, but there was something magical about the bleary dawn, their shared isolation, the two of them torpid and satiated, their bodies still imbued with the scents and secretions of their lovemaking, without the distancing barriers of clothes, combed hair, cosmetics. She felt it every time.

Ruth sipped the scalding coffee. 'Mmm. It burns all the way down.' She leaned back luxuriously on the pillows. 'Nothing like a stolen night of passion, I always say.'

Owain touched his lips to her shoulder, grazing her pleasurably with the roughness of his beard. 'It's this early-bird stuff I can't take.'

Once she was fully awake, Ruth found it no hardship to get up and dress, do her hair and put on make-up, resuming her public persona. She'd discovered a private enjoyment in taking a taxi or, better still, walking through the silent, misty streets and arriving home, to her own territory, before anyone was up. Making toast and cocoa for Ben – while the early-morning sun shone hazily at the kitchen window – and waking him with it. Hugging his small frame, cuddly as a puppy's, warm and heavy from sleep. Having coffee with Becky before she left, her body still suffused with a drowsy lust at the memory of her night with Owain. It was like having two lives.

But she wasn't sure Owain would understand all this, and answered vaguely, 'The early-bird stuff's the price you pay . . .'

'Not much longer, though. Not now.' He spoke carelessly, but there seemed an underlying emphasis, as though he were opening some gambit.

'What do you mean?'

'Well, now you and Paul have finally split . . .' Owain left the sentence unfinished, as if its significance must be obvious. His eyes, meeting hers, carried the same message.

She frowned. 'What . . .?' Though even as she asked, his meaning was suddenly clear to her.

'There's no reason now why we can't be together.'

She stared ahead of her. 'I hadn't thought of that.' Oddly, it was true. She'd not related her decision about Paul to any further action. He didn't reply. Ruth drained her coffee, the gulping, swallowing sounds noisy in the hush. The silence that followed her words gave both of them time to reflect on their implications.

'That's a strange thing to say.' Owain's voice held a measure of cool hostility.

'Yes,' she conceded. 'I suppose it is.' She had a mental picture: coming home to the quiet sunlit flat, her own place, being her own mistress.

She turned to Owain. His face was expressionless. 'I love you,' she said. 'I love us how we are.' She was terribly aware, suddenly, of the way in which their relationship permeated the fabric of her days. It was a thing apart, but vital, like the sun, a source of energy and pleasure. As she picked Ben up from the baby-minder or cleared the tables in the restaurant or shopped in the market, the thought of him was there, to be returned to

329

at will. At any time she could picture his slow smile, his hands on her body, and be sure of his friendship and support. Yet she resisted bringing them further into her life. 'I love us how we are.'

'Christ.' Owain put his cup down on the bedside table. The simple movement was invested with a kind of savagery.

There was another memory. One she didn't want to talk about. Their evening at the theatre. The Osborne play. The power of her gut reaction that night had stayed locked inside her, fuelling a determination that she was going to have that magic for herself again. Her responsibilities to Ben would slow her down – she allowed that – but nothing else. Living with Owain would take time and energy. It would confer obligations she hadn't room for.

'Aren't we fine as we are?' she suggested. 'Think about it, Owain. We're together, but . . .'

'God.' He turned on her a look of total incredulity. 'Can you really be so . . . You know bloody well I want more from you. I want you as my wife.' He drew his knees up under the sheet and rested his chin on his arms, a brooding restlessness in the attitude. 'I've waited. Not patiently, but I've waited, for you to get rid of that prat of a husband of yours . . .' He faced her with a sombre honesty. '*You* may be fine as you are, but I'm not. I'm thirty-three. I want you. I want a family.'

He looked tired. She loved him fiercely and couldn't imagine not loving him. And maybe she was mad not to fall into the ease and simplicity of living with him as if into a warm bath. But there was a clawed resistance inside her that wouldn't let go.

Soberly she tried to explain. 'Look, I've just said goodbye to something that was . . . cramped, and sort of stifling, and ruled all of my waking thoughts, and now I'm on my own, and it's such a relief.' She touched his hand. 'I'm not sure you can understand. It's an ecstasy of relief.'

His hand closed over hers, though his face remained set and unresponding. Through the curtains the dawn was brightening, hazy as yet, but full of promise.

'Look, Owain. I love you, but I don't want to lose this freedom. Not yet. Not for some time.' As she spoke the words they became truth for her, and she knew that she believed them.

Owain got up from the bed and began to pull on his clothes. When he was dressed, in a black sweater and jeans, he turned to face her. She sat watching him, half-covered by the sheet, arms clasped round her knees, hair falling forward, shading her face like a curtain.

He said, with a bald finality, 'Then there's no point in our going on.'

34

During the following weeks the Hungary project that Owain had proposed casually to Rebecca over Sunday lunch became the focus of his life. He made repeated visits to the Legation to sort out the necessary visas for himself and Becky, and was constantly on the phone making travel arrangements. He commissioned articles right, left and centre to make sure there was enough material to tide the magazine over during their absence.

Rebecca guessed that the relentless action was a form of therapy. He looked tense, and was distant and withdrawn, as though the wound he carried inside nagged at him constantly. The atmosphere of the office was affected. He made valiant efforts to join in the day-to-day badinage, but it was with an air of strain and reserve.

He was less patient than usual and quicker to find fault. Bobby, Ella and Max were fond of him and made allowances, but all of them confided privately that they'd be glad to see the back of him for a couple of weeks.

'Let's hope a change of scenery will improve his temper,' Ella remarked in her glum fashion to Rebecca as she munched on a dry-looking walnut rissole from her lunch box.

'I'll let you know.' Rebecca was agog to view an Eastern bloc country, but less enthusiastic than formerly about the personal aspect of the trip. The prospect of travelling abroad with Owain had filled her with anticipation but, given his current mood, she was more apprehensive than anything else. Though there was a month still. Time for him to recover some of his normal spirits.

As usual, she was caught in the middle. Back in

Marshall Street, Ruth was pale and sometimes irritable, but she still claimed that, in refusing to set up home with Owain, she'd done the right thing.

Rebecca was surprised by her decision, but respected her determination to go it alone. She had misgivings on her own account, though. She'd thought for a long time that Ruth, with her speculative grey eyes, was aware of her interest in Owain. As long as Ruth and Owain were happily wrapped up in one another, Rebecca could live with the knowledge. But now she became self-conscious, in case Ruth should imagine that her attitude towards their split was in any way self-interested.

She had the distinct impression, too, that under the circumstances her friend was cool about the proposed Hungarian trip. Previously she'd been happy for Rebecca and bright-eyed with curiosity. Now she missed Owain painfully and seemed less than thrilled at the prospect of his and Becky's joint departure. Probably she visualized the journey as a carefree jaunt, though Rebecca was convinced that, with Owain in his present frame of mind, it was likely to be anything but that.

The situation led to an awkwardness between the two of them. Ruth was withdrawn and Becky felt embarrassed to talk much about the impending trip, although it was overwhelmingly on her mind. There were silences between them, an atmosphere of small talk, yet neither felt able to bring the problem out into the open.

During September Tony Taylor was in London on a short three-day leave. He'd completed his tour of duty in Germany and was currently at a training camp on Salisbury Plain. He came to see them in Marshall Street bringing Linda, a girlfriend. They'd met in Andover where she was a secretary with a firm of lawyers.

Rebecca and Ruth liked her immediately. She was trim, smart and commonsensical, with short, dark curly hair and a dry sense of humour. Tony appeared inordinately proud of her. He'd mellowed since Rebecca had seen him last. His body had filled out and looked powerful. He seemed expansive and pleased with life, and kissed Rebecca with daring familiarity.

'You're so little!' he exclaimed wonderingly. 'Were you always as small as this?' He introduced her to Linda. 'This is Becky, my ex-guardian angel. If it wasn't for her I'd be the oldest juvenile delinquent in the Elephant and Castle.' He seemed to have forgotten, she reflected ruefully, that she'd not been at all keen on his urge to join the army.

He asked after Paul in an unembarrassed fashion, open but concerned. Rebecca remembered that Tony used to refer to him as a piss artist and now she was impressed with his down-to-earth tact. She knew Ruth was fed up to the back teeth with well-meaning enquiries about her husband. But Tony seemed to hit the right note and she answered his questions fully and seriously.

They bought fish and chips and beer, and sat round on the living-room floor and played some of Paul's jazz records and a Presley disc he'd bought just before he was taken into hospital. Linda seemed to find the informality surprising, but fun.

Ruth was more relaxed than Rebecca had seen her for some time. She was currently rehearsing with her drama class for a cabaret evening to raise funds for a crumbling theatre in Bethnal Green, and she entertained them with stories and sharp impressions of Ryan, the teacher, and some of her fellow actors. Ruth warmed to an audience, becoming not loud, but mocking and subtle, her face lit up with an inner glow, her mimicry startlingly accurate.

After the meal Tony helped Rebecca carry plates into the kitchen, wash up, and make coffee. It was an excuse to talk about Linda and confide that they were getting engaged.

'I don't know what she sees in me,' he proclaimed with euphoric pride.

'Wish I could tell you, Tone,' she teased.

'She's so . . . just right.' He gave a sweet, sheepish smile. 'You like her, don't you?'

'Yes, I do.' She was touched by his devotion and didn't want to make fun.

After the meal he had some more beer. Rebecca told him and Linda the story of the fight in the park over Nasser. Tony was slightly drunk and began to drop knowing hints about possible army involvement in the Suez situation. 'Not yet, of course, but if Nasser keeps on pushing his luck . . .' There was a youthfully canny look on his face as if he knew more than he was telling.

Rebecca was scornful. 'Eden wouldn't dare. You've read too many war comics, Tony. He might rattle a rusty sabre or two . . . But there'd be an international outcry. The Americans . . .'

'Tell me all that in a couple of months, Becky.' Tony stood his ground. 'And you're wrong about Eden. The army's full of his type. Can't stand pushy foreigners. Do anything to show them who's boss.' He drained his glass and set it down beside him, still with the shrewd, secret look.

Rebecca dropped the discussion. It was merely his opinion versus hers. She thought his man-in-the-know posture rather sweet, but was unconvinced by his argument. She side-tracked. 'What do you think, Linda?'

The girl smiled. 'I'll send Eden a stiff letter on the firm's headed paper if he tries to send Tony anywhere.'

They left about ten. They had to get back to the Elephant, where they were staying with Tony's family. Rebecca walked with them down the fire escape and they chatted for a minute or two in the street below. Autumn had set in. It was dark and getting chill. Rebecca crossed her arms protectively against her as she stood there.

Linda huddled next to Tony in her chic little jacket and skirt, her patent-leather high heels. He put his arm around her like a shield, as if to protect her, not merely from the cold, but from anything else in the world that might threaten her.

'Take care of yourself, Beck, among the commies.' He was dubious about her proposed trip. The army seemed to have planted in him the seeds of its own cold-war paranoia. She'd never seen it in him before.

Rebecca rolled her eyes heavenwards. 'They're only people, Tony, like you and me. Journalists go there all the time. And we've got all the right visas.' But his scepticism awakened a little pin-prick of doubt in herself, which she resolutely suppressed. 'You ought to go,' she said. 'Linda looks cold.'

He bent and held her in a warm bear-hug. 'Good to see you, Beck. I'll write, but I'll be in touch come Christmas anyway. The family are having some sort of a do for Linda and me. You'll come, won't you?'

She watched their figures receding in the purplish neon haze, arm in arm, Linda tottering a little in her high heels to keep up. Back upstairs in the kitchen, Ruth was ironing a shirt and trousers for Ben. She looked up and grinned, still open-hearted in the aftermath of the visit. 'Aaah,' she said. 'Aren't they sweet? Ain't love grand?'

Rebecca and Owain left one Thursday morning in mid-October. They planned to meet at the airport. Ruth got up early, before dawn, to make coffee and a couple of chunky ham sandwiches, which they ate sitting together at the kitchen table, heavy-eyed under the electric light.

Rebecca was already dressed in a sweater, trousers and ski boots. Her holdall stood packed by the back door. She shivered slightly, feeling leaden, in need of more sleep. She and Owain had stayed late at the office the previous night, making sure they left everything just so, and her brain had remained active until the early hours.

Another thought occurred. 'Do you think you could open my mail?' she asked Ruth. 'And deal with anything that needs action. Just leave the rest on my desk till I get back.'

'Course I will.' Ruth was huddled in a warm dressing gown that had once belonged to Richard. One way or another, Rebecca observed wryly, she seemed to have appropriated half the poor man's wardrobe. 'I'll enjoy that. You know what a nosey devil I am.'

There was a short silence. The wall clock ticked loudly. 'This trip'll be good for Owain. You're so much on his mind, you know. Still.' In the dawn kitchen Rebecca abruptly offered Ruth a line of communication. A fumble towards breaching the coolness there'd been between them.

Ruth gave a rueful smile, seeming to accept the overture. 'I know how he feels.'

'Don't you think you might have made a mistake?'

'No. Not at all.' Ruth shook her head with slow emphasis. 'I'm not over him. I won't pretend I am. I'm missing him terribly. If it weren't for rehearsals, work, Ben, being busy all the time . . . I just haven't got time for a nervous breakdown.' She poured Rebecca another cup of coffee. Her hair straggled becomingly over the shoulders of the over-large dressing gown. Rebecca had the quick, familiar impression that Ruth was the heroine of some neo-realist film. 'But even now the cosiness of marriage or even living together looks to me like a snare and a delusion. A warm, comfy trap.' Her unmade-up face had an early-morning pallor. Rebecca thought she looked wanly heroic.

Ruth got up to swill their plates and dry them, then came and sat down again. 'I've been a pig, haven't I, recently? A horrible dog in a manger.' There was a kind of appeal in her eyes and the sense that this was something she wanted to get off her chest. 'I didn't want to be. But the thought of you and Owain swanning off . . .'

'It's not like that.'

'I know, Becky. But I wasn't thinking straight. I want you to understand . . .' She gave a tentative smile. 'You're my best mate. You know that, don't you? I don't want us to part bad friends.' She touched Rebecca's hand on the scrubbed table top. 'Forgive me?'

'Nothing to forgive.' Rebecca shrugged. 'How do I know I wouldn't have acted the same . . .?'

'I want you to have something. Sort of a good-luck thing.'

'Oh?'

Ruth fumbled in the pocket of her dressing gown and brought out a cheap St Christopher medallion Ben had got in a cracker last Christmas, and swapped with her for a plastic gun. 'Don't laugh,' she said. 'I know it's hideous. But wear it for me till you get back safe.' She stood up and came round behind Rebecca, fastening the chain round her neck.

'Night or day. I won't be parted from it. Promise.' She pushed the locket down inside her sweater, then stood up and gave Ruth a quick kiss. 'Thanks – honest. But I'd better rush now, or there won't be any trip.'

35

Rebecca's fears about Owain's moodiness turned out to be unfounded. Away from his home environment the tension seemed to evaporate, though she imagined it might return when he resumed his normal life and found it wanting. On the plane to Vienna he was charming and sociable. Once they were off and rolling, seatbelts loosened, they'd chatted and had a couple of drinks, agreeing to ignore any lingering anxieties they might have about the smooth running of *Red Lion* in their absence.

Rebecca deliberately brought up the subject of Ruth. Now was the time, if any, to break her taboo. Since the two of them were going to be close for the next two weeks, it seemed absurd to make a no-go area of the one person above all that they had in common.

'How are you feeling nowadays? About Ruth, I mean,' Rebecca asked him after a Dresden-complexioned air hostess had brought their order. It was more than two months now since he'd last seen her.

She thought she glimpsed an expression of relief in his eyes at the question, as if he'd found her embargo on the matter a strain. He looked thoughtful as he poured his miniature of Scotch – he only ever drank it on planes, so he told her – into the glass provided. He said, 'For the first three weeks I felt as if I had a raw, bleeding wound under my clothes. I couldn't understand why there wasn't a spreading patch of blood on the front of my shirt, seeping through my jacket.' He raised his glass to her, with a gleam of self-mockery. 'And all the time I was trying to behave normally – not an easy trick under the circumstances.'

Rebecca sipped her gin and tonic, another unwonted luxury, and smiled at him. 'We couldn't see the red patch, but it's been pretty obvious you weren't at your sunniest.' She sipped her drink and ate a salted nut. How strange and rather pleasant it was, this leisure at eleven o'clock in the morning, discussing one's feelings at goodness knows how many thousand feet. She asked Owain, 'Are you feeling any better? With time, I mean.'

'Perhaps. I'm not certain. It's strange, but recently, in the last couple of weeks, the time I spent with Ruth is beginning to feel unreal to me. Like another life.' He took a slug of his drink, looking reflective. 'At first I'd pretty near have killed to keep . . . But now I'm not so sure.'

As he spoke Rebecca thought he looked attractively haggard. She made no comment. What he said interested her, and she didn't want to break his line of thought.

He carried on, almost as if he were thinking aloud, working something out on his own account. 'I think Ruth's always represented something for me. Right from the first time I met her. I've always been on a certain course in my life, and I suppose I've met a certain kind of woman. Down-to-earth and politically motivated . . . Well, Ruth's not interested in politics, as you know.' He paused. 'She stood for all the things I hadn't really encountered much. Fantasy, style . . . A kind of classy eroticism.' There was an ironic look in his eye as he said it, as if he were distancing himself from his words. He added, 'She's not a superficial person, but maybe all the things I wanted in her were superficial.'

Rebecca listened, fascinated by the flow of confidences, finding herself aroused by his unprecedented openness, fearing that her eyes were glowing with a too-naked interest. Their area of intimacy, between the serried rows of high-backed seats, seemed uncomfortably small for a moment. Almost claustrophobic.

'Like I said, I'd almost have killed to keep all those things for myself. But now I've lived without her for a couple of months. And it's as if, gradually, I'm going back to normal.' Owain shrugged his shoulders. 'Maybe it's a cop-out. Settling for second-best. Maybe not. It's hard to see straight. Ruth's apolitical. Maybe that mattered more than I thought at the time.'

'Suppose she came to you now and said she'd marry you . . .'

He thought, then said slowly, 'It's hard to say. I'd have to be in the situation. But now I'm almost certain that I'd say no.'

'You surprise me,' she said, the quiet comment covering a turmoil of emotions.

His smile had an edge of bitterness. 'I surprise myself.'

'Bye, Mum. Don't come in.' Reluctantly Ben allowed himself to be kissed at the school gate.

'Sure you're okay?'

'Yes.' A note of impatience.

Ruth watched with affectionate amusement as Ben crossed the yard towards the school door, sturdy and self-contained in a Fair Isle sweater knitted by Maggie, a satchel holding his elevenses slung diagonally across his small body. She was fervently grateful for the fact that he seemed to be taking the upheavals of the year in his stride. The baby-minder, Paul's mysterious – to him – defection, though he saw him most Sundays. Always, almost subconsciously, she scanned him anxiously for signs of disturbance, but found none. Maybe they'd surface later, but for now she could only wonder at his childish resilience.

Halfway across the playground his friend, Chat, caught up with him, throwing an exuberant arm round his neck. Ben had been at school for a month now and so far seemed perfectly happy. Having Chat in his class helped, no doubt. The advent of school came as a relief for Ruth, easing the financial burden of nursery school and Mrs Francioli, though the latter was still in the offing for nights when she was rehearsing.

'I think they've forgotten us already.' Annette, Chat's mother came up beside her, smiling, her thick black hair ruffled by the wind. She was half French and half Chinese. Ruth thought she looked about eighteen, and marvelled that she could have, not only a child of five, but another aged almost ten. They gazed with shared maternal approval as the twin figures of their sons were absorbed into the bobbing, multi-coloured current of children streaming towards the entrance door.

'I wish I could be a fly on the wall . . .' Ruth mused. She still found it hard to come to terms with the idea of Ben having a world outside her, and his laconic snippets of information hardly satisfied her curiosity. 'You're picking them up today, aren't you, Annette?' They took it in turns to collect and feed the boys after school.

'Sure.' Annette's pretty, smooth-skinned face seemed always crinkled on the edge of laughter. She nodded with a smile Ruth thought of as flower-like. 'Today I'm doing the honours.'

It was time for Ruth to hurry towards the restaurant in Old Compton Street where she worked. As well as waitressing, she helped prepare the food beforehand. It was a bright, blustery autumn day. The walk through Soho was always a pleasure, with shops opening and the restaurant owners mopping their floors and front steps.

'Duck on the menu again today, Ruth?' Dino, the skinny son of an Italian cook, paused in the act of cleaning the family's plate-glass frontage, to quiz her. It was their current joke. From some mysterious source Monsieur Berteaut, Ruth's boss, had acquired a job lot of boned and rolled tinned duck and was now forced to invent recipes to accommodate it.

'You bet. Till Christmas at the very least.' She smiled up at him as she passed. After five years here she had acquaintances at every turn. Her way to work was punctuated with greetings and brief, laughing conversations.

Tonight she had a dress rehearsal for the cabaret the drama group were presenting in aid of Ryan's pet project, the dilapidated Bethnal Green theatre. She was intrigued by the way it was shaping. Ryan was dedicatedly avant-garde, opting for bold, startling effects. Often Ruth was sceptical, but she thought there were some interesting things in their entertainment. Next week was the full-scale performance, and she'd heard that all the tickets were sold. With Ryan's contacts there should be quite a sprinkling of famous names among the audience. She contemplated the night with a kind of nervous elation.

It occurred to her, with surprise, that the thought of Owain was gradually becoming almost painless. Her life was full up without him. During much of her time with Paul she'd relied on consoling factors to buoy her up – Richard's admiration which had tickled her vanity, her Thursday mornings with Owain in the shop. Now, with the new vigour that filled her, such distractions weren't necessary. There was no longer the vague aura of dissatisfaction that had to be compensated for. Although it would still be good to see Owain at night after a busy day, to laugh together and make love. But Owain wouldn't be satisfied with the simple ease and pleasure . . .

She'd joked to Becky that morning about being too busy for a nervous breakdown. It had been one of those instant remarks, a cliché serving to oil the wheels of conversation. The truth was, she realized with a sense of discovery, that deep down inside she'd never felt stronger.

In Vienna Janos's journalist friend, Wolf, had hired a Volkswagen for them and left it ready at the airport. They stowed their luggage on the back seat and set out for the border post of Nickersdorf, thirty-five miles away.

Now they were on their own Rebecca was gripped by a sense of adventure. Their conversation on the plane had cleared the air between them, banishing the unresolved spectre of Ruth. They were back in harness. Their talk now was spare and functional, of the journey, routes, frontier formalities. There was no need for more. As in Red Lion Square they meshed on some instinctive level.

They reached the border at about three o'clock. On the Austrian side the road was barred by a red and white pole, which was raised to let them out. The two frontiers were separated by a mile or so of no-man's-land. It stretched away in front of them, an uncluttered exercise in perspective. Their slow advance across the space struck Rebecca as momentous. Behind them was the West, their own element, a known quantity. Ahead of them was Iron Curtain territory, a terrain invested since the war with a kind of awesome mythology, a superstitious dread. In spite of her scepticism Rebecca couldn't shake off a chill of apprehension.

She tried to joke about it. 'I feel as if I'm entering the hall of the mountain king.'

'I'm pretty blasé myself.' Owain glanced sideways at her, parodying a debonair grin.

The red, white and green Hungarian barrier was raised by an official in military uniform. They pulled up in front of the large, anonymous, yellowish frontier post. Rebecca felt like a character in a Kafka novel, humbly dependent on the mysterious whims of those in authority.

However, the passport examiner was a pleasant-looking, young man with brown wavy hair. If he had a sinister side he didn't show it, though he examined their documents with unhurried care, as if they might be written in invisible ink. At length, though, his face relaxed into a smile of approval.

He spoke German. '*Gute Reise.*' Rebecca smiled back at him, with the quick impression that she was bridging ten years of history.

It was just over a hundred miles to Budapest, through peaceful agricultural landscape. Fluffy silver-white banks of clouds stood out against a strong blue sky. They passed through neat, attractive villages, where cars seemed a rarity and children waved. For part of the way the road ran alongside the wide, placid Danube, and the autumnal yellow and russets of the trees were reflected in its glittering surface.

'It looks so idyllic,' Rebecca said. 'And yet somehow you want to read something more sinister into it.'

Talk of the devil. Ryan appeared in Le Carrousel, where she worked, that lunch time. She spotted his wild, piratical curls before she realized who they belonged to. He sat at a corner table, in the angle of the dark panelled walls. His companion was a dapper older man, whose skin had a pink, pumiced look, his appearance a contrast to Ryan's cultivated scruffiness.

'You've rumbled my disguise.' She appeared at their table, menu in hand.

'Good God. You!' Ryan's surprise was not quite convincing. Probably he hadn't meant it to be. He introduced her to his friend. 'Godfrey, I'd like you to meet Ruth Law, star of my Bethnal Green contingent.' The older man gave her a quick cursory nod. She was amused to notice that both of them ordered the duck.

Halfway through the meal Ryan approached her on the pretext of asking for a glass of water. 'I'd like a word, Ruth, later. If you've got the time. Over a drink maybe?'

She was intrigued. Annette was collecting the boys, so that was no problem. 'I could meet you outside. At about half-past three?'

In fact she offered him coffee back at Marshall Street.

She liked to be home at about that time in case anything went wrong with Annette's arrangements.

'Love the flat, Ruth.' Ryan lounged on the brown plush sofa as she brought in a tray with coffee. He lounged aggressively, with a larger-than-life languour, his heavy-set body clothed in green corduroys with a polo-necked sweater. He had presence, she admitted grudgingly, though there were times when she thought him an awful phoney.

'Glad you approve,' she replied, glancing round the familiar room. She was fond of the place. It had witnessed so much upheaval. She could almost imagine dumb eyes watching the changes in her life. The room was less chaotic since Paul had left and Ben was out more. Sunny and homely, with samples of her son's splodgy, colourful artwork tacked to the walls.

'It's always fascinating to discover other people's lairs.' He took the mug of coffee from her hands, glancing up at her with a subdued look of sexual interest. 'You can deduce so much about them.'

'What did you want to talk about?'

'You as an actress mainly.' He didn't elaborate, leaving the bald statement to speak for itself, resting his gaze on her, his eyes holding a frankness she saw as somehow spurious.

'Go on then.' She met his look blandly. Ryan reduced some of the younger actresses in the group to jelly. Ruth had never been able to take him quite seriously, so was spared their anxiety. But she couldn't deny his talent, though she thought it misguided sometimes, and deliberately perverse. He had it in his power to advance her career. His contacts were legion. But she closed her mind deliberately to that thought. Better to regard him, as she did, as something of a charlatan. That way she could stay detached.

'That older guy in the restaurant today . . .' He paused provokingly.

'Yes,' she prompted. He would say guy, she reflected. Unnatural for an Englishman.

'He's rolling in it. And he sees himself as a pretty avant-garde member of his generation. He's titillated by the theatre scene. I think he fancies me actually.' A sly look of amusement. 'And he wants to back my little scheme. There's nothing in London quite like the Manchester Experimental Company . . . I see the Bethnal Green theatre as potentially the London end of that. With strong ties . . .'

Ryan assumed a new position, leaning forward on the sofa with his elbows resting on his knees, hands cupping the mug of coffee, the posture suggesting a reined-in energy. Reaching the nub of what he had to say, the actor lowered and intensified his voice. 'There are two or three people from the group I'd like to join me. Terry. Kate.' He mentioned a couple of co-actors. 'And you, Ruth.' A telling silence, his words seeming to hang portentously in the air. 'You're the other one.' He paused again and grinned disarmingly. 'Someone told me where you worked. I confess I wasn't there by chance.'

Ruth was silent, riveted, as though he were telling her a story.

He raised his hands in a graceful, disclaiming gesture. 'Look, I'm not offering you anything definite yet. There's a whole lot to be worked out. It won't be huge money, you can imagine. But if Godfrey turns up trumps it should be enough to live on. And there'd be a certain prestige . . .' A glance of conscious seduction, confidentiality. 'I think we work well together . . . I mean – in theory – would you be interested?'

Listening, Ruth was filled with a discreet jubilation. The offer, as he presented it, was profoundly desirable to her. It was like an improbable stroke of luck in some story. But she must guard against the instinctive leaping of her heart. This was a notion, miles yet from fulfilment and fraught with obstacles. Ryan could be romanticizing. She couldn't vouch for his credibility. Yet her heart ran ahead of these reservations and soared.

She managed to retain an appearance of judicious poise, smiling at him with a circumspect, willed charm. 'You can write me down as definitely interested, Ryan. The idea's extremely inviting. I understand that it's very much pie in the sky at the moment. Also I've a young son and I'd have to be sure I could combine the work . . .' I ought to say I'll talk to my agent, she thought, with a gleam of self-mockery. But it had been years since such an animal existed.

'Good. Good.' With a burst of restless energy he hauled his stocky body upright. 'I've said my piece. I'm glad you're interested, Ruth, and I respect your scruples . . . I must rush now, though. See you tonight at rehearsals.'

She stood up, ready to see him out. His bull-necked figure seemed very close. 'You're married then, are you, Ruth?' She found herself strongly aware of his physical presence. He was phoney, she thought, and mildly ridiculous at times. But you couldn't lightly dismiss him.

'I'm separated.' She didn't elaborate.

There was a silence. Then he repeated softly, 'I'm so glad you're interested. I think we could work really well together.' His eyes held hers and he unveiled, as it were, a conscious look of sexual invitation. A complicity, deliberate and brazen.

Ruth acknowledged the gaze, meeting his eyes with a kind of neutrality. He was attracted. That was useful, making it easier for her to stall over a decision if necessary. She felt calm. It was useful. Nothing more. She smiled, breaking the spell. 'See you tonight.'

* * *

'*Luxe, calme et volupté.*' Janos Molnar leaned back on his chair, teetering perilously on the two rear legs. He drew luxuriously on a Gitane cigarette – remembering his fondness for them Owain had brought him a whole pack – and quoted beatifically from some French poem, Rebecca supposed.

'Idiot.' Eva shot him a forbearing, wifely glance as she cleared the dishes from the table. A few days after their arrival in Budapest Owain and Rebecca had been invited to dine with the Molnars. Eva had served a satisfying meal of home-cooked chicken and a beetroot and caraway salad, followed by a shop-bought strudel, all of it washed down with a couple of bottles of wine. Rebecca guessed that the lavishness of the meal was not something they commonly indulged in.

All that evening the Molnars had been elated, Janos almost skittish. There'd been news for some days of an uprising in Warsaw against the Stalinist harshness of the prevailing regime. Russian tanks had rumbled into the city, threatening and purposeful. But today they'd heard the wondrous tidings that the Russians had backed down, granting concessions to the rebels, and the tanks had left. To the watching Hungarians it was like the ending to some fairy tale.

'*Incroyable*,' Janos kept repeating throughout the meal. 'I don't believe it.' Rebecca thought him likeable, with his owl-like spectacles and impish smile and the enthusiastic way he seemed to relish his home comforts, the food and the drink.

'You've put on weight,' Owain had told him, smiling, when they met, gesturing with his hands to show what he meant.

'I try.' Janos had patted his stomach modestly.

The Molnars had no children and their flat was small. Two rooms, a cramped bathroom and a galley-like kitchen. 'It's big enough for us,' Eva claimed. Most of the furniture had a functional, government issue look to it, though there was a handsome, hand-carved sideboard in the living room that had belonged to Eva's grandparents.

Space was at a premium. Neat piles of papers and folders were stacked under the bed and any other items of furniture high enough to take them. Clothes were ranged behind a rustic-looking embroidered curtain. The table they were sitting round folded back into the wall when not in use.

'I made it. Me,' Janos had told them with a droll smile, making sawing movements with his right hand.

Rebecca enjoyed the mixture of French and English, signs and gestures they used to communicate. It made the conversation between them strangely direct and child-like. The silliness of it broke down barriers and put her at her ease. She found Eva a touch awe-inspiring. She was a nurse and looked sternly capable of dealing with any crisis, but even she seemed far more approachable, laughing frankly at herself, as she stumbled over the complexities of English grammar.

Now she carried a tray, which held a bottle of liqueur and four small glasses, to the table and set it down. Without speaking she poured drinks for them all. She was a thin-faced woman in her early thirties with a long, narrow nose and elegantly arched eyebrows. Her dark hair was drawn austerely back from her face.

With a grave courtesy that Rebecca thought very European, Eva handed each of them a glass. 'Please,' she said. 'It's Barack. It's our liqueur.' She remained standing at the head of the table. 'Let's drink,' she proposed, 'to the events in Warsaw.'

'*Volontiers.*' Janos took up the idea eagerly, his eyes, behind the uncompromising spectacles, suddenly serious. He held his glass high. Owain did the same. Silently Rebecca raised hers. She was sombrely impressed by the moment. At home she'd have been pleased by the news from Poland. But here, with Janos and Eva, its crucial importance for millions of people came home to her with a sharp immediacy.

'To Warsaw.'

'Freedom and Warsaw.'

Janos, Owain and Eva tossed their small drinks back in one go. Rebecca sipped hers, cautious of its fieriness.

'Maybe it's the start of something,' Owain said, replacing his glass on the table. She could see that he had the same sense as she did of a more conscious involvement. Then he smiled, raising one eyebrow. 'Maybe you could lay on a revolution here,' he joked to Janos. 'For two visiting journalists. We're available until the first week in November.'

Janos stubbed out his cigarette and gave his boyish grin. 'I have friends. I'll see what I can do.'

On the Sunday after Becky and Owain left for Budapest Paul came for lunch with Ruth and Ben in Marshall Street. He'd taken a room in Clapham and was resignedly plying his trade as a plumber until something better came along, although he didn't specify what. Now earning regularly, he presented Ruth with a welcome financial booster. Any unexpected windfall was immediately earmarked as rent money, so that at least she could be sure of a roof over her and Ben's heads in the foreseeable future.

Paul seemed flesh and blood again, without the otherworldly translucence he'd had in the aftermath of his stay in hospital. He hadn't touched a drop of anything for months, he told her. There seemed a certain ambiguity in his view of the achievement. 'It doesn't half make the days seem long,' he admitted with a rueful honesty. He was quiet at first, and seemed depressed, though he didn't talk to Ruth about his feelings. There was a hoarse, rusty edge to his voice that worried her. He'd always been exuberant in the way he spoke.

He had a piano in his digs and was experimenting with a modern jazz style. Paul was disillusioned with the world of Trad, as some people were beginning to call it. The disloyalty of the Wailers had hit him hard, but that wasn't the only reason. Traditional bands were beginning to seem quaint and cosy. 'Just a crowd of middle-aged lads doing their thing,' he described them sourly. The thought was anathema to Paul. Modern jazz had a cool and dangerous image that appealed to him far more. But so far he was only tinkering and dreaming.

He cheered up a little over lunch though, and made Ben laugh with *Goon Show* impersonations. Ruth joined in, and Ben was ecstatic. All of them had the brief illusion that nothing had changed and they were a family again.

Like Tony Taylor he seemed fascinated, in a sweeping, emotional fashion, by the Suez situation. 'You mark my words, they'll clobber the wogs in the end.' Wryly he parodied the received wisdom of the man in the street.

She laughed shortly. 'What, just for being wogs?'

'Yeah.' He was adamant. 'That's what it boils down to. They can't get away with defying the mighty British lion. We'll have to prove we've still got teeth.'

His claim made her pensive for a moment, but she began to tell Paul about Ryan Jaquier's offer and it slipped from her mind. Paul was interested, but reacted typically. 'He only wants to get into your bloomers.'

'You're pathetic.' The masculine dismissiveness of the remark riled her. 'I'm the best in the group.' Without his provocation she'd never have made such a statement, but it was a fact, she thought suddenly. Though she admitted to herself that there could be some truth in Paul's words.

'Sorry. That wasn't a nice thing to say.' He became conciliatory. 'Still, this bloke sounds more your type than Abe Lincoln. He was always too moral for you.'

'You're wrong.' She pictured Owain fleetingly, with an ache of tenderness.

After the meal Ruth made coffee and they played some records. Paul put on Elvis's *Blue Suede Shoes*. 'Dance, Marlene?' He approached her with his old, odd smile.

She stood up. They'd always enjoyed dancing together. He led her in a playful, buoyant jive. Their eyes met as they moved with a bruised but stubborn friendship. Ruth had the impression that she knew him through and through. Ben got to his feet. Each held out a hand to him and he joined their cavorting. There was a feeling of rightness about the dance. Eventually there'd be a divorce. She recognized the inevitability of that. And yet, in some immovable way, the three of them belonged together.

Talking to Janos and Eva in the privacy of their small apartment – as Owain and Rebecca managed to do twice during their first few days in Budapest – brought everything they'd ever read about the European satellite countries abruptly to life. Annexed by the Russians after the war, Hungary, Poland, Czechoslovakia and others longed to assert their national identity, and craved freedom of speech and their own free elections. You didn't have to be politically aware to know that. But the knowledge had no particular immediacy for people in Britain. It was, like a nursery rhyme or a fairy tale, something you absorbed without thinking about it. Now suddenly Rebecca and Owain found themselves talking to two people for whom these longings were as pervasive as the air they breathed.

Over recent months Janos had made clear in his letters to Owain that a new hope was bubbling beneath the surface. It had been there ever since Stalin had died. Under Khrushchev there'd been early signs of relaxation, and then a hardening. But earlier that year there'd been an astounding breakthrough. At the Twentieth Soviet Communist Congress Khrushchev had loudly and lengthily denounced the policies of Stalin, publicly revealing the extent of his executions, imprisonments and repressions. The drama of the event had rocked both East and West.

'Nothing's changed,' Janos told them wryly. 'But all the time you think it might. The writers and the intellectuals are always busy . . . talking and scribbling resolutions.' He himself was a sports writer. No intellectual, he protested. But they guessed he was more involved than he claimed.

In fact there *had* been changes in Hungary. That summer the hard-liner, Rakosi, had been dismissed by the Kremlin, but he'd been replaced by Gero who was almost as bad.

'We hoped to have Imre Nagy back,' Eva told them. 'He's *sympathique* and he wants the things we want.'

'He's the people's choice,' Janos agreed. Rebecca was amused by the colloquialism in his mouth.

Both of them talked with hatred about the AVH – or the Avos, as they called them – the highly paid secret police who propped up the current regime, a byword for torture and cruelty, answerable to no one but the most high-ranking officials.

'They're like poison gas. They creep in everywhere. If they knew we were speaking to you like this . . .' Janos drew down the corners of his mouth and made an abrupt chopping motion with his hand against his throat.

The Avos were detested with a blind ferocity. Ordinary people were often on better terms with the occupying Russian troops, who after all were mere pawns in the game. The Avos were Hungarian. They had a choice. And they'd used it to inflict a reign of terror on their own people.

No one else talked to Owain and Rebecca with the same frankness as Janos and Eva. For much of the time they were simply on the receiving end of the approved official treatment for visiting journalists. This world was self-contained, a round of factory tours and lectures and polite, guarded, well-meaning faces. Lunch with a trade delegation. An afternoon at a conference on the manufacture of railway cars. Men in double-breasted suits, women in square-cut blouses and skirts, with, seemingly, not a frivolous bone in their bodies. Heavy-handed, careful jokes from both sides that had to be painstakingly rendered into the opposite language and officially laughed at. A little judicious sight-seeing with Miklos and Amelie, their guide and translator, both wary-eyed and mildly touchy.

So much of their time was monopolized, organized. From their official car they could see the broad Danube glittering in the autumn sun. Wide avenues curved alongside, with trees fluttering their yellowed leaves. Steep, fascinating medieval alleys snaked away from the main boulevards. Real people with real faces talked and laughed. Children scuffled and played, while in the stuffy vehicle they conversed ponderously with Miklos and Amelie.

Being with Janos and Eva was like a breath of fresh air. There were no traces there of the official guarded mask. Their faces reflected their moods and thoughts. They could be silly and joke, then talk with fervent passion about their hopes and dissatisfactions, voicing openly to these sympathetic listeners from the outside world what they and so many others were really thinking.

36

Owain sat opposite Rebecca at a table in the large, old-fashioned Duna Hotel as they waited for breakfast. He liked the dining room. It had a gloomy spaciousness, and along one side was a plate-glass window which looked out on to the Danube and its riverside boulevard. This morning the sun shone, piercing the autumnal haze with a magnesium whiteness which was reflected in the river below, making the surrounding water shine like dark glass. There looked to be a seasonal chill in the air. Most of the work-bound citizens who bustled past wore coats or thick jerseys.

They watched the passers-by with a shared curiosity. 'Funny, isn't it,' Owain said, 'how when you're abroad people you'd take for granted at home look interesting. Mysterious.' A woman passed, half-dowdy, half-beautiful, in a boxy brown coat. She had tragic eyes, he thought, or so you could imagine, deep-set and dark-ringed.

'Not just abroad – but behind the Iron Curtain.' Rebecca spoke the words with dramatic emphasis. 'That adds even more of a *je ne sais quoi*.'

The head waiter brought coffee and dark, sour bread. He was an austere and forbidding-looking man in his forties, with rimless spectacles and grey hair cut *en brosse*. He monopolized the sprinkling of foreigners staying at the hotel, smiling at them with frosty ingratiation. They'd christened him Dimitri, for no particular reason, since it was a Russian name. It just seemed to suit him. A couple of days ago Rebecca had seen him outside the dining room, batting some fresh-faced underling across the cheeks with what looked like a damask napkin. Seeing her, he'd broken off to incline his head unctuously and insincerely.

He had a smattering of international phrases. '*Bon appétit*, Mr Roberts . . . Miss.' There was always the shade of a hesitation before he included Rebecca in his good wishes.

Owain looked at her across the table with a private flash of affection. He'd always liked Rebecca, but recently, given their proximity during the last few days, she'd come to occupy the foreground of his attention. Habitually he'd viewed her in relation to something else – as an efficient colleague on *Red Lion*, as Ruth's best friend. Since they'd been here she'd infiltrated his consciousness as her own person and nothing more.

With her professional competence it had barely occurred to him how young she was. Twenty-two? Twenty-three? His junior by a decade. Even when dressed more formally than usual in a grey jersey dress she looked like a student, black hair brushing her shoulders, the gleam of the snake earrings he'd given her as a joke. There was an appealing demureness about her that was belied by the slightly sceptical brown eyes below her straight fringe of hair, which seemed to gaze out shrewdly at the world and sum it up with an air of private amusement. Her eyes had always interested him, but since they'd been here he'd had more time than usual to observe them . . .

He dismissed the thought and instead he mentioned to Becky a feeling that had nagged at him for the last couple of days. 'There's something in the air, don't you think? Ever since Warsaw last week. I'm not sure what. A kind of nervous energy . . .'

'Yes.' She pounced on the idea. 'I feel that too. Even with Miklos and Amelie. Even when they're wearing their most official suet-pudding faces – they're restless. Not quite believing in themselves when they trot out their stability and growth statistics.' Her eyes shone with a hint of conspiratorial laughter.

A flash of memory came to Owain: Ruth one night at his flat. 'Becky likes you,' she'd said in a tone that held unexplored implications. He'd not thought of it since.

But there was no time to pursue the recollection. Out of the corner of his eye he glimpsed Miklos and Amelie entering the dining room with their usual faintly truculent air, as if they suspected their charges of wanting to give them the slip. He and Rebecca were due to visit an industrial complex just south of Budapest, at Csepel.

'Don't look now,' he said. 'It's our minders.'

Driving back from their visit in the grey mid-afternoon, it seemed that their suspicions of that morning had been justified. Something was going on. They saw nothing dramatic and yet there seemed to be an abnormal number of people on the streets in the centre of town. On some corners young people stood, offering duplicated sheets of paper to the passers-by. In Museum Avenue a young woman with a pale, intelligent face and dark eyes – she was like Becky, Owain thought – stood holding a sheaf of the papers and talking earnestly to what looked like a father and son. The man, in a prosperous-looking black overcoat, stared at the pavement as he listened, nodding curtly from time to time. His son kept his eyes on the woman's face with an air of rapt attention. A couple of streets later they saw two students pasting broadsheets on to the baroque facade of a large, sand-coloured building. Passers-by gathered at once to read them.

Inside the car Miklos and Amelie ignored their questions and sat stony-faced, rather as if they'd been caught in some kind of embarrassing *flagrante delicto* and could think of no adequate explanation. Eventually their car pulled up outside the Duna Hotel. Owain and Rebecca got out and thanked them and arranged to meet the following morning.

It was dark, with a soft dampness in the air. Old-fashioned standard gas lamps cast a photogenic light over the sea of figures, silhouetting a head blackly here and there against a slightly lighter sky. There was shouting somewhere in front of them, the revving of some large vehicle, then cheers and isolated staccato cries. Rebecca couldn't see the source of the hubbub. She was faced with a wall of backs.

'What's happening?'

'My God!' Owain was taller than most. 'It's the Stalin statue. They're trying to topple it.'

'No!' She gave a shiver of delighted disbelief. The statue was, to her, the most recognizable landmark in Budapest. Miklos had pointed it out on their first morning, a towering bronze monstrosity on a pinkish pedestal, at least fifty feet high, she reckoned, arrogantly dominating a square named after it. Janos hated the monument with a deeply personal animus. 'I would like to . . .' he'd begun savagely, completing the sentence by imitating the sound of an explosion and gesturing graphically with his hands. Even Miklos, who seemed to toe the party line, had indicated it with a strangely ambiguous expression on his face.

The people who thronged the streets were elated. Rebecca wasn't personally involved, but she caught the mood. Owain held her by the hand. In the milling crowd they could easily be separated.

He craned further. 'They've fixed cables to it. And to a truck . . . Something's going!'

There were roars from onlookers closer to the scene of the action, and a cataclysmic crash.

'The head's gone, but the rest is still standing.' Owain glanced down at her. 'I'll lift you if you like.' Placing his arms round her body, he hoisted her so that she could see over the heads of those in front. Her perch was precarious. They were jostled by the crowd.

Rebecca saw the sudden flare of a pale flame. 'The head's hollow. They're making a fire in it.' Anonymous figures fed the blaze, silhouetted dramatically as the fire became stronger, licking vigorously upward. She couldn't make out what they were burning, but the scene reminded her of some obscure Halloween rite, with a sense of almost pagan exultation. As the flames leaped, the watching crowd cheered and screamed, giving rein to a full-blooded defiance that had been bottled up for ten long years.

Some time later the body itself plunged downward, toppling dizzily like a huge felled tree. By then Rebecca and Owain had insinuated themselves further forward. They watched as men and women rushed to hack crazily at the statue, breaking off chunks to take as souvenirs. On the plinth the bronze feet remained, immovably planted in an attitude of command. Eventually the head was loaded on to a truck and driven off in the direction of Parliament Square.

They drifted away, then, towards the centre of town. Everywhere the streets were alive with people, young mostly, but with a fair sprinkling of older faces. There was a good-natured lawlessness in the air. On the fringe of a group of students talking and laughing excitedly at the tops of their voices, a round-faced, curly-haired lad gambolled like a dancing bear. Watching, Owain grinned down at Rebecca. In the street lighting his bearded face was a play of white and black. The crush was less dense here, but they continued to hold hands by a tacit mutual consent. The contact was warm and companionable. She was put in mind of the rough and tumble gaiety of a night at a funfair.

Two minutes later, turning into Lenin Avenue, they

heard a distant sound, explosive and staccato, like the rattle of gunfire, and they stopped in their tracks.

Rebecca was aghast. 'Is that what I think it is?'

'There'd have to be retaliation.' Owain barely seemed surprised. They strained their ears, but the sound didn't come again. Most of the people around them seemed not to have heard, though a few stood listening, their faces intent and uneasy.

Owain and Rebecca carried on walking. 'We couldn't have been mistaken?' Rebecca suggested.

He shook his head. 'It was definitely firing.' He was in no doubt. 'But maybe just a single incident.'

A couple of turnings later they saw a truckload of soldiers parked on the corner. The men looked decidedly unmartial, leaning over the side of the lorry and joking with a crowd of students of both sexes. The atmosphere between the two groups seemed relaxed and cordial. As they watched, a skinny youngster was hoisted up by his friends, and a couple of soldiers gave him a hand up on to the truck. He raised his hands like a victorious boxer in a gesture to the students below. Rebecca wasn't sure how to interpret the scene. The soldiers, presumably, were there to uphold law and order, yet they seemed on perfectly amicable terms with the rebel youngsters.

However, the good humour was abruptly dispelled by a fresh outburst of gunfire. It was closer this time, a long, protracted volley of machine-gun fire. Rebecca recognized the sound from countless films, though she'd never heard it in real life. Everyone reacted, listening, heads cocked, conversing urgently, uneasily. Rebecca would have expected the military contingent to disappear with alacrity towards the scene of the fray, but they stayed put. She saw one of their number, inside the cab of the lorry, speaking into a walkie-talkie, but his face showed no emotion.

The students, though, made their way towards a side-street that led in the general direction of the sound. They talked excitedly among themselves, but their advance was cautious. Owain and Rebecca followed in the same direction. The dark side-road was lit with a quivering apricot glow, and they saw, at the far end, an overturned van, around which flames licked. Rebecca gazed, awe-struck, seeing in the scene a stark, cinematic beauty.

'Avos,' one of the students, a bold-looking, black-haired boy, said loudly. He spat on the ground and drew one finger savagely across his throat in a universally understood gesture. Rebecca recognized the word Janos had used for the secret police, with the same tone of venomous loathing.

'The kids must have captured one of their vans,' Owain guessed.

The situation had escalated dramatically from the rowdy, but essentially peaceful protest it had seemed to them earlier. The rising commotion came, they now realized, from the direction of the radio station, a building they'd toured decorously with Miklos and Amelie two days earlier. By now the gunfire was sporadic, but sustained. Their earlier gaiety had spiralled into a clenched excitement. All this was real, Rebecca told herself. Here and now, momentous, real events were taking place. And yet a lifetime of unthinking security made it hard for her quite to believe the thought.

The students turned the corner by the burning van, then reappeared abruptly, driven back by a group of five armed men. They were in uniform and held sub-machine guns levelled at the young people, though Rebecca's first startled impression was that they were threatening rather than intending to shoot.

'Avos.' This time Rebecca spoke the word.

One of the men was tall, with a reddish moustache, and as he motioned the students to turn back his expression was almost fatherly. The youngsters raised their hands to shoulder height, elbows tucked close to their sides. They retreated readily, yet somehow managed to inject their flight with just a trace of lingering defiance. The black-haired boy spat again. Rebecca marvelled at his rashness. There was nothing for herself and Owain but to retrace their steps as well. Rebecca crossed the cobbled street to the pavement and almost stumbled over two figures she'd not noticed before.

A boy in a black cloth cap sat silently in the gutter. Next to him, half in the road, a young woman lay on one side. Her right arm, loosely extended, supported her head. The woman's face was smooth, white and waxen. She wore a green quilted jacket that was partly open. Rebecca saw, with a horrified, gut-wrench, that the grey jersey and slacks that she wore underneath were saturated with a thick, dark patch of clotted blood. Her stillness was unearthly. She was dead.

The boy sat bemused, his head in his hands, passive as a watching dog. He showed no reaction to the jostle of students, the barked commands of the Avos, their weapons. As Rebecca skirted him and the body of the girl, he raised his eyes and looked blankly into her stricken face.

Owain was concerned about Rebecca. She was silent as they walked home from the place where they'd seen the dead girl. From time to time he heard her catch her breath with a kind of shuddering gulp, as if caught unawares by some powerful emotion. He assumed that, almost certainly, this was the first time she'd come face to face with violent death, and it pained him to think that he'd been – however indirectly – responsible.

For himself, the sight of the woman's body had revived feelings he'd almost forgotten, but which were familiar. In France as a young soldier, in the final year of the war, he'd seen deaths which were brutal, gruesome, sudden. He'd learned the hard way that you could cope. Rebecca seemed stunned as they walked along dark streets which were now almost empty.

'Come and have a drink with me, Becky,' he urged when they were back in the hotel, and prayed privately that she'd agree. He didn't think she should be on her own. 'I've got that bottle of Scotch I bought on the plane,' he added, trying to make the invitation sound casual. 'It's got to be drunk sometime.'

She nodded wearily. 'Okay. Thanks.'

He smiled. 'Don't forget your tooth-mug.'

A few minutes later she knocked on his door. As he opened it, she held up a glass like a begging bowl, wanly teasing. She'd taken off her coat and shoes and her hair hung in rat's tails on the shoulders of a dark green sweater. She looked young, a waif. He would have liked to put his arms round her, comfort her with physical warmth. But she was her own person and didn't ask for his protection. Instead he touched her shoulder, seeing himself in a flash of self-awareness as a caring teacher perhaps, offering some young pupil a restrained show of sympathy. 'You all right?'

She shrugged. 'I've been better. But what does it matter about me? Seeing kids like that against guns. God, they must be desperate.'

He poured her a generous measure of Scotch. Rebecca sat down on the edge of a green wicker settee, a strangely rococo item of furniture, one of a set. She swallowed a large mouthful and grimaced at the taste. 'It's vile. Like medicine. But it warms you up.'

Owain sat on the floor opposite her, cross-legged. 'I feel responsible, you know.'

She mocked him gently. 'What, for bringing a gently bred gel like me into . . .?'

'I mean it.'

She smiled a little sourly. 'I'm touched by your concern. Honest. I like it. But it's irrelevant. I just can't get over . . . I mean earlier in the evening it seemed fun almost. And then . . .'

'It may stop here and it may not. There could be worse to come, Becky. I think tomorrow I ought to drive you to the border.' I sound like some tight-lipped prat in a British B-movie, he thought.

'Oh, no you don't!' A full-blooded certainty that sounded more honest to him than his own lip-service to the conventions of male chivalry. 'I'm not going to beat a cautious retreat.'

'You must.' He spoke soberly. 'If it goes on like this you could actually be killed.'

'You're staying?'

'Yes,' he admitted.

'So you're pulling rank?'

'I won't be responsible for endangering you.' He sounded pompous, less and less like himself. In reality the last thing he wanted was for her to go. Yet the decent thing was surely to persuade her.

'I resign then.' She looked across at him provocatively. 'Okay? So I'm staying as a private person.'

Their eyes met with a challenge that melted slowly into friendship, relief, laughter. He parodied the blimpish persona he'd briefly tried to adopt. 'This is all highly irregular . . .'

Owain crossed to his bedside table and picked up the bottle of whisky. He offered Rebecca a refill. She held out her glass with a reckless theatrical gesture. She'd drawn her feet up on to the strange wicker settee and lay propped on a cushion. Owain took a pillow from the bed and lay on the floor, leaned on one elbow, his glass beside him. Rebecca stayed talking for a long time. There'd been a shift, Owain thought, in the atmosphere between them, a deepening of intimacy. Their conversation was sporadic, unemphatic, like people who'd known each other for years. He found her beautiful in the muted light, though her eyes were shadowed with tiredness. He thought of her as someone self-contained. Tonight she looked vulnerable, her defences were lowered.

With unnerving clarity he could imagine himself standing and crossing the few feet of carpet that separated them, bending to kiss her unmade-up lips, touching the supple shoulders below the soft sweater. He was powerfully tempted, but a spectre prevented him. The repellent image of some office lecher taking advantage of a young colleague was potent in his mind, and he stayed put.

Around half-past four she got up to go. 'I'll be like a limp rag tomorrow.' She stood up. 'Thanks for the drink. It helped.' She grinned. 'I'll be out like a light.'

But abruptly, from outside, they heard a distant rumbling and shaking. As they listened it came nearer until their own building began to vibrate subtly. Bewildered, they crossed to the window. Owain drew back the thick, rust-coloured curtains. Outside, in the darkness, the wrought-iron street lights shone through a drifting haze. And below on the avenue, picturesquely illuminated, stood the uncompromising silhouette of a tank.

37

'A boiled egg.'

'Okay.' Ruth reached for the small saucepan.

'No.' Crouched on the kitchen floor, Ben began the absorbing daily chore of tying his shoelaces. A lock of fair hair flopped forward as he peered down at his fingers. 'No. I think I'll have shredded wheat.'

'Make up your mind.'

It was difficult at that moment to give her full attention to her son's wavering over his choice of breakfast. With an absent air she went to the cupboard and reached for the packet. Nowadays she seemed to be living inside her head. The routine things got done, but she hardly knew how. Her thoughts were focused elsewhere, on rehearsals, the cabaret. It filled her mind. In a couple of days she'd be performing again in public. After years. Details of the show – her lines, dancesteps and bits of business, as Ryan called them – impinged on her mind graphically at every moment.

But there was something else now as well . . . Something more important, though not quite as real. The news from Hungary. Ruth had known nothing about it – she never seemed to have time to read a paper or turn on the wireless at the right moment – until Monsieur Berteaut, her boss at the restaurant, asked excitedly, 'Your two friends, they're all right, are they, with all this argy-bargy going on?'

'What argy-bargy?' She had to smile. His French pronunciation of the phrase was irresistibly comic.

'You know. Hungary. The Russkis.'

He'd explained and made her listen to the next news

bulletin. Straight after work she phoned the Hungarian Legation, who were unforthcoming, and anyway the telephone lines from Budapest were out of order, they told her stolidly, refusing to speculate on the reason why.

Ruth was more shaken by the news than she would have believed. World events had always seemed to her impossibly remote, and yet her two closest friends . . . She could only hope they were lying low. They must still be there or they'd have phoned. Her imagination ran riot. There was fighting in the streets . . . She felt hugely ignorant, and for the first time in her life wished she'd taken an interest in international affairs, to be able to assess the situation less wildly. A small paragraph in the *Manchester Guardian* referred to their presence in Budapest, but without further comment.

'Mum.' Ben was battling with two chunky pieces of shredded wheat. He crinkled his face up with a calculated, melting charm. 'Cut them up for me.'

Her thoughts jerked back to the here and now. 'No.' She shook her head smiling. 'Never again. You're too big for that.'

At the same time a memory crossed her mind from years ago. When the Tories first came to power Becky had been dejected and angry and Ruth had teased her, claiming that politics was a world of its own and didn't affect nobodies like them. And in fact the idea of Owain and Becky trapped in somebody else's struggle still seemed unreal to her, like a book or a film. But it wasn't. The understanding came to her every so often in a cold, ugly flash.

'Letters!' It was Ernest Broadbent calling from downstairs, his voice hoarse this early in the morning, not yet lubricated by the pints of strong tea he consumed through the day. He always left the mail for Rebecca and herself on the stairs up to their flat.

'Thanks, Ernest.'

There were two envelopes, both for Becky. One a bill, the other a hand-addressed letter. Rebecca had given instructions for Ruth to deal with her post. She slit the first envelope, standing by the kitchen table with a half-finished mug of Nescafé. The letter was short and written on a single piece of cheap, lined paper. It came from Tony Taylor and was dated more than a week ago.

'Dear Becky,' it said. 'Just a quick scribble. I'll leave this for my brother to post. Hope he gets round to it before Xmas! Just to let you know we're off to Cyprus. Top secret. Not supposed to say why. But remember our talk last time I saw you. Eh what? You see, Becky, I said I knew a thing or two, but you wouldn't have it. No time for more. Linda's fine. Love to Ruth. I'll write. Tony.'

Ruth put the letter down on the table, feeling jumpy and oddly rattled. She was in a strange frame of mind, and put it down to nerves about the cabaret, the anticipation, the pressure. She took a sip of her coffee and made a face. It was tepid and tasted unpleasant.

She touched Ben's dish. 'Finished?'

He put down his spoon. 'Yes.'

'See. I knew you could do it.'

She crossed to the sink and threw away the rest of her coffee, then washed the mug and Ben's bowl. The news from Hungary had stirred a kind of awakening, a sense that the outside world was impinging. Tony's letter confirmed the feeling. Maybe if she'd taken notice, read the papers, she'd have been more aware of what was going on. It wouldn't all have crept up on her like this. She felt powerless, bewildered. He was a pawn too. Tony, the youthful lover, with his sweet young fiancée. This transfer must be something to do with the Suez thing he'd been hinting about last time he was here, she thought. It was stupid really. In the cabaret she was doing a satirical number on that very subject. She performed it with cheek

369

and charm, but, in truth, until this moment it had meant almost nothing to her.

'If they try to send Tony anywhere, I'll write Eden a stiff letter . . .' Linda had said that. Ruth could picture the wild-rose flush on her face, her petulant prettiness. But she was powerless too. All of them were.

She gazed out at the sea of faces. Pale blobs in the darkness, a corporate *them*. She was the individual, alone on the stage, illuminated by a white spotlight, the focus of all attention.

Ruth was dressed in black. A plain, close-fitting top and a long skirt, her hair centrally parted and drawn back to the nape of her neck. Her reflection in the dressing-room mirror had presented a classic gravity. The outward image influenced her mood, so that she faced the warm, unknown multiple presence of the audience in the ram-shackle theatre with an unhurried calm.

Ryan had kissed her cheek just before she went on. 'Go to it, Ruthie. You'll slay 'em.' He was red-faced and over-excited, trying to be everywhere at once, but oddly his presence was comforting. You trusted him.

'Course I will.' She warmed to him and smiled, miming a nervousness she didn't really feel.

The performance she was about to give was a gamble, but she felt equal to it. Up to now the evening had been freewheeling and deliberately anarchic, spiced with rowdy political satire. A little while ago Ruth herself, dressed in a red tutu and a mask, had led a rousing, silly song called 'Don't Panic, Mr Eden', about Nasser, Suez, and the huffings and puffings of the British prime minister, bellow-ing out the words with a brassy verve, backed by a chorus line of men wearing – for reasons clearer to Ryan than herself – multi-coloured Harlequin costumes. In these surroundings she barely thought of Tony's letter and it all went down a treat with the audience. They cheered rapturously, obviously tickled by a sense of sharing in something rather subversive and irreverent.

Then she'd gone and changed into the austere black clothes and immediately felt different, standing apart from the backstage chaos and cultivating a stillness that remained with her.

Now the moment was right. By her appearance, her waiting, she'd imposed a silence, a tangible expectancy. Deliberately Ruth delayed for a second longer. Then she began to speak.

'What then have you done that I have not surpassed a thousand times? You have seduced, ruined even, a number of women, but what difficulties did you have to overcome . . .?'

She could hear her voice, clear in the void, each word falling, unhurried and crystalline, like a perfectly shaped raindrop. At the same time she was keenly aware of attentive eyes, ears, minds, and she offered them a controlled passion. There was a hush beyond the foot-lights that was deep and receptive.

'. . . As you may suppose, I was like all young girls and tried to guess at love and its pleasures . . .'

The tone of her recitation was quite unlike anything that had gone before. The text was taken from a book Guy had lent her once about the sadistic mind games played by a group of French aristocrats. Her monologue was taken from the pen of a Marquise, revealing to a male lover the calculation and cunning she was forced to use in order to survive the artful cruelty of the society she lived in. The speech was formal and elegant, but it smouldered with a dark intensity. Ruth had had proof before now of its impact. Last term she'd prepared it for an exercise in class and spoken it with a harsh simplicity, reducing her fellow actors to awe-struck silence.

'Lawks. Fair wrings your withers,' Ryan had commented in a foolish country bumpkin's accent when, after the space of several seconds, all of them had come back down to earth. He was covering, so he explained later, for a sense of . . . dazzlement. 'You were very powerful,' he told her soberly, his eyes holding an earnestness that was deliberately seductive, but also sincere. And he asked if she'd repeat the performance in the cabaret.

Since then Ruth had hugged the prospect to herself with a chill of anticipation. This was an opportunity which she mustn't waste, a chance to hold the attention of a discerning audience, including professionals, people it would be advantageous for her to impress. She wavered between elation and fear, waking often in the night. Logically there was no reason why she shouldn't produce, in a larger context, the stunned reaction she'd seen in class . . .

Now, on stage, her fears had been replaced by an all-or-nothing recklessness. But she was calm and conscious of the effects she wanted to achieve. With one part of her mind she could visualize the whole scene, as if she were floating somewhere above it, picturing her own erect, austere black figure, sharp in the cold spotlight, and the blur of attentive faces. She paced herself – she'd rehearsed it a hundred times. The monologue had a rising intensity.

'I desired you before I had seen you.' She allowed a shade of controlled languour into her voice, yet retained the hostile, challenging tone that the text demanded. Always love was spoken of in terms of war. 'Seduced by your reputation, I felt you were lacking to my glory. I burned to wrestle with you hand to hand . . .' She paused a second for the words to settle in the darkness, and added with a cool reflection, 'This was the only one of my inclinations which had even a moment's power over me . . .'

As she spoke Ruth was keenly aware of how lucky she'd been to stumble on this text. It was fresh and unknown. Its impact had never had the chance to dull into cliché. She was conscious too of how much – how very much – she'd missed this feeling of being a focus, projecting a mood on an audience, convincing them. She had the power, and could do it.

She moved into the last defiant phase of the monologue. '. . . After I have raised myself above other women by painful labour, should I consent to crawl, like them, between impudence and timidity? Above all should I fear a man to the extent of seeing my safety nowhere but in flight? No, Vicomte, never. I must conquer or perish.'

The final words rang with a fierce clarity in the warm darkness of the auditorium. Ruth knew that it was going to be all right. Much better than all right. The silence that greeted her had a coiled vitality and erupted into a storm of applause.

38

All yesterday there'd been fighting in the streets. They'd heard the muffled crump of guns, explosions, shouting. It was too risky to go out. They'd been warned to stay away from the windows, but upstairs in Owain's room they stared out and saw, in Buda, on the other side of the river, vigorous eddies of grey-black smoke rising into the pale sky. Much of the fighting, they heard later, had taken place on the opposite side of town near the East Station, close to where Janos and Eva lived.

In the early afternoon, though, the hotel was shaken again by the rumbling of tanks. The boulevard outside was deserted as they passed, massive, grim and anonymous.

While Owain and Rebecca watched, a young boy – he seemed no more than that – had come running out of nowhere. He wore a royal-blue sweater and his complexion was rosy with the fresh air. As he ran towards the tanks he looked desperate and wildly exhilarated. About twenty-five feet away he lobbed something at the first vehicle. A bottle? There was a blurred flash and it broke against the side of the tank, falling to the ground. A startling sheet of flame reared up and bright, forked trails of burning petrol trickled down the side of the vehicle where the Molotov cocktail had struck it.

The orange, flaring vitality of the fire was dazzling and dramatic in the damp afternoon, though the tank was barely threatened. But almost before the bomb had hit the ground, a volley of machine-gun fire was loosed, apparently at random, spraying trees, the sides of buildings, a fire hydrant, and stopping the boy dead in his tracks with a shocking finality. In a second his body lay, humped and totally still, on the pavement.

They watched passively from the grandstand comfort of Owain's room, too stupefied to react. What could anyone say to cap the enormity of the absurd, sudden death? Later, though, as the afternoon dulled into dusk, Rebecca felt herself begin to shiver.

'Oh, God.' She caught her breath sharply to suppress a sob that was gathering in her throat, but it forced an exit, gracelessly loud like a hiccup. Her hands pressed against her eyes, as if to blot out what she'd seen.

'Becky, come here. Becky.' Owain's arms went round her, one hand cradling the back of her head and pulling it to him. She felt rigid, unyielding, her eyes were burning. She closed them, leaning her forehead against the hardness of his chest.

This morning the city was calmer. You could walk around cautiously, skirting burned-out tanks, through streets torn up to make barricades, wading at times through broken glass. Wherever you went women were plying brooms, sweeping the glass into ordered piles, attempting to impose traces of normality. It was drizzling and flags hung, heavy and wet, from windows and balconies. Mostly they were the red, white and green Hungarian tricolor, with a slit in the middle where the red Russian star had been torn out. But here and there a black banner of mourning trailed starkly. Across the road Rebecca saw that the side of a square, official-looking building had a jagged, gaping hole. Inside you could glimpse chairs, upended, and shards of white, splintered wood. The stillness was oppressive. Rebecca thought there was a feeling in the air of waking from a nightmare and finding that it had been real.

'Look at that.' Owain pointed at the gutted shells of two vans, and close by a charred body. It was blackened, and you could no longer tell whether it had been male or female, old or young, yet the essential shape was perfectly preserved.

Warily she gazed in the direction indicated. 'I see it.' By now she'd passed other corpses, lying in the streets, shattered by bullets, or burned by the homemade fire-bombs the students were using. She'd seen blood in the gutters, coagulated and dusty, crawling sometimes with sluggish flies. Amazingly it seemed that the Russians hadn't had it all their own way. Rebecca remembered Janos laughing that, if the revolution ever came, the Hungarian kids knew a thing or two about partisan warfare. They'd been trained at school, from Russian manuals, ready for the Western imperialist aggressors.

They'd received a message from him that morning at the hotel – how he'd got it to them was a matter for conjecture – asking them to meet him outside the plush Hotel Astoria, on the corner of Rakosi Street and Museum Avenue, which the Russians had commandeered as their headquarters. They knew the place. Their guide, Miklos, had pointed it out to them. It was a prosperous-looking building, always with a row of shiny foreign cars parked in front of it.

'My God, it's taken a bashing!' As it came into view Rebecca was thunderstruck. The hotel was shelled and shattered. A large hole gaped in the façade, and not one window, it seemed, remained intact. The smart cars were festooned with jagged slices of broken glass.

'The Hungarians've got hold of some pretty hefty guns then,' Owain said. Till now they'd only seen kids involved in the fighting, but in this bombardment there was evidence of professionalism.

Several Russian tanks were stationed outside the hotel, but their crews stood neutrally by, seeming indisposed for the moment towards any kind of warlike action. Quite a crowd had gathered and they couldn't see Janos at first, then Owain spotted his stubby figure dressed in a corduroy cap and jacket, talking earnestly to a tall Russian soldier with the mournful eyes and flaccid cheeks of a bloodhound. The soldier had inclined his head a little towards Janos, lending a stately ear, while the small Hungarian harangued him, gesticulating eagerly.

'He's a lad.' Owain grinned with ironic affection. Out of the corner of his eye Janos caught sight of them, and gave a small wave. They waited at a distance, not wanting to draw the Russian's attention to their own foreign presence. After some minutes of animated conversation Janos shook hands with the soldier and with two of his comrades, clapping them heartily on the arm. Then he turned and came towards them, pink and beaming at his own bravado.

'They say we're justified,' Janos reported as he drew level with them. 'They agree with us.' His glasses were spotted with drizzle. He took them off and rubbed them vigorously with his handkerchief.

'They're not going to disobey orders, though,' Owain pointed out. 'If they're told to shoot, they'll shoot.'

But Janos was elated and ignored the remark. 'The police have come over to our side, you know. And many Hungarian soldiers . . .' He replaced his spectacles and shook hands now with the two of them, as if suddenly remembering his own social obligations. 'It's good that you're here. There'll be a demonstration, I think . . .' He was enthusiastic that they should see as much as possible and give a firsthand account of it all back in the West. Janos nodded towards the gathering crowd. 'They think to see Nagy . . .' He looked sceptical. 'But I'm not so sure.'

Owain and Rebecca already knew that, in the wake of the unrest, Nagy, the people's favourite, had been created prime minister. He'd talked yesterday, on the radio, so

Janos told them, but he'd sounded strange and disappointingly indecisive. Janos's expression became dour and knowing. 'I think he's forced to say what others want him to.' His guess was that Nagy's promotion had been a sop to appease the rebels, that – behind the scenes – the real power remained with the Kremlinite hardliners and their henchmen, the Avos.

By now, more people had gathered round the scattered groups of soldiers, many of them youngsters who spoke halting Russian. Since the war the language had figured prominently in the school curriculum. Painstaking conversations were taking place, in apparent friendship. A large proportion of the crowd were older people, many of them middle-aged parents accompanied by their children.

A commotion from behind made Rebecca and Owain turn sharply. They saw a group of young Hungarians climbing aboard one of the Soviet tanks. The soldiers grinned and hoisted them up. A pretty dark girl planted a Hungarian flag in the turret of the tank, laughing over her shoulder at a crop-haired Russian. After a minute or two the tank began to move slowly through the crowd. A good-humoured cheer went up. From his vantage point next to the turret a skinny lad with foxy, excited eyes announced, so Janos explained, that they were heading for Parliament Square. Two other tanks followed suit and the spectators began to walk behind them in a ragged procession. There was a buzz of exhilarated chatter in the air.

As the crowd crossed one end of Lovolde Square they saw the dark, skulking shapes of further Soviet tanks. A silence fell gradually. The marchers waited to be challenged. Straggling past, they were watched warily. You could sense a sullen air of threat, but it remained unspoken.

Parliament Square was already crammed with a crowd thousands strong. The small column of Russian tanks came to a halt in one corner. Officially demonstrations were banned, but today no one seemed much bothered by the thought. There was a hopefulness in the air, which seemed to Rebecca bewilderingly at odds with the previous day's blood-letting. Close to her, a father lifted his young son on to his shoulders to peer at the tanks with more curiosity than dread.

'Look up there, though.' Owain pointed discreetly at the top of a large, columned building facing the Parliament. Above the line of the roof two figures were visible. Men in the uniform of the secret police.

Outlined against the sombre, churning clouds, Rebecca thought they looked sinister, but by now the Avo uniform had fixed in her a conditioned response. 'Maybe they're just here to keep an eye on law and order,' she said dubiously.

Suddenly a voice cut across the hubbub of the crowd. It was magnified by a loudspeaker, which lent it a hollow, echoing quality. An Avo addressed them from the steps of the Parliament building. Neither Rebecca nor Owain had any idea of what was being said, but the crowd responded with jeers and whistles.

'He says we should go home,' Janos interpreted helpfully. The expression on his face showed what he thought of that idea.

The message was repeated and the derision of the crowd grew. Even the boy on his father's shoulders shouted with the rest, his immature face twisted with scorn. For good measure he waved a small, clenched fist, clothed in a red woollen glove.

Without warning the sharp stutter of machine-gun fire sliced through the commotion and, even before Rebecca had framed an understanding of the sound, the child next to her was knocked from his perch. Those closest to him side-stepped. Still disorientated, Rebecca stared down at the boy and caught the look of surprise in his eyes before he died.

In an instant of horrified concern, she fell to her knees next to the child, along with his father. The boy's body appeared almost untouched, but from underneath him thick blood was already seeping. She saw this in a flash before someone grabbed her arm, pulling her upright, and she realized that the guns still crackled.

'We can't stay here! They're shooting at anyone, every-one.' It was Owain's voice. He dragged her in the direction from which they'd come. But almost immedi-ately they were halted. A separate burst of gunfire came from the tanks. From the same men who, half an hour earlier, had been laughing, pulling bystanders up beside them.

The crowd wheeled in total confusion. Rebecca saw a middle-aged woman in a thick brown winter coat lying dead in front of them, a hat tipped rakishly alongside her head. Two men stepped across her as if she'd been a bundle of soiled washing. A boy of fourteen or so sobbed in great breathy gusts. As she ran, Rebecca glimpsed from the corner of her eye a dismembered arm, trampled and disregarded like meat.

A distraught young woman attempted to hold on to her injured daughter and a wriggling toddler. Owain took the girl from her mother and carried her, holding the child's body against him, protecting her head with his right hand. All was panic. There was no shelter and still the guns sounded. Someone stumbled against Rebecca, a girl of about eleven in a white wool hat, her expression wild and lost. With a simultaneous instinct she and Janos grabbed the child's hand, pulling her along with them. Behind her Rebecca heard a sharp, blood-chilling cry of grief, but she kept on running.

* * *

Janos, Owain and Rebecca stood and stared through the rain and drizzle with a dull, repelled curiosity. On the opposite side of the road a body hung by its feet from a tree. The corpse was shirtless, its chest and back a mottled mess of black and purple. The skin of the face was liver-coloured, with the consistency of patent leather, the mouth and one eye pulped and monstrously swollen.

'It's an Avo,' Janos told them flatly.

'Bastard,' Owain said wearily, the single word holding unplumbed depths of contempt and revulsion. Rebecca could detect no trace of pity in his expression. She too gazed at the body, unmoved. Only this morning she would have turned away, unable to look. Since then she'd witnessed a surfeit of horror and violent death.

Contemplating the Avo, she could identify completely with the national loathing for the secret police. It was a hatred so deep and savage that ordinary people experienced a thirst to kick and beat the mercenaries to death, denying them the impersonal efficiency of guns and bullets.

'After this morning I think many will be killed like this,' Janos said. His voice sounded hollow. Whenever Rebecca had met him before he'd been smiling. Even over matters he regarded as serious. Now his face looked gaunt and much older.

When the morning's chaotic nightmare violence had subsided and they could think clearly again, the demonstrators understood that the massacre had been carried out by Avos, from the roof of the Ministry of Agriculture, opposite the Parliament building. Owain had spotted two of them early on, but there'd been more, many more. They had sprayed the peaceful crowd with bullets, repeatedly, irrespective of age or sex, on and on, until the square was littered with hundreds of bodies. In their zeal they'd shot down some of the Russians who were there in all friendliness. The Soviets suspected an ambush, so they too began to fire into the crowd.

Now the panic was stilled Rebecca was conscious of a kind of hopelessness, a drained indifference. Dusk was falling and it was cold. Over the road a group of men stood talking, shoulders hunched, hands in pockets. The mutilated body swayed a little in a sudden gust of wind. They paid it no attention. An old woman passed, stumping along the pavement in a long, black coat and heavy boots, spitting on the ground below where the corpse was hanging.

They sat in Janos's small living room, all three of them still wearing their outdoor coats. The curtains were open and two rectangles of bleak, dark sky showed. Every so often came the muffled report of gunfire. Sniper shooting, by the sound of it, not the crackle of big guns. Janos poured them all a hefty drink, from a large, anonymous bottle without a label. Some kind of vodka, he said. Rebecca sipped it gratefully. It tasted raw and burned her throat, but glowed comfortingly inside her, thawing out the numbness.

'You want some?' Janos offered the bottle again for refills.

'Never wanted it more.' Owain held out his glass. Sitting forward, as he was, on the edge of his chair, legs braced, he seemed restless, as though he'd found the days events somehow invigorating. Ruth had always said that with his thin, intense looks he made the perfect revolutionary. But the thought seemed trivial to Rebecca. They were in contact now with the real thing.

'You, Becky?' Janos smiled.

She nodded wordlessly and lifted her glass. Maybe the drink would make her feel human again. Janos poured her another large slug.

He seemed different, too, as if he'd laid aside a

comforting mask and behind it was someone much harder. Rebecca noticed that he'd dropped the French phrases that used to pepper his speech, as if they'd been an affectation, suitable only for less stirring times.

'I must go out soon,' he told them. Janos worked on the newspaper *Szabad Nep*, the official government mouthpiece, but in the last couple of days he and some colleagues had been putting together a news-sheet in which they could speak from the heart. They compiled it and ran off copies during the night. Janos luxuriated in the joy of free speech. 'I never feel tired,' he confided expansively, 'when I can write the truth.'

Eva, too, was working all hours. With the cataclysmic happenings the hospital services were cruelly over-stretched. Janos urged them to stay put for the night. It would be dangerous to walk across town after dark. The flat would be empty until early tomorrow morning. 'Our bed is yours. And there is bread.' Food was running out fast in Budapest. 'It's old, but you can eat it. And Hungarian cheese. That's all, but it's better than nothing.'

Rebecca welcomed the idea. She felt physically and emotionally exhausted, and didn't relish the prospect of a long and risky walk across the town. To her relief Owain seemed happy to accept the offer as well.

'I'll go then.' Standing in the doorway, his hair dirty and dishevelled, a growth of stubble on his chin, Janos looked ruffianly and tired, but intensely alive, happily contemplating a night of work after the nightmare experiences of the day. Rebecca's heart went out to him, with a surge of liking and admiration, almost of envy. His role was clear to him.

'Take care, Janos,' Owain said.

The Hungarian's smile was faintly mocking, as if caution had small place in his current scheme of things.

'I feel useless in this situation,' Rebecca told Owain sombrely when Janos had left. Maybe the drink hadn't been a good idea. Perhaps numbness was the best option at a time like this. She was beginning to feel perilously emotional. 'There's Eva working thirty-six hours at a stretch, and Janos existing on two hours' sleep a night, and I'm sitting here . . .'

'How can you think that?' She was startled by the forcible reproach and surprise in his voice.

'Don't you?'

'The simple fact of our being here is an incredible chance.' He was vehement and it was obvious that he had no such doubts. 'We didn't plan it. It happened. But we're living through something that's just hearsay to almost everyone in the West.' Owain leaned forward in his chair, convinced, and wanting urgently to convince. 'We're one of the few links with the rest of the world, and when this is over, for better or worse, we'll know what it was like, and we'll be in a position to *tell* what it was like . . . That's what's important. Not the fact that here, at this particular moment, you've got no role to play.'

Rebecca was only partly persuaded, but in her battered state of mind she was heartened by his certainty and by the physical familiarity of him here, among this alien, almost unbelievable mayhem. 'Maybe you're right. Maybe you're thinking clearer than I am. I don't know.' She shrugged and hauled herself to her feet. 'I'll tell you what, though. I'm famished. I'll go and cut some bread. It's about the only form of action open to me just now. Do you want some?'

Rebecca lay between the worn linen sheets of Janos and Eva's bed. In her underwear and a sweater she felt cold. Exhausted and craving sleep, she was powerless to suppress the teeming activity of her brain. For more than an hour, in the hard, high bed, she'd been tormented by hellish visions. In her mind's eye a succession of graphic images danced: writhing bodies, children with wild, panic-stricken eyes, flesh strewn like so much meat around the square. It was never-ending. On the large, firm, rectangular pillow she turned her head this way and that.

Owain was still in the adjoining room. His waiting was diplomatic, she imagined; to spare her the embarrassment of undressing in front of him, to give her time to get off to sleep. Rebecca heard him moving next door, crossing into the kitchen. A tap ran briefly. Then he was back in the living room. Taking his shoes off, she guessed. The door of the bedroom opened, admitting a shaft of light, which was quickly extinguished.

She lay facing away from him. 'I'm awake. I'll put the light on if you like.'

'Okay. Thanks.'

She reached for the lamp on the bedside table and found the switch. A dim light shone. Amazingly, in spite of the chaos, the electricity services still functioned.

'You all right?' he asked. Lying with her face averted, she could hear the faint friction of clothes being removed.

'I can't sleep.' She noticed suddenly that tears had started from her eyes, wetting her cheeks.

'I'm not surprised.'

'God, Owain. I feel as if I was living in a dream before I came here . . . A safe, stupid dream that everything could be sorted out by fair play, democracy, things like that. And then today . . .' Her voice was toneless, unemphatic. It faltered. A chance memory drifted into her mind of some foolish film she'd once seen. An old woman – a gritty stock character – had admonished a sheepish juvenile lead. You young folk, you don't know you're born. Rebecca had used the words often herself, in derision. And suddenly, tonight, they meant something.

Owain lifted the coverlet and climbed into bed, weighing down his side of the mattress. He laid a neutral, comforting hand on her shoulder. She lay still, not acknowledging the warm weight that filtered through the fabric of her sweater. The tears were still wet on her cheeks.

'I'll turn the light out.' Rebecca leaned away from him and flicked the switch.

In the blackness she turned towards him, slowly, then moved closer to the warmth of his body as if drawn by some magnetic field. Abruptly they were clinging together in the sightless void like drowning men, and neither could have said which of them had made the first move. Rebecca buried her face in the solidity of his shoulders and chest. Clumsily Owain kissed her forehead, then shifted and found her lips. She strained against him as if, by sheer force, she could exorcize the satanic visions of the massacre. His arms round her, his warmth close to her were an anchor, a blessed relief. In the darkness her eyes were shut tight. She rejoiced in the simple, solid fact of his physical presence, the whipcord of muscle, hardness of legs and thighs, rib cage enclosing the vigour of his heartbeat. Becoming aware, too, of the bulge of his erection against her belly.

His tongue entered her mouth. She experienced the snake-like uncoiling of an insidious excitement, beginning to take the place of her blind, instinctive need for comfort. One of his hands caressed the skin above her waist beneath the sweater. She luxuriated passively in the intimacy. His leg insinuated itself between hers.

But he paused. 'Hey, Becky.'

'What?'

'It's okay, is it? You want this?' He kissed her softly. 'I wouldn't like to take advantage . . .' There was an edge of satire in his voice, and yet she knew the enquiry was in earnest.

She found it meltingly erotic, this combination of kindling desire with chivalry. She experienced a stirring of memory: Ruth once, one evening, describing him, with a secret smile and an unusual lack of discretion, as so sexy and at the same time so . . . decent. Her own lurch of envy, resolutely suppressed at the time. Rebecca smiled in the darkness, reaching for his penis with a deliberate, lingering precision. 'I thought it was me taking advantage of *you*.'

39

The next few days were extraordinary, full of a high, bright euphoria, in spite of the guns which still echoed dully in the streets and the increasing scarcity of food. There was a purposeful optimism in the air, which Rebecca found contagious, helping her to shake off the despair she'd experienced in the wake of the Parliament Square carnage.

'Gero is *out*,' Janos told them the following morning, when he returned to the flat. He was dropping with tiredness, but full of a giddy pleasure. 'And Imre Nagy is his own master.' Gero was the hardliner, the Kremlin's man, a figurehead for the current repressive regime. Nagy stood for nationalism, liberalism, a measure of freedom. It was impossible to know about the hidden power struggle taking place in private, but surely this was a hopeful sign. The radio reports were frankly jubilant, no longer shackled by the hypocrisy of the party line.

Owain and Rebecca jettisoned the worthy, uninspiring material they'd gathered under the auspices of Miklos and Amelie. They began to work on a passionate and purposeful account of their personal experiences of the uprising. At the same time they interviewed as many witnesses as they prudently could, collecting vivid, firsthand reports on a host of different aspects of the struggle.

Janos was tremendously enthusiastic about the project and very helpful, introducing them to journalists and acquaintances who were directly involved in the fighting, translating for any of them who had no knowledge of English or French. Rebecca no longer had any doubts about the usefulness of their role. Janos and his friends saw them as a direct line to the outside world. The Hungarians felt grievously isolated. The Soviet propaganda machine held centre stage, while their own national voice went unheard.

However, the revolutionaries were heartened by the radio messages of support they received from countries all over the world. They felt less alone. Their courage was praised, moral support pledged. 'Though what they could really do with is something a bit more concrete,' Owain remarked privately to Rebecca. 'Not that they're likely to get it.'

At that time the greater part of the freedom-fighters' energy and effort was focused on the secret police. The day after the Parliament Square episode there had been a further massacre in the nearby town of Magyarovar. Again, a group of Avos had fired on a crowd of their countrymen who were peacefully demonstrating. They'd killed over a hundred and injured many more, transforming a peaceful village green into a writhing sea of agonized bodies. Anticipating the frenzied backlash, many Avos had gone into hiding or holed themselves up in their headquarters. Patiently, persistently, they were being winkled out.

While searching for Avos, the partisans made discoveries. They found underground cells full of emaciated political prisoners, many of whom hadn't seen the light of day for years. And now, abruptly, their doors were flung open and they were free to go. One of the detainees was a friend of Janos's called Joszef, a writer who'd been imprisoned two years earlier for a foolhardy, almost desperate criticism of the system.

Rebecca and Owain met him in Janos's flat. A tall man with pale blue, milky eyes and a brutal prisoner's hair cut. Yellow-grey skin stretched tightly over his bones, giving him a skull-like look. He agreed, via Janos, to be interviewed, but as they questioned him he began to weep silently, covering his face with one hand. His distress was shocking, shaming, and they abandoned their efforts.

'If you'd known him before . . .' Janos was terribly shaken by the physical and mental ravages his friend had suffered. 'Such a gay dog.' Behind the spectacles his eyes filled with tears. 'A real Lothario.'

Janos spent his time in a whirl of activity, working by night on his brainchild, the underground newspaper, and by day, in his official capacity, on *Szabad Nep* – though hardly anyone bothered to buy the latter any more, he told them with a dry malice. There was such a wealth of choice. Independent broad-sheets sprang up like mush-rooms. Every group, so it seemed, produced its own. Often it was expensive and too complicated to print them in large numbers, so they were pasted on the walls of shops and public buildings for passers-by to read at their leisure, along with cartoons of a truly stunning irreverence.

The temporary lack of censorship gave rise to a kind of intoxication. It had been years since people had been able to write freely and frankly. The reckless days inspired outpourings of poetry, displayed on walls, or duplicated in inky profusion and sold in the streets.

'Some is excellent,' Janos said. 'But some . . .' He looked askance. 'Very serious, but good to line the *poubelle*.' He had a small, lingering regret; one he saw as paltry and unworthy. As a sports writer he'd been looking forward to a scheduled soccer international between Hungary and Sweden, but, given the current mercurial political situation, the match had been cancelled.

Rebecca surfaced into a state of semi-consciousness, her mind clouded with a vague, unspecified anxiety. Slowly it came to her that she'd been sleeping, dreaming. She mustered whatever shreds of concentration were available to her and pictured Ruth as she'd looked in her dream, sitting in a café, motionless behind a plate-glass window, staring out at her with heavy, resentful eyes. The memory was chilling. Instinctively she turned towards the body next to her, pressing herself closer to the warm, live flesh.

Owain. The realization dawned again, as it had each morning since . . . Filling her with an almost painful gladness. She laid her face against his shoulder, feeling him stir.

'Becky.' His voice was full of sleep, his hand shifting and finding her hip. Drowsily she opened her eyes, raising her head, so that she could see his face on the pillow next to hers. He smiled slowly. 'You're still here. *We're* still here. I didn't imagine it.'

His incredulity echoed her own. They'd lived alongside one another for so long, sharing work, beliefs, concerns. A good team, as everyone said, as they themselves recognized. And now this physical intimacy, which she saw at some moments as right, inevitable almost, but simultaneously astonishing, the unreality heightened by her awareness of the dangerous uncertainty of the world outside the dowdy, comfortable womb of Owain's hotel room.

She laughed sleepily. 'Maybe you did imagine it. Perhaps there are more layers, like the skins of an onion. And waking up like this is a dream too. Just something one of us imagined.' Turning towards him, she kissed him softly, tangling her fingers in his hair, marvelling yet again at the casual way she now did things that until a few days ago had been taboo.

Her body glowed with physical well-being. She had never felt like this before. With Carl there'd always been a sense of half-buried disappointment. You read books and heard songs about the wonder of love and sex, and it had occurred to her that perhaps it was all a mighty conspiracy, making people yearn for something that didn't exist. But then there was Ruth with her dreamy, satiated smile. She'd wondered if ever in her life she would feel as Ruth looked. And now she did. But it wasn't a languorous feeling. She was energized by Owain's body, the sensuousness he'd initiated. It brought her further to life. The private pleasure of their nights seemed to her in some way the reverse side of the focused daytime activity.

Owain raised himself on one elbow, tousled, his eyes still holding the vagueness of sleep. She drank in the marvellous unfamiliarity of seeing him stripped of his daytime mask. He looked at her for a moment, a smile of affection in his eyes. 'Christ, I love you, Becky. I could eat you. You're so pink and warm and . . .' Tracing the line of her collar bone, tugging gently at the tarnished St Christopher she wore round her neck, he grinned. 'Though you'd be even lovelier if your skin wasn't turning green. Why d'you wear this thing?'

'I promised Ruth. She gave it to me before I left. Sort of a peace offering.'

'Oh.' Rebecca sensed a tightening at the mention of her friend's name, the shade of a withdrawal.

She was conscious of a twinge of anxiety that wasn't altogether new to her. A couple of nights ago she'd lain awake. Owain was sleeping soundly and some words he'd once said had drifted into her mind. Something about how Ruth had been, for him, the embodiment of style and fantasy and eroticism. And in the discouraging small hours she wondered whether, by taking up with herself, he'd made a deliberate decision to live without those qualities. The thought had hurt. But she was resilient, not given to brooding, and in the bustle of the following day her doubts had seemed cowardly and negative.

She told him, 'I dreamt about Ruth last night.'

'Oh.' His tone was neutral.

'I dreamt she was in a café with a big glass window – a bit like the restaurant downstairs – and I was outside in the street. She was staring at me through the glass, quite still, with a hostile look on her face. When I woke up I felt miserable.'

He said nothing, though his eyes, locking with hers, were steady and thoughtful.

'I wonder how Ruth'll take it. Our being together.' Several times the mental question had pierced her haze of happiness and purposeful activity, but there was never time to think about it.

'It shouldn't be a problem.'

She was stung by his nonchalance. 'It might well be.'

He shrugged. 'Not *our* problem.' There was a faint hardening in his voice.

Rebecca lay back on the pillow, staring up at the old-fashioned cornice ceiling, noticing a cobweb clinging to one of the elaborate curlicues. There was another stumbling block. The question of Ben's paternity, or possible paternity. If she and Owain were going to be together, she could no longer push the knowledge into some dusty corner of her mind. Secrecy was impossible now. She had to tell him and betray the silence Ruth had kept all these years. She felt guilty at the thought, and also apprehensive. Perhaps Owain would see the revelation as an honourable tie, binding him morally to mother and child.

'Ruth's my friend,' Rebecca said. Her tone was strangely hollow. 'My *best* friend.'

'*I'm* your friend. Don't forget that. *And* lover.' He smiled at her with a wolfish lustfulness, breaking the solemnity, and pulling her close so that the length of her body was in contact with his. The live feel of his skin galvanized her. She could no longer be bound by Ruth's wishes.

'There's something I've got to tell you.'

'What's that?'

Rebecca hesitated. 'Something Ruth never wanted you to know. And maybe I shouldn't . . . but it's too big a thing to ignore.' His eyes scanned her face curiously. She shifted slightly, moving a little away from him. 'It's this. You see, Ruth never knew who Ben's father was.' She paused for the words to sink home. 'She never knew if it was Paul – or you.'

He frowned, not understanding.

'She got pregnant after that time in Llandudno. When you and she . . .' Rebecca shrugged. 'But it could have been Paul equally well. Ruth never wanted you to know. I mean, to all intents and purposes Paul . . .'

'Paul knew?'

Her heart bled for the look of confusion in his eyes. 'Yes. He knew.'

Owain's expression was one of cold disbelief, reviving her night-time anxieties.

Janos stood framed in the doorway to his flat, gazing at them with a sentimental affection. There was a gleam in his eyes that looked as if it might spill over into tears. He was so much thinner, and with the lack of sleep one eye had developed an intermittent tic. Rebecca thought how fond of him she'd become over the last tense, over-wrought week.

'You'll drink with me,' he said, with a small, secret smile.

'We always seem to be doing that,' she said. 'For one reason or another.'

'This will be the last time.' He gave her a look of exhausted triumph. 'Nagy was on the radio speaking to us. The Russians are leaving. They've agreed, like in Poland.' His voice sounded hoarse with fatigue. Then his face crumpled and a large sob erupted from his throat.

'Janos, don't. Don't cry. It's wonderful news.' Rebecca stepped forward and put her arms round him. He embraced her, patting her back like an awkward uncle, convulsed with tight tears which he attempted to master.

'You're sure, are you? There's no mistake?' Owain

seemed to stand aside from their emotion, as if he thought it somehow reckless.

Eva appeared in the hall. They'd not seen her for days. She'd practically been living at the hospital. Her eyes were dark-ringed, but deep and glowing. She looked exhausted, but her presence had a quiet grace. 'We must believe,' she said. 'What else can we do?'

In the living room Janos poured more of the paint-stripper he called vodka. They'd drunk it the evening of the Parliament Square massacre. They raised their glasses soberly, like old comrades. If Owain still harboured any doubts he kept them to himself. Rebecca braced herself to take a slug. This time the raw abrasiveness was familiar to her, already with a nostalgia of its own. She swallowed. The liquor burned inside her and the sharpness in her mouth was the taste of hope.

Rebecca had to admit that there was a stark, science-fiction beauty to the landscape as, five days later, she and Owain walked down Szent Istvan Street in the morning mist. The jagged, irregular shapes of shelled buildings loomed through an autumnal haze, along with the skeletal outlines of burned-out tanks; tram cables looped and dangled in the streets, and the desolation was haloed fiercely by the veiled white glare of the sun. The Danube had a glassy darkness. A group of Russian tanks still guarded the entrance to the Margaret Bridge. The high-cheekboned, Mongolian features of a Soviet soldier in a long greatcoat seemed wholly in keeping with the savagery of the scene.

She gazed impassively for a moment at the tanks and troops. There were infantry too, Rebecca noticed. 'Why the hell are they still here?' she asked with *sotto-voce* fury. The question was rhetorical, since Owain had no more information than she.

'God knows what discussions are going on behind the

scenes, here and in Moscow.' He shrugged. He'd had doubts about the general euphoria from the very start. 'I don't suppose we'll ever know. All anyone can do is wait.'

Nevertheless, there *had* been action. They'd seen it for themselves, sharing in the jubilation as guns and ammunition carriers rumbled along the Danube Embankment, pulling out. It was just that so many Soviet troops still remained.

A semblance of normal life had returned to Budapest. The streets bustled with people on their way to work. They cast bewildered, wary eyes on the tanks and soldiers. The Mongolian passed some remark to a fair-haired colleague, and their laughter had a callous sound.

A young woman in a red coat – a splash of colour in the sombre surroundings – said something to a male companion. The unease of the whole city seemed mirrored in her face, and Rebecca was filled with a hot anger. They were victims, these people, with no vestige of control. She pictured the fragile, incredulous joy in the eyes of Janos and Eva at the announcement of the Russian withdrawal, and now this fearful doubt – like children, to whom a picnic had been cynically announced, leaving them to discover the practical joke for themselves.

She and Owain changed direction, heading downtown, towards the hospital where Eva worked. She'd invited them to come and talk to a couple of trusted colleagues, adding further material to their panoramic view of events.

As she walked in the brisk, hazy sunshine after a night of making love, through wrecked streets still shadowed by an inscrutable military presence, Rebecca was suddenly aware of a palpable exhilaration, a sense of closeness to life. It filled her, almost suffocating in its intensity, expanding until she had the feeling that it might crack her rib-cage. The situation in which they found themselves was ambiguous, ugly with implicit violence, but for better or worse she felt triumphantly alive. Perhaps she would never have the feeling so directly again.

As they walked she contemplated Owain, in love with him, with everything about him, with his unconscious, imperfect elegance. A Renaissance portrait, made human by hair in need of a trim, eyes still half-drugged from sleep, the morning pallor of his skin, a purplish bruise on his neck, inflicted, she imagined, by herself in some oblivious moment of passion.

He glanced sideways, catching her eye. He looked distant. It was clear that his mind was elsewhere. He spoke suddenly. 'I felt betrayed, you know, by what you told me the other day. I still do.'

Rebecca was unprepared for his words. His silence had covered thoughts so far removed from her own. But, in a sense, she welcomed them. They opened up the possibility of discussion. At the back of her mind the unresolved question had lurked like a shadowy figure in a doorway. She shrugged her shoulders. 'I understand how you feel. You two were close . . . You loved her,' she added, with an effort. 'All the same . . .'

'I had a right to know.' There was an echo in his tone of the harshness Rebecca had heard in his voice the other morning.

It triggered a protest in her. 'You're looking at it from your own angle,' she told him with an edge of acerbity. 'I'd have thought Ben's was the important point of view. Being the innocent party . . .' Rebecca slipped her arm through Owain's as if the physical contact could add weight to what she said. 'Hundreds of times – literally – Ruth came within an ace of telling you.' He glanced sharply down at her. 'That kind of secrecy's not in her nature. But it was better, for Ben's sake. She saw that. God knows, I admire her self-control . . .'

There was a silence and then she spoke again. 'Ruth would never hear of a blood test, you know. She'd chosen the father. She and Paul were Ben's family. And he loved Ben, come what may. He still does. There's a bond. He's the father even now they're separated. For all his . . . Paul was a good thing in Ben's life.'

Owain kept his eyes on the road ahead, saying nothing. He was uncommunicative, but perhaps she'd given him food for thought. They walked for a while in separate silence. As they passed a low archway leading to a narrow alley Rebecca thought, with a small, random part of her brain, what an excellent hiding place it would make for street-fighters. She marvelled simultaneously at how the last couple of weeks had altered her perception of the city landscape.

They crossed a road, picking their way between loose bricks, strewn glass and cobblestones. Owain put his arm round her shoulder. Through her coat she felt the warm, welcome pressure of it. 'I love you,' he said, as they skirted a large lump of concrete with metal struts protruding from it.

On the far side of the road he halted and looked down at her, his face pale in the cold sunlight, and his eyes very clear. He said, 'It's got nothing to do with us, has it, all this? Ben, Ruth . . .?'

She grinned up at him buoyant with relief. 'God, no.'

Ten minutes later the hospital came into view. As they got closer they saw a coterie of freedom-fighters standing close by. It was rumoured that a sprinkling of Avos was concealed in the hidden reaches of the building. As Owain and Rebecca approached the gate, a male figure emerged – shortish and stocky. Familiar somehow.

'Janos!' Owain exclaimed. 'What are you doing here?' The greeting froze on his lips. Janos looked terrible. Through all the gruelling exhaustion of the previous days he'd kept a smile. Now his features were twisted, drawn into an unconscious grimace of desperation and grief.

'Eva's dead,' he told them.

40

On the Sunday after Eden ordered the bombing of Egyptian territory, Ruth attended a political rally for the first time in her life. She was restless and anxious with wondering about Becky and Owain, incredulous at the thought of smiling young Tony Taylor poised to plunge into the grim reality of military confrontation. The bland, impersonal voice on the radio relaying news of the bombing had been the final straw. The proposed demonstration seemed the answer to her sudden thirst for some kind of action. It was just about the only thing she could do.

Trafalgar Square was already jammed with people as she approached from the direction of Charing Cross Road, virtually swept along by a comradely tide of would-be demonstrators. She was lucky to find a place on the steps of St Martin's-in-the-Fields. The speeches weren't due to begin for another hour, but already it was impossible to get closer.

'Over here, love.' A beery-looking man with unnatural, angelic blond curls and a missing front tooth manoeuvred her confidently to a more favourable position and offered matey advice. 'Use yer elbows if you have to, girl. Don't stand on ceremony.'

From her vantage point the scene was awe-inspiring. Huge, dark clouds rolled across the sky with a doomsday menace. Below, a vast living sea of heads stretched in all directions, and above them massed placards teetered, proclaiming 'No War Over Suez' and 'Eden Must Go'. Here and there she could see the larger colourful splashes of trade-union banners. There was a great deal of shouting, much of it rhythmic and synchronized, like the chants of the cheerleaders at an American football match.

'Eden out! Eden out! Eden out!' the curly-haired man standing behind her bawled suddenly. His mouth was close to her ear and she jumped, as did several other people in the vicinity. He wasn't popular. You could sense a shared, unspoken antipathy to his cheeky charm. 'Didn't frighten you, did I, love?' he cackled, laying one hand on the shoulder of a woman next to Ruth. She was prim in a navy felt hat and a double-breasted coat, and she endured the familiarity with undisguised distaste.

Gazing round her, Ruth was warmed by the size of the crowd. The news of the bombing last week had filled her with a sense of outrage that was new and surprising to her. She'd been caught off balance by the strength of her own reaction. It was heartening to realize that other people felt the same. Thousands and thousands of them. And they were here, like her, to demonstrate the fact. She was cheered by a sense of solidarity, and it crossed her mind that it would be nice if Becky were there to witness her incongruous awakening to political involvement.

'God, you're hopeless, Ruth.' She recalled her friend's exasperation on so many occasions. If only Becky could see her now. The wish was accompanied by the prick of anxiety that nowadays always followed any thought of Rebecca or Owain.

In a sense, though, Ruth felt a charlatan. All summer the Suez crisis had threatened and she'd ignored it blithely. Her understanding of the situation was decidedly shaky. It was just that she'd been overtaken by this strange, new vulnerability, what with people she was close to suddenly becoming caught up in world-shaking events. And the jingoistic, strong-arm tactics peddled by Eden and the French prime minister had been the final straw.

'You're like Sleeping Beauty,' Becky told her once, not altogether kindly. 'But something's going to shake you up one day.' Apparently, Ruth thought, with a mild sense of astonishment, that day had come.

The curly-haired man standing behind her began to sing suddenly, in a raucous, crackling voice. 'Rule Britannia! Britannia rules the waves . . .' He gave the song a humorous jazz beat and jiggled his body in time.

'Oh shut up!' someone yelled from the back of the crowd.

Ruth thought of Becky again when Aneurin Bevan began to speak. He'd always been Rebecca's hero. Even at this long range his stocky, white-haired figure was enormously impressive, standing four-square on the rostrum, flanked by slogans and banners. From the bits of information she'd gleaned from Becky over the years, Ruth was expecting a fiery speech, but it wasn't like that. He spoke in a measured tone and didn't settle for easy, black-and-white definitions.

He was unsentimental about Nasser. 'I'm not saying,' he proclaimed stolidly, 'that because Eden is wrong Nasser is right. I'm not saying that for a single moment.'

Ruth was struck by his air of sober realism. One of the earlier speeches had been a rabble-rousing harangue that never achieved the tumultuous ovation it seemed to demand. She noticed a youth standing to the left of her, and was touched by his look of rapt attention, head tilted slightly back, lips just parted. There was something almost feminine about the delicacy of his profile. He'd be slightly younger than herself, Ruth thought, in his early twenties perhaps. Her eyes lingered on him for a moment before returning to the rostrum.

Bevan talked on with the same unemphatic shrewdness, surprising and pleasing her. He was a controversial figure, she knew, much reviled in the newspapers, but today she was impressed by his solid common sense. The young man to her left glanced her way. He caught her eye and smiled, as if taking for granted that she too approved the logic of the speech. Ruth was cheered by the feeling that Bevan was putting her own ideas into words. Things she'd thought in a muddled kind of way, and never really sorted out, but which lay at the root of the revulsion she felt for the Anglo-French bombing.

'We are stronger than Egypt,' he barked, the amplified words echoing above the massed ranks of listening heads. 'But there are other countries stronger than us. Are we prepared to accept for ourselves the logic we are applying to Egypt? If nations more powerful than ourselves accept this anarchistic attitude and launch bombs on London, what answer have we got?'

The young man turned to Ruth, shaking his head with a smile that lit up his faun-like features. 'No bloody answer at all,' he said.

Afterwards many of the diehards surged down Whitehall towards Downing Street, with the object, Ruth supposed, of delivering their message to the Prime Minister in person, though somehow she doubted that he'd be there waiting for them. She was carried along on the tide of the demonstration, too excited to go tamely home.

'Eden out! Eden out! Eden out!' The shout rose, brief and staccato, with an edge of menace to it. Ruth was stimulated by a vague lawlessness in the air, though the march was perfectly legal. She was flanked by animated faces, as though the rally had provided an excuse for the demonstrators to shed the well-behaved masks they wore for most of their lives. She saw something heroic in the naked faces, recalling a Russian film Becky had dragged her to see once, about the Revolution. The marchers walked and chanted, grouped and regrouped with a kind of dynamic restlessness.

Ruth had thrown in her lot with the young man who'd been next to her earlier. His name was Howard. It was comforting to have a companion, however temporary, and she sensed that he felt the same. 'Eden out! Eden out!' they shouted in unison, made bold by their makeshift alliance.

At the entrance to Downing Street they encountered a police cordon which was barring access. There were scuffles and one of the policemen lost his helmet. It was seized by a demonstrator, a pert young woman who clapped it on over her own poodle curls. Ruth thought the policemen looked very young, with raw, boyish faces. She felt a sneaking sympathy for them in the frightening press of the crowd. A group of demonstrators rushed them, trying to break through, but the cordon held. They began to shout insults at the bobbies instead. Ruth was a little shocked. She didn't share the general hostility. In her view they, the public, were stating a point of view, and the police were keeping order. There was no need to make it personal.

In the ensuing jostle she and Howard kept hold of one another. They were pushed towards another group of policemen, standing off to one side. In the thick of the crush the two of them were forced against a burly young copper with black, Brylcreemed hair and ruddy cheeks. He stood firm as they regained their balance, staring with an expression of cold dislike into Howard's pale, almost pretty features.

'Why don't you go home, nancy boy?' he said finally, in a tone of brutal, gratuitous contempt.

Ruth was astonished, and for a second or two she could think of no riposte. Then she heard herself exclaiming, 'That's awful! You can't talk to him like that!' To her own ears the reproach sounded shrilly middle-class and mildly ridiculous.

Immediately she felt a tug on her arm. Howard was pulling her away. 'Don't get mixed up in a slanging match,' he warned. 'It won't do you any good.' The copper watched them with steady, inscrutable eyes until their two figures were swallowed up in the mêlée.

Halfway back up Whitehall they were stopped by a woman in a maroon coat, her face framed by wispy side-locks which had escaped from a bun at the back of her head. 'Have you heard the latest about Hungary?' she asked them avidly.

'No,' Ruth said, not liking her hot, over-excited eyes.

'They're back. The Russians are back in Budapest. Thousands of them, with tanks and reinforcements.' She told the news almost gloatingly, gratified to be the bearer of such momentous tidings.

'How do you know?' Ruth asked. Her voice was sharp as a whip.

The woman was self-important. 'One of the organizers told me. He asked me to pass it on . . . There's no mistake,' she added huffily.

Ruth turned away, feeling sick, and continued on up Whitehall. She shivered and hunched her shoulders, plunging her hands deep into her pockets. It was almost completely dark. 'I'm cold now,' she said.

Howard asked, 'Are you all right?'

'Two of my friends are out there,' she told him. 'Journalists.'

'Oh.'

She liked him for not making a fuss. They walked on in silence, threading their way through splintered groups of demonstrators, many of them still chanting and shouting, unwilling to call it a day.

'I wish I could buy you a coffee,' Howard said plaintively. 'But there's not much chance of that on a Sunday night.'

In a side street off the Charing Cross Road a brazier glowed orange in the darkness and the warm scent of roasting chestnuts floated on the air. Beyond it a small mobile canteen was parked, probably illegally, Ruth thought, but then the police were otherwise engaged.

'Someone up there likes us,' Howard said. He bought two thick china cups of coffee and gave one to Ruth. 'This'll put new heart in you.'

She wrapped her hands gratefully round the cup. She was warmed by the glowing coals of the brazier, and Howard's face reflected the muted orange light. His pale hair blew wispily across his forehead, and his eyes looked dark and deep-set. In spite of everything there was a kind of poetry in the scene, and in their casual companionship. Ruth sipped the coffee. It was made with essence and ready-sweetened. Usually she hated it like that, but at that moment the cloying drink had the power of a revivifying drug.

'If they're journalists they'll be all right.' Howard tried to offer words of comfort. 'Foreign journalists are a special case.'

'I've been trying to convince myself of that all the way here.' There was more than a grain of truth in what he said. 'I'll phone the Foreign Office tomorrow. They might know something. Or failing that I'll try the Hungarians again.' With the hot coffee and the prospect of action she felt a touch more optimistic.

'I could've killed that copper, you know,' Ruth told Howard suddenly. 'The one that insulted you.'

He shrugged, looking vulnerable. 'It's not the first time I've been called that.' He gave a wry grimace. 'It's not even true. I used to kick up a fuss, but I know better now.' She sensed a wealth of unspoken experience behind the words.

In the aftermath of their shared afternoon, she was curious about him. 'What do you do in real life?'

'I'm an actor.' He couldn't suppress a small gleam of pride.

'Honestly?' Ruth was enthusiastic. 'Where?'

'The Old Vic at the moment.' He smiled. 'You know at the bottom of the programme where it says revellers, courtiers and men-at-arms? Well, that's me most of the time. Though I played Lancelot Gobbo a little while ago.'

'I act,' she said, diffident for a moment, and not sure why.

He looked interested. 'It's not often you meet an actress who wants to set the world to rights.'

She accepted the accolade without comment, liking the sound of it, though she could just imagine Becky snorting with derision. She was bucked at having been to the demo. True she'd been one of thousands. An ant. But in however small a way she'd stood up for her opinion. And she would again.

'Are you working at the moment?' Howard asked.

'I'm joining Ryan Jaquier's group. In the old King Edward Theatre in Bethnal Green.' Till this moment she'd deceived herself, going through the motions of hesitating, weighing up the pros and cons. But had there ever really been any doubt?

'You're not!' He was hugely impressed. 'Some people have all the luck. That's just the kind of work I dream of. That company's going to be just about the most exciting . . .'

Ruth nodded modestly, warmed by his enthusiasm. She'd talked to other people about the job, but no one who was in a position to appreciate its specialness. She took another sip of the sweet, thick coffee. The glare of the brazier was hot on her cheeks. She was abruptly conscious of being enviable, the way she used to feel a long time ago. Her own life beckoned to her, chancy and exciting.

41

'Eva's dead,' Janos had repeated.

Saying the words out loud triggered an agony of weeping. The tears rolled down his cheeks unchecked while his face twisted in ugly, naked pain. Watching, Rebecca had felt ashamed, as if she were witnessing something unbearably private.

That had been three days ago. She and Owain had accompanied Janos back to his flat. Rebecca's arm was round his waist as they walked slowly through the streets. He'd gripped the material of her coat, like a man on a cliff face clutching at a handful of grass to stop himself from falling. People stared with mute sympathy as they passed. Such desolation wasn't a rare sight in Budapest nowadays.

Back in the flat, Janos sat dazedly on the edge of a chair in his overcoat. He murmured to himself in Hungarian and the tears came again, subsiding gradually into a kind of stupor. He took off his glasses and began to wipe them. His swollen eyes looked achingly defenceless. Neither Rebecca nor Owain offered any words of comfort. They had none.

Rebecca kept picturing Eva as she'd been last Sunday, when the news had come through of the Russian withdrawal. Unmade-up, her hair drawn haphazardly off her face and touched with strands of grey that Rebecca hadn't noticed before, haggard with the long hours spent at the hospital, but glowing from inside with a half-fearful happiness.

Brokenly, in fits and starts, Janos explained that a Russian tank had opened fire that morning on a group of freedom-fighters. It was an isolated incident, the first for several days. He thought it was in revenge for something, but he didn't know what. Eva was caught in the cross-fire on her way to work, along with a group of women queueing for bread. She was dead before she reached the hospital.

They were like a force of nature, Rebecca thought, the Soviet will, the Soviet war machine. Impersonal, undiscriminating and unstoppable as fire, flood and earthquake. You could rail against them, but what was the good? The only effect was a deeper understanding of your own powerlessness.

'I didn't say goodbye,' Janos told them. Behind the spectacles his eyes were anguished and as uncomprehending as a child's before he closed them in pain.

Around midday Janos's friend Joszef, the released detainee, knocked at the door. With his gaunt face and the dun-coloured raincoat flapping round his scarecrow frame, he made Rebecca think of some hollow-eyed soothsayer, a creature of ill omen. He'd already heard the news about Eva, but his condolences to Janos were almost perfunctory, as if such tragedies were only to be expected. But he spoke volubly in Hungarian, occasionally nodding in the direction of Owain and Rebecca. For a time Janos was jerked out of his grief, asking Joszef questions and looking tense and concerned. They heard the word Russki used repeatedly.

Joszef left almost at once, as if he had other calls to make.

'It's bad,' Janos told them. 'I think you can't stay in Budapest.' Joszef had come from the Kilian Barracks, he said, where most of the partisans had their headquarters. He'd been informed on good authority that huge numbers of Russian troops were pouring across the border into Hungary and that within a day or so no one was going to be allowed to leave the country.

* * *

'For God's sake,' Owain urged, 'come with us.'

It seemed brutal, in a sense, this pressuring of a grieving man, but time was so short. Janos stood by the window. The daylight harshly revealed his puffed face and reddened eyes. He stared out dully, as if his sight were focused inward and the familiar streets were merely a grey void.

'Think about it, Janos,' Rebecca pleaded.

'Christ, Janos, I know this is the worst time . . . But obviously we can't wait.' Owain stood too. An urgency was visible in all his movements, but he tried to control any impatience in his voice, to reason with Janos. 'If the Russians come and crush this rebellion, and if everything goes back to what it was before, to worse than before, then think about what's in store for you. You haven't exactly sat on the fence. Your views are no secret. You published them for all the world to see . . .'

Janos continued to gaze out of the window, showing no reaction. It was hard to judge whether he was pondering on Owain's words or simply lost in a world of his own. There was condensation on the glass. Idly, with one finger, he traced some letters, then obliterated them with his hand before Rebecca could see what they were.

'I'm certain the uprising's over.' Owain, deliberately, was cruelly blunt. 'Only the retribution's still to come.'

Janos said tonelessly, 'I've been in prison before.' He sounded indifferent to the thought.

Something in Rebecca protested violently at this resignation. 'You can still do something. Act. Talk. Write about all this. Influence people . . . if you come with us.' Her voice cracked slightly. She was overwrought.

'You've got no children to think of,' she said. 'No parents.'

'No wife,' Janos added.

A silence fell in the room. It seemed tactless, pointless to persuade further. Janos was his own man and he knew the situation. His decision would spring from a private tangle of reason and emotion. It could go either way. Only there was so little time. Outside a woman's voice could be heard calling stridently, then laughing with a neighbour. Janos turned away from the window. 'I'll come with you,' he said, the same hollow lack of emotion in his voice.

Rebecca parted the heavy, rust-coloured curtains of Owain's room in the Duna Hotel. It was almost six in the morning. Outside, flurries of fine, dry snow whirled through the dark air. She watched for a moment, her eyes hypnotized, while her mind churned with a confusion of conflicting emotions.

Apprehension knotted the pit of her stomach at the prospect of the unknown risks that lay ahead of them and, at the same time, she was filled with an elegiac regret because this intense, extraordinary episode of her life was coming to an end. There were other feelings, too. A black conjecture as to the fate bearing down on the people of Budapest, and a helpless, useless guilt that this wasn't her struggle, and she was leaving.

'D'you honestly think the Americans and the United Nations will just stand by and let it happen? Let people be battered into submission?' Abruptly Rebecca turned away from the window with a burning, almost childlike sense of outrage.

Owain looked up with an air of dry disillusionment. 'Yes, I honestly do.' He was in the middle of packing the sheaves of interviews, notes and impressions they'd compiled over the last fortnight carefully into a khaki, waterproof satchel Janos had provided. He shrugged his shoulders. 'They'll talk a lot and be morally damning and pass resolutions. But I'll be amazed if it goes any further than that.'

'God, it's so unfair!' In the early-morning hush her

words echoed back at her, a fractious, foolish understatement, and Rebecca reflected that there were times when all the savoir-faire and sophistication you'd gathered to yourself painstakingly over the years simply evaporated, and you were left with the moral certainties of a child of five.

'Wicked,' he agreed, with a kind of despairing cynicism. In the half-light of the dawn bedroom Owain stood at the table, deftly taping, folding and wrapping, making sure that their manuscript was as weatherproof as it could be. There was a depressing ordinariness to the activity. It was the final necessary chore before they quit the heightened world they'd been sharing and returned to the bathos of real life.

'I feel like a rat leaving a sinking ship.' Rebecca sat down on the edge of the unmade bed and began to lace her boots.

Owain looked up, with a brief, frosty smile. 'You haven't left it yet.'

What with the presence of Janos, and the fat, incriminating bundle of notes, leaving Hungary was going to be risky. From the rumours they'd heard, there was likely to be a considerable Russian presence at the border. Without a shadow of a doubt if they were seen escaping they'd be shot at. But Janos claimed to know a likely spot where they could cross the border with minimal risk. Eva was from a village close to the frontier, and he remembered a secluded, wooded place, not landmined, unlike many of the open fields near to the border . . . It was where he and Eva used to do their courting, he told them bleakly.

It occurred to Rebecca that if she and Owain were to leave Janos behind and jettison their manuscript, it was still quite possible that they'd be allowed through the frontier post without too much trouble. But neither of them considered this course of action even for a moment. Over the past fortnight they'd seen so much of the

411

Hungarians' desperate last-ditch courage that it had become, for them too, the natural, the only way to behave. Anything else was compromise. Their emotions were engaged. For better or worse, they were embroiled in the struggle.

I'm scared, though, Rebecca thought. Yet, in spite of everything, she was still protected by her twenty-three years of sheltered living. Lulled into the illusion that nothing really bad could happen to her.

'You ready?' Owain asked.

She pulled a jacket on over her trousers and the two sweaters she wore. It was hard to know whether the snow would turn out to be a help or a hindrance.

'Funny. I'll miss this place.' Her eyes scanned the old-fashioned, dilapidated grandeur of the room that had been their refuge from the mayhem of the streets, housing their privacy and pleasure. The stuffy furnishings had a personal significance for her, and she tried to imprint on her brain an image of the dusty drapes, the high, moulded ceiling, the ornate wicker furniture, and the rumpled bed. Already they seemed invested with a kind of voluptuous nostalgia.

'High times we've had here, Becky.' Owain came and stood next to her, as if to share her view of the room. His arm circled her shoulder. Their bodies were separated by layers of cold-weather clothes. He shook his head. 'God, it's an unlikely love nest.'

'Will it ever be as good again?' The words slipped out without her having willed them and she was taken aback by the wistfulness in her voice.

But Owain seemed not to notice. 'It'll be better,' he said. 'You'll see.' He hoisted Janos's waterproof bag on to his shoulder. 'If we get out of Hungary it'll be the beginning of the rest of our lives.'

'Oh, we'll get out all right,' she said with a conviction she'd have found hard to justify.

* * *

You couldn't buy petrol for love nor money, but Owain thought there was just about enough in the hired Volkswagen to take them to the frontier. They picked Janos up in Engels Square as they'd arranged the previous night. The snow was becoming thicker and more insistent. Janos wore a cap and a grey muffler tucked into the neck of a thick tweed jacket and he carried only the briefcase that he used for work.

Owain slowed the car and Janos climbed quickly into the passenger seat. His face was ashen and he looked like death. As they drove in the direction of the river he stared fixedly out of the window. 'I'm trying to understand,' he said suddenly, 'that this is the last time I'll ever see this place.'

With the snow and the heavy grey sky the passing streets had the look of a black and white film. Rebecca gazed out too, trying to view the scene through Janos's eyes, but it was impossible. To her the city was inescapably foreign.

They crossed the Danube via the Chain Bridge. In Buda Owain was forced to detour a couple of times because the main roads were still choked with rubble and fallen masonry. Janos peered ahead and gave instructions, directing them through a tangle of backstreets. He had a lifetime's knowledge of this town, Rebecca reflected, yet soon it would be merely part of his past. The thought weighed on her like a responsibility.

Eventually they reached the outskirts of the city. 'You're certain about this, Janos?' Owain asked him earnestly. 'It's not too late to change your mind.'

Janos shook his head. 'What's here for me now, Owain?' He shrugged, with a chilling air of indifference. 'No. Drive on.'

They advanced to the border via a series of country roads. It was safer. This way they were unlikely to encounter Russian patrols. With the snow and the rutted roads, the going was slow and hard. Rebecca was sharply alive to the beauty of the smooth, white fields, which were bordered by the black shapes of skeletal trees. Her awareness of them seemed heightened by the anxiety that writhed slowly in her stomach. They passed small groups of children on their way to school who waved to them, pink-cheeked from the cold. Later they saw the odd villager or farmer stumping along the rough track, and once a shaggy horse walking doggedly between the shafts of a rickety cart.

In the small villages there was no sign yet of a Russian presence. Janos assumed that they would concentrate their strength in the border area. The mechanics of their escape gave him a preoccupation, taking his mind off Eva. All the same, there was a dead tone to his speech, as though the mental processes involved in remembering and planning their route were automatic, carried out with one small part of his brain while the rest of his being was hunched in a quiet, inert despair.

Owain began to be anxious about the petrol situation. The back roads twisted and turned far more than the main route, and the mileage mounted up. 'I don't think we're going to make the border on what we've got,' he warned them. He frowned, as if calculating, and shook his head. 'We'll just have to leave the car at some point and keep going on foot. Just keep your fingers crossed it's not too far from the frontier . . .'

Around eleven o'clock they parked close to a small village. Janos went into a café and bought hot black coffee. All of them were cold in spite of their layers of clothing, and the coffee thawed them out and warmed their hands. They ate some tinned meat Janos had brought from the storecupboard at home. It was gristly, and had an odd aftertaste, but they munched it grimly to keep their strength up.

At about midday it became obvious that the petrol was almost gone. There was no one around and Owain drove

414

the car into a clump of mixed trees where there was a good chance of its remaining undiscovered for a day or so.

'Could be worse,' Janos said, in his dead, distant voice. 'I think fifteen, eighteen kilometres till we come to the place.'

It sounded a huge distance to Rebecca, though she didn't say as much. As they climbed reluctantly out into the ankle-deep snow, the reality of their situation hit her fully for perhaps the first time. They were stranded in the middle of nowhere, with the white fields stretching as far as the eye could see, and somewhere out there was the anonymous presence of an enemy who'd shoot them for two pins if their plans were known. They faced a freezing, arduous walk, and then the risky unknown quantity of the border crossing. She was filled with a sense of disbelief. What was she, Rebecca Street from Llandudno, doing in this place, at this time?

Are we mad? she felt like asking, but she bustled instead to hide her discouragement. 'We'll leave the suitcases. They'd be heavy, and they'd draw attention to us. The manuscript's the only thing that's really important.'

Janos brought his briefcase. There was further tinned food in it and, so he'd confided earlier, all the photographs of Eva he'd been able to lay his hands on. Abandoning the car, they began to walk. At first the physical activity put new heart into Rebecca. The sun had come out and the snow glittered. The movement of her body was warming and in spite of everything she found herself exhilarated.

'God, but it's a slow way of getting around, this walking,' Owain grumbled wryly, as they plodded along, leaving three sets of footprints behind them in the softening snow. 'You put one foot in front of the other time after time after time . . . You'd think they'd have discovered something more streamlined.'

'Like rollerskating?' She grinned at the sudden mental image of the three of them . . . But immediately she was aware of Janos again, silent, his face set and grey, unable to participate in their moments of good humour.

After a couple of hours, in any case, the temporary exhilaration faded. The sun disappeared and the sky was sullen again, as if, at half-past two in the afternoon, the prospect of nightfall was already in the offing. Their energy flagged and they began to feel the cold again, yet there was nothing for it but to trudge onward, inching their way towards the border.

They'd arranged that Janos would greet the few people they encountered. It would be unwise to reveal the fact of their foreignness. The Hungarian's terseness and his closed expression were an advantage to them in this situation, discouraging closer contact.

'How much further?' Rebecca asked. It was well gone four by now, and darkness was beginning to fall.

Janos pursed his lips and considered. 'A couple of kilometres only.'

At length the border became visible, marked along its length by a wide area of ploughed earth. It had snowed less heavily there, and in many places brown soil broke the surface of the white. For the first time that day they came face to face with the dark silhouettes of Soviet tanks, stationed at intervals along the edge of no-man's-land. They paused, then, to stare at the looming shapes and ponder on the threat they held. Rebecca could feel a kind of prickling in her body. She was hideously aware of its vulnerability. Inconceivable as it seemed, those guns could and would rip her to shreds, and Owain and Janos, if they were seen so much as setting foot on the innocent expanse of worked soil.

'This way.' Janos led them off in a northerly direction

towards a wooded area, which was crossed by a hard-packed mud path. The snow muffled sound, so that they heard footsteps only seconds before the two young soldiers rounded a bend in the track and walked towards them.

They were Hungarians, but doubtless under the command of their Soviet overlords. Rebecca's stomach lurched with the sensation, remembered from childhood, that the game was up. At the same time she, Owain and Janos continued along the path with apparent unconcern, though Rebecca was certain that their intentions must be absurdly transparent. As she walked and waited to be challenged she could feel the strength draining from her legs. In the twilight wood the Hungarians came closer, their features becoming clearer with every step. Their faces looked rigid with the cold. One of them had clear grey eyes that made her think irrelevantly of Ben's. They drew level and still nothing had been said. As the soldiers walked past them, one of them turned and muttered something. Janos nodded to him wanly.

'What did he say?' she asked when the men were out of earshot.

Janos shrugged. 'He wished us luck.'

They hid in the wood until it was fully dark, eating some more of Janos's dismal tinned supplies. His fingers were so cold and clumsy that it took minutes to open each can and he cut himself and bled copiously on to the snow at their feet.

Rebecca was chilled to the bone. Her numbed hands could hardly feel the chunk of pressed beef she held between finger and thumb. But it was better that way. If you chafed your hands or breathed on them the pain was worse than the cold. Owain's face was drained of all colour as he wolfed the greyish-pink slab of processed meat. They sat on a log that saturated their trousers, adding further to their physical discomfort.

Freezing and exhausted, they barely spoke. Rebecca felt dull and brutish, like an animal enduring because it can do nothing else. In a sense this was a blessing, partially stilling the fear that gnawed her insides.

Around nine o'clock Owain said, 'Let's do it. Let's go.' He stood painfully and tried to rub some feeling back into his legs.

Rebecca uncoiled from the sitting position with difficulty. Her body was numbed and stiff, but the adrenalin began to flow, sharpening her reactions.

'Through here.' Janos led them along a small, rough, winding track for about a mile. In the dark they stumbled continuously against tree roots and tussocks of vegetation. Once Janos slipped and fell full length on the uneven floor of the forest. Rebecca recalled briefly that he used to walk there with Eva in days gone by.

They reached the edge of the wide, ploughed strip of no-man's-land and paused. Some way in, on the other side, they could see the lights of an Austrian village, as serene and desirable as some legendary Shangri-la. The empty field lay spread beneath the dark sky, innocent somehow, and yet imbued with a silent, ominous significance.

Rebecca became aware of the violent beating of her heart, the tension in her body and limbs. Set one foot on this ground and it was a justification for killing, she thought, pressing her balled fist hard into her mouth. It was too dark to see the Soviet tanks positioned half a mile or so away to their left, but Rebecca knew they were there and also that, at any given moment, the flat, featureless landscape could be brilliantly floodlit.

'Now or never.'

They began to walk cautiously across the rutted mud. Janos went in front, oddly citified with his dangling briefcase. Owain and Rebecca walked side by side. To Rebecca each step was precarious, an exploration, as though she were a long-legged colt just learning to walk. In the open land, after the shelter of the woods, she felt monstrously exposed.

They trudged forward, made clumsy and slow by the unevenness of the furrowed earth that crunched frostily under their shoes. Rebecca perceived her numbed feet almost as separate entities. She could hardly feel them. They carried her forward step by step, but barely seemed part of her.

'Okay, are you?' A low, spare enquiry from Owain. Even in her state of suspended, terrified tension she was comforted by his presence, the disconnected thought fleeting through her mind that she'd rather die with him than without him.

She shot him a smile of fellow feeling that he probably wouldn't see in the dark, but might hear in her voice. 'So far, so good.'

Janos turned his head briefly, whispering with a cautious wonderment. 'This is too easy.'

'Sh-sh.' Superstitiously Rebecca laid a finger to her lips. He was tempting fate. Soviet guns were half a mile to their left, and at any time one of the Russian patrol cars could come, picking them out like petrified rabbits in its headlights.

An owl hooted mournfully across the moonlit landscape. Then behind them, in the woods, someone shouted. Instinctively they froze, turning sharply to look back. Rebecca strained her eyes in the gloom, but could see nothing, no movement, just the black outline of the trees.

'Keep going,' Owain urged.

Another shout from behind galvanized them into movement. Rebecca's knees were like water. She stumbled, expecting her legs to buckle at any second. Yet incredibly they kept going.

In the unreality they heard the flat, whining crack of rifle fire, seeming not close but somewhere in the void around them. Strangely, the danger seemed less alarming to Rebecca than the terrors manufactured by her brain, almost as if the gunshot were meant for someone else. On the edge of her consciousness she heard another shot but no more voices.

Stolidly they kept going, conscious again of the limitations of their legs. The stretch of bare earth seemed endless, their progress across it snail-like, infinitely protracted.

And then miraculously in front of them stood a row of posts, each topped with a small pointed flag. It was the Austrian border. Janos turned, smiling. 'This is it!' Then abruptly he fell. And only afterwards they heard the sharp, whining report and realized that a bullet had hit him.

'Janos.'

Rebecca spoke under her breath, falling to her knees beside him. She was aware of Owain on the other side of him, dumping the bag with the manuscript, kneeling too. With frozen, gloved hands Rebecca cupped Janos's face. In the grey light she could see that his expression was still mobile. Puzzled, pained. But his eyes met hers with full understanding as one of his hands crept, in an exploratory fashion, across his breastbone.

'I'm shot.' His surprise and indignation were almost comic.

'How bad is it?'

'I don't know.' The shadow of a smile crossed his face, checked almost instantly by a rictus of pain. 'But we got here.' The smile flickered back into tentative life.

'We'll have to get him to a hospital,' Owain said. 'No waiting.'

'We shouldn't move him.'

'I'll get hold of someone from that village.' Owain pulled her to her feet. For a second they clung together, clumsy in their thick coats. She was sharply aware of the wide, dark, starry sky and a singing, soaring sense of relief. Also of her own numbed body, the wet clothing clinging to her legs, the rasp of Owain's beard against her frozen face and his cold lips on hers.

42

Ryan Jaquier stood centre stage, bulky in corduroys and a polo-necked sweater, braced on his short, stocky legs – an aggressive stance assumed, Ruth guessed, for his own benefit rather than that of his audience. He was in mid-flow. An improvised monologue about a trip he'd made last year to Hollywood to play the painter, Hogarth, a minor role in some costume drama. A sprinkling of British accents had been imported to lend the project a spurious air of authenticity.

Ryan and Hollywood hadn't hit it off. Quite unwittingly he kept bumping up against the right-wing paranoia that currently gripped the movie capital. In these surroundings his woolly liberalism had taken on a sinister, radical colouring. He'd had some worrying run-ins with stern-eyed executives, and been relieved when finally he'd found himself on the plane back to England.

'Someone actually called me a goddamn pinko,' he said. 'I thought they only used that word in books. I imagine that's why most of my bits ended up on the cutting-room floor.' He told the story in a self-mocking, self-deprecating style, quite unlike his usual bumptious manner. Ruth found it rather endearing, though she suspected that his ruefulness was something of a ploy, designed to foster a feeling of equality in his new band of actors. At the same time there was a discreet edge of hysteria in his voice that revealed how much the experience had shaken him.

The empty King Edward Theatre seemed a warm and welcoming place to Ruth. You could imagine the shades of Edwardian music-hall regulars thronging backstage, watching, with their tough, resilient grins. The very cobwebs strung between discarded pieces of scenery held a dusty, historical glamour for her. She had a quick, crazy fantasy of spraying them gold so that they'd hang there, a kind of glittering testimony to the theatre's past.

This was their first rehearsal as a company. Not a rehearsal really; more a kind of Sunday lunchtime get-together, Ryan had said, so they could start to get to know each other. As he talked, the rest of them sat round cross-legged on rugs on the stage, eating cheese sandwiches and drinking Spanish plonk from waxed paper cups. It would be someone else's turn to speak next. The monologues were another of Ryan's suggestions. What if each of them stood up and talked for five or ten minutes about anything they liked? Something that meant something or had touched them emotionally, either recently or years ago. It didn't matter. It would be a way of breaking down the barriers, a beginning of their learning to trust one another.

For now, seeking familiarity, Ruth sat with Kate and Terry. They were the only three members of the old drama group that Ryan had invited to join his new company. Next to her – skinny, sandy-haired, smoking continuously – Terry watched through narrowed eyes. Kate, in repose, had a sulky, evaluating look that belied the audacity of her on-stage persona. Her eyes were dark-ringed and elongated à la Juliette Greco, her hair straight with a heavy fringe. Already, in the wake of more than a year of shared improvisation, the trying and rejecting of new ideas, the taking of risks, a bond existed between the three of them – a love, almost, when things were going well – the kind of feeling that Ryan wanted to extend to the whole company. Ruth was strongly aware of it now, and conscious that *their* reaction to Ryan was the same as her own – a mixture of admiration and scepticism. But when the chips were down you could trust him, rely on him. All of them knew that too.

His chapter of accidents came to an end. Mock-diffidently, Ryan inclined his head with its wild curls, then sat back down on the floor with a crooked, engaging smile. Nobody clapped. It wasn't that sort of performance. But there was a general ripple of approval for his fluency, his turn of phrase.

'Nice one, Ry,' Terry murmured, raising his paper cup with a negligent flourish.

Now a woman that Ruth didn't know stood up to speak, introducing herself as Evelyn. She looked about thirty-five and had black hair and a genial, horsy face. She was brassy and played up a kind of native cockney breeziness. Ruth had the vague feeling that she'd seen her in films, in bit parts, character parts. In Ealing comedies perhaps. Something about the woman made her think of Alice from the Illyria Theatre with her matinees, the common touch.

Evelyn was from these parts. She'd lived in Bethnal Green as a child, and she began to reminisce about her first-ever visit to the theatre – to this theatre – with her grandparents in the Twenties. They'd seen some kind of variety show and Evelyn had retained a mass of vivid, disconnected images of the evening, of comedians, singers, jugglers, conjurors, which she proceeded to act out for them in rapid succession with a dizzying versatility.

'She's fucking good,' Terry muttered as if to himself.

As she performed there was an exhilarated smile on her ruby-painted lips and a reckless sparkle in her eyes. Ruth was dazzled. As she sat and watched and listened she was filled with a sense of incredulity, a shiver of delight, that she, too, belonged here among this exuberance and talent. It was as if she'd spent years in the wilderness and at last was exactly where she wanted to be, doing exactly what she wanted to do.

Next to her Terry lit up a fresh cigarette. He smoked Gitanes like Owain did, and the scent of the tobacco sent Ruth's thoughts drifting hazily to the two of them, Becky and Owain, reactivating the now familiar sense of relief that they were safe, but also stirring more ambiguous feelings.

When Becky had telephoned from Vienna nearly a week ago, a massive sense of deliverance had at first ousted all other emotions. But later, when she'd become accustomed to the idea that her friends were no longer in danger, a secondary reaction had set in.

'There's something I've got to tell you, Ruth,' Becky had said cautiously. 'I hope you won't be upset . . . You see, Owain and I are together . . . In love, I mean. We love each other . . .'

Thinking about Rebecca's words that evening, Ruth had been badly shaken. More shaken than she'd have thought. As she told Paul later, semi-jokingly on the phone, with friends you like to imagine you're the sun and they all revolve around you, and you feel a bit left out when they get together among themselves . . . But she'd been understating the case, putting a brave face on her disarray . . . That night in the Marshall Street flat she'd poured herself a stiff drink and stood in the dark living room, staring down through the window but seeing ghosts from inside her own head, feeling desolate and very alone. In time, though, the shock had mellowed into a kind of sentimental melancholy, and she'd taken a conscious decision, vowing to accept the *fait accompli* with a good grace. Dog in a manger was a thankless role and she was determined not to play it.

The actress, Evelyn, wound up her *tour de force* with a bizarre impression of herself as a child, in the audience, watching a troupe of acrobats. Uncannily, from the look in her eyes and the movement of her head, you could tell exactly what the imaginary performers were doing. Ruth and the other members of the company were open-mouthed, riveted, like children at a Punch and Judy show. Evelyn had them hanging on every lift of her eyebrow, each shift in her expression. You could have heard a pin drop.

Finally she broke the spell, bowing to them with a look of shy, breathless triumph. 'I told me Gran there and then,' she proclaimed, 'that I was going to get a job here when I grew up. Well, it's taken a bit of time . . . But here I am.' She treated the assembled actors to a long, teasing, challenging, confiding look before returning to her sandwich and her place on the rug.

The hubbub that followed her monologue was wondering, animated. Her bravura performance had certainly broken the ice. A man of about forty whom Ruth didn't know – arty-looking with long, wavy hair, a burgundy velvet jacket and amused brown eyes – leaned towards her and remarked, 'Damnedest thing I ever saw. How does she do it? Evelyn's a kind of holy fool, don't you think?' His voice was suave and confidential. Consciously so, Ruth thought, but there was something about him that she warmed to.

'She was walking a tightrope,' Ruth said. 'Above a ravine. That's how I felt. But she didn't fall in, or even seem in any danger of it. That's what's so amazing.' The woman's performance had left her feeling exhilarated, and ready to take risks on her own account.

'Who's going to follow that?' Ryan challenged.

For now Ruth hung back. She still hadn't decided what she was going to talk about. But she wasn't worried. A year of workshops with Ryan Jaquier had convinced her that she'd find something. Just a spark was all it would take. She was secure now in her ability to think on her feet.

Terry leapt up from the rug they were sharing. 'I'll go next.' He could never resist a challenge. 'I want to talk

426

about the night my son was born,' he said. There was a hint of defiance in the statement, as if he still felt the power, the after-shock of Evelyn's flamboyance, but was proposing to use other tactics: candour, a quiet simplicity, the appeal of his youth.

Ruth watched him with affection. Terry overflowed with emotions, explosive laughter, anger, tenderness, sentimentality. In that sense he was sincere. But he knew how to use his temperament for effect and was fully conscious of his own charm. Often he reminded her of Paul when younger.

Now he took centre stage, a slim figure with short, sandy hair, a pleasing shyness, an attractive hesitation in his speech. He'd married just recently, a young actress of eighteen or so. She'd been six months pregnant. Ruth knew already the story he was about to tell. He and his wife had been staying with her grandparents in the country, in a primitive cottage without electricity or indoor plumbing. The baby had come prematurely and hurriedly. It had been too late to get his wife to hospital. Terry and the girl's grandmother had delivered the child together in a tiny bedroom under the eaves by the light of an oil lamp. He'd been enormously and genuinely moved by the experience.

As he spoke, Ruth's mind drifted again, back to Becky, to her second phone call from Vienna two days ago. She'd been crying, terribly upset . . . Janos, Owain's Hungarian friend, had died unexpectedly from some kind of internal bleeding brought on by his bullet wound, which at first hadn't seemed to be terribly serious. Becky's emotion at the death of this man, who to Ruth was a stranger, just a name, had made a huge impression, bringing home to her the enormity of the experiences her friend and Owain shared. They'd talked for some time – the call must have cost a bomb – and Ruth had been moved by the depth of

Becky's identification with the Hungarian cause, her determination to publicize what she and Owain had seen.

Afterwards Ruth had been thoughtful and seen the relationship between Rebecca and Owain somehow in a new light, laying her own feelings aside. The love between her two friends had seemed inevitable in a sense. Inevitable and right. Mentally – as she ironed and folded the washing in her small kitchen, below the bare electric light bulb – she'd given them her blessing.

'It was magical,' Terry was saying. 'More . . . important . . . than anything, ever. I felt . . . just so close to life. We all sat there when it was over, and I held him, my kid, and I cried and cried . . .' His soft, hesitant speech had changed the mood of the gathering. In a quite different fashion from Evelyn, Terry held his audience in the palm of his hand. When he resumed his seat there was a profound hush. They were spellbound, like children wrapped up in a fairy tale, losing themselves in the narrative.

'Thanks, Terry,' Ryan said quietly. And in the silence that followed, the company surfaced slowly, and with reluctance, back to full consciousness.

An impulse seized Ruth, fuelled by her thoughts of Becky and Owain. Almost without willing it she rose to her feet and looked round at the expectant circle of faces that over the next months would become well-known to her, close, familiar. Colleagues.

'I'd like to tell you about two friends of mine,' she said. 'Who've just escaped over the border from Hungary. My closest friends in fact . . .'